RIVER BOY

LYLE MORGAN

Publishing Coordinator – Sharon Kizziah-Holmes
Cover Design – Jaycee DeLorenzo

Paperback-Press
an imprint of A & S Publishing
Paperback Press, LLC

ISBN -13: 978-1-960499-36-3

DEDICATION

I wish to acknowledge those individuals who served as mentors, great friends, and supportive colleagues. The late novelist Warren Fine, who called himself "the foremost unpopular American novelist," author of numerous books, among them *The Artificial Traveler, In the Animal Kingdom, Their Family, American Confession*, and many short stories and poems, who served as my writing coach while both a doctoral student and faculty member at the University of Nebraska-Lincoln. A good man, gone too soon. Dr. Laura Franklin who never ceased to encourage me in my many pursuits and remained a staunch friend and supporter until her death. H. Neal Sievers, MD, for his many years of close friendship and constant encouragement. Decades-long dear friends Drs. James and Kathryn Bellman, two more outstanding individuals one cannot meet. Dr. Paul McCallum, consummate scholar, dedicated teacher, great friend, and valued confidant. To my many colleagues throughout the years in the Department of English and Modern Languages and the Colleges of Arts & Sciences and Education at Pittsburg State University. Fine, decent, and dedicated persons all.

Special gratitude goes to my outstanding parents, Lyle W. and Ione E. Morgan, now long departed. Whatever I needed and whenever I needed it, they were there. Better, more caring and supportive parents one could not hope to have. I pray in some small way I have made them proud.

PROLOGUE

―――――――――――――

An Ending and a Beginning

"I'M SORRY, BOY," MR. MEYERS said to me as we watched Pop's coffin slip into the soft soil of the cemetery on the knoll above Hortonville, five miles from where Pop and I had lived.

In the shallow valley below, the river flowed somber-slow and quiet, shrouded in an early morning mist.

Ronnie Meyers was there, too, looking groundward, watching the men handle the coffin straps, Pop's pine board box slowly disappearing into the shoulder-deep hole.

We weren't friends then. As I watched the men and Pop's coffin, I glanced at Ronnie, too. Sober-faced, his dark hair slicked back, he heeled pock-mark furrows into the bare ground near the graveside. His shoes looked too big for his feet and, the way they curled up at the toes despite the paper he'd stuffed inside, I judged they were his brother Johnny's. Why Ronnie had come I couldn't reckon unless Mr. Meyers felt it was somehow proper for another boy my age to be there to mourn.

The Parson Briggs was there, his strong voice rolling over the hillside, but I only caught snatches of his speech: "for this good man, Father, we pray. Grant his soul may find rest and nurture in Your kingdom." A hollow thump sounded up from the hole as the men spaded in the dirt.

There hadn't been a church funeral. Just the service on the hill. Only the Parson Briggs, Mr. Meyers, who'd known Pop since they were boys and worked the river together, and Ronnie and I were there. And the river flowed silently past Hortonville, and the fog

1

began to lift.

Pop hadn't left any money, so of course there wasn't any stone. "I'll carve out a marker," Mr. Meyers told me following the service. "It wouldn't be fitting for John Clayton not to own a marker."

I thanked him for his kindness.

"I'd like to take you in, Clayt," Mr. Meyers said, looking down at me. "But with Molly laid up constant, the twins to care for, and all the mouths to feed–well–it just ain't possible." He stopped and pawed the ground some, like Ronnie. Thinking. "Maybe Emma Hawkinds could use a boy around the house. I could ask her for you. Leastwise I will if you're willing to promise to work for your keep."

"I'm passing good at getting along alone," I told him. "I've had experience." Mr. Meyers nodded. Knowing.

"There won't be any need for the boy to go living with strangers," a voice boomed out behind us. It caught all of us by surprise, and I jerked around to see. The voice was Uncle Frank's. He stood tall and gaunt, his gray hair flopping in an easy breeze flowing up the hillside from the river.

"You'll be staying with the boy I reckon," Mr. Meyers asked, looking directly at Uncle Frank, "seeing' how John Clayton's gone?" From the bolt-jawed look on Mr. Meyers and the steely quiet in Uncle Frank's eyes, it wasn't hard to see there was no friendship lost between them.

"For a time at least," Uncle Frank said. "Trading isn't easy these days, and it wouldn't be any easier having a boy along. I'll be staying," he nodded, "'till things get settled. And if I leave, I'll make arrangements."

Ronnie hadn't spoken to me all along, but, when his father turned to leave, he shot a soft look toward me then walked away.

The Parson Briggs, recognizing Uncle Frank, took him aside and they talked at length. I shuffled over to where Pop was laid. The ground was mounded up soft above the level of the hilltop. With the rising breeze I could hear the river. It seemed to moan and gurgle gently, but I knew it didn't mourn for Pop.

It didn't rest easy–the thought of staying with Uncle Frank and him raising me as his own–but he was Pop's brother. And kin. Besides, there was no place else to go.

Uncle Frank's discussion with the parson done, he came striding over to the graveside. It wasn't his way to be sentimental, but the way he bent his head over and clawed the hair back from his eyes seemed to show he cared.

"I'm sorry about your pa, boy. I just heard tell of it in Hortonville this morning and came straight here."

"Pop was a good man," I said, speaking mainly to myself.

"He was. But he was weak in the ways of liquor·." It burned me to hear Uncle Frank say it, but I kept quiet because I knew his words rang right.

Uncle Frank plopped a firm hand on my shoulder, siding me around to face him. "I'm not here to take your pa's place, boy. I never raised children and in general, I don't like boys–always whining, running off, not pulling their share of work." He slid his hand off my shoulder, laid his thumb under my suspender strap, and pulled me toward him. "You do what I tell you, when I tell you," he punched his words, "without back-talk and belly-ache, and we'll get along." His gray eyes burned against mine. "You understand me clear, boy?"

"Yes, sir," I whispered.

The breeze from the river had vanished, and with it the fog. The sun shone golden-bright in the east and was rising higher. The hilltop lay silent except for a gathering of honeybees which jerked and flitted among the dandelion and blue bell spray Emma Hawkinds had sent along with Mr. Meyers to lay against Pop's grave. The sun was rising hot.

I felt cold.

The wailing of the newborn infant is mingled with the dirge for the dead.
    –Lucretius

CHAPTER 1

Reflections. Early Life. Ronnie's River Gang.

MY FATHER DIED FROM A LONG SICKNESS WITH DRINK WHEN I was scarce fourteenand I never knew my mother. Pop had told me she died bringing life to me and that no finer woman ever lived and that most of the times they spent together were happy times even though those early years were hard.

I'd heard told around Hortonville they were never married legally, but I preferred to believe Pop's own word and be damned to those old gossips in town.

Pop and I were real poor, he being just a riverman, and things were none too easy for us in those early days. We might have been poor but I never really knew it. Living by the river, a body never needs go hungry, and Pop provided the rest for us as best he knew how.

Looking back on it, Pop was a rich man in every way but having money. Because I worked alongside Pop for a time, the folks in town had gotten to calling me "River Boy," but my Christian name is Clayt–short for Clayton–but I didn't ever use it because it sounded too formal and all.

I was born on a late August night in 1873, shrouded in a fog so thick you couldn't see the lamps in the few sparse cabins straight

4

across the narrowest part of the river bend.   Pop had built the cabin himself with logs he'd hewn by his own hands out of cottonwood and pine which grew dense along the riverbank in a clearing some five miles downstream from Hortonville, a village in those days of about three hundred hearty souls. Being too young to recollect those first times with any accurate clearness, I have to go by word of say from what Pop told me and what I've heard from other folks that knew us best.

I was born amid much uncertainty about my mother's health: whether one or the other, or both of us, would live through the experience.

Mom had been in awful pain for some time, no doubt from the strain of river life and of carrying me as I was a big little brute when I first popped into the dim lantern light of that awful night. Old Doc Severine says Mom labored for three days and that he never left her side but to eat a bit with Pop just outside the door to her room.

Doc had hired a Mrs. Emma Hawkinds, a peerless neighbor woman of good reputation and some experience in these affairs, having raised ten children of her own, to care for her those few days before my birth. She cooked for the doctor and Pop, managed the house, and looked after Mom, ofttimes holding her hand and sitting for hours at her bedside, reciting stories from the Bible to take her mind off the pain.

She had no worry about affairs at home, her oldest children on their own and the two youngest, eight and ten, taking good care of themselves, and with her eldest daughter on hand to keep things straight,

I was born shortly after supper. It was a hard delivery from what old Doc recalls. He said the strain of birthing caused her heart to burst and that she was dead before I was born. So, on that dreary night, I came into the world half orphaned.

When the matter of being born had come and passed, Pop was pacing nervously outside the door back and forth like a caged raccoon, wearing the old jute carpet thin with long, uneasy strides. As it was told to me sometime later, first Mrs. Hawkinds emerged from the dim-lit room and brought Pop the news.

"How is she, Emma?" Pop asked, his face pale and awash with sweat. "You've a fine little dauber," Mrs. Hawkinds said, forcing herself to smile, then casting her eyes down quick. "He must weigh nigh on to a full ten pounds."

"A boy! I got a son!" Pop nearly shouted. "But" he said, seeming mighty worried, "how's Mary Ella?"

With this, Mrs. Hawkinds, unable to form the words, and a flood of tears welling up about her kindly, deep-set eyes, was saved the news by Doc.

"You have a fine son, John," he told Pop, emerging from the room and standing in the doorway wiping the sweat from his forehead with a big white rag. "A son you can be proud of." Then he drew his doctorly hand across Pop's shoulders and motioned him toward the table. Pop knew what he meant already.

"Mary didn't pull through the delivery," Doc droned kind of soft. "We did all we could, believe me, John. I'm sorry."

Mom's death was a great shock to Pop who loved her very much. The only time he was ever far from her was when he went out on the river fishing, and he always took her with him into town when he rowed down to sell his catch at the market. Pop was heart-sick after that, and that's when he took to drinking heavy.

Leaving me to the care of Mrs. Hawkinds, or to one of her older daughters, Pop would go off to town, sell his catch and buy some needed provisions, a couple of jugs of good drinking whiskey and come back upriver. As I was growing up, he always made certain I was fed as good as possible, but he would seldom eat but a scrap, saving all he had for the drink he poured down every night. Soon it came a time when he was taking a jug out with him on the boat, and those were the times, when I was about ten and upwards, when I'd be alone for three-four days at a stretch, fending for myself as best I knew how until he got back.

"I was kept upriver a spell," he'd say when he came back. "The fishing' was especially good." Then he'd wrap his broad, brown arm around my shoulders and say, "Clayt, you're a mighty fine son for a man to have. I'm proud of you, knowing' how's I can leave you alone and trust you'll be looking' out after yourself." Those were lonely times, but despite the bad days, Pop and I had our mutual share of good times, too.

Pop was a loving man, given to hugging and kissing, which he did in large amounts, and he was a kind man, interested in what I did and learned. He seldom drank heavy around me, save for what he termed a "sociable short," and I never saw him sick drunk until toward the last when the sickness hit him worst.

Pop always stood up for me when I played hooky from school to loiter along the river, sending notes telling the schoolmaster I'd been sick that day or had to be attending to chores at home. But then Pop didn't make a habit of me missing school. No way. And while he never whipped me for cutting school, he made it mighty clear he wanted me in the schoolroom.

"Clayt," I remember him saying to me, "I want you to get that schooling' of yours. Schooling's mighty important and I don't want you to grow up being' just a stupid riverman like me."

Well, Pop might have been just a riverman, making his living selling fish, but he wasn't dumb by any stretch. Pop was a born riverman, but he was educated; could read as good as most and write with some ease. But mostly he was self-taught in the ways of the world.

Pop was my real schoolmaster, having taught me more about the river and its ways than any of those schoolbooks ever could. And, after all that, I had a deep hankering for the river and its way of life.

Oft times I'd just lie out on a raft I put together with saw logs, some binding rope and pegs I carved myself with the whittling knife Pop gave me before he passed away. I used to lie out on that old raft with my shoes off and my shirt folded beneath me for a pillow and fish for catfish or sometimes just lie back and watch the big clouds float off in the sky or watch the flatboats heading for town with their cargo heaped high and those brawny polers working so hard.

Those notes Pop sent with me to school saved me from some vicious whippings. Old Mr. Dodson, the schoolmaster in those parts, was a real stern and humorless man, giving to raising welts on a body's hide, boys and girls alike, without much want of a reason. He believed if you spared the birch, you spoiled the child, and no one knew of any spoiled children when Mr. Dodson was around! If we talked out of turn or didn't have our lesson done or rough-housed too much at recess, he'd take out his switch which was so shiny it must have blessed the bottoms of many a scholar before us and clobber a body mercilessly. Oft times it was Ronnie Meyers, a boy about my age but some months older, who got it most.

Ronnie wasn't given to schooling much, and every chance he got he'd play hooky to beat it down to the river and go swimming or fishing–just about anything to get away from the doldrums of having to sit in school the best part of a warm spring or a hot fall day and read and cipher. Sometimes when I felt right about it, which was more times than Pop approved, I'd join him on the river and together we'd swim or fish or prance about acting out the part of real western cowboys and Indians. Through our association, Ronnie and I became good friends. But that wasn't right off.

Ronnie, he'd never tattle on me or anybody else, even those he didn't take a particular hankering to. Whenever we'd both done something which we were likely to get punished for, he'd take the blame wholly on himself and lie so's I'd escape the worst of it. Ronnie took all the brunt of Old Man Dodson's whippings and never complained, except to give off a tear or two and wipe his nose on his shirt sleeve. Of course, he did it while his back was turned so no one was like to see. Mr. Dodson could blister the butt of a bull, but he could never injure Ronnie's pride.

Ronnie was a boy a body could look up to and admire, just like his older brother, Johnny. Ronnie was a natural leader and had his own gang which was totally loyal to him. It's hard saying what makes a leader of a man and delegates the rest to followers, but Ronnie had the magic. Looking back on it, I'd reckon it was something within him.

All the guys that ran around with him were about the same age, except Sam Johnston who was nearing sixteen and Mike Dearson who was seventeen, but he didn't count. Ronnie wasn't any brighter than the rest, including me, but he was strong as a young tug mule and hairier than anybody around his age I'd ever seen. For a body some months shy of fifteen, he was the hairiest boy around, and to tell the truth, we were all mighty envious of him.

The big doings for some times were for the gang to go off by the river on a weekend and hold a pow-wow. Of course, Ronnie was the chief and no one seemed bent on taking the honor away from him. There we'd all curl around a circle drawn by dragging a stick around behind and Ronnie would sit in the middle real commanding like with a look of pride and importance shining across his face and we'd test one another. Mostly the testing was for strength and skill, and it was Ronnie who always came out on top. Pop always said that a hairy man was a body to be reckoned with and Ronnie was one of them for sure.

The beginning of the ritual at these pow-wows was always the same. After we were all gathered tight into the circle and Ronnie had taken his chief's place in the center, one by one we'd all open or pull off our shirts to see who'd grown the most hair. I guess this was Ronnie's idea to begin with because he knew what he had, and it always made him the center of admiration. When it came my turn to show, I always held back, and it took some prodding for me to comply with the ritual because of all of Ronnie's gang I had the least—only a few sparse sprouts under my arms—and they were so light a body could scarce make them out. The last of us, before it came Ronnie's turn, was always Mike Dearson. Old Mike, he'd be itching for his turn, and in a long-drawn-out manner and with the greatest of ceremony, he'd carefully lift his shirt and puff his chest way out and point with the greatest pride to a tiny patch which was growing high up on his breastbone like a clump of tree moss or a triangle of cat's fur. Of course, we'd all gather around and make a big to-do about it. Even Ronnie would join in the praise, all of which was important to Mike because with his lisp and twisted lip, that was the only thing he ever had going for him to make the truth known.

But Ronnie was the real man. He was never one to brag but, come his turn, he'd throw off his shirt and we'd all gape and smile and compliment him because he was covered with curls as black as a moonless night. He had hair on his upper chest, nipple to nipple and a narrow strip which ran down past his belly button. He was a real sight to see! Oh, how we envied him. Hairiness must've run in his family because I remember the first time I met his brother, Johnny.

A bunch of us were down on the river one Saturday fishing for cats and sunning ourselves in the process, when this big kid comes stalking up to where I was lying out. I didn't know him at the time, but I sure sat up fast and took notice of him.

He was big, about nineteen at the time, with shoulders like a plough horse, muscles rippling all over and a face as handsome as any to be seen in picture books of long-ago Greece which Mr. Dodson kept in the schoolroom. He'd been swimming and was in his altogether, browned over like deep-tanned leather, and hairy like to beat all count. He came up and stood over me awhile without saying anything—real strong and silent like.

"Catch anything?" he asked.

I didn't answer back but held up a little cat about the size of a woman's hand. He smirked then burst out laughing loud.

"If I was you," he said, "I'd toss it back. Its momma might be looking for it." He smiled. His voice was deep, like a shout from a dry-well bottom. He said something else too, I can't recall right off.

Then Ronnie came running up and put his arm around this big kid's waist and introduced Johnny to me real formal like. It made me nervous–them standing over me like that–and I admit I felt self-conscious because of Johnny's size and all that hair. But then Ronnie wasn't doing badly for himself either, sporting much of the same equipment, and he was only fourteen then. It made the rest of the gang and me look just like newborns standing beside them.

After the opening ritual we'd all go about holding our "Olympic Games" just like the ancients did, except our games were wrestling and Indian Back Flip where two guys lie down opposite and link arms and on a steady count lift their legs together then try to flip the other crosswise over him. The arm wrestling and seeing how far out we could swing over the river on an old rope strung up from a thick cottonwood near the riverbank before we dipped into the water made up the remainder of our games. We all had a good time and Ronnie was always crowned champion. As long as I knew Ronnie, he was never whipped.

Of course, getting in tight with Ronnie and the gang was a different story than just being allowed to tag along. Before Ronnie and I became real friends, I trailed him around like a pup to its mother. I know it bothered him at first, but then he seemed to get used to it, me being around all the time and looking up to him. He seemed way older, and a whole lot smarter than me, and me following him gave him a sense of importance he seemed to like. Before I got in really good with Ronnie, whenever the gang held a secret meeting, I wasn't invited. Of course, I knew about the secret meetings because there were times when I'd be with the gang and they'd all gather and talk silent like then go off back into the woods and leave me sitting on the riverbank, dangling my bobber in the water or heaving dirt balls among the ripples. I tried everything I knew to do to get in tight with Ronnie and the gang so to be accepted, but nothing ever worked. Whenever I could, I'd cover up for Ronnie with Old Man Dodson. But it seldom did any good.

Mr. Dodson had eyes for any kind of trouble, and he always knew, somehow, that it was Ronnie behind it all.

The gang never fully accepted me until the day I saved Ronnie's life.

The gang was down on the river one afternoon after school just lying out and telling stories about the old river pirates or talking up stories some of the guys had heard sitting around back behind the tavern in town and listening in on the drunk talk there. Ronnie was off alone that day, fishing as usual, noodling out cats from a cave in the riverbank. Pop showed me how to do it, too, but had always warned me of how it could be dangerous business and that it wasn't any business for a boy. The cats in the river grow to be over a hundred pounds in places and some have mouths as wide as supper plates. Pop had told me tales about how men his size and bigger had jammed their hands down the throats of some of those big cats and how those cats just clamped their broad mouths tight and swam away, hauling the men away to drown. It seemed all in all a pretty big tale, Pop being given to telling whoppers on occasion, and I never put much stock in it until that day.

Ronnie had fished that cave before and tickled out some small cats by wiggling his finger in the mud while lying with his shirt off, belly wise on the bank. You see, when a cat smells out the bottom for food, it can't tell a worm or such from a body's fingers. Well, there was a big cat lurking the cave that day and when he sniffed out Ronnie's hand, he opened that cavernous mouth of his and clamped down hard, taking in Ronnie's whole hand and arm near up to the elbow. Ronnie pulled, but that big cat held fast and retreated into the cave. Ronnie hadn't any choice but to follow along with him. Well, the gang and I were some distance away, sitting in on a story Sam Johnston had heard at the pool hall in town. It was a mighty good tale, full of gore, about a woman who'd been murdered by a man up the river in Waytown, and things were just coming to a head when we heard poor Ronnie just a screaming and a hollering and a carrying on something terrible. We thought he was being murdered! All of us gaped and scrambled up and beat it lickity split to where the shouts were pouring from. By the time we got there, all we could see of Ronnie was a pair of muddy feet barely hanging above the bank. By then, that old cat had tugged him neck and shoulders under water and, as I've been told since, if it wasn't for me diving into the river like I did and rapping that cat on top of the head with my fist,

Ronnie would have drowned for certain. When I'd pulled his arm loose, Michaels and Johnston took hold of his feet and hauled him up the bank.

"He looks 'bout dead," Michaels said, rolling Ronnie over. "He's scarce breathin' neither," Johnston said.

"He ain't breathin'!" another member of the gang gasped, looking down close at him. And he wasn't. There was no rise and fall of his hairy chest, and no color to his lips.

"I think he's dead!" Michaels gasped again. A deathly hush fell over the whole lot of them, and they just stood fixed, staring down at Ronnie.

I'd been standing waist deep in the river near the bank watching and had just shaken my head like a spaniel after a swim, when I heard Michael's last words.

"He can't be dead!" I shouted, bounding to the bank and bending over him. Ronnie was gray as cold ashes all right, and a stillness lingered over him like the grave. It was then I got down on my knees, bent low over Ronnie's face, and put my mouth over his and began to blow gusts of wind into him.

"Whataya doin'?" Johnston asked. "It's scarce no sense a-kissin' a corpse!"

I paid no heed to Johnston, nor to Michaels's comment either. It was something Pop had taught me, part of his long experience along the river. In healing, Pop was always better than a doctor, except in cases where cutting had to be done, so I kept blowing, taking breaths, and blowing again until I heard a whistling sound coming deep from Ronnie's mouth. I laid my head down closer over him and I could hear him breathing.

Michaels suggested, "Ain't we got to put him 'cross a barrel or something?" and Mike Dearson who'd been sitting nearby on a log fall gnawing on his bottom lip, lisped, "We ain't got no barrel."

"Yeh," I said, "but we've got that log you're sitting on," noting its similarity to the barrel that'd been suggested, so we hauled Ronnie limp along the ground and slung him belly-wise across the log, rolling him across it back and forth like a saw, me at his arms, and Michaels pulling on Ronnie's feet. It was but a short while later when Ronnie came around again. He lay there, opening his eyes and looking about like a man come back from the brink of death. At that moment, Johnston bellowed, "It's a miracle!" and I stepped back while the rest of them crowded in around Ronnie, all scrambling for a place beside him and speaking at once. Well, then and there, I was in, and Ronnie and I became the best of friends. The next day in school, Ronnie got up in front of the whole class and told how I'd saved his life and all. And the way he said it, it sounded mighty fine.

Meet the first beginnings; look to the budding mischief before it has time to ripen to maturity.

                    –William Shakespeare

CHAPTER 2

The Initiation

I HADN'T SEEN THE GANG for several days since the afternoon along the river when I saved Ronnie from drowning, except in school, of course. Uncle Frank had kept me real busy around the cabin, cutting, hauling, and chopping timber into kindling for the cooking fire and for heat at night when the river turns cool and damp. I did some straightening up around the cabin, too. Uncle Frank, he'd made it clear in his 'special' kind of manner, that as soon as school was out, I hiked my way back home and set into tending chores.

"You've got responsibilities 'round here, boy," he'd told me one night as we sat around the room after the supper hour. I'd fixed the meal because he was busy reading through a parcel of store goods catalogs he'd gathered from the post office in town.

"This place is beginning to look a mess," he droned, not looking up from his reading matter and speaking out one side of his mouth, the other being occupied with a gnawed-on stub of a thick cigar. "There's more wood needs chopping, and" he added unenthusiastically, "the privy reeks when the wind blows 'cross the river." Uncle Frank was none too glorious when it came to using words, except when he was selling. Then, Pop had told me, there were few traders better at the gift of gab and selling than Uncle Frank.

I'd grown up around Pop in the spirit of mutual co-operation–he doing most of the heavy work around the cabin with me settling for the lighter chores. Of course, as I'd grown older and Pop taught me how to wield the ax and use the chopping block so the wood wouldn't bounce up and fly, I kept the wood pile stacked high beside the cabin and made certain the kindling box was full. With Pop and me, the chores were always fifty-fifty. With Uncle Frank it was my fifty and his half, too. He didn't hanker much for working–unless it made him money.

It was the end of May of my fourteenth year. Uncle Frank had settled in, and summer recess had begun. School was over at last! No more sitting quiet as a rock, no more reading or 'rithmetic, no more dates to memorize and no more Old Man Dodson. Summer had finally bloomed.

The air was sweet as new-cut grass and the river flowed lazy and snake-like amid rich green swathes as far as an eye could reach.

Old Man Dodson stood before the class on the final moment of that last day peering over the wire edge of his spectacles, making his final, droning speech. The schoolroom was dead silent as he talked, everyone teetering on the edge of the slick school benches just waiting to storm away as soon as he was done, but no one daring the wrath of the schoolmaster's switch in the final minutes before our long-awaited freedom.

With his speechifying ended, he signaled Jody Wintels, whose duty it was to ring the final bell. Mr. Dodson worked his pocket watch from out his vest, twisted it around the fob, and glowered at its face for several seconds. He wasn't about to let us loose a second sooner than the school board allowed.

Finally, he announced, "Miss Wintels, you will sound the bell on my signal." He adjusted the spectacles on the bridge of his spoon shaped nose. "This school year has been mildly rewarding," he spoke slowly, "and it is my fervent hope some of you have profited. Others, of course, are beyond redemption." His glance fell straight on Ronnie when he said it. With a sharp slap of his pointer finger at the air, the school bell clanged loud and long, Jody Wintels jerking up and down like a clockwork monkey I'd once seen in the general store in Hortonville with Pop. We had half jammed through the doorway at the first resounding clang.

Most of the girls, dainty and smart in their calico aprons and linen pinafores, proceeded in orderly fashion from the schoolhouse, some laughing, some in bunches talking quietly. Rose Martin, the mayor's daughter, lingered around the steps talking with Sally Madsen. And Lucy Stern, Old Man Dodson's pet, stayed behind to haunt the room and help the schoolmaster in collecting books and slates and setting the room up right for the summertime.

The boys, of course, were different. Blustering with one another, slapping backs, and laughing over jokes which, had Old Man Dodson overheard, would for certain have brought on the whipping switch, school out or not, rushed out the door, jostling, stampeding, and knocking into one another. Once outside, Ronnie was the first to doff his shoes and feel the play of dust beneath his toes. Johnston and Michaels followed suit–Michaels with a bandaged toe where he'd meant to kick his dog and struck the porch post instead.

I was dogging my way toward home, having a powerful lot of chores to do, when Ronnie came sauntering over, tall and prideful and smiling broad. Slinking his arm across my shoulders he said, "Clayt, seeing' how's you saved my life an' all the other day–I'd a drowned for certain if it hadn't been for you–the gang's elected you to membership. Of course, you got to be 'initiated first," he added.

To tell the truth, I'd been expecting it and it came as no surprise, but I acted out my part first rate. I smiled, joked, and laughed with Ronnie for a spell and with some of the gang which had gathered around and played my role like a first-rate actor. Mustering my words carefully and as formal as I knew how, I said to Ronnie, "I accept your offer with humbleness and pride."

Ronnie grinned ear to ear and said, "We'll meet at Burtram's Levee," Burtram's Levee being close to the spot where I'd freed Ronnie from the cat.

I was all excited and scampered off for home with no more than a 'by your leave' to Ronnie. I tended to the chores Uncle Frank had set for me and started supper, too. The gang and I were to meet at six o'clock for certain, and I wasn't to 'dally on the way as Ronnie put it. But, by the end of the supper hour I was late because Uncle Frank had a hankering I tend to the dishes and put everything neat away at first.

I washed while Uncle Frank sat in his favorite chair, Pop's old chair by the woodstove, puffing on his pipe and reading some merchandizing literature on a new line of goods he was considering. The work was drudgery; I was itching to escape and worried about being late. I dried the dishes as fast as possible and stowed away the frying skillet and utensils on the shelf above the stove.

"Uncle Frank? Can I go out for a while?" I asked all polite.

His only answer, glowering up at me from atop his reading, was, "You be home by ten you hear, or I'll have the strap awaiting when you do."

"Yes, sir," I said, and scampered out the door and into the dimming light toward the river as fast as my feet would move.

Darkness had fallen quicker than usual it seemed, and the moon glowed dimly through the willow thicket as I half bolted, half stumbled through the blackness toward the levee. I knew the river well and the area surrounding it, but in my scurry, I tumbled down a steep embankment, nearly rolling off into the river. But I was soon up the bank again and well-nigh onto the levee about to meet the gang. When I arrived, I spied Ronnie first, shadowed in the darkness but illuminated by a small campfire. By the scowl on his face, he didn't seem too pleased. Sam Johnston and Charlie Michaels were there, too, standing in the shadows by a sagging, half- downed cedar.

"You're late!" Ronnie snapped.

"I'm sorry, but–"

"Silence, slave!" someone shouted from the darkness. It was Michaels.

"You've a-kept us waitin' near on to midnight," Johnston said, exaggerating.

"I'm sorry," I gulped in my excitement, "Uncle Frank …

"Silence! Michaels sounded again, more commanding than I'd ever known him before.

Ronnie stepped up, coming to stand in front of me, his arms folded across his chest.

"You're our slave," he announced, all seriousness. "A slave does what his masters tell him, and he never complains," he added. The others emerged from the darkness and assembled around me forming a lazy sort of circle. There was another body which they edged in near me. Skipper Knox, a boy whose folks had moved mid-

17

February from Illinois. He was near on to my age, but a year in school below me. I guessed he was being initiated too.

"Whaddaya have to say for yourself, slave?" Michaels asked, reaching out his hand and grabbing my shoulder hard. As I began to answer, Ronnie shouted me to silence.

"So, you want to join us?" Johnston said, laying his hand against my back and shoving me into Michaels. Michaels shoved me back.

"Down on your knees, slave," said one. "And bark like a dog," said another.

I glanced toward Skipper. I guessed the gang had shoved him around some too, but earlier. He just stood by kind of wide-eyed and pale. I took a breath and swallowed my last bit of pride and dropped down on my knees in front of them and barked and howled at the moon, too, to further act the part. The gang laughed and snickered, then got really serious again.

"Who do you think you are?" Michaels called out.

"A dog," I answered, and this time there was no calling for my silence.

"A dog!" Johnston laughed. "You're a mongrel cur. And when a cur don't obey, whaddaya do with it?"

"Beat him!" shouted the rest in unison. Skipper joined in too, seeing how he'd most likely been through this before.

"Beat this mongrel then," Ronnie ordered.

No sooner had his last word escaped, but three of them pounced on me, grabbing my shoulders hard and hauling me arms and ankles toward the deep woods. Michaels, who was my size but thicker, hoisted me up off the ground from behind so my toes barely touched turf, and Johnston hauled my trousers down. Michaels from behind shouldered me into Johnston then grabbed a stick that was lying by.

"Grab your ankles," Ronnie ordered, which I did, not liking the position, then Johnston laid to and paddled me several times. Hard.

Then the rest joined in, Michaels striking harder than old Johnston, then Ronnie at the last, the hardest of them all. My pride—and my behind—were appropriately bruised.

"That's the treatment we give to slaves and curs," Ronnie announced, promising more if I wasn't careful.

I scarce had time to button up when they grabbed me once again, tied a blindfold around my head, and hurried me off up the levee.

They half dragged, half carried me along a piece then scampered up a slope and well into the trees where they'd built another fire. I could smell the sweet scent of pine sap burning. The gang came to a dead halt. I stood still; the only sounds I could make out being my own labored breathing and the crackling of the fire. Then someone came up behind me, sneaking Indian quiet, and pushed me down hard by the shoulders.

"Sit quiet and keep your eyes shut tight," a voice ordered. It was Ronnie's. He took off my blindfold and I kept my eyes shut as I'd been warned. I sat close by the fire. Its heat grazed against my cheeks, and I could make out swirling balls and streaks of colored lights which played across my lids.

I sat beside the fire for some time, growing more and more uncomfortable because of the heat which I imagined was about to turn me pink on the front side like a slice of roasted ham. The gang had slunk off deeper into the woods, but I could make out their voices barely whispering from somewhere back behind me. After a time longer, there was a cracking and popping of cedar twigs and pine needles under their feet as they came back.

"Open your eyes," Ronnie ordered me. I opened my eyes, which ached because the fire shown so bright against the blackness of the trees. Before me stood Sam and Charlie and Ronnie–all dressed up like Indians–and naked except for breechcloths made from gunny sacks and painted white and red and yellow with grease sticks like clowns from a carnival. Ronnie wore a kind of bonnet, two chicken feathers and a red hawk's tail held on by a band of string tied around his head. Michaels and Johnston had one feather each. Ronnie was the chief.

I could've burst out laughing because Ronnie made the hairiest Indian I'd ever seen, Indians having scarcely any hair at all except on their heads. He stood there rigid, staring down at me real seriously, his brown arms folded across his hairy chest. First Ronnie mumbled some nonsense words. I guessed they were supposed to be Indian language, but I knew Ronnie didn't know any language except his own, and I guessed he'd made it up. Then the gang broke into a circle. Skipper Knox sat squat legged directly in front of me across the fire. The five of us formed a tight bunch around the fire which was slowly dying down. Ronnie brought out an old pipe made of real briar which he'd borrowed from his pap, and which would've made a fine pipe except the bowl was cracked. "Before you prove yourselves worthy 'enough to join us, first we got to smoke the pipe," Ronnie announced, still posing serious.

He took a grease-blotched leather draw-string pouch about the size of a fist from off his waist and filled the bowl with great ceremony. He knocked a flaming stick from out the fire, and soon a large, gray cloud of smoke billowed from his mouth. The smoke smelled kind of harsh–like a mix of stale tobacco and sweet sumac not quite cured. Ronnie sucked it in, making sort of a rushing noise. He passed the pipe to Johnston who did the same, then it passed to Michaels, to Skipper, then to me.

"You got to pull the smoke down deep," Ronnie ordered, and I did.

I'd never inhaled a pipe before. The smoke smelled awfully sweet, and it burned my throat going down. I held it about a second before I sputter-choked, coughing hard, then passed the pipe to Ronnie. For some length we handed the 'peace pipe' from one to another around the circle in silence broken only by the popping of the fire and the whistling rush of air as we inhaled.

It wasn't too long before my head set in to growing woozy, my eyes lost sharpness and the dying fire began to fade. The ground around me began to shake and quiver and my head spun like a crazy top turned loose. I was feeling dizzy and green-sick. My heart hammered in my chest and knocked against my ribs, and I could hear myself breathing hard. Across from me, Skipper pursed a gag-sour look, squeezed his belly tight, then bolted upright from his squat and scampered for the trees, sounds of gagging and choking followed. Ronnie, Johnston and Michaels all set in to laughing. I felt sorrier for Skipper than humored because I was feeling much the same. But he came back a short while later looking none the worse except for a sag-jaw and sour look.

Ronnie, who'd been sitting beside me, stood up once Skipper rejoined us, and gave a sign. The two of us were lifted by both arms and led into the trees. Michaels gave the word to strip, and Johnston slapped some grease paint on our face and chest with a couple of stripes down each arm and leg, all in different colors. Then they led us back, painted all over and wearing burlap breechcloths, Indian fashion.

The two of us stood before the fire to which Ronnie had added a few small sticks which soon caught and blazed up quick.

"To join the gang, you've got to do a danger," Ronnie said.

"You got a choice," he said, "swim the river to the oak snag and back or steal an egg apiece from Slink Snipe's coup. Seeing there's two of you, you can confab together and decide."

Neither choice was good. The oak snag was plum out near the middle of the river where the channel was the deepest. That oak had bottomed deep into the sand during the last river flood. Only the top bare branches tipped the water by some five feet, and no one, except the steamboat pilots, knew how deep the channel water was.

The river sloshed and eddied near the stump and practically boiled near the branches when the river flowed full like now. It was a danger to boats and foolish swimmers–especially at night.

Our second choice–stealing eggs from Slink Snipe's chicken coup—seemed about as dangerous. 'Slink' Snipe (none of us knew his real name) was a river hermit who had no hankering for people, especially kids. In July they'd try to swipe a melon from his patch, in October snatch apples from his trees. He never seemed to sleep and had a mean mongrel dog to keep watch besides. And his scattergun was always loaded at the ready. Skipper Knox and I talked a piece about the choices.

"Clayt," Skipper said, "I'm not too good a swimmer in the light, and I don't cotton much to swimming in the dark."

We talked a while longer, weighing our choices carefully, then came to a decision.

"Ronnie," I said, walking up to him and the gang, "we choose eggs."

Finding Slink Snipe's place was no problem. Getting his eggs without being caught, bitten, or shot was. The cabin sat back in the woods in a narrow clearing a quarter mile from the levee and beside a shallow crick fed by a fresh spring which emptied into the river. Snipe's place wasn't much of a cabin, just a clutter of warped clapboards, some hand-sawed logs, tar sheeting and pine bark shingles.

Skipper and I poked a path through the woods, scarcely speaking. It's a wonder what a body can hear at night when he's quiet. An owl hooted somewhere in the darkness from among the pines. It sounded like it was perched right on my shoulder. A cricket chirped and a wood mouse scurried past through the leaves. Ahead, scarce a rock-throw's distance, was the cabin with the henhouse right alongside. I was wishing the moon wasn't quite so full, the glitter of stars not quite so bright.

A light glimmered inside the cabin. It must've been nine or past, with Slink Snipe not gone to bed. It felt a might strange crawling knees and hands along the ground wearing only a strip of gunny sack.

Alongside me Skipper voiced quietly, "I wonder if the Indians felt like this?" Guess he was thinking the same as me. "You think those stories 'bout Slink Snipe shooting folks is true?"

"Can't say for certain." I had to allow the thought was troubling. "But he can't go around killing people. He'd be hanged for certain. I'd be willing to bet two bits his scattergun carries a rock salt load."

"That's worse than being shot."

"Or chewed?" About thirty feet away I caught sight of a dark shadow trotting near the cabin door. It was supposed to be the meanest cur around those parts. If I had my choice, I'd rather face a scattergun with rock salt than a dog.

But we had to do something, and sitting around wasn't getting Skipper or me any closer to the eggs or to membership into the gang. It was time we went and go we did. We were dressed as Indians and we moved as quiet, keeping low down to the ground and slinking belly wise toward the dark side of the coop. By the feel of the breeze against my face, we were down wind. The dog couldn't smell us, but of a sudden he set into yipping, then growling, then set off a string of barks and snarls that sent chills up my back. Skipper's too by the looks of him. We froze ice block still where we were–some fifteen feet from the coop. We heard the door latch snap open and the tromp of heavy boots on Slink Snipe's porch.

"What is it, Samba? What is it, boy?" The dog stopped yipping. I couldn't figure right off why it hadn't given chase but when I dared glance over, I could see how it was tied.

"What is it, boy? What do you hear?" Slink Snipe stopped asking questions and looked around slowly.

Lucky for us we lay in the shadows of the coop. "Keep your butt low," I whispered to Skipper. Any closer to the ground and we'd been under it.

"Too early for melon thieves," I heard Snipe say. "You barkin' at squirrels or coons again?" He gave the dog a pat on the head and traipsed back inside. The dog gave out one last growl before curling up on the porch.

We moved ahead slowly on knees and hands against the soft grass and dirt near the coop. Slink Snipe didn't have many hens and he would have sorely missed them if we'd come to steal any. A couple eggs were no loss. The danger, of course, is there's no way to steal an egg from under a nesting hen without raising Hell's own cackle, and Ronnie and the gang knew it. We knew it, too, and it didn't make us feel at ease. The best way is to grab the hen, grab the egg and run!

Inside, we did just that. I snatched up a fluffy red one, palmed an egg and started for the coop door. Skipper did the same. "Clayt! There's no egg under this one!" The sound of Skipper's voice, and our snatching up the hens raised a war-whoop of clucking and cackling.

"Grab another. Quick!" I yelled.

We were barely out the door, each holding firm to a precious egg, when the dog set into barking amid the chicken clucks and Slink Snipe stomped out on his porch again.

"What the–?" His eyes tried to adjust to the darkness. He took one look at Skipper and me scampering through the shadows at the house and let out a howl louder than his dog. "Chicken thieves!"

"Run like the Devil's own!" I yelled to Skipper. Behind us sounded the blast from a scattergun muzzle. We dove for the crick bed, lay out belly-flat and panting. The yipping bark echoed through the woods behind the scattergun.

"Follow the crick and run!" I bellowed out. In the dive, Skipper skinned his knee up and was running side slip from the oozing blood and pain. I'd snagged my breechclout on a tree root and, except for the grease patterns painted on me, was prancing naked through the knee-deep water. I didn't care. All I was worried about was Slink Snipe and his dog.

Sloshing through the water would (I hoped) keep the hound off scent. And though we were making noise aplenty of our own, I doubted Slink could hear our thrashing over the yaps, barks, and howls of his dog. I was winded and Skipper was nearly bent double out of breath. We passed the initiation.

Life is not a spectacle or a feast: it is a predicament.

–George Santayana

CHAPTER 3

Uncle Frank. Bottoming. The Old Woodshed.

WHEN POP DIED, MY UNCLE Frank came to live with me and he tried his hand at raising me, but without much luck. You might say we had a disagreement. Perhaps my most unpleasant experiences in growing up after Pop was gone were with Uncle Frank. Franklin Pierce Sievers, as he liked being called by strangers, was Pop's eldest brother; Pop coming from a large river family of four brothers and six sisters. As Pop was the last boy born, most of his family had grown up and moved to other parts and, because of that, Pop's family was never very close.

Pop's youngest sister, Emily, was always his closest friend, and Pop was mighty hurt when she up and died a most miserable death as Pop described it, from being bit by a mad dog when she was ten.

"She just couldn't eat or drink toward the last," Pop once told me, "And went into the raving fits and died."

The picture Pop painted was mighty horrible; enough to give a body the cold shakes just thinking about it. Since then, I've made it a firm point of staying clear of any stray mongrels that looked suspicious. A body can't be too careful. Old Doc Severine says some scientist in France has discovered a cure for the hydrophobia, but that the cure's often as bad as the fits and is mighty painful. So, it doesn't pay either when everything's all told.

When I was younger, Uncle Frank used to come by on his way down river and, from time to time, pay Pop and me a visit. Pop and he would get together over some drink and sit around the table in the middle of our cabin, discussing matters of 'grave' importance, carry on and on about some silly matter of a sort, and play stud poker. I never entirely understood grown-ups who can sit over cards for hours, talking but saying little, and say they're having fun.

Uncle Frank was a trader by profession, mostly carrying his wares up and down river by barge or steamboat and selling to shopkeepers along the way. It was no doubt interesting work, but none too steady seeing how he could never seem to make his mind up on what it was he sold. First off it was tobacco and cigars, then dry goods and ladies' wares and finally, pots and pans, dinner plates and flatware. Leastwise that's what he was peddling the last time I set eyes on him. There's no telling what he's selling now. But it didn't seem to matter much because he always made good money and was always dressed just fine. In my recollection I never saw Uncle Frank except he was trussed up fit to bury in starched white shirts and silver links and a fine black suit with matching trousers that shined like a tin plate in the seat. Oh, he was mighty fine! I used to dream what it'd be like wearing clothes like that and being someone a body could respect. To tell the truth, he didn't look the part of being born along the river, and only those folks from around these parts knew he was the rest thinking he'd come from somewhere East. Uncle Frank had a way of fooling people most of the time and he was proud of it. It was something he was good at.

Uncle Frank used to tell Pop and me stories about his adventures with the river pirates and gamblers in the old days before the war. Looking back on it, I have strong suspicions he'd never met up with any river pirates, but his tales were always entertaining and plenty scary. I used to climb in bed at night and lie wakeful in my bunk and shake from fright and pray to the God Almighty I'd never meet up with any of those river pirates.

One of Uncle Frank's favorite stories he told was about a trading man like himself that was way-laid along a river bend where the channel grew narrow. They'd lured him onto shore by setting out a false distress. Those pirates had laid hold of his trading wares, but when he refused to tell where he'd hid his money, they hung him from a hook in the ceiling of their cave-front hideout by a rope slung under his arms and trimmed off parts of him with Barlow knives until he told. Uncle Frank swore to the truth of it because he met the man, minus some parts, along his travels. The man had taken up gambling after that, an equally hazardous profession.

Oft-times, when I'd heard that or similar tales, I'd go to bed and dream and wake up in a sudden start and pray loud and long to my Almighty Maker to be spared from horrors such as that.

My favorite tale, though, was the one Uncle Frank talked about, a sunken riverboat and the treasure she had carried. When he first told it, Uncle Frank was musing over a jug of whiskey set between Pop and him and was feeling mighty good.

"Her name was the *Channel Belle*," he began, "and she ran a snag and sank in mid-channel just near the start of the War 'tween the States. She was loaded hull-full of cargo and headed south to New Orleans."

Like all his stories, I was all ears for this one, and I listened closely. "What cargo was she carrying?" I asked,

"Some copper ingots, silver bars, quicksilver in pony barrels, and hogsheads of quality sipping whiskey." That must've reminded him of something because he paused and took a pull from off the jug. "But her serious cargo was gold–coins–some newly minted that'd been stored in holding banks in St. Louis and was shipped out secret to support the war against the North." He paused long enough to take another swig from the jug and look toward Pop who sat impassively in his chair, no doubt having heard the tale before.

"How much gold was she carrying?" I asked. I was all excited. The only real gold I'd ever seen was the watch Uncle Frank carried on an elk's tooth fob in his pocket and once when Pop brought back a Half Eagle piece for me to hold.

"I reckon plenty. Some say thousands of dollars' worth, but I've heard tell it was nigh on to half a million." Uncle Frank paused again to take another drink and light up his cigar. "When I was younger and traveling down the river, I used to look for her."

"Did you ever find her?" I asked,

"Never did. Come close a few times. That I'm sure of. I passed by her rotting hulk enough times heading up and down the river. If I'd have found her, do you think I'd be selling ladies' wares?" he added kind of gruff, nearly grunting out the words. "But I know where she lies."

"But if you know where she is, why don't you look for the gold?"

"The river changes every day. It's changed a powerful lot in twenty-five years. She's covered with tons of mud and sand by now. No one will ever find the *Channel Belle*.

For days I dreamed about finding sunken treasure: silver bars, quicksilver, copper, and GOLD. I used to sit out along the riverbank dangling my feet in the water, gazing out and thinking about the *Channel Belle*. The very water that lapped my feet was flowing over the wreck of that treasure boat somewhere upstream. The thought of it was enough to make my body tingle all over with excitement. I even planned out how I'd find her, and I'd take Ronnie with me, too. But, like most dreams, it was a boy's easy fantasy and was soon forgotten.

Uncle Frank might have been a storyteller, but he wasn't a cheery soul by any stretch. Overall, he was cold and hard. His face looked like it'd been cut from a block of granite, and his eyes were cold and gray as a polished rifle barrel. He was a big man, too, and that made me even more afraid of him. Standing a whole head taller than Pop, who wasn't too short himself, Uncle Frank was a most impressive sight. He was nearing sixty- fifteen years older than Pop-- and had a limp he said came from a miniball he'd caught in the thigh during the war and a slight stoop in his shoulders which came from rheumatism in his joints. He was at the funeral when the Parson Briggs laid Pop to rest and afterwards, he took me back to the cabin and stayed with me a short piece before I escaped and went to living with Ronnie along the river.

After Pop's death, Uncle Frank was none too kind to me, he being cut from a different bolt of cloth than Pop. From their differences, you would've never known that they were brothers.

A short spell following the prayers at graveside and the lowering and covering of the pine box that Pop was in, he held a talk with me.

"Your pap's dead, boy," he said. His voice wasn't somber and sweet like the rest of the handful of mourners had been. Mrs. Hawkinds and her eldest daughter attended, Ronnie Meyers' pap and Ronnie too, and a half a dozen other folks from Hortonville that knew him best. When we got back, Uncle Frank was already lighting into the bottle. Unlike Pop, who'd always called me 'Clayt,' Uncle Frank always called me 'boy.' "I ain't saying," he continued, "it ain't gonna be rough on you, losing your pap like that. And to be respectful we'll have a decent time of mourning. But there's things needing to be done 'round here, and I expect you to cut your share. I won't bide by any carrying on and horsing. And when I say 'jump,' you jump! Any backtalk from you and I'll peel your hide." 'Course I listened, saying 'yes, sir,' and 'no sir' all the while, and he rambled on a while longer, telling me the don'ts and dos. I knew I was in a lot of trouble living with Uncle Frank.

Uncle Frank was a sitter, not a doer. He'd either be sitting in the cabin thumbing a deck of playing cards with pictures of powerful-looking women painted across the backs and drinking whiskey from a brown-stone jug or playing cards and drinking at Gursey's Saloon in town when he felt like company. Oft-times he'd get himself all liquored-up drunk like Pop had done, but unlike Pop, you weren't safe anywhere around him. He'd get powerful drunk and, instead of falling asleep like Pop had done, Uncle Frank would go about the cabin raving and ranting and bellowing like a mad bull that just been cut, calling out unimaginable foul names and swearing like I'd imagine Satan himself was like to do. He'd always have me fix him supper and then find fault, telling me that the meat's too tough, the beans too cold–anything to raise a ruckus. And when I'd answer back, being pleasant as I could, he'd get really mad and come after me and when he'd caught me, which was most times, too, he'd lay it on me real good. Uncle Frank believed in laying one on a body for no good reason–just like Old Man Dodson.

"This is for your own good," he'd often grumble as he was about to skin me out. "It'll clear your soul." Uncle Frank was a God-fearing, church-abiding man, "and someday when you're all grown up, you'll be a- thanking me for what I'm about to do."

Well, I'm pretty grown up now, and, looking back, I can't say I thank him for it any.

Uncle Frank believed in 'bottoming.' Whenever he thought I'd done something bad, or whenever he was in a mood, or drunk, he'd tell me to stand by the table until he fetched his razor strap then he'd tell me to drop my trousers to the floor. When he got me helpless, with my trousers puddled at my feet so I couldn't run, he'd stand behind me and to one side and lay it on me. I didn't mind the bottoming so much as when he missed his aim when he was drunk and switch me about the legs and back.

It hurt something fierce, and if I whimpered, he'd lay it on again, telling me to be a man and that "grown men don't beller so," to use his words. Well, grown men don't get whipped, and I'd set to bellowing anyhow. When he got tired of swinging at me, he'd go back to drinking and playing solitaire and I'd hoist my trousers up and slip quiet and unnoticed from the cabin and head down along the riverbank, cry something fierce, then swim and let the river kiss the hurts away.

I remember the time just before Uncle Frank left for good–just after an awful row with him, I'll never like to forget it so long as I might live.

It was a Sunday morning and Uncle Frank, being a God-fearing man and a good churchgoer, was getting set to oar upriver to meeting. He got all trussed up in his Sunday-go-to-meeting best and I was supposed to go with him and sit in Sunday school where you learn about Noah's Ark and Jonah's whale and other such mythologies. Well, the night before, Ronnie Meyers and I had decided we weren't going to Sunday school anymore. We were older than the rest of the kids and the tales were old and so unreal nobody could set much truth in them. Uncle Frank believed in the word-for-word fact of the Good Book. Of course, Pop had been religious too, in his own way.

"Son," Pop once told me as we were sitting alongside the riverbank poling out carp and channel cat, "I can't speak for the certain truth of it, but I'd say the Bible's mostly fact. It's a good book to carry and read as often as you can. It teaches a body how to live upstanding and beholding to his Maker."

We talked more and I asked him about the truth of the tales I'd heard in Sunday school. Pop sat quiet and thought hard and long on it before he answered.

"It's hard for a man to believe in all those stories he reads about. I doubt a man can be swallowed by a whale and live to talk about it. Your ma saw the fact in it, but I never did. But that don't make a man any less God-fearing. Jesus Himself talked in riddles. If your ma was living, she could tell you 'bout it. Believing you was made by a Maker more powerful than yourself, and you've got a purpose in being's enough for any man."

After that, I'd go off to Sunday school and listen to those stories and try to find the truth in the riddle of them. But it was a powerful trial and I'm not certain I ever did.

That morning, early, before Uncle Frank had finished dressing, I skipped out the cabin door and met Ronnie in the willow break behind our place, and we scampered down along the river some piece away where it was quiet.

The day was glorious. The sun had been up for hours; the air lay warm and heavy around the river. We sat, Ronnie and me, along the bank, our naked feet dangling in the soft current, making eddies where it lapped our ankles. As we watched the flowing water, a flatboat drifted past in mid-current on the other side. It was so still and calm we could make out the flatboaters' song echoing off the far bank and sweeping back toward us.

I'm working my way back home, Honey, I'm working my way back home.

I'm working my way back home, Honey, I'm working my way back home.

Barrels don't grow too heavy for me, and bales too heavy to stack.

All that I crave for many a long day, is your loving when I get back.

On a calm day along the river, you can harken to sounds really clear, and Ronnie and I listened to the plaintive song until it faded out as the flatboat moved on out of sight.

With the boatmen gone along and the river again silent, save for the easy lap of water against the bank and the chirping of sparrows in the trees, Ronnie and I stripped down and waded along the bar, the water coming to scarce above our knees.

All along, Uncle Frank thought I'd been waiting for him in the skiff, but when he didn't find me there, he called and called and went about searching because he didn't get an answer. Well, angry as a bull from looking high up and low down along the river for a quarter of a mile, he finds us stretched out, side by side, along the bank. Well Uncle Frank, he blew up. He let out a bellow, stormed over to where we lay, raving and ranting like to beat anything I'd ever heard before. In all my days with him, I'd never seen him so mad! He called us names the both of us flushed red at and not at all fitting to repeat except in the crudest company; told us we'd both be punished, spouted Hell Fire, and it sounded really bad indeed. Then he stalks up to Ronnie and grabs him by the naked shoulder, lefts him to his feet, and steams him out real but good.

"You ought a be arrested!" he shouted, rocking Ronnie back and forth like a rag doll, "going about corrupting my boy like this."

"My boy?" I'd never heard him say that before. I guess he thought Ronnie was a sight older than he was because of his hair and all. And Uncle Frank and Ronnie had never met except at Pop's funeral. Ronnie had his clothes on then. Uncle Frank goes on shaking Ronnie until his teeth clattered and demanding to know his name.

"Ronnie Meyers, sir," he said and started whimpering.

"'Bank' Meyers's boy?"

"Yes'r," Ronnie said. I'd never seen him so red-faced!

Realizing then Ronnie wasn't older–he being just a boy like me– Uncle Frank ceased his talk about the law.

"I ought to skin you out right here. Peel that sinning hide right off," he steamed.

Ronnie was mostly in tears. After he was done with his shaking and spitting, Uncle Frank tells Ronnie to get on home and quick, and that he'd be calling later on his father to tell him what he'd seen.

"You boys ought to be in church on the Sabbath and asking forgiveness for your sinful ways, not fooling around. You're most like to get yours good," he said to Ronnie.

Well, Ronnie picks up his clothes and scampers off into the woods naked as a newborn and scared to beat the Devil. Then Uncle Frank turns and grabs me. "Get your trousers on, boy," he said, which was a might rough, him shaking on me so. Before I can get the rest, he tows me back to the cabin. I must have been some sight, Uncle Frank dragging me near naked through the trees, preaching about God's righteous wrath when all we'd done was wade, lie out to sun, and talk.

When we reached the clearing and the cabin, which wasn't long with the rate Uncle Frank was dragging me, we went directly to the woodshed alongside the cabin. He pulled open the wood-slat door and most to shoved me inside.

"You get over by that post and strip them trousers off," he stormed, "I'll go fetch my strap."

I didn't see I had much choice and escape was impossible because I'd heard him slip the bolt. I sauntered over by the post, taking my time about the trousers, knowing just what to expect. Uncle Frank was such in a storming mood I could still hear him a-ranting about inside the cabin, and I laid up a silent prayer to the Great Almighty, begging His forgiveness for whatever I'd done so wrong and asking to be spared. About the time I said 'Amen,' Uncle Frank came back, swishing his leather strap like a buccaneer.

"Be thankful for this licking," he snorted real stern, "and be eternally grateful that the Good Lord hasn't seen fit to strike you dumb when you ought a be in church a-praying. And worse," he added, "you made me miss service too."

With those words, he reared his strong arm back and laid one on me. I winced and he laid another on me, harder than the first.

"Spare" ...whack... "the rod" ...whump... "and spoil the" ... crack ..."child," he quoted from the Bible. The razor strap stung like a swarm of angry hornets. Uncle Frank wielded it like half a dozen Mr. Dodsons slapped together. Hot tears flowed down my cheeks.

I don't rightly remember how long he whipped me, but after a time I went sort of numb and it didn't hurt as much. All the while he wailed loose words and quoted from the Good Book. And each passage from the Scripture brought another strike.

Then it was over. He left me lying on the hard-packed floor and locked the door. Tears flowed and I could scarcely move. I finally managed to pull my trousers on and spent the whole day in the shed, cold and without supper. Sometime later I heard Uncle Frank slam the cabin door and leave, and I heard him still mumbling something under his breath when he returned many hours later.

It wasn't too long after that he started into drinking.

Uncle Frank got powerful drunk, raved throughout the night, and swore at God, and the other traders, and the authorities, and the blacks and whites alike with no difference between them. He'd gone and said everything the parson says is a sin against the Almighty. I thought for a time he was going to come back and lay it on me again, but he didn't, and I was thankful for it, too. If he'd returned, he might have killed me he was in such a condition.

Despite what Uncle Frank said about sinning against God with Ronnie, I think the Almighty was with me that night. Anyhow, Uncle Frank carried on until the early hours of the morning. I could make out nearly every word and sound from the cabin because the woodshed lay right alongside with scarce a space between. Finally, it got quiet, and Uncle Frank fell asleep I guess, because he didn't make any noise other than a wheezing sound, like a drunken snore.

Come early morning, just before first light when the sun rose over the east bluffs, I made out a shuffling outside the shed. There was no window to peer through to see what was making the scuffing sounds, but then I heard Ronnie's voice, barely a whisper, coming through the slats.

"Clayt. You in there?"

"Yeh," I whispered back.

"Don't worry 'bout making low voices. I looked through the cabin window and your uncle's fast asleep."

"Can you open the door?" I called.

"It's locked, but I think I can jimmy the latch."

After a time, he jimmied the latch with his jackknife and shot the bolt open. We slipped back into the woods and headed toward the river and, when we were at a safe distance, Ronnie showed me the marks his father had put on him when Uncle Frank showed up and told him about what he'd seen.

Ronnie looked a mess: welts cropping up along his backside like new-shelled peas. The sight of it made me sick. I told him what he looked like from behind since, of course, he couldn't see.

I lowered my trousers down for him to see. "Judgin' from what you say, I reckon you appear the same," he said. "You got welts the size of two-bit pieces and turning all black and blue."

I volunteered to skip back to the cabin and get the green salve Pop used to heal up wounds, but Ronnie said no. He took the whole thing like a man.

In case Uncle Frank came looking for me again when he found me gone, we spent the whole day along the river a far piece from the cabin, wading in the shallows and fishing with a make-shift pole.

We caught a nice-size cat and baked it in mud and leaves, using matches Ronnie had brought from home to start the fire. We sat around the fire for a long spell afterwards, not saying much to one another. Ronnie whittled on a piece of willow, real thoughtful like, while I hunched up against a log, digging my toes into the soft, warm sand. At some length, Ronnie broke the silence.

"Clayt, I've been a-thinking' and I'm not going' back home. There just ain't no good use in it." He carved his willow until there wasn't anything left but shavings which he picked up one by one and tossed into the fire. "All I get is whippings," he added, thoughtful and quiet, "from my pap, from Old Man Dodson, too. It just ain't worth it."

Ronnie went on as to how he was going to live like his brother, Johnny, alone somewhere where nobody'd bother him, and he could do what he darned well pleased. Of course, I agreed with him because he was right.

"I don't have a real father," I said to Ronnie, "and my mother lies bones and dust in her grave." I decided then and there to swear the same. "If you'll have me, I'll head along with you."

Ronnie had been waiting for me to say that. "Just think of what we can do!" he said, his voice swelling with excitement. "I got this secret place down along the bluffs near the Indian caves," he added. "I go there when I want to be alone but seeing' we're brothers-in-blood and all, you can stay there, too." We had mingled blood from a cut on our palms at my initiation.

Well, we talked it out some and laid out our plans.

"Uncle Frank can do without me and probably wouldn't care if I never come back," I told him.

"Yeh, your Uncle Frank's a whiz-bang of a tyrant – worse than Old Man Dodson. I reckon my pap's 'bout the same. With all the mouths Paps got to feed at home he won't be missing me none either."

So, the plan was set. We'd leave come first light for Ronnie's secret place.

It gets cold by the river at night, and I wasn't dressed but in my trousers, so Ronnie and I went back to the place we'd been when we were caught, and I slung on my shirt, which was wet with morning dew. Stupidly, I tossed my Sunday socks and shoes into the river. I weighed them down first though so they wouldn't float and chance be seen by anybody because I didn't want anyone thinking I'd gone and drowned by accident, or out of desperation. We spent the rest of the day in the deep woods, huddled back-to-back for warmth, and when the sun rose, we headed downstream toward Pop's old cabin.

Freedom is to live one's life with the window of the soul open to new thoughts, new ideas, new aspirations.

–Harold Ickes

CHAPTER 4

The Meyers Boys. The Escape. Heading Upriver to Freedom.

RONNIE CAME FROM A GOOD family, good at least as river folk go.

His father was a good riverman, the best in those parts now that Pop was gone. Mr. Meyers made a decent living by selling his catch at the local market and doing odd jobs in town. He was a tall, rugged, dark-looking man with deep-set gray eyes and curled hair, who enjoyed the companionship of his jug now and again, but he wasn't the heavy drinker like Uncle Frank. Like him, however, he was stern and powerful. Outwardly, Ronnie took after him a lot, but inside he was as different from his father as much as he was from the rest of the family.

Ronnie's mother was a kind and quiet sort of woman, born and bred up along the river, and a good, understanding, and God-fearing Christian soul. Being born to the river, she'd been a strong woman once, but she was none too healthy anymore. Her rheumatism kept her in bed a lot of the time and Ronnie's father would wait dutifully on her as best and often as he could. His work kept him away along the river during the daytime, though, so Ronnie's sisters took care of her until he got home. I guess she'd been strained raising all those children, and the hard life of a river woman had laid her low.

Ronnie had five brothers and a scattering of sisters, all younger except for Johnny and his sister, Annabel. Michael was the youngest-- 'Micky' as his mother called him–being barely five at that time and was a real mamma's boy who always stayed close to home and wasn't much interested in what the older children did. Then there were the twins who were ten and always with their pop along the river. Annabel, who was nearing sixteen, and Crystal, who was twelve, took care of their mother, cooked the meals, and cleaned up about the cabin. Ronnie, of course, was my age, fourteen, but older by about three months. He was full of fun and liked high adventure and doing things up different. I liked Ronnie a lot– especially listening to him talk and dream. Then there was Johnny.

Johnny was the oldest of the Meyers' clan, nearly nineteen, when I knew him best. He was most of six foot tall and really strong and handsome. Ronnie and I used to wrestle him, and the both of us together were no match for his powerful legs and arms. Like his father, Johnny was a fisherman, but the two of them had personalities as different as the meanderings of the moon. Johnny waxed bright and full while Mr. Meyers waned darker, like a declining crescent,

They used to fight with one another something fierce, never coming to blows, but with words all the time as Ronnie told it, so Johnny moved away down river and lived alone. No one really knew Johnny well, but there were a lot of tales about him, spouted mostly by the tavern bums in town. We never knew if the tales were true, but knowing Johnny like I did, I think they were mostly truthful.

Johnny fancied himself a real ladies' man, He used to go into town and try to make time with any girl he saw who caught his eye. Of course, Johnny caught many a girl's fancy, too, being tanned brown and swarthy like a Turk. It had been only a short few months after he'd left the nest that a story began circulating along the river that he'd taken up with the mayor's daughter in Cloverville, about forty miles by river north of Hortonville.

The story went that he'd been sneaking the girl out at night against her daddy's orders, and the two of them had set to frolicking together. I guess they were pretty serious, because after a time, word spread that Johnny had gotten her with child and the whole town was in an outrage, the mayor being a particularly popular and powerful man in those parts. The mayor sent his daughter east apiece to live with a well-off aunt, but the hurt he felt and the fierceness of the uproar didn't settle. Lucky enough for Johnny, no one knew his last name, nor where he lived, so nobody could do anything about it. It's said the mayor threatened to hang Johnny, but sporting with a girl wasn't a capital crime. Rumor had it he was going to cut him somewhere it counted most so he couldn't ever sport another girl. Taking the mayor at his word, Johnny didn't set foot in Cloverville again and hasn't since. I've heard since he headed to Ohio, having stolen away the mayor's daughter and their child and married her legal and proper.

After Ronnie and I had decided for certain on leaving, me to escape Uncle Frank's heavy hand and Ronnie to avoid the trouble he felt at home, we settled our plans and set off for the secret place. It was a goodly piece away upriver, nestled along the high bluffs and the Injun caves where the old river gangs used to camp as Uncle Frank had told. Getting there wasn't any easy task. The river path grows steeper the further upstream you go, and the young willow shoots grow so thick along the bank and the thickets so snag-ball tangled, a deer can scarce meander through. The only easy way (which wasn't an easy way at all) was by boat. But neither of us had a boat. So, we sat for some while, stumped, stretched out along a log fall which laid out over the river apiece, silent and thinking hard.

"We got to have a boat," Ronnie said, breaking our mutual silence. "It ain't no good use in walking'–a rabbit couldn't scarce get through them thickets, much less us."

I asked him how he'd gotten to the secret place before, and he tells me, "I ain't been there since Johnny left. I always used his skiff."

When I, having done some heavy thinking, suggested we build a raft, Ronnie, who was always more practical than me, says, "Clayt, a raft won't do. A raft's too heavy to pole upstream for the two of us. It'd only be good for going down."

We laid back and pondered some more on it, and it was getting mighty wearisome lying there and thinking and letting all our plans go to ruin. At last, after some length, an idea fired my mind like a lantern overturned sets the straw in a barn to burning.

"I got it!" I nearly shouted. "We'll borrow Uncle Frank's skiff and row our way upriver."

"That's a great idea!" Ronnie allowed, "so long's your Uncle Frank don't catch us."

As it was nearing dusk, Ronnie and I decided we'd wait until nightfall to sneak back to the cabin and get what was needed and borrow the skiff. Knowing Uncle Frank like I did, I was sure he'd be drunk asleep around midnight and that would be the best time to make our move. So, Ronnie and I camped out along the bank, roasted up a carp he'd caught, and swapped yarns until it was time to go.

"If Uncle Frank catches us," I said to Ronnie as we snaked the pathway toward Pop's cabin, "he'll blister the both of us good."

Save for the monotone of the river slow flowing past the cabin landing and the chirping of the crickets on an early summer night, everything was still. An easy breeze fluttered the treetops along the river, but made no sound, and the full moon was out, large and yellow faced, floating light among them.

Though we could live well off the river, catching then roasting or baking, even smoking channel cat, or blue cat, a carp, or an occasional paddlefish, we needed some provisions. We needed flour for slap-dough bread and biscuits and matches to get our fires going. I'd learned from Pop several ways to start a fire, and Ronnie knew them too. The best was finding a piece of flint and striking it against the steel backside of a knife blade, setting sparks into a nest of dry, fine-torn cottonwood or cedar bark. If conditions were right, in no time a body could have a fire. But though the early settlers had used it with success, it wasn't nearly so easy as a match.

Other staple items were needed too. A canvas sack of dry beans would come in useful, and a few pockets full of coffee beans which we could grind ourselves. All those things were in the cabin. The only problem would be getting in past Uncle Frank, who, even when he was drunk, was no easy sleeper.

The important thing was staying tomb quiet as we approached the cabin. The least unusual noise might set Uncle Frank into waking.

Nearby the cabin, a horseshoe bend of heavy cedars near ringed the clearing. Ronnie and I moved death quiet, like the Indians had when they stalked the settlers sixty years before. I was just rounding a full-branched cedar, Ronnie at my heels behind, when a shape flashed up in the moonlight. There was a wild snort, like a bellows blast in a blacksmith's hearth, and a pawing at the ground. My heart near leaped up with a start and a shout was about to cut loose when Ronnie slapped his hand over across my mouth and held it tight. A deer! A huge buck deer–the biggest one I'd seen all year–was standing not three-foot distant, head bent low, his antler rack glistening in the moonlight surging through the trees. My heart thumped like a steamboat piston and Ronnie's weren't quiet either. With his hand laid across my mouth and his chest heaved up against my back, I could feel it pounding hard.

Ronnie and I stood frozen. The big buck just kept a baleful eye toward us–not moving. Then, with a sudden start, he flung his head full back, reared up on his hind legs, and crashed up through the trees, stopping only long enough to turn again and snort the air in warning not to follow.

"Whoa! That was close!" Ronnie whispered.

"You said it! Thought for a minute he was going to charge."

"Ever been run down by a buck?" Ronnie asked, his voice still quivering.

"No. "

"Well, Johnny has. Knocked him clean unconscious. Gave him headaches for a week."

We reckoned quietly how we'd both been mighty lucky in our encounter with the deer. They can be mighty mean.

Once we'd recovered our wits and our hearts stopped racing, Ronnie and I sneaked fox-quiet around the cabin. I knew the door'd be bolted shut so we tried a window on the shed side. Peering in through a crack between the window coverings, I could make out in the darkness the bunk Uncle Frank used. He was sleeping on it, his legs jackknifed against his upper body with one arm thrown across his eyes. A crock jug of sipping whiskey sat on the table beside the bunk.

I knew that to slip in and get away without him noticing, I had to be so quiet all he'd hear was the steady tock, tock, tock of the windup clock on the beam above the fireplace. Whispering to Ronnie to crouch down and wait for me beside the shed, I dusted my feet up good in the fine, loose dirt which lay by the stone foundation. The dust on my feet would make the skin dry so my feet wouldn't squeak across the floorboards once I was inside.

Pulling up the window was a painful task–and slow–but I raised it high enough to crawl inside. Ronnie told me to do it quiet as a mouse, but I did it quiet as a ghost walks. In the dead stillness of the night, you can hear a mouse scurry across the floor. With a ghost, you can't.

The window frame yawned a groan when I set my weight on it, but the creaking didn't muster Uncle Frank. Having done all the cooking and the cabin cleaning, I knew where everything we needed was right off. Most of it was right out in the open on the low shelves beside the cookstove.

I slipped my shirt off carefully, all the while keeping a steady stare at Uncle Frank who was sleeping peacefully, not moving. He was snoring some and breathing out the smell of stale liquor. The cabin had the musty odor of urine and spilled whiskey–just like it had before Pop died.

The matches, beans, and coffee were easy enough to find, and I laid them carefully together inside my shirt that I'd made into a bundle to carry things off easy. The flour was another matter. It was in a huge, fifty-pound sack, near full, and standing in a corner with a beam of moonlight striking it directly. If Uncle Frank woke up, he'd see me standing there for certain. There was an empty canister sitting on a shelf nearby, so I took it, pulled the top off easy, and scooped the flour in it. All the while I kept my eyes pasted on Uncle Frank's limp body.

A wheezing grunt shot through the gloomy silence of the room. A chilling sharpness jolted up my backbone and lodged against my skull. I froze. With no further sound coming, I turned slow and shot a quick glance toward Uncle Frank. He flopped over on his back and folded his arms across him like a laid-out corpse. For an instant I could have sworn his eyes were open and he was glaring at me, but he didn't move or seem to see me. I waited, frozen still like a winter pond until I saw his head roll downwards and his chin butt against his chest. He was asleep.

Clutching the bundle close to me, I didn't waste any time getting to the window and lowering the things out to Ronnie. Then I slipped out myself and, still not making any sounds, Ronnie and I headed off together to the landing where Uncle Frank's skiff was moored.

Having loaded ourselves and our provisions, I took the pocketknife Pop had given me, edged the blade lengthwise along the rope, and cut us free. I did it so it appeared the rope was frayed, not cut, and that the skiff broke loose and drifted downstream. When we were free-floating, the current started carrying us down river, but we grabbed the oars and headed north. Ronnie oared first for a time, until he was winded, then I took over.

We hugged close to the bankside. Upriver, the main current cut away from the land and churned in mid-river, and once we were free of its tug and rowing was easier.

It's dangerous to be floating along the river at night, but we were out of the current where the most danger lay. Snags —"sawyers" as the riverboat men called them--could snap up anywhere. The sawyers were great logs and sometimes whole trees which had toppled into the river and were carried along downstream. Often times a body wouldn't see them until he was right on top of them, and then it was too late. They'd often lay just underneath the surface, soaked through with water but not heavy enough to sink. Then, if the movement in the river was just right, they'd bob up to the surface where a boat could slam into them. One large sawyer, caught in the pull of the current, could rip the bottom of a great steamboat clear through. It would have taken only a small log to snare our skiff.

But snags weren't the only danger along this stretch of river. There weren't as many paddle-wheelers as in the years past, but the traffic was brisk enough at times. Sounding their steam whistles when they churned along a bend, or at night when they neared a landing to let off passengers or cargo, they were easy enough to hear. They'd be generally lit up well, too, unless they were carrying cargo only, and you could see them soon enough to steer away. But when the fog blanket came up along the river, it was a time of nerve-jangling tension for anyone caught along the water.

When Ronnie's pop and mine were swapping tales once, Ronnie's father had said how he was nearly run down and drowned by a great side-wheeler in a fog.

He'd been out fishing in his skiff and the catch hadn't been good that day. Staying out longer than he normally did, he'd rowed toward home at night. He'd hugged the east channel bank tight but had come to the point where he needed to angle across the river and point toward the opposite shore. The fog had come up quick and in no time there was nothing but swirling gray all around him. The light from his lantern didn't help much and, by all accounts, he was rowing the river blind.

As Ronnie's pop told it, he could hear the clanking of the piston rod as it turned the paddle wheel on the boat but couldn't tell where the sound was coming from exactly. Fog plays tricks on your ears – sounds can be close in or far away. You can scarcely tell. Mr. Meyers listened close for the sound and kept on rowing, the clanking and churning noise growing louder, then nearly disappearing,

A light from the bow loomed up suddenly, just ahead, and he pulled for all he was worth. But it wasn't any use, the bow sprung out of the fog bank and was almost on top of him. The wheel churned up the inky water and shuddered like thunder rolling between the banks. He made the choice tween his boat and himself and jumped just as the wheel slammed past. The skiff was caught up in the undertow and pulled down beneath the steamboat. Mr. Meyers used all the strength in his powerful arms and legs to stay afloat and keep from being swallowed under, too. Half drowned, and with no other choice but swim, he struck out for shore. Of course, his skiff was crushed into splinters which floated up about him, and his catch was gone. But he made it to shore and home. There's scarce any love between rivermen, like Pop and Mr. Meyers, and the steamboats.

Ronnie and I pulled along for several miles. We were about five miles above Pop's cabin with about seven more to go as Ronnie figured it. The going wasn't easy, so we oared into shore and rested up a piece.

The river was restful and quiet. Ronnie rolled out two thin blankets he'd squirreled away from home which we used to help keep warm. We wrapped them across our shoulders to keep off the chill and dampness of the night air and laid back, Ronnie resting his head at the bow and me at the stern of the skiff.

The skiff rocked gently as the river flowed and lapped against it and near lulled us into sleep. The moon floated down lower over the river, and I could see the silver patches of light reflecting off the water and the bare outline of the tree-studded bank on the opposite side. A fish jumped, breaking the surface near the skiff. Its soft sound drifted past me and off into the darkness below. The river and the land were beautiful yet, but I set into wondering what it'd been like a hundred years before, before the settlers came, before the paddle ships scurried and thundered along its banks when only the Indians were here.

"Ronnie," I called out softly, "you awake?"

"I'm just resting," came his equally soft reply.

"You ever wonder what it was like before we come here, before our folks came and before their folks?"

"The river? Oh, I guess it was 'bout like now. Quiet."

I was interested in what he planned on doing when we got to the secret place, and I asked him. Ronnie was silent for a minute, thinking to himself before he spoke.

"We're going to live off the land and do for ourselves, and fish a lot and swim some and adventure awhile I guess."

"And after that?"

"And after that?" he echoed me. "What more can a body want to do?"

"We can't swim and fish and lay out along the river the rest of our lives," I said.

He paused for thought some more, knowing it was true. "Guess I'd like to be like Johnny. I'd like to live somewhere 'long the river, maybe marry and raise up a family." He began to stir and rustled himself into a sitting position. There was a far-off look about him. "I don't want to be like Pap," he said. "I don't want to be a riverman all my life. Guess I'd like to be somebody important."

Neither of us talked for a while after that, save for some mundane passings, and a short while later we were up and on our way again, rowing easy up the river.

My turn had come at the oars and as I pulled it was almost like rowing on a still pond. The river didn't seem to mind our being on her. In fact, she seemed to help us along.

As dawn began to break, the darkness lifting up and off the water and the morning light set in to filter past the trees, my mind set off on daydreaming. It was Ronnie I was thinking about mostly. Ronnie was strong, not just in his body, but strong where it mattered most—in his heart. He was a dreamer, sure, but he was a doer, too. Thinking about Ronnie married up and living somewhere along the river, raising up a fine, large family and being somebody of importance—a sheriff maybe, or a mayor—set me into thinking about myself. What things lay ahead for me? Would I live forever along the river; be a riverman like Pop? There were no answers coming. At least not yet.

A boy's will is the wind's will. And the thoughts of youth are long, long thoughts.
　　　　　–Henry Wadsworth Longfellow

CHAPTER 5

Ronnie's Secret Place. We begin a Search.

A SHORT WHILE AFTER DAWN had broken, the skiff pointed toward a piece of land which jutted out from the level bank and into the river like the pointer finger on a hand.

"That's it, Clayt!" Ronnie yelled out, excitement in his voice, "That's my secret place."

The riverbank along this stretch was steep. The land finger rose up at a sharp pitch from the level to a height of about fifty feet.

Pointing out like it did from the clean lines of the shore on both sides of the river, it looked somehow out of place. Young stands of willow thickets lined its banks, prancing their way down near the water. A strip of bare sand, scarcely two yards wide, rimmed the finger, and here and there along it, clusters of yellow flowers sprung out around it.

From a distance, the bank line lay out like a green and yellow and gray-brown patchwork quilt running narrow right along.

As I was rowing, Ronnie took charge as pilot and pointed me in toward 'his landing' as he called it.

The landing was a cove, like a 'U' scooped in at the land end of the finger, about ten yards wide at the mouth then curving inwards at the center. Clustered clumps of half-grown cottonwoods stood lined up and gathered like soldiers standing at the morning ready. Their smooth, pale trunks glinted gray and shot short shadows over the water. Beyond the young tree stand, the older cottonwoods soared up sixty feet or higher, their tops fanned out above the hill peak. Their bark was pale like the younger trees but deep-furrowed, giving away their age.

The landing was on the down-current side of the river, so the water here was calm and even-flowing, near as still as a farm pond, with scarce a ripple on it.

"Tween those trees," Ronnie called out, "set her in 'tween those two trees."

My backside to the landing spot Ronnie wanted me to pull toward, I slung around side-saddle on the board I was sitting on to see. Two sentinel cottonwoods, greater around than both of us linking hands together could circle, rose skywards so high I couldn't see their tops. I pivot-oared and pointed the skiff in between them.

The skiff bellied in on a mud slope. Ronnie leaped out, his bare feet sinking in the soft, deep mud, and he pulled the skiff, front end high, up on the slope then looped the bow rope around a stump jutting up from the bank. We loaded up our provisions and I followed Ronnie's lead up a winding path near overgrown by brush.

"This was Johnny's secret place before he passed it on to me," he said, huffing his way up the winding trail. "There's a slab hut he built himself up just ahead a piece."

Near the peak of the hill, the trail leveled off some and wasn't nearly so steep. The hiking was easier going. A small clearing– natural I think, though it could've been hewn out years before by a good, strong back and a sharp-bladed ax–loomed up just ahead. Between two tall cottonwoods, a slab-boarded hut lay its backside up against the hillside. It was Ronnie's 'secret place.'

The hut sure wasn't a place to spend any time in and expect to be comfortable. The clapboard walls leaned sideways like two young willows in a gale, and if it hadn't been for a well-weathered two by ten attached to the back of the hut and nailed tight to the two trees, a good wind would have pushed it over.

We lay up our provisions inside the hut and lay out on the hard-packed floor to rest a spell before heading off and having a look around.

The hut was a cramped-up place about eight feet wide and the same long. It was old and had been put together quickly. The boards gapped in places wide enough to fit your hand through, and the sides, like I said, tilted at an angle to the south. To make the truth known, it looked like a storehouse shed about to topple over. Ronnie, though, thought it was mighty beautiful.

Having not eaten for nigh on to an entire day, Ronnie and I set into stirring up some breakfast. Eaten and having rested up some, about mid-morning we stopped lounging around like two tired porch dogs and set out to explore the hideaway.

The finger point was like an island except it was connected by its backside to the land. Climbing to the top of it, we gazed out over the entire river. About five miles further north, the bluffs rose up high from the riverbank on one side like the walls of a picture book fortress, the only difference being that these walls were made of clay. Below, the river stretched out like a sunning silver snake and slid off into the distance, twisting and bending as it flowed. From the hillcrest we could see the river valley from some miles clear in both directions. As Uncle Frank had said, the old river gangs hid out in places like this and from their vantage could overlook the entire river and set out traps when a cargo boat was coming.

Ronnie had never seriously explored the entire finger, so we set out to do just that. But not until after a cooling swim in the cove where the skiff was shored.

The water in the quiet cove was warm but still refreshing considering the heat from the sun beating down on the land point. Ronnie and I set to frolicking some in the tree-shaded, chest-deep water. I got it in my head to challenge him to a wrestling contest in the mud shoal near where the skiff was moored. Long as I'd known Ronnie, he'd never been whipped at wrestling. He won. I just wasn't an even match for his powerful legs and shoulders. Of course, we were covered head to foot with the gooey mud and swam to wash it off before it hard-caked dry.

"Ain't it great," Ronnie said as we were washing off the mud, "freebooting' along the river with nobody to worry about but ourselves?"

"If Pop was still alive, I'd most likely be somewhere else but here," I said, and I reckoned it was true, "but I don't think I could've stayed much longer around Uncle Frank."

"Nor me 'round my pap. I ain't never been whupped like that. I can still feel his shaving strap when I think about it." A thoughtful, far-away sort of look beamed up in Ronnie's eyes. "Clayt, I'm mighty glad it was you who came along with me. Sam and Charlie– even Mike's okay–but you're the most special friend I got."

"Aw, Ronnie, cut it out." I said. "You're starting to sound as gooey as this mud."

Ronnie threw a fist strike at my shoulder, real playful like, and I struck him back, and before long we were rolling one another around in the mud like before.

After lulling out around the cove, soaking in the sun and growing browner than we were, we wandered off down the shoreline a piece and looked around. There wasn't a thing in sight along the river. The rippling water lapped easy against the land, flowing southwards a thousand miles toward the sea.

Ronnie was better acquainted with the land side of the finger point than with the side the current flowed against. So, after meandering up the sand strip a piece and seeing nothing that interested either of us, we headed back to the shelter of the cove. We gathered up our clothes and dressed, then hiked the hill up the winding trail to the hut, Near the top, the sun beat down without mercy, so I tossed my shirt inside the hut. That was later to prove a big mistake. Ronnie left his shirt on, but open-fronted.

The backside of the land point was nothing like where we'd landed. Trees here grew up close together: the cottonwood and basswood and willow, with some twisted scrub oak and stunted cedars which the light couldn't reach. It was hard making headway through it. Ronnie was in the lead, dodging the gooseberry tangles and the ivy creepers, with me following near behind. There wasn't so much as a deer path, so we were forced to make our own.

"Think anybody's been around here before excepting us?" I asked.

"Guess, except for Johnny maybe and some Indians years ago, we're the only ones. I ain't seen so much as ashes from a cooking fire in the times I've been here," Ronnie answered.

It was easy enough to see how Ronnie was probably right. Most folks, unless they're traveling by steamboat, head down river, riding along with the current. Anyone coming up would most likely have ridden the opposite shore which wasn't as steep and where they could land easily and set up camp.

This side of the land point was one of the most inhospitable I'd ever seen with its twists and tangles and shallow-water bogs. The only reason a body would land here without a purpose was by accident.

It was getting toward dusk. The sky, which had been stark blue earlier, was beginning to turn gray-white. Down in the deep part of the trees the light was dimming fast and in some parts was almost black. Ronnie and I parlayed together a time and decided we'd have enough light yet to look around and finish our exploring. We'd come down toward the shoreline, about ten yards from the water, when Ronnie, who was still ahead, caught sight of a glint, like fading sunlight striking metal. Of course, there's nothing more curious than two boys out exploring, so we forced ourselves along the downslope toward it. There, just ahead, on the other side of a low willow hedge, was what looked like a pipe jutting up. We pushed closer, me nearly toppling over when my foot caught in a mess of rotting deadfall.

"Clayt!" Ronnie sounded out a sudden surprise streaming from his voice. "There's a boat down here!"

Sure enough, there was a boat. She was slung up on the bank, her bow end rising up three feet above the water with her stern end sunk down and mired in the thick mud bank. An old boat, her stern wheel higher than Ronnie and me standing shoulder to foot together, rested silent, the paddle boards splintered and useless.

She was a small boat, scarce fifty feet from bow to stern, and about one-third wide. The upper deck was all that was visible from the land side as the vines and creepers grew up around her thick and heavy. Her rotting deck was sunk nearly out of sight. Atop the wheelhouse was a large brass fitting, like a knob atop a pole. It's what caught Ronnie's eye and lead us to her.

Excitement shot through both of us. She was a packet boat, not built for passengers, though there was no doubt some room for them. She was a cargo-carrier mostly, and she was old; probably older than my and Ronnie's ages put together and then some.

We pushed and shoved and shouldered a pathway through the creepers and willow shoots until we stood beside her.

"Ain't she something'!" Ronnie exclaimed. And I had to allow, she was.

I asked, "How long you suppose she's been setting here?"

"Johnny built the hideout when he was fourteen," Ronnie said, "and he never mentioned no sunken boat. Guess she's been mud-holed here for quite a piece from the looks of her."

The packet boat sat mired in the thick mud ooze of a cove which was just exactly opposite the one we'd landed at. But this cove was on the current side. A jam of heavy logs had scattered up against the open mouth and because of it, the river most near dammed up tight. There was scarce two feet of actual water there and what there was, was stagnant. But the mud was maybe knee deep on me.

The sun was dimming fast. "There's nowhere to stay here tonight," Ronnie said. "It don't make no sense camping on that boat without having' a look around her first and make sure it's safe." There wasn't anyone around except us, and it was certain the boat wasn't going anywhere. I wondered what Ronnie meant by 'safe.'

"Let's get back to the hut," I said. "It'll be pitch dark in half an hour. I don't want to get caught here in the dark. It was hard enough to get here in daylight."

We started back toward camp, not longing to leave the wreck, but deciding to return and explore her some length come morning.

I'd said it was a mistake, me not wearing my shirt. The air was growing chilled, but that wasn't the worst of it. The stagnant, slime-green waters of the cove was a haven and breeding ground for skeeters and, with nightfall coming, they rose in swirling clouds like a thick fog around the wreck site. I couldn't scarce begin to fight them off–there were too many of them. When I'd swat one dead and bloody, another two would land and take a bite. Ronnie, he'd fastened up his shirt and laughed and howled at me as I beat a fast retreat, the nasty, stinging devils nipping at me all the way.

I lay wakeful nearly half the night, and the part I did sleep was filled with dreams about the sunken wreck. Ronnie wasn't sleeping either, so we laid back on our blanket rolls and talked a piece.

"Ronnie, you reckon that wreck might be the *Channel Belle*? I've heard Pap talk about it, but she sunk right down. This wreck's grounded."

"Maybe that's what the authorities wanted folks to think. So's they wouldn't go looking for her. And if it is the *Channel Belle*, maybe there's still some treasure on her."

Ronnie yawned. "Well, maybe. I didn't see any nameplate on her, but there ought a be one somewhere. We'll look for one come morning."

I don't right recall when sleep came on me until morning came and waking time, but the dreams came back. Those dreams called up Uncle Frank sitting around the cabin table with Pop and me, talking about the *Channel Belle* which was said to have sunk near here. Thoughts of barrels filled brim-full with whiskey, cases of copper and quicksilver casks danced through my mind like a thunderstorm. The warming fire crackled up inside Pop's cozy cabin. Uncle Frank was telling us the tale about gold coins, thousands of dollars' worth. Some say as much as half a million.

We rose up early–just after dawn. I was first because of all my excitement, while Ronnie lounged lazy for a time. After breakfast-- slap-dough cakes and coffee–we started down the hillside to where the wreck was shored. Having felt our way along the day before, and in the dark, the going wasn't nearly so rough, and we reached her side in no time flat.

The boat was all over decay and ruin. We shinnied up onboard and surveyed the deck. In places, the boards were rotted through and where they weren't, they were soft and spongy, sinking down and mushing up as we stepped over them. Green moss–like what grows on dying trees–covered the deck planks and was creeping up the outer walls. The cove hung heavy with the river's morning fog and the air around the wreck site was thick and foul-smelling.

There were a couple of cabins on the upper deck, their louvered doors hanging crooked on busted hinges.

"Looks like they've been picked clean," Ronnie noted, glancing inside of them.

Probably her crew had taken everything of value when they'd abandoned her. All there was, were stacks of yellowed, crumbling newssheets with names of towns further up the river. The newest dates were nearly thirty years before the time the *Channel Belle* was lost. "How come Johnny never found this wreck?" I asked Ronnie.

"I never said he didn't. If he did, he just never saw fit to tell."

We checked the other cabin, which must have been the captain's. It was bigger than the first, and through a door which opened toward the stern, a crumbling stairway led up to the pilothouse on top. Doors which slid on roller grooves in the floor and ceiling and opened out, lay at the far end and opened up to closets.

"Look, Ronnie," I said, opening one of them, "a coat!" On a bar inside, a dark-blue coat hung limp, its sleeves near eaten through by mold.

"Must've been the captain's," Ronnie allowed, "judging' from the gold braid laced around the cuffs."

A walnut desk sat near the cove side of the wreck, its back against the windowed wall. The drawers, with cast brass pulls, were open and empty.

I was first to venture up along the sagging stairway, being careful where I placed my feet, and entered the small wheelhouse at the very top. Ronnie followed me up. From that high up place, we overlooked the cove with its mud shoal and fallen trees and the path we'd trampled through the woods where the willow shoots bent back.

"Ronnie!" I sung out, looking at the giant wheel. I was the first to see them. "There's bullet holes here and what looks like bloodstains!" Sure enough, along the wheel rim gaped a splintered hole with a lead ball lodged in plain sight. Ronnie took out his pocketknife, dug it out and pirated it away in his trousers pocket as a souvenir. Beside the wheel was a dark black stain large enough to stand inside with both feet set together.

"It's too old to tell if it might be blood," Ronnie said, plying at it with his knife blade. "But the bullet hole says this boat was pirated."

It looked it sure enough. There was nothing in the cabins except for the captain's jacket and a pile of crumbling papers. The wreck had been picked clean of anything of value. The bullet hole in the wheel rim and others we found in the window frame proved there'd been a tragedy.

We set off to explore some more. Below, the boiler was a mass of flaking rust, but there was a wood pile stacked up neatly against it, the logs split and looking ready to feed a fire they'd never see.

The hold below the upper deck was like a cave, pitch black in its oozing darkness and empty save for a half-dozen vacant casks which had been split open. Sticky ooze sucked about our ankles, and it wasn't long before we discovered leeches latching on to us, clinging about our legs like squirming black patches and looking like fat garden worms. We hauled out of the hold but quick, and Ronnie scraped them off with his knife blade. Those leeches were harder to get off of him than they were off me because of his hairy legs. He squirmed and yowled some whenever he snagged a hair.

Two great logs–dead trees with leafless, bleached-out branches that reached outwards like stark ghosts from the mud shoal–had jammed against the cove-side hull. No doubt they'd been carved out from the banks upriver and carried downstream by the current during flood time. The trunks of both had pierced the rotting hull which was filled with foul-smelling silt.

I stalked over to the bow end of the wreck and examined the single smokestack which had tilted forward over the deck. It balanced like a half-drunk tightrope walker, held in place by a rusting steel line.

Atop its twenty-foot height was a fluted metal piece like a king's crown, too big to fit a human head. Then I caught sight of it. A name plaque made of brass, bolted half-way up the stack. And I could read it plain: *CAPTAIN GEORGE* it read. The beached wreck wasn't the *Channel Belle* as Ronnie had thought.

A small wooden box lay up beside the fore rail. Beside it, a lump of blackened, rusting metal caught my eye. It was a pistol. I stooped down and held it in my hands and examined it. The hammer lay cocked back like it was about to fire, but the works had rusted shut. A once deadly bullet still lay chambered in its lifeless cylinder. At first, I thought I'd keep it as a souvenir–like Ronnie's bullet–but I reckoned I hadn't any use for it and laid it back where I'd found it.

As I set the gun back down, my heart near leaped a foot! A thick, black shape like a piece of rubber lay coiled beside the box. A moccasin! And it wasn't the ordinary water snake a body sees all along the river either, but a cottonmouth. And its bite is deadly. That snake was poised to strike, and my hand was scarce a foot from its deadly head!

The snake must've been five foot long and at its thickest part as large around as my upper arm! Its thick head perched forward in the midst of its circled body, its stark-white, cotton mouth propped open. That snake cut loose a hiss like water spattered into hot grease, and I lurched back, nearly tumbling over my own legs, which had turned to rubber. I cut loose a war-whoop which brought Ronnie scrambling from the stern-side.

"S-snake! Moccasin! There," I stammered, pointing a shaking hand bow ward.

While I sat quaking on the molding deck, Ronnie moved slow and careful toward the crate. The moccasin lay coiled, frozen, its white mouth flared open, its cold, black, pinhead eyes staring balefully at him. I'd gotten back my wind and the heart-shakes were subsiding now, so I stepped up to Ronnie. The moccasin, seeing how it was outnumbered, unwrapped its body slowly and slithered around the box then pitched itself over the side, headways into the slimy water.

"That snake was probably as scared of you as you of it," Ronnie laughed as we watched it slink a path through the water plants.

"There's no way of telling that!" I reckoned; a might upset at Ronnie making fun of me. If the truth was known, it was. Snakes don't cotton to humans any more than humans to them. But I couldn't scarce believe how close I'd come to being bit.

We'd explored the packet boat wreck from stern to stem and, finding nothing of any value, decided we'd had enough of the exploring. On our way back to camp, Ronnie and I set into talking, asking one another questions and speculating on what we'd seen.

"From the looks of her I'd say she didn't run aground," Ronnie said. "Looks more like she was lured in."

The best answer we could think of was river pirates.

"I'd guess the land point was a hideout for a gang of river pirates long before Johnny came to claim it," I told Ronnie. The finger, with its high-peaked hill and dense forest cover, was the perfect vantage point to overlook the river and not be seen.

"Bet that river gang set up a trap to call the packet in toward shore, then attacked her," Ronnie allowed. "The bullet holes we saw was evidence of that."

"I reckon so. And I bet they killed the captain and the crew, then stripped her bare and left her sitting against the shoal." Then, on second thought, I said, "But wouldn't there be bodies aboard–bones at least–if that was true?"

"Maybe they buried 'em. Most likely though they weighted 'em down and heaved 'em in the river."

We wandered back. The *Captain George* lay resting in its murky graveyard, being slowly reclaimed by the river and the land. It wasn't the *Channel Belle*, and there hadn't been a treasure. In that we were disappointed. But we'd had quite an adventure on her.

The night approaches ... Bringing dread of that irrevocable journey to Eternal Sleep. Is it so awesome? Ask the dead,

–Lloyd Hartley

CHAPTER 6

The River Floods. We Witness a Disaster.

RONNIE AND I SPENT OUR DAYS along the river and the land point in much the same ways we had when the gang was together. Fishing took up a load of time, both for pleasure and the necessity of eating, and it gave us the chance to sit out along the riverbank and talk or be quiet and think to ourselves. There were times when one or the other, sometimes even both of us, would want to be alone, but Ronnie and I were fast friends and seldom tired of one another's company. But a person needs to be by himself at times.

All cramped up and squeezed together as Ronnie's slab hut was none too large, oft-times I'd take a blanket roll and head out by myself to sleep. On especially warm nights I favored a tiny clearing near the nail point of the finger, right at the very tip where the land slid downward toward the river. The sky was nearly always cloudless and bright, and the distant stars shined like white jewels sparkling against a jet-black curtain.

At these quiet times, I'd often ponder on the moon's face, picking out the features, dreaming some on what they were: mountain ranges (which I'd never seen except in picture books), valleys wide and deep, and lines that looked like rivers flowing across the face. Beneath that dark-jeweled curtain, I felt small and lonesome.

By gazing close, I could make out colors in the stars. They glowed not only white but sparkled yellow and red and blue like fine diamonds and fine jewels in a wealthy woman's ring.

More often than not, Ronnie and I were together, though. We laughed and joked and carried on. Ronnie loved to swim and, of course, so did I, and we frolicked a lot together in the cove or somewhere along the land point. I'd turned a deep brown, like a polished leather saddle, and Ronnie said my hair had turned a light and silky yellow with the sun. Of course, without a mirror to see myself I couldn't tell.

All things good don't last. We'd been on this land point going on three weeks when the good weather finally broke. The sunny days turned sour; great black cloud puffs rolled up on the north horizon, then floated in from the west and south. The rains followed, pouring in on us and, for a time, we were more than a might uncomfortable.

In our excitement about finally being free and resting easy–me away from Uncle Frank and Ronnie from his folks–we'd forgot to fix the hut. Thick rain, with the wind behind it, drove in through the cracks on one side. When we managed to get a blanket up to stop it, the rain would change direction and blow in from another angle, and the roof leaked something awful. Finally, we were forced to make a trip down to the wreck of the *Captain George* and pry off parts of her to use as patching for the hut.

The weather was foul, and it rained for days and days without a stop. Our blankets were damp and our clothes were soaked, and the small fire we built inside the hut was but little comfort. Together, if a body could have seen us, we must've appeared like two soaked spaniels, wrapped up naked in our blankets while our clothes were strung up above the fire to dry.

Ronnie said it looked like Noah's Flood from the Bible stories we'd both read.

Suddenly, nearly as quickly as the rain had come, it stopped. But the sky didn't brighten any, remaining dull-gray and overcast. The river was rising though, and higher every hour.

"I'm worried 'bout the skiff, Clayt," Ronnie said one afternoon as we stood peering out over the rising river. "I think it's best we pull it up some."

Together we scampered down the trail to the cove to pull it higher up on shore.

When we reached the cove, we saw the water had risen near four feet; the mudbank the skiff was on was gone and under water. Our skiff was floating up and tugging at the mooring line and the stump it was anchored to was nearly out of sight.

"If we haul it up another ten or fifteen foot, it should be safe enough," he said, and we did. There was no doubt now but that the river was in flood stage.

We lingered around the cove a while longer, catching glimpses of the river rising, then stalked back up the hill where we could look out over the river on both sides for some miles. The river churned up wild, dark-brown, and muddy from bank to bank. Opposite from the finger point where the shoreline sat low, the river had overflowed and was widening with the passing hours. Soon, the river had grown near a quarter mile wide, murky water flooding through the woods with only the tops of the taller trees jutting out above it.

I'd seen floods before and I remembered one spring when I was six the water rose right up to the landing of our cabin, totting Pop's boat away. It had kept on rising near up to the door. Mrs.Hawkinds' cabin, which was down a piece on lower ground, was flooded out. The river had moved on in, right to the top of her cookstove. She and her daughters had had to tote and haul all the household goods up to the second floor. It was quite a mess. Pop had lent a hand when the water receded and I did, too. Scooping out the mud was the hardest thing. It was foul-smelling and clung to everything.

Pop and I were luckier, our cabin being set upon a stone foundation about two feet above ground level. The landing was pitched higher, too, which helped. There was a trap in the cabin floor and Pop used to store his fall potato diggings in the cool dark. After the flood went down, I spent hours snaring out crawdads with a cheeseball tied to a length of string.

This time the flood was different though. I'd never seen the river so wide and wild.

There was little for Ronnie and me to do except hole up and wait for the river to calm down. We went about our business and, at about five o'clock, warmed some beans, made some cornbread, and cooked supper. It wasn't but a short while after eating that we heard this awful noise out along the river. Right away we dropped what we were doing and sprinted out to have a look.

About a half-mile below the land point, a steamboat churned upriver, no doubt bound toward Cloverville. Though it wasn't uncommon for riverboats to plough upriver during flood times, the captain of this boat had misjudged the situation and now was in real trouble.

Apparently, the pilot, having seen how the main channel was clogged with floating logs and whole uprooted trees, tried to steer cross-current and come up on the calmer side below the point. That had been his deadly error.

From where Ronnie and I were standing we could make out where the channel had shifted and, in doing so, had stirred up a shoal bank. From atop the Texas deck in the pilothouse, neither the pilot nor the captain had seen the shallow water. It wasn't near deep enough for the steamboat to churn over. Now her bow-belly was beached fast, her great sidewheel shuddering to a halt. Great streaming clouds of jet-black smoke belched from her stacks and the boiler whistles were full open and piercing the air with long, shrill-sounding shrieks.

Her bow end bellied fast, and her engines stopped, the stern end twisted sideways to the raging water. She was a dead wall target for charging trees and logs. The railings along the upper deck were crowded with passengers. Even above the rushing sound the river and the boat's steam whistle made, we could hear their frightened screams.

While we stood dumb-struck, watching, a whole tree–near as big as the sentinel cottonwoods which stood guard at the cove–lumbered down current, swept past the shoal with the charging water, and slammed stump-end broadside into the paddle housing. Wood shattered and splintered everywhere; the paddle housing and wheel buckets flew in a thousand pieces through the air.

More passenger shouts and screams followed. More piercing whistle shrieks.

The engineer about this time was racing below decks like a man who'd heard a death knell, fighting to douse the boiler fires before the river came rushing in on them. Too late! An explosion, the likes of such I'd never heard (and hope never to hear again), split the air like a thunder peel and set the land to rocking. A moment later, a ball of blazing fire rocketed skywards big as the boat itself.

The blast wrenched away the stern third of the boat, and human bodies, or pieces of them, flew everywhere. A searing pain gripped my stomach and held it fast. The screams and shrieks of the passengers grew louder. Ronnie and I were helpless but stood by fast and watched.

Confusion raged rampant all along the boat. The river glowed crimson where the flaming timbers had scattered out along the landside and much of the exploded wreckage was being jolted downstream by the sweeping flow of the surging current.

Ronnie and I didn't speak for the longest while–like we were frozen in a trance. We knew we had to act. Somehow.

"Ronnie," I said, turning toward him and still horror-struck, "we've got to do something!"

"Let's get the skiff," was all he said, and we lit out running full tilt down the narrow trail to where the skiff was moored.

We wouldn't have been able to reach the wreck at all if it hadn't been for the land finger protecting us from the raging current and the sand shoal which kept a lot of the water back. Ronnie rowed because he was stronger in the shoulders and could pull the skiff along faster.

Ronnie hugged in tight to the land side, keeping the bow end pointed downriver so we wouldn't slither sideways against the current and maybe capsize.

The closer we drew toward the steamboat, the worse the disaster looked. Bodies which had been blown skywards by the blast lay crumpled up limp along the portside deck. Some of the bodies, their clothes shredded and charred, lay heaped against the sand shoal or were being quickly swept away to disappear downriver. A fire raged along the afterdeck and passengers and crew, faced with the burning flames or the charging river, were in panic.

Some of the crew and passengers manned bucket lines and doused the fire, Others, choosing water over flame, leaped overboard, clinging to anything that would float. Some were on planks, some on barrels. One man gripped a latticed rail section. All were being jostled backwards down the river, the way the boat had come.

Aboard, it was a riot, every man for himself, women and children be damned. I saw one sturdy brute throw a screaming woman overboard to scramble into the boat's yawl that was being lowered. Two men, holding tight to one another, straddled a great hogshead cask. There was barely room for both, and they were fighting fiercely to stay upright. The hogshead bounced and dipped down along the churning water like a cork float on a fishing line. Suddenly there was only one of them.

Ronnie managed to get the skiff close in on the bow end of the boat. I shot the tying line over a rail post and tied her fast. The skiff bounced along the boat's windward side then settled out, tugging against the current flow.

Once we climbed onboard, we saw most of the crew had abandoned the fire-fighting effort, preferring to leap overboard into the red-dyed darkness of the river. A few passengers still bucketed the fire aft, but it was pushing slowly forward and I could see it wasn't any use. The fire-fighters were mostly men, but some women were with them, too. One man at the lead line had set his coat afire and was beating wildly at the flames. A woman, scarce half his size, was sloshing water on him.

The river was alive with the cruel sounds of screams and the piercing shrieks of the injured and the burned and the dying. Prayers crowded heavenwards in the growing darkness.

We scrambled along the rail. "I'll stay up top to help, Clayt," Ronnie called out. "You run down into the main lounge and see what you can do."

I went down as Ronnie suggested. No one was below. Most likely they were all on deck. I thought I'd check out the cabins first before going back with Ronnie to see if anyone by chance was trapped and needing help. All the first-class cabins I came to were empty and I headed toward the second class.

The two rooms I first came to were clean. The third was empty, too, but on the floor near the louver door was a lady's jewel box, open and half-empty. A woman's bracelet, a pair of rings, an orange and brown hairclip and a hairclip which looked like it was made of silver lay inside it. The cabin was a mess, looking like whoever'd left it had left it in a mighty hurry, but not before gathering up a load of dresses with her. There was part of a torn dress caught beneath the door. The jewel-pieces which had been abandoned, with no one there to claim them and no one likely to return, I gathered up and stuffed inside my trousers pocket. A quick search of the remaining cabins proved useless, and I dashed back to Ronnie.

There weren't a lot of people left on deck, most having abandoned the wrecked and burning boat overboard to save themselves if they could. Smoke and flames still heaved up from the aft deck and crept forward like a gray-white cloud of fog. I found Ronnie standing by the leeward rail on the upper deck, He'd gathered up a woman and her daughter, a straw-haired, cream-skinned girl about my age. She was uncommonly pretty as girls go, and she caught my eye right off.

"I couldn't find anyone in the cabins," I said, shouldering up to Ronnie.

"Guess we'd best be leaving," Ronnie said, glancing sideways and noting the smoke fog drifting along the rails. "This here's Mrs. Ellis and Marie," he said, nodding toward the mother. "We can take them with us in the skiff."

The two women appeared remarkably calm and poised, except for a puckered look of worry around the mouth of Mrs. Ellis. Her daughter's face was pretty, but mostly blank and pale. Both women were bearing up mighty well considering the horror that'd been going on around them.

There was no warning of the horror that was about to happen next.

We were about to take the two women off the deck and lead them safe into the skiff and put them up in the slab hut until the river calmed. Everyone was set to go when the boat exploded a second time. Most likely the fire that'd been burning aft hit the pine pitch kegs which the boilermen used to feed the fire with to call up extra speed. When they fired, they shot up like rockets on Independence Day. The steamboat shook from its belly upwards, shuddered, then lurched violently to leeward. Mrs. Ellis, who was standing by the rail, let out a wail and was nearly pitched backwards over it. I'd laid a clutch around the girl's waist when the explosion sounded and kept her steady, though we both fell forward on the deck. Ronnie, though, wasn't so lucky.

The older woman rocked backwards against the rail and only Ronnie's reaching out quick and grasping her around the leg saved her from falling overboard. Ronnie pulled and tugged. Mrs. Ellis screamed and wailed loudly, not stopping until she was sprawled out lengthwise along the narrow deck and safe.

Meanwhile, Ronnie had scrambled to his feet and was stooping forward to help her when the boat pitched violently again. Ronnie slammed back hard against the rail lattice. With a splintering and cracking sound, the rail, weakened by the explosions, fell away, dropping Ronnie backwards into the river. The girl I was holding let out a fearsome shriek and for a moment's time, I was horrified and frozen. An instant later, where Ronnie had been standing, there was nothing but a gaping hole!

I scrambled to my feet as fast as my body would let me and rushed over to the hole. The river was sweeping fast past the starboard side, muddy, dark, and angry. Ronnie was nowhere to be seen. I raced down along the rail side, pulling myself along the rail top and peering down into the water. Ronnie's voice! Suddenly I heard his call. It was Ronnie calling from out of the blackness.

Somehow Ronnie had managed to grab hold of a wooden plank that jutted out along the water, one end still anchored to the boat. He was bouncing with the current like a cork float and the plank piece was giving way.

"I'm coming, Ronnie!" I yelled. But I was too late.

In the rapid sweep of the churning water, a snag log came bounding by and before either of us saw it, it came crashing broadside into Ronnie. There was a dull thud like a flour sack dropping to the floor. Then, save for the rumbling tune the river made, Ronnie and the plank he was holding onto were gone!

A voice welled up inside me. Ronnie's a good swimmer. Ronnie's going to make it. I kept repeating over and over like a body sick with fever rages in his delirium: Ronnie's a good swimmer. He'll make it. I felt sick. I was sick.

The women! I had to get to the women and then to the skiff. That's what Ronnie would've done. I peered off out into the river again, but there was nothing there; nothing except dark water and emptiness.

Mrs. Ellis and her daughter were still sitting where I'd left them-- all crumpled up together and hugging one another tight. They were crying and they were scared. I gathered up both and we lit off together toward the skiff.

When disaster strikes it doesn't dribble down, it pours. The skiff was still tied to the lower rail and still tugging against its line. I got

Mrs. Ellis lowered down in the skiff first, then helped her daughter down and saw that she was in. Then I was about to step down and launch us off when, out of nowhere, a brutish-looking man, raging fire in his eyes and terror on his face, came charging up like a wounded steer.

With one quick shove he knocked me back and sprawled me along the deck, then leaped like a madman into the skiff amid the women's screams and cut the line with the Barlow knife he was brandishing.

When I'd scrambled to my feet, the skiff was off a distance below the boat and racing down the river. An instant later it had vanished into the blighted darkness of the night.

I was numb. Ronnie was gone. The skiff was gone. The women too were gone. And all of it had happened of a sudden. The wrecked steamboat still dripped fire, hot flames drifting forward about halfway toward the bow. The river glowed an eerie red all around me.

It didn't take me long to find a stock of pony barrels that were empty and being shipped upriver, perhaps to store molasses in. I cut the rope that bound them to the wall and lashed two around me at the waist. I hoped if the current caught me as I leaped overboard, the barrels would keep me up so I wouldn't go under and drown.

The swiftness of the current didn't catch me though. The sand shoal and what was left of the flaming steamboat blocked the river's swiftness. The rampaging water had cut a new path in the main, mid-stream. It wasn't too long before I reached the shore.

With all that'd happened, once I'd reached the safety of the land, I must have collapsed into an exhausted sleep. The first thing I noticed when I woke was the glowing of daylight and the powder-blue sky with trailing wisps of white.

At first, I thought the whole ordeal had been but a dream, but when I looked out toward the river, I knew it wasn't so. The waters had receded some and the river was going down. A short piece away, the charred bow end of a riverboat lay on a sandbar that had risen up from the falling water. Everything was still and silent save for the calls of crows and catbirds and the slow drifting of a circling hawk and buzzards floating high up overhead. How did I get here?

Somebody pushed me. Somebody must have set me off in this direction and clusters of other hands must have touched themselves to the controls at various times, for I would not have picked this way for the world.

– Joseph Heller

CHAPTER 7

Swainville. • A Rivertown's Violence. "Mother Lewis."

SWAINVILLE WAS LIKE A HALF-A-THOUSAND other towns all along the nation's rivers. Once, when Pop and I were floating past the landing on the channel side of one of them when I was most of ten-years-old, Pop, who'd been silent and thoughtful for a long while, called my attention to it.

"Clayt," he said in that soft but commanding way he had whenever he wanted me to learn something new, or special, "notice that town close and remember it. It's like any of dozens just like it along these banks."

I turned and looked at it closely as we drifted by on our old log raft.

There was nothing special about it in any way that I could see. There was just a collection of white frame houses settled back a short way from the riverbank. The houses and store buildings were all small, most of 'em no bigger than Pop's cabin. Low-peaked shingle roofs glinted mossy green in the sunlight. The only difference between the peoples' houses and the few flat-roofed storefronts was the houses had pickets around them.

A narrow dirt-packed and curving street between the buildings on both sides finally twisted up a low hill at the edge of town and wandered out of sight. I noticed stacks of lumber along the bank, some higher than two full-sized men standing feet-to-shoulders together. But most of the wood was banked in pallets held together by loops of thick rope circled around the logs.

"There's a lot of lumbering going on along this river," Pop said, anticipating my question before I asked it. "This is a lumber town—one of dozens 'round these parts. The sawmill's yonder–up that road a piece," indicating with his pointer finger the roadway I'd seen before, the one that snaked and vanished in the hills.

"Log boats, rafts, or flatboats bring the cut timber down from the bluff tops after they've been sluiced into the river and dump them here. Wagons cart the logs up the hill to the sawmill yonder. 'Course, it's quite an operation. Those flat rafts," he added after a pause "are raw timber lashed together and drifted down. Those are a two- or three-man operation."

"The town's so quiet," I said, noticing not a single soul anywhere about.

"Oh, there's people hereabouts. Just don't see them often unless a steamboat stops to drop off a passenger or pick one up. But that's but seldom. This town may see a dozen steamboats churning up along the bank or smoking down mid-river. They probably have one stop twice a month to set off cargo–dry goods and whiskey mostly. Then you should see that town; the whole population empties to the landing."

I'd been surveying the location closely while Pop was talking. Some of the houses were set right up against the hill slope and some were spaced a piece apart. Most had waist-high pickets around them, their white paint fading and peeling in the sun. They almost seemed set apart to invite no visitors and I didn't suppose they received many either. They looked so inhospitable. But I knew they must have people in them, and children, and mothers and wives baking bread and pies or simmering stew for supper. But as Pop and I floated by I didn't see anyone.

The town which had loomed up so suddenly, disappeared as fast and was soon no more than a distant memory, framed like a picture in a brown and moss-green frame, chipping and peeling at the edges.

"Don't allow the quiet looks deceive you, son," Pop said, starting up again after some silence. "There's a lot of wild things go on in towns like that one. Tokentown, a village no bigger than a blink and a whistle, saw a murder just last month, and the place we just passed had a lynching the year before. A man's got to be ever watchful–on the lookout all the time. There's the good and the bad all over, and it's all mixed up together."

I recalled those words of Pop's, and I don't mind saying, they set me a might uneasy as I shuffled past the shingle sign which read: SWAINVILLE, POPULATION 302. But I was tired and discouraged, so it didn't matter much.

I hadn't slept in nearly a couple of days, although it seemed like I hadn't seen settled sleep in weeks. I spent most of my time roaming the river along the channel side thinking maybe I'd happen on to Ronnie. I kept on hoping, though he'd been swept away, that maybe he'd made it into shore and was alive and was maybe looking for me, too, all along. But in the hind part of my mind, I knew better. I'd seen that snag log come cutting to leeward past the boat and thunder headlong into Ronnie. And I'd heard that whoomph of wind go out of him when it struck, and him rolling down under water with that great log on top of him, carrying him under toward the bottom. He'd been swept away sure enough and he was dead. I knew the fact on it as near as a body can be sure of anything.

And hadn't I searched and hunted along the banks for miles, combing every brush pile and log jam I'd come across, hoping to find his corpse and give it as Christian a burial as I could? But I knew better. Ronnie was buried sure enough, lying under twisted brush and mud and sand, maybe as far as a hundred miles downriver below the wreck site.

"The Good Lord gives," I recalled Pop telling me when I'd asked him once about my mother. "He gives life to everything around–the trees and flowers, the birds and animals, and to people, too. And the Almighty takes what he gives in turn, but He never does it out of spite or vengeance. Remember that, Son." And, as I entered Swainville, I remembered pausing at the town shingle, I sent up a silent prayer for Ronnie and for all the others that had died, too, and I knew in my heart it wasn't out of spite that they were gone. That prayer brought on a glowing comfort inside me and, for a time at least, Ronnie was forgotten and allowed to rest in peace in the flowing eddies of the river.

SWAINVILLE, POPULATION 302. Certain enough, it was like many another river town. There were the moss-overgrown shingled roofs and the graying whitewashed houses with their picket fences bending in toward them or outwards toward the road.

The naked dirt street led up from the river landing and angled at a slope into the center of town. I passed by a few houses, their insides dark though twilight was coming on, and sauntered on up the street, my bare feet kicking up patches of dust behind me. Up ahead, music rang out from one of the flat-roofed buildings, and knowing there were people there, I guided toward the sound.

The music I'd heard was sailing past the doors of a saloon set slap dab in the heart of the community. A piano tinkled out a tune and there were muffled voices singing. The town and street were both dark.

There weren't any lights along Swainville's main street except what glowed out from the windows of the saloon and glimmered off the boardwalk in front of it.

My stomach was gnawing at me, and I realized I hadn't eaten for the most part of two full days. Maybe the saloon served food. With that thought and little else on my mind, I walked right briskly, stepped up on the boardwalk and swung myself inside the saloon's low swinging doors without so much as a look inside.

I'd never ventured inside a saloon before, and I hadn't given it any thought to what my welcome would be either. All I could see was a single large room, scattered here and about with round, bare wood tables and straight-back chairs, Sawdust lay in scattered sweeps across the floor. At one end, farthest from the windows shining on the street, a woman in a faded green and wrinkled dress danced her slender fingers across the yellowed piano keys. She, and four dilapidated men accompanying her, were croaking out the singing I'd heard earlier. A parcel of other men stood up along the bar and in the near corner at a green felt-covered table, six men played at cards. No one noticed me.

I stopped short when I caught sight of the man behind the bar. He was about the biggest man I'd ever seen, near as big as Pop and Uncle Frank and Ronnie Meyers's father all put inside one skin. He was graying-haired and bald on top. The bare skin atop his head shown shiny like the chimney of a lamp from the oil lights behind the bar,

The bar in front of him was lined with glasses he was washing, and he was gazing puppy-faced toward the woman in the green dress at the piano. He slathered the rag he was drying the glassware with in and out of the openings, keeping beat with the piano's tinkling keys.

As I passed the green-felt table, one of the card players glanced up a rapid shot at me, looked back, called, "I'll see that ante," and resumed his game. He was different from the other men gathered around the table. They were older and sort of shabby looking– logging men or rivermen. He was young, narrow-waisted, smooth-faced, and pale about the cheeks.

I moved past the poker game and stood at the far end of the bar, actually a thick oak plank about twelve feet long set atop four hogshead kegs about five feet from the back wall. The woman in the green dress had broken her playing long enough to sip her drink, then skipped up another tune with the half-drunken men gathered around her joining in.

The barman took a long time in noticing me standing there, but when he did, he came stalking over. He rose above me like an old cottonwood along the riverbank, towering straight up toward the ceiling. He studied me over a moment without uttering a word, then, in a voice deeper than an echo from a dry well, grunted, "Out kinda late, ain't you, sonny?"

"I've come a long way. I'd like something to eat," I said. When I looked down, the level of my eyes caught him about mid-chest.

"This ain't no eatin' house, sonny. All we got is beer 'n whiskey, and they ain't none of it for you."

"Is there another place in town where I can get some food?"

"Town's closed up, and there ain't no eatin' house in Swainville. You'd best be movin' on, sonny, afore the sheriff comes or afore I throw you out. We don't allow no brats in here."

From behind me at the card playing table, one of the players sung out, "That's a-tellin' the welp, Max." Then he added in a drunken slur, "Throw 'im out. Might be fun to watch."

The barman's face was hard-set and when he talked, his lips were tight-set and drawn back against his teeth, giving him an especially fierce look. "You best be leavin' now," he said. I'd found I wasn't welcome in the Swainville saloon.

As I was shuffling out, there was an awful ruckus started at the table where the men had been dealing cards.

"You cheated me on that call," hollered one of them, a short-set man with a shabby growth of whiskers.

"I ain't never cheated you nor anyone in my life," said the other one. He was bigger, a sort of greasy-looking man, clean shaven. His belly popped out of a grease-stained leather vest as he stood up.

There was more deep-voiced shouting between the two, and considerable name-calling, too. I hunched over near the door where I'd come in and watched. The young man I'd seen earlier skittered his chair back away a piece and sat there watching. Neither of the grumblers had a pistol showing–no belt knife either–so they had to come to blows. The other men who'd sat in at the game, except for the young man, had moved aside and were now standing at the bar. The huge barman stood calm behind the hogsheads, drying a glass on a towel.

"I didn't cheat an' I told you that," the big-bellied man bellowed out,

"Cheat!" the smaller man shouted back. "I saw you slip that Jack in. Saw it with my own two eyes." He glanced to the other men, as if searching out support. There was none.

"Then you're blind as that damned dog a yours," belted out the big belly. "An' you're a liar to boot."

"Cheat!"

"I ain't no cheat!"

"A cheatin', lard-bellied liar's what you are." The short man stood his ground.

They were hollering at one another at the top of their voices. Of course, the singing and piano playing had stopped, and everyone was huddled around and watching the scene. The woman in the green dress had sauntered up to stand beside the barman and her small hand was slipped inside of his.

Just when it appeared the squat man and the big belly were about to come to blows, the barman stepped out and collared both of them and marched them toward the street. The big belly's feet dragged along the floor, scuffing tracks in the sawdust sweepings. The short man's legs danced wildly through the air like a puppet's, held high above the ground.

They were still cursing and bellowing fiercely at one another. It was more than a might comical seeing them carried through the saloon like two potato sacks.

"There ain't gonna to be no fights in my saloon," the barman growled. He held them both from behind their necks and was all but lifting the big belly off the floor as he quickly moved past me. Still holding to them, he set both men none too gently on the boardwalk.

"You got fighting to do, you stay out here 'til you get it settled," he warned, "one way or another."

When the barman walked back inside, I slipped out behind him and glided past the building front and edged into the alleyway. Neither man had settled down.

"I saw you slip that card into the deck."

"I did no such thing."

"Liar!"

"I ain't no liar!"

"You bristle-headed fool!" the big belly cried, no doubt pointing fun at the short-cut man's hair. "Iffin' I was gonna cheat, I'd a slipped in an Ace."

"An' that shows how smart you are. I saw you do it. 'Sides, it don't matter."

All of a sudden, the little man bent low and aimed a head butt, throwing himself full weight into the taller man. Both men were drunk. The big belly wheeled at the blow. There was a dull thud as the smaller man's head busted full force into the taller man's midsection. The big belly, recovering quick from the blow, bent low and dashed forward, slamming his head like a ram into the smaller man's middle. Whump! A gush of wind sailed out of the smaller man and he slammed back into the front wall of the saloon. He regained himself fast though, being wiry, and aiming another head butt, rushed full gallop into the larger man. Thwap! His head sounded as it crashed into the taller man's middle and sent him bounding off his feet, flying and sprawling along the boardwalk.

"I ain't no liar!" the smaller man called now, coming up and standing over the one that fell. "Now you take it back or I'll butt you harder."

The big belly tried to clamber to his feet but was having a might of trouble. He sagged back down and lay on his back staring up. I thought the fight was done.

"Admit you cheated an' we'll call it even," the small man wheezed.

"I ain't gonna admit to nothing I didn't do," the big belly groaned, finding strength, and lumbering to his feet. He loomed up over the short man like a sand crane above a frog.

They stood back a pace from one another, scowling and glaring at one another. They shouted names at one another not fit to hear.

The big belly finally said, "I'd dropped that card and was just putting it back into the deck." He brought one hand up to rub across his belly.

"I call that cheating."

"It weren't cheating! I was picking it up."

The one man yelled "cheat" and the other man bellowed "liar," then the whole thing started over. Suddenly, the bar doors flew open. The barman, face red and polished with sweat and anger, came stomping out, shaking the boardwalk with heavy steps. He was brandishing a club in his tight-clenched right hand.

"I've had 'bout enough of this," he growled, waving the axhandle in the air. Then, without so much as a warning, he cracked the big bellied man square across the head. The man let loose a groan and sagged in a heap to his knees.

"You can't do that! We was fighting fair," the small man yelled, defiance glowing about his eyes.

"I can and you'll get the same," the barman yelled back. He was mad as a breeding bull without a heifer. He aimed that club and swished it down on top of the small man's head like to split a melon open.

The small man just stood there, glowering. The barkeep aimed another blow which had the same effect.

"You can't split my skull and you know it. My head's made of cast iron."

The barman looked a might amazed and let his club arm fall. "What a club won't do, a scattergun will," he growled. "Now get out or I'll pepper your butt for certain."

The smaller man just stood and looked at him, then went stomping off down the darkened street. "Take that sagging sack of cheatin' blubber an' dump him in a horse trough," he said, turning back once more.

The spectators who'd gathered around the barroom doors

wandered back inside, all except the younger man who'd stood apart from the other players. He glanced flat-faced at the big belly who still knelt on the boardwalk, trying to recover from the barman's blow, then ambled away on up the street, looked back once toward the saloon and disappeared.

It was quiet on the street again. The woman in the green dress, who'd been all the time standing alongside the other watchers, stepped outside the saloon and bent down low over the fallen man.

"Max, help me up with him," she called to the barkeep. "I'll get a towel and some water." She examined a purple lump swelled up on his forehead. "Did you have to hit him so hard?"

"I'll cotton to no fighting here," was all he said and together they disappeared inside.

I lingered around outside a while. When the fight was over and everyone had gone back to drinking and gambling at cards, I sauntered on up the street.

Just when things seemed settled down, another ruckus shot out from the saloon. Three men, the poker players that were left, ran out on the boardwalk breathing fire.

"Curly, you take the river. Jake an' me'll check the alleys." The one man, Curly, lumbered off toward the river landing. The other two shot up the street, pounding the dust toward me.

"Hold it there, young'un," the one man called, stomping up and collaring me about the shoulder. "You see a young feller pass by here?"

"No, sir," I said.

"You sure 'bout that?" the other man asked. By his voice I could tell he was the one who wanted to watch the barman throw me out.

"Yes, sir. I haven't seen anyone,"

"The one that was playing cards with us. That's the one."

"Think this here kid's in cahoots with 'im?" the other man asked.

"You in cahoots with him, sonny?" the man that had grabbed me said.

"No, sir. Not me," I said, being truthful and hoping they'd accept it.

"Well, during the fight, that young feller made off with the playing money. Two hundred dollars, an' most of it mine," the shoulder squeezer said.

Because I hadn't paid much attention, I hadn't recalled the man they were speaking of. Then, of course, I remembered.

"I did see the man from the saloon leave short after the fight and wander up the street. He didn't seem in a hurry, though." The man let loose of my shoulder. "Which way?"

"That way," I said, pointing toward the nearest alley.

"You'd best be right, boy," the other man warned. "Iffin it turns out you're in cahoots with 'im, when we catch up with that there thief, we'll hang you up 'long beside 'im."

"I'm telling the truth," I said. I didn't cotton much to hanging, especially if it was me they were talking on.

"We've wasted enough time with the kid," the one said, "An' all the while he's getting away." And again, the two of them were off, dashing down the alleyway I'd pointed out.

I didn't go in for thieving. In no way. But I was hoping they wouldn't catch him and hang him.

Once again, Swainville was quiet. I noticed there wasn't any singing and music coming out of the saloon. It's an eerie feeling pacing through a darkened town you've never seen before at night and where you don't know a living soul.

"Boy." I heard a call behind me–a woman's voice. I stepped around and saw the green-dressed woman from the saloon pacing steadily toward me up the street.

"I couldn't help between songs but overhear your talk with Max," she said as she walked up. "He's the bartender there back. Are you hungry?

"Yes'm," I said. "I sure am."

"I've finished playing for the evening and as long as I've found you, how about coming home with me for a home-cooked meal?"

"Yes, ma'am! That sounds mighty good."

There wasn't much to Swainville, though I allowed it was larger than a goodly number of other river towns with a population of over a hundred, so it didn't take long to reach her house, a tight little two-room frame just up the street.

"I have some leftover beef stew from yesterday," she said. "It's all I have, but I'll warm it and bake up some biscuits while you're cleaning up."

With the rumblings in my stomach, I told her I could sure enough use the stew and biscuits, and when I stepped up to the tarnished, gilt-framed mirror, I could see I needed washing, too. My hair was all a-muss and my face was smudged. I'd lost near all the buttons off my shirt and my trouser legs were torn near off at the knees. I couldn't do anything about my clothes, so I washed up at the porcelain basin while the lady warmed over the stew and set the table.

Her name was Maggie Lewis and she'd lived in Swainville most all her life she told me as we ate. She'd been married once to a river pilot and, for a time, she'd lived with him aboard the steamboats he guided up and down the river. But he'd fallen for another woman and one day left her high and dry in St. Louis and run off. That was five years back. Maggie had come back to live in Swainville with her mother who'd taken sick and died shortly after. She'd fallen into hard times.

Max, the giant barman and the owner of the saloon, offered her a job singing and pounding the piano, and she'd been at it ever since.

"That was some fight tonight," I said, trying to make conversation after she'd told me about herself. "Does that happen often in Swainville?"

"Too often to please the church folk. Swainville can get wild on a Friday night."

"Who were those men fighting?" I asked between bites of sourdough biscuits.

"Regulars," she said. "Sam and Erik. Sam—he's the short man—brags he has the hardest head in half the counties along the river. Erik used to be his logging partner a few miles upriver until they had a falling out a while back. Now they fight like dogs whenever they have the chance."

"Is it true during the fight one of the card players stole two hundred dollars?" I asked, telling her about my experience with the men on the street.

Maggie sighed. "There was a young drifter there tonight playing cards with Sam and Erik and the others. And the money was gone when they went back to play."

"They were talking of hanging him," I said. "You think they would?"

"Swanville's a rough town. It's hard telling what they might do," Maggie said.

I'd downed two bowls of thick stew and a small plate of buttered biscuits and was feeling full at last. Maggie got me into talking about myself. I didn't see fit to tell her about Pop or my leaving Uncle Frank, but I did tell her about my adventuring with Ronnie and about the steamboat wreck. Maggie had heard about the wreck. News travels fast along the river. She allowed how it all sounded like the things boys were like to do, and she was honestly sorry about Ronnie, too, when I told her how he died.

"You'll be going home now, I suppose?" she asked.

"Yes, ma'am," I lied. I didn't want to bother her about not having a real home and setting her to worrying over me. Women always seemed to worry, least that's what I'd gathered from my limited experience. But I allow that men do too, though they seldom want to show it by fretting about too much and showing no emotions.

Maggie was a young woman, in her early thirties somewhere, but looked older in the face and around the eyes where small wrinkles had formed.

"They call me 'Mother Lewis' around these parts," she said, "because I'm apt to take in all the strays that come through town. Dogs and cats and people, too, that wander through and need a warm meal and a place to stay."

"Like me?" I asked. She smiled.

Maggie's place wasn't any too elegant, but it was functional.

There were only two rooms; the back was a small bedroom with from what it appeared, scarce enough room to slide sideways between the bed and the dressing table and clothes cabinet. The larger front room served as the living space—the parlor and dining room and kitchen all in one. There were two square windows at either side of the door and over the windows were flour sacks hung as curtains with some embroidery work–small butterflies and flowers–she'd done herself. But the house was spotless, clean, and dusted, with not a scrap out of place.

Between the eating and the storytelling, it was near on to ten o'clock. I thanked Maggie for her kindness and her hospitality and told her I'd best be going.

"Do you have a place to stay tonight?" she asked.

"No, ma'am, but I make do."

"Well, I can't offer you a bed, but I've got some blankets and a feather pillow you can use."

"I reckon I could stay the night, if it's all right with you," I said.

"It gets mighty cold along the river at night."

Her kind face beamed a wide smile, and the crinkles around her eyes grew deep as she smiled. "I'll put on a pot of tea to warm and get the bed things for you." From the other room, a short time later, she came out carrying a pillow and a blanket.

"Thank you, ma'am. I sure appreciate your hospitality."

"If you aren't too modest, I'll take your shirt and pants and mend them as best I can and sew some buttons on," she said.

I allowed I'd have to keep the trousers because I was wearing nothing underneath. Maggie just sort of chuckled.

I gave her my shirt, grateful for her offer, and knowing she was tired. She strolled into the other room with her tea and sewing basket and shut the door. I set out the blankets on the floor beside the wood stove which still had a small fire going and was putting out some warmth and took my trousers off and slipped in between the blanket folds. I was warm–the warmest I'd been in some days–and I dropped quickly off to sleep.

I'd slept sound and peaceful throughout the night, but I woke up early, around five o'clock I'd guess, judging from the light outside.

I pulled on my trousers quick as I could, not because I thought Maggie might catch a sight of me naked, besides--her bedroom door was closed--but because the morning chill from the river was thick, raising goosebumps across my skin. On the chair beside the table, I found my shirt. Sometime during the night, Maggie had finished her work on it and brought it out. I'd slept so sound I hadn't heard her. It was mended beautifully. There was a calico patch stitched over where the biggest rip had been, but the remainder of the mending had been done so carefully you could scarcely tell where she'd done the sewing. And there were four bone buttons, three white, one blue. I guessed she'd run out of buttons because there was still one missing.

I pattered about the main room, quiet as I could. I folded the blanket and laid it across the cane rocker in the corner and tidied up the dishes from last night's supper meal which Maggie hadn't had time to do. And I gathered up some wood and laid a fire in the cookstove and heated up some water for morning tea.

At seven, I heard noises from the other room and soon Maggie had come out. She was surprised, and thankful, too, at seeing the cabin straightened up without me even being asked.

"When you're grown up, you'll make a woman a fine husband someday," she smiled. With a kind of sad look in her eyes, she added, "So many men are helpless when it comes to sharing duties around the house."

I told her how Pop had raised me, giving out no hint that he was gone, and she allowed how lucky I was to have such a fine and caring father who was seeing fit to bring his boy up right.

We shared a breakfast of biscuits, grits and tea and talked some more.

"I have to leave at eight. I put in a full ten-hour day at Max's," she said. "I guess you'll be leaving for home."

"Yes, mam," I said, "I guess I will."

I thanked Maggie for all she'd done, but she wouldn't hear of it. "It's my Christian duty to help whenever I can. I was happy I could feed and house you, Clayt. Have a safe journey home and when you get there, tell your father for me how I said he has such a fine young son."

"Yes, ma'am, I surely will."

We left her house together. Maggie headed off down the street toward the saloon and her piano and I wandered on down the street to have a look around.

The greatest difficulties lie where we are not looking for them.

–Goethe

CHAPTER 8

Ramblings Around the Town. I Meet a River Sheriff.

WHEN MAGGIE WAS OUT OF sight, I felt I should pay her something for her kindness to me. All I had were a few things–some jewelry pieces--from the steamboat wreck. I fished my pockets and brought out a fine-looking, genuine silver ring with a great blue stone that glinted fire in the sunlight and, looking around and seeing no one, I sneaked back into the house and set it on the table where she was sure to find it.

Swainville was beginning to come to life. Men were up and heading off to work and, by mid-morning, women and a handful of children coursed up and down the street. As I was all cleaned up now, looking less a waif and more a visitor, I felt I could look around the town without being gawked at.

The village of Swainviile had a livery barn and blacksmith's shop, a lumber yard and bank, and a store whose heavy sign read: CROAKER'S DRY GOODS, MEN'S AND LADIES' WEAR. GLASSES FITTED. Since I wasn't planning on remaining over any longer, I decided I'd try and swap the jewelry at Croaker's for some provisions: flour and matches, a bag of coffee, some dried beans, and maybe some bacon and salt pork, then be on my way.

There weren't many customers inside the dry goods store. I wandered up and down the several rows and found a canvas sack of flour and the matches, then made way to the man behind the counter.

"What'll it be for you today, son?" he asked. He was a pleasant looking man who wore a long, white apron and gold wire spectacles which hung low down on his nose.

I told him what I needed and after he'd gotten me the things, he reckoned out the bill which came to $1.20. I told him that I didn't have hard money, but that I'd swap for him some valuable things I had.

"Where did you come by these?" Mr. Croaker asked after I'd fished out the remaining pieces from my trousers pocket and handed them to him to look over.

"They were my mother's." I told him that she'd died and left them to me as remembrances, but seeing how Pop and I were riding the river together and hadn't any money, I'd have to trade them now.

He looked the pieces over for the longest while, like he was carefully considering the deal.

"I have no right idea what they're worth," he said finally. Looking over the ring he noted, "I'm certain these stones are crystals or rhinestones and not diamonds. But the metalwork is silver. Tell you what, son. I'll take the bracelets in trade for what you have, and I'll buy this tortoiseshell hairclip and the small ring for a dollar."

The trade and the dollar sounded fine to me, so I accepted. About the time Mr. Croaker had finished packing up my order, a woman sauntered over with a bolt of printed cloth which she laid up on the countertop. The jewelry I'd traded was still sitting beside the register. The woman scanned the pieces over, then glanced at me, then studied the pieces again.

"Where did you get this jewelry, boy?" she asked, looking at me real hard.

"From my mother, ma'am. She died of the fever a while back and now Pop and I are out of money and have to sell."

"This boy's a liar," she asserted to Mr. Croaker as he came over from helping another customer, "and a thief," she added. My heart nearly leaped through my ribs. What did she know about those jewel pieces? "These are some of the pieces of jewelry I had on the Aster Queen when she hung up, caught fire, and sank last week. I barely escaped with my life. I didn't have time to fetch my jewelry."

"Are you certain they're yours, Mrs. Billington?" Mr. Croaker asked.

"Certainly, I'm sure. I'd know my own jewelry, wouldn't I?" She was in a huff. "This tortoiseshell comb is mine, and so is the silver hair clip, and the bracelets, too. This boy's a thief!"

"I'm not a thief!" I spoke. "I found them on the boat."

"Found them, my sainted mother!" the woman shouted. "You stole them from me."

Though I hadn't stolen the jewelry--they'd be lying at the bottom of the river then if I hadn't rescued them--I could see I was in a tight spot. The only solution was to run and get away from the dry goods store and Swainville as fast as possible. I made a dash for it, leaving the provisions and the jewelry and Mr. Croaker's silver dollar on the counter and bolted for the door. But just as I was about out the door, another woman with two small children was stepping in and I slammed into her, sending her a flying. She let off a shriek and her little girls started crying. The woman who'd accused me of stealing from her let out a wail.

"Stop that thief!" And before I could get running again, Mr. Croaker had come up behind me and grabbed me tight and I had no way of breaking free.

"You hold him, Mr. Croaker," the jewelry woman said, "and I'll go fetch the sheriff."

She stalked right out and hurried off down the street, mumbling 'thief' with every step. The dry goods keeper had a firm hold on me and was shaking me by the collar like a dog playing with a rag.

"You little scamp! Try to sell me stolen goods. You just wait 'till the sheriff comes. He'll make short work of you."

With Mr. Croaker's shaking, the buttons Maggie had sewed on began to pop and I'd nearly struggled free of the shirt. Leaving my shirt behind in Mr. Croaker's hand would be little enough if I could get away before the sheriff came. But Mr. Croaker saw what was happening so he grabbed me around my chest and by the trousers back which wouldn't give and held me fast.

It wasn't but a few minutes, but the angry woman came stalking back with a large, balding man in tow. It was Max the barman. He was Swainville's sheriff.

It turned out that Max the barman, who'd thrown me out the night before, wasn't the sheriff after all. He only acted the sheriff's part when the real sheriff had gone out of town on business. But it didn't make no matter. I was caught.

"So, it's you again!" he grunted, as he took me over from Mr. Croaker and gripped me tight around the arm, his large hand wrapped all the way around. "So, we caught us a little thief?"

"I'm no thief!" I protested, "I found that woman's jewelry on the sunken riverboat."

"That don't make no matter," the barman sheriff said. "You took 'em and you're a thief. I should've known this boy was trouble when he come into the saloon last night looking for a handout," he announced to Mr. Croaker and the jewelry woman and a dozen other lookers-on who'd by now gathered around inside the store and outside along the boardwalk.

"I didn't want a handout. I was going to pay for it."

"With stolen jewels?" I knew he had me there.

"How old are you, boy? Where'd you come from? Who's your folks?"

"Fourteen," I said, "from downriver. My folks are dead," I blabbered out.

"So, a no-account river scamp!" the jewelry woman said, nodding her head at me. "You're going to arrest him, aren't you, sheriff?"

"I'm a-goin' to do just that. It's a jail cell for you, boy," the barman growled, giving me a shake that near set my teeth on edge. "An' it'll be a long stay 'till the circuit judge rides in and hears your case."

"He told me his father's sitting down along the river," Mr. Croaker told him.

"Is that true, boy?"

"No, sir," I said. "Pop's dead."

The barman looked toward Mr. Croaker. "I'll check it out. If he's there, he's just as guilty as his boy."

I tried once more to make a break for freedom, but the barman had me fast and there was no escape.

"Please," I wailed. "I'm not a thief! I found those things. I'm not a thief!" But my protests didn't do any good. Max, the barman-sheriff, wouldn't listen.

He hurried off, dragging me down the street toward the jailhouse. "You're a liar, boy, a born liar from the looks of it," he growled, yanking me harder by the arm. "I've half a mind to whip you 'till you bleed, maybe beat some of the sinning ways from you." The barman was beginning to sound a lot like Uncle Frank. But he didn't whip me and was I ever thankful.

All things come to him that waits- even justice.

—Austin O'Malley

CHAPTER 9

The Old Stone Jail. Maggie Comes to the Rescue. An Unexpected Visitor. A Hearing Before the Judge. Redemption.

I'D LAID UP IN THE jail cell all day with nothing to do but lay back on the wood slat cot which was covered by a straw-ticked mattress no thicker than my hand and count the heavy stone blocks that surrounded me. I must've counted them a dozen times to take my mind off my troubles. There were a thousand and twenty-three in all. The only light in the cell flickered through an iron-barred window too small for even a boy like me to crawl through. The window was high up on the wall near the point where the heavy-timbered roof joined the brown- streaked, granite-gray walls. When I stood up on my toe points and stretched up my arm, I could just touch the bottom of the sill.

No sooner had the barman, as acting sheriff, clanked the door closed and twisted the key in the lock, but I was left alone. I knew that Pop had never been thrown in jail, or Uncle Frank either that I could recall, but here was Clayton Sievers himself, locked away for thieving. It was an awful fix.

I'd wanted freedom from Uncle Frank. That's why Ronnie and I had been on the river together. Now he was gone, and I was locked away.

There was no more freedom, and I'd been gone all of two days past a month away from home. My first visitor called on me about seven o'clock that evening. It was Maggie Lewis. She came trotting into the jailhouse alone, carrying with her a wicker basket. She was still wearing the same faded green dress she'd worn the night before.

"I brought you some supper," Maggie smiled, setting the basket down. She found herself a high-legged stool inside the sheriff's office and brought it in and sat down next to the jail bars. "The least I can do is feed you." She appeared a little nervous. And her kind eyes were sad.

Never having had a pocket watch, I didn't rightly know the time exact, but when a body grows up living along the river, he gets an inner sense for telling time by the position of the sun and the shadows it casts down. It was something Pop had taught me, and I'd used his teaching ever since.

"How'd you get off to see me?" I asked Maggie, knowing by the light it was too early for her to be away from work.

"Max wasn't planning on feeding you tonight, said he'd wait until the sheriff gets back sometime in the morning. Max is a kind enough man in his way, but sometimes he can be thoughtless. I told him I wasn't feeling well so he let me off and I cooked you up some supper."

Maggie passed me some chicken pieces in a folded napkin through the bars. They were thighs and wings, my favorites, and I told her so. They were cooked brown and golden, and she'd made up powder biscuits and wilted greens. The meal tasted mighty good.

As I was eating, she also fished from out the basket the ring I'd given her.

She asked me, with a kind of sorrowful look, "Does this belong to Mrs. Billington, too?"

"I can't rightly say. I found it in the same stash on the boat. But it's yours now. I want you to have it."

"I can't keep it, Clayt. It doesn't belong to me."

"Maggie," I said, "I'm not no thief. I found those jewelry pieces, and if I hadn't taken them, they'd be lying at the bottom of the river now." I searched her face closely for a sign that she might agree but didn't see any sign. "Isn't stealing when you take something someone wants?" I questioned her.

"Stealing's taking anything that doesn't belong to you. I'm sure

Mrs. Billington would have gone back to claim her things if she could have."

I pondered over Maggie's words for a time. I knew down deep she was right in what she said. I was a thief, at least in the law-book sense. But I hadn't intended it.

"Maggie, what's going to happen to me when the judge gets here?"

"I think you're too young to be sent to prison, but it won't be easy. Mrs. Billington's very angry with you and has sworn out a complaint," After a pause for thinking, she said, "I don't rightly know what the judge will do."

"You believe me that I didn't take those jewel pieces intentionally, don't you, Maggie?" Maggie nodded her head yes. "Isn't there anything you can do?"

"I'm afraid not. My word doesn't hold much sway in Swainville. You see, in the eyes of the town, I'm not a very good woman."

"Just because your husband left you?" I questioned her.

"Because I work in a saloon." Maggie looked a bit downcast, and I wasn't certain if it was because she couldn't help me, or if she'd been reminded of the past.

"What's wrong with working in a saloon?"

"Oh, it's honest work enough. I make it honest work. But the townsfolk don't view it as a fit place for a single woman."

I thought all she did was play on the piano and sing out songs and make music that makes folks happy. There sure wasn't anything wrong with that. But Maggie said she served drinks to the men who came inside and was working around a lot of drunken rabble-rousers. And there were fights always breaking out like the night I wandered in. If the men liked her playing, some of them would tip her pocket change or buy her drinks.

"Some of those men are husbands to the womenfolk in town," she explained, "and the womenfolk of Swainville don't take kindly to what I do. If I didn't have to make a living here, I wouldn't do it, believe me."

It didn't seem fair. From what Pop had told me about my mother, Maggie took after her a lot, giving of herself and doing things for people and not ever expecting a reward. And the folks in Swainville looked down on her because she worked in a saloon. I didn't see the justice in it.

We'd talked together for about an hour and Maggie thought she'd best be leaving in case Max should saunter over to look in on me at the jail.

"He might want to see that you're keeping out of mischief," Maggie said. We both laughed at that, but it wasn't funny really. What mischief could I get myself into with the window barred and the door to the cell latched tight? After Maggie cleaned away the supper things, she left and I went back to pondering my predicament.

The jail cell was dark now, reminding me of a moonless, starless night along the river. The night chill off the river was settling in on Swainville and pushing against the damp walls of the cell. I had only one small blanket, shot through with holes where the mice had gnawed.

I thought a lot about what I could do and came up blank. It was useless trying to make a break. The walls of the old stone jail were a foot thick. The jailcell bars were flaking rust, but it'd be another hundred years before they'd rust through enough to let me out, and only a raccoon could've slipped through that window hole anyways. I pulled at the cell door bars a dozen times, putting my whole strength behind the effort, but that was useless, too. The door jiggled some but held fast and wouldn't move an inch.

In the morning, the sun rose up along the eastern shore and the creeping silver mist that rolled from bank to bank slowly dissipated with the sun's arrival. I knew it was happening though I couldn't see it. I'd seen it a thousand times before.

About nine o'clock, Max had turned over his duties as acting sheriff to the real sheriff who'd arrived just a while before. He brought me breakfast–eggs and coffee and a slice of buttered toast.

After he'd served it up, he pulled up the same long-legged stool Maggie had used, propped himself up against the far wall and commenced interviewing me.

Sheriff Wortman was a kindly man enough, not gruff like Max, but he took his office seriously. He was a large-boned man, considerably plump about the middle and growing plumper. I could see where his belt-- the part his belly didn't overlap–had been loose cinched more than once, and he'd bored out extra holes. In our talk, I found out he'd been born and grown up in Swainville and had ventured out along the river much like me, so he knew and understood some of the things I said.

I laid the whole thing out for him–about the flood and the steamboat sinking and about the jewels and about Ronnie's drowning, too. And I talked, too, about Pop, and me leaving Uncle Frank, and brought the whole story up to date.

"There's nothing I can do," Sheriff Wortman said after hearing my story out. "Since Mrs. Billington has sworn out a formal complaint, I'm cuffed and tied near as much as you. I'm bound to uphold the law."

I asked him the question, same as I'd put to Maggie: What would the judge be like to do with me? I didn't like the answer he gave. Not one bit.

"Seeing that I don't make the law–I just uphold it–I can't speak for what Judge Bellman will say exactly." He echoed Maggie's words, "I think you're too young to go to prison," he said. "After all, you didn't commit a murder, nor break into some folks' houses at night. But," he added, "seeing how your papa's dead and all and you've run off, Judge Bellman will most likely put you in the county orphan home, least until you're sixteen and able to work things out for yourself."

Orphan home! The words slapped against me like a beaver's tail striking water when danger's coming. I'd always worked things out– from the times when Pop was drinking heavy and leaving me fending for myself. And I'd taken care of Uncle Frank more than he'd cared for me. Ronnie and I had ventured along the river hadn't we–cooking our own meals and camping along the river--traveling and meeting the good and the bad of it? I'd taken care of myself just fine and I told the sheriff so.

"Don't make no difference, boy," he drawled, stretching his arms out after listening to my long tale. "A young'un's got to have his folks, or leastwise someone old enough to take care of him until he's grown, and for these parts that's sixteen. That's how the law looks on it."

I thought about that for some minutes and didn't see an answer. An orphan home! That'd be little better than a prison; living with a bunch of strangers, walled in, windows barred, the whole place gated up. No. There had to be another way. Even if I had to go back to living with Uncle Frank, although I doubted he'd have me back. So, I pondered on it some more. In the meantime, Sheriff Wortman, having finished his talk, ventured out and shut the door between his office and the cell room.

I thought and thought on it a long spell, still seeing no way out.

Then an idea hit, rocking me like a thunder blast. "Sheriff! Sheriff!" I called out loud.

"What's all this yammering 'bout, boy?" Sheriff Wortman drawled, ambling in and forcing up his trousers higher around his waist as he walked.

I was all excited and explained my idea to him nonstop. "I'm certain Maggie Lewis would take me in," I said. The sheriff looked skeptical. I told him about Maggie taking me in when I'd first tramped into Swainville. Me, a stranger. How she'd cooked up a fine meal and mended my shirt and set me up for the night. "Maggie Lewis is old enough. She could take care of me. I could get a job right here in Swainville and you could keep an eye out on me and see I didn't get in trouble."

Sheriff Wortman listened tight as I rolled right along, explaining the sense of it. When I quit talking, the sheriff stood silent for a moment,

"Maggie Lewis is a good woman all right," he said finally, "and she's seen her share of hard times." He paused, seeming to collect his thoughts. "The trouble with your idea, boy, is the townsfolk would never go along with it. Maggie Lewis raising up a boy!" He hit the sentence hard. There was an explosion of air, nearly like a bitter laugh, as he spoke it. "The town would never accept Maggie Lewis raising up a young'un not her own. Not so long as she's working in a saloon."

What the sheriff said was what Maggie had said before. In the eyes of the good citizens of Swainville, she was a fallen woman.

I'd done worn out my ideas. Settling back with little else to do except sleep and stare up at the bare stone walls, I resigned myself to wait for Judge Bellman to send me off to the orphan home.

The chilling dampness of the jailhouse had been my home in Swainville for a week and there was still no sign of the circuit judge. Sheriff Wortman allowed that "Judge Bellman will be here any day." I wasn't looking forward to his arrival, though I didn't welcome remaining in the jailhouse any longer, either.

When the sheriff wasn't riding out, tending to his lawman's duties, or talking to townsfolk along the street, he'd come in and talk with me. He brought my breakfast every morning at seven, served up the mid-day meal around one. Maggie had made arrangements with Max, who I guess was in a better mood, to cook me up supper meals. She never could stay long but following the end of her work in the saloon, she'd stop by again and gather up the supper dishes and stay a while to talk.

It wasn't any use hiding the truth from her any longer, so I told her all about myself. I laid the whole story out.

"Maggie," I said, "I lied to you the night you took me in, about my family, and my conscience's been troubling me ever since Pop died," I told her, "from drinking himself to death. My mother died when I was born, and he never got over her loss."

Maggie was mighty sympathetic. "It's hard for a boy growing up these days without a mother to care for him or a father to teach him the things he needs to know."

"Before he died, Pop taught me a lot about the things a boy needs to know," I said. "He taught me about the river, and how to fish, and about the Bible as best he could, and the importance of an education. I really miss him, Maggie. I wish he hadn't died."

"Clayton, I guess most people feel the same. No one wants their folks to die. Most folks wish their parents could live forever. I know how you feel, I guess as close as anyone can know another's feelings."

I lost my father when I was a little girl, and I told you about my mother dying five years back. I know what it feels like to be alone with no one to share your joys and troubles with. It's a deep hurt, but it goes away."

I knew all about sharing and the hurt that sometimes follows because of my adventuring with Ronnie and his death.

Maggie and I never spoke about my talk with Sheriff Wortman—about her taking me in. I didn't want to trouble her and I knew it couldn't happen.

Several nights later, Maggie came in to bring my supper and said she'd be late picking up the dishes. The town was holding a revival meeting in the church, and she was planning to attend. Some preacher from upriver (she couldn't recall his name) had arrived in Swainville and was going to lead the services. "Half the town's turning out for it," she said.

I'd never attended a revival meeting. If I'd been free, I might have gone–mostly out of curiosity. The town was quieter than ever that night–Swainville being mighty quiet most nights, save for an occasional ruckus from Max's place, and I imagined the populace had turned out in force to hear the preacher.

There wasn't anything to do but sleep, which I did a lot of, and following supper I dozed off deeply. I don't rightly remember what I dreamed, but I recalled I was sitting out along the river listening to the current lap the bank, my campfire glowing bright among the trees. The blast of a deep-voiced steamboat whistle ripped the stillness and echoed off the shoreline at a distance. Everything was silent after that.

I slept peacefully for several hours. Around midnight I was startled from my dreams by voices floating past the window bars. A few moments later, the jailhouse door groaned open. The voices were less distinct, then more distinct. One belonged to Sheriff Wortman, the other to Maggie Lewis. I didn't recognize the third. It was a man's voice, that was certain. It had a different sound than the sheriff's tenor drawl. That voice became clearer now. From somewhere in the past, I was certain I'd heard that voice before.

The door between the office and the inner cell room groaned open. Maggie was the first to enter. Sheriff Wortman followed her close behind.

"There's someone here who'd like to see you, son," the sheriff said. I looked at him, then glanced at Maggie who couldn't keep from smiling.

A man stepped in from behind the door. I judged he was going on toward fifty, maybe older. His graying hair was slicked back on the sides and glinted with silver specks in the lamp light. Long, slender legs hidden in the cut of a black frock suit moved with deliberate strides to the cell door. A low, flat top, wide-brimmed hat shaded his face. When he removed it, I recognized him right off. It was Parson Briggs. The very same preacher who'd laid Pop away to rest!

"I'd like to speak with the boy alone if I may," he addressed the sheriff. Sheriff Wortman, seeing no harm in that, snapped the lock and swung the cell door open. Parson Briggs stepped in, stepped over, and sat beside me on the cot. I couldn't have been happier to see anyone than the Parson Briggs just then.

He patted out the mattress lumps and made himself comfortable.

The black hat he wore he hung carefully over the low post at the cot foot. The sheriff and Maggie left, closing the jail room door behind them.

"It was Sister Lewis who told me you were here," Parson Briggs began. "I wouldn't have known about you if she hadn't come up following the services and asked me to look in on a boy she knew who'd happened on to hard times. When she told me your name was Clayton Sievers, we found the sheriff and hurried over as soon as we could." He paused and smiled. "The Lord works in mysterious ways."

The Parson and I talked together for near an hour, he asking a parcel of questions and me answering them. He wanted to know what I'd done after Pop had died. Hadn't I gone to live with Uncle Frank?

I told him about life with Uncle Frank, about his swearing and his drinking, the whippings he'd given me and how he never did a lick of work at home and how I couldn't stand it any longer. The Parson listened close to what I told him and, by the time our talk had ended, I'd told him everything.

He stood up to his full height—a little over six foot–and stretched his thin arms out a bit. "Well, Clayton, the sheriff has informed me the judge will be here tomorrow afternoon. I don't know yet what I can do, but I will try. I feel the Lord guided me to Swainville for this very reason." Even though his presence reminded me of Pop's passing, I was glad to see Parson Briggs again. "Have faith, my boy. The Lord's put you here and the Lord's plan may get you out. His works are marvelous and beyond man's ken."

Before he left, Parson Briggs preached up a prayer over me then opened his thumb-worn Bible and read aloud a passage. It was Psalm 139: "In Thy book all my members were written, which in continuance were fashioned, when as yet there was none of them."

At one o'clock the following day, my hearing before the circuit judge began.

The courtroom was Sheriff Wortman's office. The judge was there, seated at the sheriff's desk. There wasn't any jury. It was just a hearing. I was settled in a slat-back chair, sandwiched between the sheriff and the Parson Briggs. Maggie was seated just behind me and to the left where I couldn't see her without craning my neck around. Having sworn out the complaint against me, Mrs. Billington was present, too. And Mr. Croaker, the dry goods keeper, was there to act as witness.

Judge Bellman was a man in his middle thirties, an ample enough man without being fat like Sheriff Wortman. I'd heard him talking with the sheriff earlier and he spoke with the practiced ease of an educated man. I'd been told that judges always wore flowing robes when they were holding court, but this judge was dressed in a starched white shirt, string tie and black frock suit, the same as Parson Briggs except without the collar.

The judge cleared his throat a couple of times, looked up from a paper he was reading, then asked, "Is the defendant in the court?"

"Yes, Your Honor, he is," Sheriff Wortman spoke, rising up and gesturing toward me. "This is the boy, Your Honor, Clayton Sievers."

The judge looked over at me, studying me close for several moments. Though Maggie had patched my shirt again and sewn on new buttons, my feet were bare, and my trousers' knees ripped. I looked a ragamuffin.

Except for some nose-blowing and a cough now and then, it was dead silent in the courtroom. "I understand from reading the deposition, this is a case of common theft. Mrs. Billington, please step forward and present your testimony."

Mrs. Billington rose out of her chair, stepped proudly forward and stood beside the judge's desk. She was dressed in a dark blue satin skirt, her blouse with a high-up, pointed collar. A large, black hat topped her head, with a wide red satin bow twisted around a wire loop in front.

"Judge. Your Honor," she began, "this boy here stole a considerable amount of jewelry from me a while back, then pranced bold as brass into Swainville and tried to sell his ill-gotten gains to Mr. Croaker there. I was fortunate enough to be in the dry goods store at the time and recognized the jewelry. If I hadn't been, the little scamp would have gotten clean away. A thief like him ought to be put away from decent folks like us where he won't go stealing from someone else."

Mrs. Billington ranted for a time, telling the judge her story, pointing her finger at me all the while. It wasn't hard to see she was feeling mighty proud of herself. The judge listened to her closely, pausing every now and again to jot some lines with an ink pen on a sheet of paper in front of him.

"And how much value do you place on the articles this boy allegedly stole?" Judge Bellman asked.

"No less than one hundred dollars, Your Honor."

The judge wrote down the figure and circled it with his pen. Then, having heard her out, he thanked her for her testimony and called Mr. Croaker forward.

Mr. Croaker told about my entering into his store and buying goods. "The boy offered to pay for them with some few jewelry pieces he said belonged to his mother who is deceased," he said.

"Is the jewelry in question in evidence?" the judge asked Sheriff Wortman.

"Yes, Your Honor. In the envelope on the desk."

The judge took the envelope, opened it, and scattered out the jewelry pieces in front of him. He examined them for a moment, prodding at them with his pointer finger. He picked up the small ring and the hair clip and the other pieces Mr. Croaker had offered me a dollar for. Judge Bellman crinkled up his brow in puzzlement.

"You place a value of one hundred dollars on these articles here in evidence?" he questioned Mrs. Billington. His voice showed skepticism.

"No, Your Honor. Those are only a part of what was stolen. That little tramp must have hidden the rest. If I may, Your Honor, Mrs. Lewis there was given another of my rings by this boy as a gift." She shot a haughty look toward Maggie.

"Is that ring in the courtroom?" the judge asked. I craned around. Maggie reached into her handbag and searched out the ring, handing it over to the sheriff who passed it to the judge. He added it to the collection.

Judge Bellman peered over at me from the tops of his reading spectacles. "Sheriff?"

"Your Honor. Those pieces there are the only ones recovered. The boy didn't have anything else on him. He did, however, give to Mrs. Lewis," he gestured, pointing to Maggie, "the large ring with the pale purple stone before he was apprehended, as Mrs. Billington said."

"It's an amethyst, Your Honor," Mrs. Billington blurted out from among the onlookers. "It's one of the finest rings I own."

The judge was silent for a moment, then began jotting notes again. "Mr. Croaker, I believe you sell jewelry in your mercantile. What value would you place on the items here in evidence?" Judge Bellman asked.

"To the best of my knowledge, Your Honor, at retail, ten, maybe twelve dollars."

"So, some ninety dollars in retail value of the alleged stolen items are still missing." He eyed the sheriff. Sheriff Wortman answered. "Yes, Your Honor."

"Thank you, Mr. Croaker. I think it's time we heard the accused's side of this story," the judge said. Judge Bellman smoked a pipe, and he stoked it full of tobacco and lit it up right there in the room in front of everyone. I was more than a might surprised, not realizing before that high-up quality folk smoked tobacco. Pop had, and of course Ronnie and I had smoked cob pipes, stuffing the bowls with corn silks mainly, tobacco when we could get hold of any.

The sheriff's chair was the rock-back kind which swiveled, too. After firing up, the judge laid back. A rolling puff of gray-black smoke drifted upwards in front of the judge's head then slid off toward an open window. During the whole time, the onlookers in the room sat quiet as death, with no one scarcely moving.

"Mr. Sievers, would you step up front and tell this court your story? In your own words," the judge added in a sideways thought.

I'd never been addressed as 'Mister' before, much less by my last name. Once when I'd sailed a chaw-wad at Laura Howells in the sixth grade when I was about eleven years old, Old Man Dodson had called me 'Master Sievers'—of course he was angry as a snagged gar then. The judge, his expression unchanged since the hearing first began, except when he'd wrinkled up his brow. He was stone sober looking.

Parson Briggs nudged me from the left and I got up to face the assembled witnesses. My knees quivered like I was about to topple over, and I could scarcely remember when I'd been more scared. Mrs. Billington, who was seated on the near side to the sheriff, next to Mr. Croaker, glowered out at me from underneath her hat. Sheriff Wortman's face was blank, reddish colored, and tight skinned around the cheeks. Only Maggie Lewis was smiling slightly and I took some comfort in it.

"Your judgeship," I began, feeling weak, "I took those things like Mrs. Billington there said, but I didn't steal them from her. Thieving's when a body takes things when he's meaning to do harm.

But Maggie, Mother Lewis there, says that stealing's when you take something that doesn't belong to you. So, I guess I stole the jewels."

I rightly didn't know what more to say. I was nervous as a tom cat in a lightning storm and sweating something fierce. Pop had told me something a long time back and I remembered it: 'When you're in a hard spot, it's best to tell the truth.' I was in a hard spot now and I didn't feel it was right to lie.

The judge listened carefully to what I said. Telling him about Ronnie drowning was the hardest thing I did, my voice quavering all the while. But I told him the whole story and the truth.

"The truth of it is I didn't find no other jewels. Those were the only ones I took. The jewel box was open when I found it."

All the while I talked, the writing pen had been resting on the desktop. Judge Bellman was quiet and thoughtful for the longest while. Taking deep draws on the pipe, he shuffled through the scribblings he'd taken earlier, pushing the smoke out between his lips in tiny gusts.

"Having heard the evidence presented here," he said finally, leaning forward and crossing his arms on the edge of the desktop, "I can't find otherwise than that the boy is..." the judge paused and cleared his throat, "is not guilty of the charge of theft."

When I heard the 'not guilty' words, I craned my neck around and glanced at Maggie. She was staring steadily at me and smiling from ear to ear. I couldn't rightly figure which of us was most surprised.

A sturdy "Well! I never!" shot out from between Mrs. Billington's tight-pursed lips. There was some confusion and commotion in the room.

Everyone, including me, thought that I was guilty.

Rapping a wooden mallet on the desktop, the judge brought the room to order.

"It's a point of law," the judge began, "which perhaps requires some explaining. American law is based upon English Common Law," he said. "The finding of Common Law upholds my judgment here." Pulling up a satchel from beneath the desk, he opened it and brought out a thick, worn, heavy, brown leather book, The judge thumbed through it some moments. He uttered a drawn out 'yeess' when he found the place. "It's right here in ARMORY V. DELAMIRIE, KING'S BENCH, 1722," he said, then proceeded to read aloud from it. "That the finder of a jewel, though he does not by such finding acquire an absolute property or ownership, yet he has such a property will enable him to keep it against all but the rightful owner."

"The jewel that this case addresses," the judge said directly to me, "was found by a boy about your own age a hundred and sixty-six years ago. The case of ARMORY V. DELAMIRIE has never been disputed. There is no evidence a theft was committed here and therefore you're not guilty. The jewelry, of course, must be returned to Mrs. Billington, who is the rightful owner."

I was all for returning the jewels to Mrs. Billington, and I didn't regret it either. I glanced over to look at her and she began squirming when she caught my eye,

"However," the judge said, interrupting the commotion which had started up again, "Sheriff Wortman informs me that both the parents of this boy are deceased and that he ran away from the home of an uncle who beat him." Once again, he turned his eye on me, "Under law, I could return you to that uncle. However, this court does not believe a boy should be viciously whipped any more than an obstinate horse or mule. I, therefore, have no other choice than to bind you over to the county orphans' home until your sixteenth birthday." Judge Bellman turned and looked at me again, "You'll be cared for there; you'll be around some children your own age, and you will receive a proper education. So ordered." The room was breath-quiet again, "Sheriff, I am placing this boy in your custody. See that he is delivered to Kenton in the morning."

The judge's sentence was over, I felt like a body about to be hanged.

Maggie had been right in what she said. Orphan home! Kenton was forty miles inland from the river. It would be nearly two years before I'd see the river after tomorrow.

Judge Bellman was sorting through his notes and about to leave when the Parson Briggs took to his feet beside me.

"Your Honor, may I address the bench?"

Startled, the judge looked up. "Identify yourself, sir, and state your business."

Parson Briggs craned his thin neck forward, "I am the Reverend Obadiah Briggs, Your Honor. I pray for the court's indulgence if I may."

"This is quite irregular," the judge sniffed. "But you may address this court."

Parson Briggs shuffled himself up front, tugging on his coat collar as he walked. "Your Honor, I've known this boy here most all his life. I knew his parents before he was born. Shortly after I came to settle in Hortonville, I met this boy's father and married him to a fine wife. I laid his father to rest nearly a year ago. The Sievers were fine folk–river folk, God-fearing, hard-working and honest. The boy doesn't know it yet, but he has an aunt–his father's oldest sister– living in Waytown. A member of my present parish. When I learned last night that he was here and the circumstances he was in, I telegraphed her. Her name is Addie Hudson, an influential and well-off woman. I have her telegram response to my communication here." The Parson reached inside his frock suit pocket and brought out a sheet of paper. "It reads, in part, "I will take my nephew in.""

Parson Briggs handed the paper to the judge who adjusted his spectacles and scanned it over for some moments.

"You are a mighty fortunate young man," he says to me. "I am rescinding my former order and placing you into the custody of Reverend Briggs. Sheriff, release the boy into the care of the Reverend here."

I could scarcely believe my ears. The room was all a-buzz and Maggie came rushing up and hugged me. Tears were trickling down her cheeks. Even the sheriff and Mr. Croaker appeared happy about the decision. Only Mrs. Billington shined sour as a green apple. She came near to stomping out of the sheriff's office in a huff and, when the door slammed shut, I never saw her again. Guess it wasn't enough for her just getting her jewelry back. She wanted to see me punished, too.

That evening, Max the barman being in a good mood and knowing it was important to her, allowed for Maggie to have the evening off, leastwise long enough for her to cook up another fine supper meal for the Parson Briggs and me. She insisted, too, we both stay over, there being no hotel in Swainville, and she set out all her extra pillows and blankets. She even offered Parson Briggs her own bed, which he graciously refused.

"I've slept on many floors and bare ground in my years. One more night won't matter much though I'm getting older," he said, and thanked her for her thoughtfulness.

The Parson curled up on one side of the cookstove when it came time to sleep, me on the other. We both slept peacefully through the night.

Come early morning, I paid my good-byes to Maggie. We stood on the bare dirt street in front of the stationhouse. Parson Briggs had purchased two tickets to Waytown. It was a journey that would take three hours.

I felt sad in leaving Maggie. She'd done right well by me. "Clayton," she said, smiling and slipping her hand around mine," if circumstances had been different for me and I'd had a son, I'd wished he'd grown up to be like you."

It was the kindest, most meaningful thing Maggie could have said. I held her hand, bent forward and kissed her cheek. She was holding back a wall of tears.

"I know your aunt will love you," she said. "Try to make her happy, too."

In the next few minutes, the stagecoach came clattering up the street. The coach for Waytown. As soon as it boarded passengers, I was bound toward my new home.

A man's reputation is the opinion people have of him; his character is what he really is.

                                        –Jack Miner

CHAPTER 10

Living with Aunt Addie. The Mercantile. A Visit with the Doctor.

IN A SMALL TOWN THERE'S no way to keep a secret long, and the news spread quick I was coming to stay with Aunt Addie. The Parson Briggs had made certain I'd be cared for "in a proper manner, befitting a boy your age," as he put it to me while I was an unwilling lodger in Sheriff Wortman's jail. The Parson had done it all up right, sending off a telegram to Aunt Addie, telling her to be expecting us on the next coach from Swainville.

It was past the middle of the afternoon when the stage pulled into Waytown, we being delayed along the way by a broken wheel. Aunt Addie was there, dressed real fine in a long, cream dress and carrying a parasol with a pale green fringe around the edge. The Parson Briggs had told me what she looked like, and I recognized her right off.

Along with her were several of the ladies from town, came out for the occasion just to see me in. Well, it was a real scene at the station house and all that furor mainly because I hadn't any proper clothes to wear. When I stepped off the stage, barefoot, with torn-out trousers' knees and a single button missing off my shirt, which was none too clean to start with, a gasping hush went up from the collected mouths of the assembled ladies and I guess I didn't make a very good impression. I didn't know for certain who all those old ladies thought I'd be, but for sure, what they were expecting wasn't me. You should've seen the gawks and heard the coughs and whisperings which came from that crowd. You'd have thought I was some kind of returned criminal–one that's paid his debts to society and come back to his old haunts only to find no justice.

Well, they cackled like chickens in the coop yard, and the polite coughs and throat clearings and whisperings made Aunt Addie nervous. The Parson saw all this, too, and found it an appropriate moment for some sermonizing right there on the street about Christian understanding and loving forgiveness for those less fortunate than themselves. He spoke on how a person who's dressed in not-so-fancy clothes is no less beloved by the Almighty than those who can afford them. And I thought to myself that, in some instances, the Almighty might love a body more, not because of what he looks like outwards, but of what he is inside. Well, that bit of sermonizing did the trick and all those ladies, put fast in their places and at length realizing the errors of their ways, gathered in around me and Aunt Addie and complimented her on the new addition to her family.

One short lady with a squat nose said, "He's certainly strong and healthy looking."

"An outright handsome specimen of boyhood," a taller woman standing balanced on the curb strip cooed. And the congratulations to Aunt Addie, and the compliments meant for me went on and on, something coming from the lips of nearly every woman there. For an instant, I thought I caught a wispy sigh and a smile crossed Aunt Addie's cream-powdered face–the kind that comes when the pressure's been lifted off.

Well, we left the stationhouse in Aunt Addie's carriage, the Parson Briggs driving, and left the hens behind who, no doubt the moment we were out of earshot, most likely set in to criticizing me again, if the truth was known.

Aunt Addie lived on the edge of town on a brick-paved street in a large, two-and-a-half-story framed house. The half-story nestled beneath the roof slope, sandwiched between two towering chimney stacks on either side. Aside each chimney stack lay a row of windows, and four gable rooms jutted from the roof which faced the street. A white, waist-high picket fence surrounded the house and walled off the long, green yard, sprinkled here and about with trees and bushes and clumps of flowers. To me, Aunt Addie's house looked like a mansion, or as I'd picture such, having never seen one in real life. She insisted though, as we drove up, it was nothing more than a large and comfortable house, the place where she'd spent most of her married years.

My first duty on arriving and bidding Parson Briggs good-bye, was to drive the rig around back and park it by the parlor door so as Clarke-Jiles, Aunt Addie's black houseman, could take the Parson home and later tend the horses. Aunt Addie had driven herself into town. When I pulled the rig up back, Clarke-Jiles met me and I handed him the reins and sprang out, giving the rig a jolt.

Clarke-Jiles was a large man, dark brown, with wide shoulders and a deep chest. He had a pleasant, handsome, full-mouthed face, and the moment I met him, I was impressed.

"So, you're Clayton Sievers, Miss Addie's nephew," Clarke-Jiles said, looking me over closely, then beaming broad. "Well, you're a fine-looking lad, Clayton Sievers." He grabbed my hand and gave it a pump or two. "I'm mighty pleased to make your acquaintance."

I liked Clarke-Jiles right off. He spoke really well–better than me, I think–and appeared to be an educated man. In those first few moments, I got the feeling I'd known him longer than just the one or two minutes that had passed. I was later to learn he was Aunt Addie's joy and pride and without exception a regular member of the family. He got paid twice again what any other houseman in those parts got and was well-thought-of in the town. Looking back, had Aunt Addie come upon hard times, she'd sooner have sold her house and furniture before she'd have parted with Clarke-Jiles. He was no mere houseman. He was family.

Of course, Clarke-Jiles was a citizen; an outright upstanding one, too. And he was as free a man as anyone, slavery having ended years before. His father had been a bailing slave in New Orleans and Clarke-Jiles was born twelve years before Lincoln's emancipation speech nearly thirty years ago.

Since Aunt Addie had no children of her own, and before my arrival (which was as much a surprise to her as it was to me) she'd taken in an orphan boy who was fast going on to twelve. His name was Jamie, and he was nearly as tall as me. For the time I was under Aunt Addie's hospitable roof, Jamie and I got along pretty good, considering he and I didn't have a whole lot in common, having different backgrounds and interests in life.

Jamie was a quiet boy, and kind of pale and washed-out compared to the brownness I'd gotten living near naked along the river. Aunt Addie was mighty prideful of him, and he was liked by all the ladies in her circle who fawned over him at every Saturday afternoon tea. He liked best to read and was always studying and getting the highest marks, which pleased Aunt Addie and heaped praise on him from the schoolteachers and every circle of town society which counted. Jamie and I were to become fast friends, but he was never a substitute for poor, lost Ronnie.

The first day I spent in Aunt Addie's house was a time to be remembered. Aunt Addie had never seen me before that day and, in fact, save for having heard of Pop's passing and not attending the laying away, she hadn't bothered with me until now. I supposed it was Uncle Frank who'd told her he'd be taking care of me as he was her brother, too, and no doubt kept in touch. But I never asked or knew for certain.

In her young womanhood, Aunt Addie was no doubt pretty, noting the gentle curve of her mouth and the healthy roundness and glow about her cheeks. She was the one member of Pop's large family that had found success having married well. Her late husband had been a dry goods keeper and had done mighty well for himself. She still ran the mercantile in town although she was seldom there in person. Aunt Addie had it managed for her by a man she'd hired, but she checked the ledgers and made all the sizeable decisions. It was the Parson Briggs who'd told her about me, and she felt it her God-given duty to take me in.

When I came inside from parking the rig and chattering with Clarke-Jiles, she flung herself on her knees and began to sobbing–crying and carrying on something awful. All the while she knelt crying over me and saying how Pop had been her favorite brother, I'd been noticing Jamie who'd been standing polite and quiet in the corner. After Aunt Addie had finished making over me and had cried herself dry, she got up, straightened out her dress and clasped my hand between hers, bent forward and kissed me on the forehead.

Then she called Jamie over and introduced me real formal.

"Clayton," she cooed, tugging me over gently toward him, "this is your new brother, Jamie."

'Your new brother' kind of haunted me. I knew I didn't have a real brother, being Pop's only child, and that the closest I'd come to having a real brother was when Ronnie and I had mingled blood.

Jamie must've felt the same because he didn't smile, but stepped up kind of hesitant and nodded his head and shook my hand like a gentleman. He didn't make like he was happy to see me.

"Now you two are going to have to get acquainted and become friends now that you'll be living together," Aunt Addie said.

I don't know how Jamie felt about it then, but I was willing to make the best of it.

When it wasn't more than an hour or two after my arrival, Aunt Addie set into a storm of cooking. I made a gesture or two toward Jamie, who'd grown a little more relaxed and friendlier, and together we hauled in two armloads of kindling from the box on the kitchen porch. Clarke-Jiles normally did it, but Aunt Addie gave it over to us to do; a sort of 'sharing the labor' you might say. Jamie, who knew the layout, started the fire in the cookstove and Aunt Addie began to set the table.

"Jamie, dear," Aunt Addie called, bending over the table and craning her neck upward to look at him, "Why don't you show Clayton around the house while I'm readying supper."

I don't know that Jamie was too keen on playing guide, but he did it without a word.

The house was mighty grand. The bottom rooms were only used for company and formal entertaining except for the back parlor and the kitchen where the family gathered. A staircase, most of six feet wide, and covered with a thin red-carpet strip which ran all the way to the top, led just off the front parlor to the second floor. The walls were all covered with cream-colored paper with all sorts of bright printed flowers. What wasn't covered by the flower prints were under pictures, some large, others no bigger than a hand. Several small wooden racks held porcelain figurines–tiny kittens romping together, miniature dogs playing with colored balls, and jewel-eyed hoot owls, some no bigger than a thumb. The house was powerful grand.

Aunt Addie believed in sunlight and the house was airy and cheerful all over. The curtains and the cream-colored velvet drapes were all drawn back, and the rooms caught the last beams of the fading sun. I was glad Aunt Addie liked the sunshine as much as I.

The upstairs were more of the same; thick curtains drawn open, Aunt Addie's large bedroom that faced the house front and connected with a sitting room, a room where she did her sewing and reading, a bathroom near as large as Pop's river cabin, other bedrooms for visitors and yet another for Clarke-Jiles, had he wanted it. A narrow, bare-stepped stair led up from the far end of the upper floor toward the attic rooms where Jamie and I would be.

Mealtime had come by the time our tour was done.

When supper was set, Aunt Addie called and we all gathered around the table–the whole family–Aunt Addie at the head, Jamie, Clarke-Jiles, and me. They all folded their hands real pious, and I followed suit only when Jamie shot his bony elbow into my side and Aunt Addie glowered at me over the rim of her silver spectacles. I guess right then she knew her work was cut out for her in raising me. Aunt Addie offered the blessing, which was a memorized one, with the others joined in. I didn't know it, so I kept my mouth shut.

Something about the blessing bothered me, not that I wasn't brought up to pray, because Pop had taught me that. But Pop always said the Good Lord wasn't happy with mere lip service; He wanted thanks given from the heart.

"The whole world's a prayer, Clayt," I remember Pop telling me one day while we were lulling downriver together. "All a man has to do is look, knowing He's in everything you see. Pray often and pray to be the best you can. And always pray from the heart."

The blessing was over soon enough, cracked off like a church hymn when the organ pace is doubled, and we set into eating. Aunt Addie had cooked up a real feast–steaming corn bread with a crock of butter fluffed and whipped to dig into, the butter melting deep down inside, and jams and homemade jellies, the main course a stew with chunks of beef and turnips, carrots, celery, parsnips, and potatoes. It was every bit as good as Maggie's and smelled better than I could remember, me having lived off fish and beans for so long, or a rabbit I'd snared and roasted. In mid-table was a plate full of home-baked apple cookies for dessert. I'd been living off my own meager ability with the skillet for some while except when I was with Maggie. Aunt Addie could cook better than most I'd say, and, considering her age, she'd been at it a long while, too.

The house had plenty of room as I've said, being the largest place, I'd ever seen–the largest one in town–and I could've had an attic room all to myself. But Aunt Addie decided on Jamie and I to share a room so that we could get to know one another better.

After supper, Jamie and I did the dishes and tableware. Aunt Addie, who loved to sew, set into making me a nightshirt of muslin cloth. She had it all stitched together by the time we'd finished. She'd even embroidered my initials onto it so that it wouldn't get mixed with Jamie's which looked the same. I think Jamie felt a little bad about it though, because his was just plain white and without a mark. Mine was monogrammed in neat, red stitching.

Everything about Aunt Addie was elegant, clean, and neat-as-a-pin proper. How she'd allowed me to eat with her that first night without cleaning up–except for scrubbing my hands good with lye soap–I've never reckoned. Maybe she was dithered from the excitement of having me, or felt I'd had enough to bother with for a time.

Now that everything was settled, catching sight of a yawn I made, Aunt Addie said, "Clayton, you've had a long enough day for any boy your age. You and Jamie go upstairs and get ready for bed. I've had Clarke-Jiles heat some water. You boys scat now and get yourselves ready for a bath."

As I learned not long after, Aunt Addie was a pure stickler for cleanliness. "Cleanliness is next to Godliness," she'd often say. It was almost a ritual. And she carried it to extremes. As Pop told me, a man shouldn't take a hot soap bath oftener than once a week because it makes a body weak. Washing hands before eating and rinsing off by swimming were fine. Aunt Addie didn't hold to that. Jamie was so clean he glowed pink; Aunt Addie, too, except she smelled of fresh violets and lavender from her toilet water.

She had kept a wooden tub, oval and high-backed, just for Jamie. Of course, she kept a fancy porcelain one for herself. She wouldn't allow Jamie and me to use it because she reckoned we'd get it grimy with dirt scum and soap. The wood tub was for 'boy bathing' as she called it, but I always felt I was sitting in a wash tub.

That night Jamie and I went upstairs and undressed together, which wasn't embarrassing because he was a boy like me. Clarke-Jiles came and poured the hot water (I swear to the point of near boiling) into the tub. Aunt Addie poked her gray head into the room from around the corner and caught me naked as a newborn before I'd had time to climb in next to Jamie who was already seated and busy with the soap cake. Noticing my embarrassment, Aunt Addie, instead of stepping out, pranced right on in!

"It's no matter, Clayton, dear," she soothed. "I've seen my share of nude boys before. I might not have had any sons of my own until now, but I was raised with a load of brothers."

I suppose she said it to put me at ease, but in truth it didn't help.

I felt a flush of red spread quick over my neck and face. Jamie giggled some, sounding girlish, and I hurried into the tub, entwining myself between Jamie's legs like a wrestler and slid down into the soapy water to my neck. The tub was plenty big for one, but scarcely large enough for two.

Sharing the space, Jamie and I were all cramped up together and it was some wonder how we got clean at all. Then Clarke-Jiles appeared for the second time, toting more water in and scalded us again. About that time, Aunt Addie, who'd abandoned the bathing room, came back, and peered in from around the corner.

"Scrub each other's backs well and be sure to wash behind and in your ears," she warned. The bathing done, Jamie and I dressed for bed and Aunt Addie came up and made the both of us kneel down to pray. I forgot to fold my hands and Jamie let me know with another of his elbow knocks. After all, I wasn't much on praying before falling asleep, and all this carrying on with the Almighty made me a might uncomfortable. Aunt Addie, who'd listened in from the bed foot, came over and tucked us in and pressed each of us a kiss on the mouth. I hadn't ever been kissed at bedtime before, or on my mouth, and I didn't like it either. Aunt Addie kissed moist.

Another thing I wasn't used to was being tied into bed all tight and stiff, like a corpse in an undertaker's box. But it wasn't too bad because the bed was soft and nice to be in–save for the fact Jamie was in it, too. He sure gave me a plain fit sleeping. He never seemed content sleeping on his own side. As soon as the shades were pulled and the gaslight turned out and things got quiet, he'd cradle up on mine. It wouldn't have been so awful except his feet were always cold, and later he'd slap his arm across my chest, toss and roll, and wheeze warm breath into my ear.

Well, that first night was a warm night, and I just couldn't take anymore of Jamie's twisting and breathing, nor the nightshirt which twisted about my legs and cramped up against my underarms. Jamie had finally settled out and was sleeping peacefully. I crawled out and clattered down the gutter pipe outside the window, cat quiet, and stayed in the carriage house. I slept well that night. Come first light, I shimmied up the pipe and slipped in next to Jamie, who hadn't noticed I'd been gone, and curled up all handsome like.

When Aunt Addie came in early to wake us, no one was the wiser for me having slept outside on the horse blankets and straw.

In the time which followed, I became as accustomed as I could to Aunt Addie and her ways. It was a powerful trying time, though, between the daily bathing and the kissing and the dressing up.

Aunt Addie was as fine and gentle a Christian woman as ever I've made acquaintance with. She and Maggie Lewis were sisters of a kind. She'd told me she'd do her God-fearing Christian best to be a fit mother to me, and I tried, but she and I never took to cottoning much to one another's ways. At times she'd be all sugar syrup and spice cake, but then she'd start in to harping about my doings and telling me to wear my shoes and keep my shirt on. "It's indecent for a boy to go about undressed like that," she'd say. Well, those shoes, they cut into my feet something awful, and those shirts were stiff and scratchy, and she insisted Jamie and I keep our collar buttoned. I had to allow how Aunt Addie, having never had a boy of her own to raise from scratch, didn't understand them and their ways.

On Saturday, exactly a week after being with her, Aunt Addie got the notion into her head I needed some new clothes. She allowed how I wouldn't be an embarrassment to her if I was always dressed up proper.

Jamie remained at home while Aunt Addie and I rode in the carriage up the main street, Clarke-Jiles all trussed up in his spanking livery, all smiles from ear to ear. He showed his natural personality which warmed everyone around him, and he tipped his hat to everyone we met.

Waytown was like no other river town I'd ever seen. With several thousand people, it was the biggest town I'd ever set foot in.

It looked–even felt–different from any other town I'd seen–

Hortonville and Swainville notwithstanding.

First off, most of its streets were paved with brick, not with naked dirt and gravel, and the streets were wide and tree lined. A large park sat slap-dab in the middle of the town with the businesses surrounding it in a square. There was a building in the park, open on one side and with a high-peaked roof.

"That's the bandshell," Aunt Addie pointed out. "There's a concert there every Sunday afternoon during the summertime."

The park was lush and green and lined with trees and built-up banks with flowers covering them. On one side, pointing north toward HUDSON'S MERCANTILE, the business Aunt Addie inherited from her late husband, sat an old ten-pounder cannon left over from the war. It wasn't any good for firing anymore. Its barrel was plugged and had become a pigeon roost.

The storefronts in Waytown were different, too. Instead of being wood frame and flat roofed, they were mostly brick and many with sloped roofs. Colored awnings jutted away from them for folks to walk under and stay free from the sun and rain. I must've been some sight, gawking and craning my neck around as Aunt Addie pointed out all the sights of interest as we rode along.

Finally, we pulled up at HUDSON'S MERCANTILE. Clarke-Jiles gave out with a deep-chested "Whoa, Gray," then bolted from the driver's seat and helped Aunt Addie down. Mr. Mertinger, Aunt Addie's manager, who'd apparently been expecting us, came right out and greeted us personally. While Aunt Addie traipsed back to look over new merchandise and figure bills and ledgers, Mr. Mertinger took it upon himself to measure and fit me for my new clothes.

I was fitted out all nice and proper, dressed good enough to bury. Mr. Mertinger selected a gray and brown-striped Cheviot suit and three pairs of trousers in tan, gray, and blue; brown buckled shoes and dark wool stockings; three sets of underdrawers complete with button traps; and three fancy linen shirts with collars and cuffs that buttoned on and off. Aunt Addie allowed I should wear the Cheviot suit while we were in town, so my other things were packed in long, flat boxes along with the clothes I'd come in. Mr. Mertinger was going to throw my river clothes away, but I wouldn't stand for it, so he packed them, too.

We stayed in the mercantile nigh on to three full hours while Aunt

Addie scoured the books. Clarke-Jiles, he'd gone on up the street to visit some friends of his, no doubt to swap tall stories, so I browsed around the huge shop a while, looking over things I'd never seen before.

The mercantile was large, two floors high and taking up an entire block, and brightly lit. It was the largest and grandest store I'd ever seen. Glass windows stretched all the way across the front from the alley to the corner, and the shelves and tables were just filled with fancy things. There were hollow-ground barber razors like Pop used to use, and Russian leather strops, soap mugs and brushes, lemon squeezers like Aunt Addie used at tea, cork pullers with fancy handles. Along other shelves were hog scrapers and cleavers for chopping meat, solid brass soap cups that looked like scalloped seashells, and even a three-wheeled velocipede with genuine rubber tires. Along another wall, in padlocked, closed glass cases, were Smith and Wesson single and double-action and hammerless revolvers, and many rifles and shotguns. Why, there was even real silver flatware in silk-lined boxes. Uncle Frank used to hawk goods from village to town along the river, but what Aunt Addie's store contained was far better quality. He'd given Pop and Mother a boxed set of silverware on their wedding day and, by the time I'd turned seven, the silver plate was flaking off like chunks of rust.

After a time of looking, I started growing antsy being around the store and all cooped up inside waiting on Aunt Addie to finish reading through her ledgers and take for home. The day was especially warm. The sun was bright along the walkways and on the street beyond.

The Cheviot suit Aunt Addie wanted me to wear was sharp, as those things go, and a lot like what Uncle Frank had worn when he dressed his best for selling. But it was hot and growing more uncomfortable by the clock. Those long, wool stockings beneath my trousers made my legs itch something fierce and the shoe buckles cut into the tops of my feet. I kept having to pull the backside of the trousers down to feel right, and all the while I kept thinking of the pleasure of being without them, free along the river, naked mostly, and lulling in the sun and water.

It wasn't too soon when Aunt Addie came out from the back, bid Mr. Mertinger farewell, and the shop ladies in the store good-bye, and wandered outside.

"Clayton, stop gaping and pulling at yourself so!" she warned. I felt like a woman must feel, all laced up and corseted in and bound up tight.

Glancing at the tiny watch she wore like a pendant around her neck on a gold chain, she said, "We have one more stop to make. It's two o'clock now. I've told Clarke-Jiles to meet us at Dr. Clarendon's office at three."

"Why are we going to the doctor?" I inquired. "Aren't you feeling well?

"I'm feeling fine, Clayton, dear," she said, smiling and looping her arm at the elbow inside of mine. Strolling up the street with me, she seemed relaxed. More than she'd been before. Aunt Addie did walk slowly and put quite a drag on me. "I've taken the liberty of making an appointment for you to have an examination with the doctor."

"I don't need no examination!" I protested.

"Any examination," she corrected. "And when was the last time you saw a doctor?"

I guessed I'd never seen one outside of old Doc Severine, except when I'd had the quinsy something awful.

"Pop was always doctoring the both of us," I told her. "And he was better than most doctors, too."

"I didn't know John Clayton was a physician," Aunt Addie chortled with a soft, warm smile.

"Well, he wasn't no phy-si-cian," I said, having trouble with the word.

"Any physician," Aunt Addie interrupted, "any physician."

"He wasn't any physician," I said. "But he could doctor better than anyone along the river."

"I imagine John Clayton could," she admitted, "but could he tell how his boy was growing? That he was normal? Could he tell if you were healthy?"

I didn't feel like answering. It wasn't any use. I could see Aunt Addie had her mind made up. I was to see the doctor, and nothing I could say was going to change the fact.

We walked on slowly, about four blocks, and I could see the sign over the doctor's door, jutting out over the street. It read: JENNINGS CLARENDON, M.D. with the words PHYSICIAN AND SURGEON in fancy gold lettering on a shiny white shingle.

It was gloomy inside the doctor's office. The only light streamed through a small window on the street side. The room was large, with a row of chairs set neatly one beside another against one wall. An open doorway led to another room at the back. Aunt Addie and I were the only ones there. The whole room smelled like disinfectant. Because of the bell above it, the front door made a chiming sound when we came through. Soon, a man I'd guess about fifty of average height and with graying hair, thin on top, and a not too large but rounded belly, came out from the other room and greeted us.

"Miss Addie," he welcomed, smiling kindly and stepping forward to greet her.

He set his hands out to take hers between them. They small-talked together for some moments before he turned to me.

"And you must be Clayton." He took my hand, too, and shook it steadily for some pumps up and down. "I've heard a lot about you, Clayton, and now here you are."

The three of us stood in the dim outer room, passing the amenities, then the doctor guided us back into his office,

The office was somewhat cramped and not like the outer room which was plenty big enough to move about in comfortably. But it wasn't nearly as dark, having a large window set into one wall which let in lots of sunlight from an alleyway running past. There was a big roll-top desk crammed full of books and papers, two large horsehair chairs, one of which Aunt Addie took the liberty of sitting in as soon as we walked in. Around the room were more books, big thick ones in walnut cases covered with glass, and above them were shelves with rows and rows of all size bottles filled with pills and powders and colored liquids. Of course, my curiosity was aroused, so I sauntered up and gandered at them for a time.

They were all cork-sealed and with names printed on the labels a body couldn't read. One bottle said Crataegus and was filled with pills no bigger than a bee-bee. And there was Crotalus Horridus and Chrysanthemum and another marked Camphora Monobrom. On the bottle of each, a label, in black or red, was printed LUYTIES PHARMACAL COMPANY, ST. LOUIS, MO. My natural curiosity was mighty high, so I asked the doctor what ho-me-o-pathic meant.

"Similis similibus curentur," he said, looking up from a pile of papers at his rolltop desk.

I guessed right off they were foreign words which doctors use so as the patient won't know what's being said. Then he added, "like cures like," which still didn't make any sense. Aunt Addie, who'd been sitting quietly in the corner, said, "Dr. Clarendon is a homeopathic physician. He cures people with those little pills."

I'd taken down a large half-filled bottle and was tilting it side to side, watching the pills avalanche from top to bottom.

"I cured a case of diphtheria with those very pills in just three days," the doctor said, "when another physician had given the patient up for dead. Miss Addie, you remember Laura Hutchins, don't you?"

"Very well, poor woman, all she went through until you took her case. Everyone said it was a miracle how she recovered. And so fast!"

The doctor nodded knowingly. "Yes, the miracle of homeopathy. But," Dr. Clarendon said, walking up and placing his hand on my shoulder. "We aren't here to discuss my practice. We are here to look you over." Go ahead and undress. I'll be with you momentarily." Aunt Addie spoke up and said, "Take off everything, Clayton. The doctor needs to see all of you."

Even though she'd seen me naked on my first night when Jamie and I bathed together, all the same, I wasn't keen on getting buck bare naked in full view of Aunt Addie sitting just a few feet away. But I saw how I was stuck. I stripped slowly, handing each piece over to her as she told me to. Red-faced, embarrassed, and nervous as I was, it was some pleasure being free from the buttoned collar, those tight-buckled shoes and woolen stockings.

A narrow table covered in padded black leather stood nearby, so I climbed up on it and waited for the doctor to arrive. Soon after, he stepped up and set into his examination. I hadn't ever been examined before--leastwise not that I recalled, and it was more than a might embarrassing.

Dr. Clarendon tapped about my back and chest with his fingers and put a funny looking gadget he called a steth-o-scope on my back, telling me to breathe deeply in and out several times, and then over my heart to listen. He allowed me to listen, too, and it was indeed a wonder to hear the thump, thump, thump of my own heartbeat. When he was done, he had me open my mouth as wide as it could. "Say aahh," he said and was like to gag me with a flat stick he shoved down my throat. He checked my teeth then had me lie back on the table and pressed and tapped and thumped some more from my armpits to down my middle to below my belly button. He felt me from head to feet, both front and back. All the time he scarce said a word save when he took hold of my pecker and tugged back on the skin. He uttered a drawn-out *hmmm* and pulled harder on the skin which moved back but slowly until I said, "That hurts a little." "I'm not surprised," he said, still holding on to it and bending lower to get a closer look. Aunt Addie overheard. "Is something wrong?" she asked, rising to her feet. "Nothing that can't be fixed," he said and set into more pushing forward and pulling back. I silently begged him to finish.

"Off the table now and stand up straight," he told me, "And cough when I tell you to." I stood and spread my legs some like he said, and his hands went straight to my balls which he rolled around for some time, then poked his pointer finger straight up in me. "Head to the side and cough," he said. I did. He stuck his finger up on the other side and had me cough again.

"How old are you, Clayton?" he asked.

"Fourteen," I told him. "But I'll be fifteen 'fore long."

"In three months," Aunt Addie added from her seat. He jotted the information down in a little leather-covered book.

"Stand against the wall so I can measure you." I propped myself up against the wall and the doctor pushed my head and shoulders back and measured me with a ruler mark.

"Five feet four and a quarter inch. You'll likely be growing above that soon enough. From the looks of you, you're still maturing. Little body hair yet to speak of and you're slender as a pole. You'll be filling out soon, too." His words were reassuring. I wanted to look like Ronnie had looked, all muscular and hairy and manly and the sooner the better.

When Dr. Clarendon was done examining me, he told me to sit tight and strode over to talk his findings to Aunt Addie.

"River life must have agreed with him," I heard him say. "He's a fine-looking boy and healthy as a spring colt." Then he gathered Aunt Addie's arm and walked her gently out of earshot. They spoke together for a spell. Still naked because Dr. Clarendon hadn't told me I could dress, I watched them conferencing in the front room. When they finished, Aunt Addie came pacing over and, to my horror, walked right up. Even though she'd seen everything, I covered up quick, both hands hiding my man parts.

"Dr. Clarendon says you're sound and healthy as can be." She seemed mighty pleased. "However," she added, "he believes you should be circumcised." Circumcised? I'd never heard that word before.

"It's a simple operation," the doctor announced.

"Operation? I don't want no operation!" I sputtered.

"I don't want ANY operation," Aunt Addie corrected. "You simply must learn to speak correctly, and I will see to that." With Aunt Addie's firm correcting and Dr. Clarendon's explanation of what was about to happen, I knew I didn't want any part of it.

"If Dr. Clarendon believes it should be done," Aunt Addie said, placing her hand softly on my naked shoulder, "we had best listen to him. In these matters, he knows what's best."

I protested, but the line of her gentle-curving jaw was set firm. I hadn't been with her long, but I'd seen that look before and knew it wouldn't do any good to argue.

"It won't take long," the doctor said. They chatted a moment more, then Aunt Addie reached inside her handbag, pulled out some bills to pay him, and they pressed hands and said good-bye.

"I'll have Clarke-Jiles drive me home, Clayton," she said, "and then come back for you."

With Aunt Addie gone, Dr. Clarendon ambled over and put a reassuring hand on my shoulder. "Now, Clayton, this won't take long at all." With that he put his finger under my chin and raised it up so he was looking me in the eyes. "I won't lie to you, son," he said, "at your age this will hurt some but snip, snip and it will all be over quickly. "That said, he had me lie back flat on the table. I hadn't noticed two leather straps hanging by hooks from the ends which he took and, spreading my legs to meet the ends, tied my ankles. "I don't want you kicking me," he said with a smile. He buckled another strap across my chest. I was held fast. He turned and took some things from a drawer. It was then I saw the instruments in his hand. "No need for chloroform," he said. "This will go quite quick."

The townsfolk might've heard me yell all the way down to the waterfront.

A half-hour later, I walked stiff kneed and bandaged tight from the doctor's office.

Clarke-Jiles was seated tall and handsome in the carriage seat. I climbed up slow and easy and sat down beside him.

Clarke-Jiles was sympathetic. On the slow ride home, taking care to avoid the ruts and jolts from the road, he tried to make conversation. It was clear Aunt Addie had told him about my circumcision.

"Want to talk about it, Clayt?" he asked. It was obvious he was interested in my operation and how I felt.

"No," I said.

After a bit, he broke the spell of silence between us. "Lan-sakes, boy, what you must think of us! You've been in Waytown scarce a week and already they're making' you over. First, it's a parcel lot of new clothes that're too hot to wear in summer, then Doc goes a-trimming on you!" I listened but wasn't much interested in talking. "You know, Clayt, Miss Addie only wants what's best for you. You're her son now and she cares about you and Jamie. Doc Clarendon does too. They's fine folk and only do what's best."

The carriage drove along, the horses' hooves clip-clopping on the brickwork. The warming sun began to lull me, and the rocking of the rig set me to dozing. But the pain, and my humiliation, weren't forgotten.

At supper time that evening I scarcely looked Aunt Addie in the face and didn't speak to her. Clarke-Jiles was right, though. I knew it wasn't her fault.

Come bedtime, I couldn't sleep but lay wakeful listening to the windup clock, its works grinding out the seconds and the minutes. I pondered on the Parson Brigg's own sermon words from when he served the church in Hortonville. If God created menfolk in His own image and God is faultless perfect, it was a puzzlement why man felt he had to improve on the Lord's own work.

Jamie, of course, joked and thought the whole thing mighty funny. He made the most of my discomfort, though it turned out while he hadn't been tight like me, Doc Clarendon had done his handiwork on him too some months before. As the saying goes, misery loves company.

From Uncle Frank to Aunt Addie, living with kinfolk was mighty bothersome. It must've been the price of living in fine society. If it was, I wasn't certain it was worth it.

The devil can cite Scripture for his purpose. An evil soul, producing holy witness, is like a villain with a smiling cheek, a goodly apple rotten at the heart.

—William Shakespeare

CHAPTER 11

An Unwelcome Guest.

AUNT ADDIE WAS A MILD-MANNERED woman, mainly. She'd never had to work hard, leastwise not like Pop, nor even like Uncle Frank in the earlier times when he beat himself up and down the riverbanks selling wares. Oh, she'd had her hand in the building of Hudson's Mercantile and done her part in making it the largest such concern for many miles along both sides of the river. The store was always packed with buyers and business was mighty brisk.

Nearly everyone who knew her called her 'Miss Addie' despite the fact she'd been married, and those who weren't part of her large and formal social circle addressed her as 'Mrs. Hudson'. From the short while I'd spent in Waytown, it seemed she had a reputation for both forthrightness and utmost honesty. If someone in the community needed help, Aunt Addie was there to do her share. If the church required hymn books to replace the well-thumbed and ratty ones, she ordered and paid for them. She was a nurse to the sick, a comfort to the lonely, and a helper to those outcasts, like me.

Once, when Parson Briggs mentioned from the Sunday pulpit he wished there were funds enough for a new altar Bible, Aunt Addie sent all the way to Chicago for one. A month of Sundays and sometime later, we sat in church together: Jamie, Aunt Addie, Clarke-Jiles, and me, in our usual place near the pulpit just left of the center aisle. Parson Briggs walked solemnly up the aisle following the choir and, when he stepped up to the altar, you should have seen his face! He beamed from nose to ear–both sides--and was like to cry. The new Bible was waiting for him.

"The Lord be praised!" he nearly shouted. "It's an answer to a prayer!" he said, gratitude and happiness ringing from his voice. He smoothed his hands lovingly over the tooled, red-leather cover and along the page edges, fronted in real gold.

The congregation was as surprised as he was. Voices mumbled through the church, everyone searching one another's faces, looking for the tell-tale glow of the mysterious benefactor. Aunt Addie sat quiet, as normal as can be, not looking innocent nor guilty.

The Parson allowed how everyone could come forward following the service and admire the new book. And, when the service ended, Aunt Addie was among the lookers-on. Of course, everyone thought it was she who did it, but she wouldn't admit it anyway.

"Miss Addie gave the Bible," Clarke-Jiles told me that afternoon, "but you're not to breathe a word about it. Not to Jamie, not to anyone." He told me how, when it arrived, Aunt Addie bid him sneak it ghost-quiet into the church after dark. "Made me feel like a thief," he smiled, "breaking into the church like that, except it was doing good, not ill."

That Sunday evening, the Parson and Mrs. Briggs ventured to the house to make a call. He tried every which way to make her confess she'd done it, but she held firm, her dead-pan expression not giving away a thing.

That was Aunt Addie, mainly, but I discovered she had other sides.

First off, she had the senses of a cat. She seemed able to sense when anything was wrong, or different, or unusual. Turned out it was me who was unusual, and usually wrong and different.

I'd grown up along the river being free minded about nearly everything. Pop had taught me well and raised me right. In no way could I fault Pop except for the drinking which had killed him. He hadn't wanted me to smoke, and I didn't until I knew Ronnie well. He saw nothing wrong with swimming naked in the river nor spending a lazy afternoon sunning and fishing along its banks. But Aunt Addie didn't cotton to it much.

One late morning, Clarke-Jiles running errands and Jamie off somewhere, Aunt Addie called me in. I was lazing beneath the shade of the carriage house overhang.

"Clayton," she began, all seriousness, "I know you smoke. Smoking is a vile and unhealthful habit, not good for anyone, much less a boy your age."

"But, Aunt Addie, I ha–"

She interrupted me, speaking with preciseness. "Now, Clayton, don't deny it. I smelled the tobacco on your clothes, and when I straightened your room. What will Jamie think if he sees you smoking? He looks up to you and you should set a fine example."

"I don't smoke around Jamie," I said. I admitted my guilt, knowing she knew, and it wasn't any use in lying. There and then she made me bring my pipe to her and throw it in the bin along with the other rubbish. First, I had to snap the stem in two. Oh, you wouldn't know how it pained me. It was like losing an old friend.

There were other times, too, I could mention.

I never could sleep well with Jamie–between his wheezing and his cold feet, so, like the first night there, I kept sneaking out. I thought no one knew. I hadn't figured on Aunt Addie.

Real casually one day she asked, "Why do you sneak outside the house at night?" She hadn't raised her voice above its usual softness, but the question struck me like a hammer blow.

"What?" I startled.

"I know you have been leaving the house at night and going off and I wondered why." Again, she'd caught me.

"I can't sleep with Jamie," I told the truth. "He sleeps too restless."

Aunt Addie stirred her tea. She was forever drinking tea. "You don't wear the nightshirt I made you, either" she said, still soft voiced and totally dead pan. I wasn't certain how she'd reckoned that. I knew she wasn't spying on me, slinking around about in darkness. That wasn't Aunt Addie's way. Guess there was still the smallest smidgeon of river woman in her, river women being a remarkably insightful lot. Perhaps she knew because mine was never soiled like Jamie's.

"No, ma'am. I haven't ever had a nightshirt before. I reckon it gets too bunchy and torments me something miserable."

"Landsakes, boy," her voice rose in pitch, but not in anger. "What have you been sleeping in all these years?"

"Mostly in my—my altogether, ma'am."

She let escape a small burst of air and smiled gently." I guess I can't expect you to change your ways overnight from nearly fifteen years of river living. Still," she added, following a pause for thought, "it isn't fitting for you to be sleeping in the carriage house." She stirred her tea and waited for my reply.

"No, ma'am. I guess it isn't."

The next day, Clarke-Jiles was set to work taking out the double bed Jamie and I used. Together, we carried up two single beds, fancy ones with quilted mattresses and brass head and foot boards, delivered from the mercantile. It was peaceful sleeping after that, and Aunt Addie never mentioned my sleeping naked, either.

What followed a few short days before my birthday proved Aunt Addie could hold her own against anyone and come out the winner.

The day was beautiful—cloudless, sunny, and warm. I'd been out scouting the town and river, not having any special place to go. Just wandering. No one was around, so I stripped off my clothes and swam and lazed until mid-afternoon, enjoying the river like I had with Ronnie. When I came back home, I heard voices drifting past the porch door of the kitchen. If I'd recognized the man's voice and paid attention, I would've never ventured in.

There, seated at the kitchen table, was none other than Uncle Frank.

Aunt Addie was sipping tea, Uncle Frank a shot of whiskey from a teacup. It looked a might laughable, that tiny cup nested in his large bony hands. Aunt Addie didn't drink hard liquor. Tea was like poison to Uncle Frank. So, they'd compromised; Uncle Frank's pocket flask emptied into one of Aunt Addie's teacups. She didn't keep whiskey glasses.

My heart took a steamboat piston thump upward into my throat when I caught sight of him. He just sat by, tall and proud and somber faced, staring over to me.

"How've you been doin', boy," he drawled, "since you seen fit to run away?" His voice was as deep and firm as I'd remembered it.

I gulped my heart back down. "Just fine, Uncle Frank."

"I see you are." His cast-gray eyes scouted me over some. He took a pull from his teacup. I'd been careful to keep my clothes neat as I sauntered out along the river. Guess I appeared a might better sight than when we'd last set eyes on one another.

"Franklin came here to talk about you," Aunt Addie said softly, inviting me to sit.

I gathered up a seat around the table opposite them. "How'd you know I was here?" I asked him.

"Didn't. Just was in Waytown on business and stopped by to pay a call on my sister." I knew if Uncle Frank had come to sell his wares at Aunt Addie's mercantile, he'd be out of luck. She only handled quality merchandise, not like what he sold.

It was like Uncle Frank to aim right to the heart of things "Why'd you run off, boy?" he asked, giving me a cold glare. I didn't answer, not feeling Aunt Addie needed to know the truth. He shifted in his chair and took another swallow. "It's just like the boy," he said, talking direct to Aunt Addie, "takin' off without a word, leavin' the chores to pile up." Then he glanced back toward me, "I reckon you took my skiff, too, stealing off in the dead of night with that thievin' friend a yours. Well, I want it back."

"I haven't got it," I told him. "It's lost."

"Lost?" he boomed. "That was a near-new skiff. Cost me twenty dollars hard money."

I was feeling helpless and looked toward Aunt Addie who sat calm and listening.

"I'll pay for your boat, Franklin," she said quietly. "But" she turned to me, "it will come out of your allowance." Twenty dollars! Fifty cents a week was all Jamie and I got between us. If Aunt Addie held back half, it'd take forever to pay off my debt to her!

I reckoned maybe all Uncle Frank wanted was his money back and to see me squirm, which I did when I first saw him and which no doubt gave him pleasure. But he wasn't done yet.

"Addie," he started up, "now that I'm here and found him, I want him back. John's passing gave him over to me to raise and I reckon a boy like him needs a fatherly hand." I was thunderstruck and numb. Living with Uncle Frank now would be worse than before, especially since I'd run off. Uncle Frank wasn't a forgiving man.

"A boy needs a woman's hand, too," Aunt Addie said.

"A woman's hand in raising him up early maybe," he drawled, "but now he needs a man's guidance, a man's firm hand to set him straight. Since he came, I bet he's given you no end of grief. 'Spare the rod and spoil the child' the Good Book says. I know you haven't it in you to whip him when he needs it. Next few years he'll need it plenty. Take the starch out of him. Make him understand." Uncle Frank glowered toward me as he spoke, looking satisfied.

"Don't preach the Good Book to me, Franklin Pierce Sievers. I know it as well as you. A boy doesn't need whipping as much as loving. I can see he gets a proper home."

"You sayin' I can't give him a proper home?" I guess he'd caught the insult and was feeling angered. "He's a river boy, Addie, just a river boy, colt-wild and needin' taming. He ain't fittin' for this fancy social living."

"He's fitting well enough," she said. "He'll learn the rest." Her mouth had taken on that firm set-jaw look. Aunt Addie was doing battle over me.

Uncle Frank held on. He was like a treed coon and wasn't going to be knocked down easy. "There's work needing done downriver, chores 'round the cabin. Who's going to tend to those?"

Aunt Addie set her pale blue eyes straight against her brother's. For the first time since I'd rolled into Waytown and come to live with her, I heard her thin voice peak angrily.

"You don't want a boy to raise," she countered, "all you want is a boy to labor, to do your work for you. Well, I won't have it. As long as I've known you, you've done your hardest to get out of work. I won't have it, Franklin. Clayton stays with me in Waytown."

Uncle Frank had polished off his whiskey and was no doubt feeling bold. "You're a fine one to talk 'bout savin' labor. You and that big Buck a yours."

Aunt Addie's gentle eyes flashed fire. A line of red rose up her neck and spread outward over her pale face. "I'll have none of that kind of talk in my house!" she shot back. "Clarke-Jiles is as fine a man as any. Better. He's paid well for what he does. You'll never get your hands on Clayton as long as I have life and breath to say it." Aunt Addie wasn't all sweet-dough soft. She had the spunk of a river woman in her. Her eyes clouded up some. "Franklin, I'm your sister and I do love you, but you've outworn your welcome in this house."

Uncle Frank gazed at her, knowing he was beaten. "Mark my words, Addie," he said, rising to his feet, "when he starts running wild, you'll wish I had him."

He was half out the kitchen when Aunt Addie called back to him. "Wait, Franklin." He stopped at mid-pace and whirled around, defeat and anger still crinkled across his face. "The money for your boat," she said, handing him two crisp sawbucks from her purse. He stared at them an instant, folded them quickly, and shoved the bills into his suit pocket. He shot a scowl toward me without even glancing at Aunt Addie and disappeared, clattering the screened porch door behind him.

Since Ronnie and I lit off along the river in search of fortune and adventure, I'd mostly forgotten Uncle Frank. It was sure neither of us had wanted to see the other.

As soon as he'd left, Aunt Addie set about puttering in the kitchen. I could tell she was still in a pique, more over what Uncle Frank had said about Clarke-Jiles than what he'd said about me. Still, Aunt Addie had proved herself to me, and I loved her for it.

Youth is a blunder, a struggle, a regret.

–Benjamin Disraeli

CHAPTER 12

Birthday Boys. Adventuring on the River. A Familiar Face.

JAMIE'S BIRTHDAY CAME TWO DAYS before my own. He turned twelve, and I tumbled into my fifteenth year. Aunt Addie, thinking it made no sense giving us separate celebrations, decided to give us a party both at once while saving herself energy and bother. She felt a formal celebration would be a good, and certainly "proper" way for us to be introduced into the town's society.

Preparations got underway two days before the date she set, and she was in a dither during both of them. Clarke-Jiles was sent hurrying and scurrying all over Waytown, buying things she needed or having them sent over from the mercantile. Invitations were written, Clarke-Jiles delivering them in person. I thought Aunt Addie was like as not to get writer's cramp from all her card signing.

She'd invited near everyone in town who counted. Of course, all the ladies of her sewing circle were invited, and the ladies from her social circle and the Bible circle, too. And Parson Briggs would come, and Nelly Martinson, the local piano teacher and organist at church, who'd provide the entertainment. Of course, Jamie, being mostly new like me, bookish and slow at making friends, didn't rightly know who his own age to invite. I hadn't been in Waytown long enough to have made any friend except Jamie, so the entire party list was made up of people, ladies mostly, except for the

Parson, who were near Aunt Addie's age.

On Friday, the day before the big to-do, Aunt Addie set into a wild storm of baking. Jamie and I and Clarke-Jiles, too, were set to work carrying in loads of kindling from the wood box and were kept busy filling up the stove and setting the fire right and shoveling out the ashes. Aunt Addie had become a near slave driver. All she needed was a whip and a gravel voice to fill out the part. We set into working hand and foot with scarce a minute's rest, she ordering us to do "this 'n that" then checking on it herself, making certain we'd done it right. Jamie and I were all bushed out and tuckered when the running was over.

The moment Aunt Addie freed us all, Clarke-Jiles was out washing down the buggy and currying the horses. It was his way of resting up. I was too tuckered to do any work and took my freedom by laying out under the peachleaf willow alongside the house and resting up. Jamie set into reading from his books and staying quiet in his room. But I grew restive and didn't know right what to do, so I went back to the carriage house and watched Clarke-Jiles work and helped him groom the horses.

We were all up at Saturday call next morning. After breakfast, Aunt Addie set into icing the cake, a grand fluffy white one in layers, spotted all over with tiny colored birds and flowers the like of such I'd never seen before. It was all I could do to keep from tasting it early.

"Landsakes, Clayton Sievers, you're into everything," Aunt Addie chided when she caught me dipping my pointer finger into the icing bowl. "Now you scat and go help Clarke-Jiles with the ice cream."

I dipped another lick while her back was turned, then skipped out to find Clarke-Jiles and Jamie.

Clarke-Jiles had gotten out the ice cream freezer, an oak bucket bound in brass with a lid and crank and a wooden paddle dangling down inside.

He'd filled it full of milk and cream and sugar and chocolate shavings carved with his whittling knife off a solid block. After he'd gone into the carriage house to fill the bucket with rock salt, the iceman came driving up in his delivery wagon. Clarke-Jiles had been expecting him.

His name was Mr. Gumprecht, or so the sign on his wagon said. His wagon rattled up the drive, stopping at the kitchen porch door, and he slung himself down heavy to the paving stones like a fat man, which he wasn't.

"Haloo there, young'uns," he greeted Jamie and me. His voice was sandy, kind of raspy like a file. He looked like a man who'd been caught up in a rooster fight the night before. He rubbed a three-day growth of salt and pepper whisker stubble with the heel of his right hand as he sauntered up.

"Where's Jiles?" Mr. Gumprecht snorted. He held a chaw wad in his cheek and talked through yellowed teeth. "That old gator hunter." His breath hit me full-faced and smelled of rye.

"Clarke-Jiles hunted alligators?" Jamie gasped. He was near bug-eyed at the thought.

"Sure did, Sonny. His pa used to tie a rope 'round his waist an' dangle him in a slough for bait. When some twelve-footer come tail-slidin' up, Jiles's pa'd yank him back into the boat and clip that old' gator right 'tween the eyes with a sledge. Yes, sir, clean 'tween the eyes." Jamie was near breathless. I couldn't tell if from excitement or fascination. "Yes, sir, used to hunt gators myself when I was your ages, down in Louisiana."

"Is that how you lost your eye?" Jamie asked, his mouth agape. It was my turn to elbow-knock Jamie's ribs like he'd done to me so often. It wasn't polite to ask a body how he'd come to lose a piece off himself.

Mr. Gumprecht fingered the eye patch thoughtfully for a moment. It was a black leather patch slung across his right eye and tied around his head with a black cord. His one good eye was shot full of blood-- like he'd been hit. He'd been hit all right–by a few shots too many of rye if his breath could talk.

"No, sir, can't rightly say it was. Lost it in the war to some damned Yankee's musket ball. It weren't but a lucky shot. Lucky, too, instead of my eye, my brains didn't come squeezin' out. 'Course, wouldn't a mattered much iffin they had. Don't use 'em any in my line 'o work." He fingered the patch cord with his pointer finger. "Wanta see what's under this here patch? Ain't nothin' 'cept an empty hole. Can't afford no fancy glass eye like some folks got." About this time Clarke-Jiles stepped out from behind the carriage house doors.

"Sinky Gumprecht!" Clarke-Jiles snapped, sounding like he was mad. "You feeding these boys some of your tales?"

"Didn't mean no harm, Jiles. Just passin' time with the young'uns here."

Jamie turned to Clarke-Jiles. "Is it true your pa used to tie a rope around you to hunt for alligators?"

Clarke-Jiles glanced serious toward Mr. Gumprecht then burst out grinning broad. "So, you're telling that old story again? I'd thought you'd done that one in by now."

"The young'uns here ain't heard it," Mr. Gumprecht said.

"Jamie," Clarke-Jiles smiled, "I haven't seen but one gator close up, but you've seen plenty, haven't you, Sinky?" he said, turning his interest to the deliveryman. Mr. Gumprecht pawed the paving stones with his boot tip and looked a might chagrined. "How do you think he got the nickname 'Sinky'?" Clarke-Jiles asked Jamie. Jamie shrugged his shoulders. "It's his daddy who used to throw him newborn naked to the gators to teach him how to swim. But Sinky here never could learn to swim, could you, Sinky?" The deliveryman was quiet. "Sinky puts his story on me 'cause that's what black folks are supposed to do to catch gators down South. There's no truth in it. Isn't nothing but a myth."

It turned out Mr. Gumprecht and Clarke-Jiles had grown up together down near New Orleans and had been fishing friends since they were boys.

"Show the boys where the gator nipped you," Clarke-Jiles said.

Mr. Gumprecht held out his left-hand pinky finger. It was lopped clean off at the second joint. The skin formed over it like a shiny pink mushroom where the nail should've been.

"That's where a seven-footer got me," Mr. Gumprecht grinned, and he seemed to be proud of it.

'Sinky' Gumprecht lingered on a while longer, he and Clark-Jiles telling tales on one another. Then he served up the blocks of ice he'd come to deliver, jolted onto the driving board of his delivery wagon, gave the reins a snap, and drove off down the drive and back to work.

Jamie and I watched as Clarke-Jiles filled the freezer barrel with rock salt, and the ice Mr. Gumprecht had delivered. Then we made turns at winding the handle crank which looked like the windlass on a water well.

Churning the freezer crank was mighty wearisome work and the three of us had to relieve one another after a spell of it. Like Aunt Addie's cake, we couldn't even taste our labors. Clarke-Jiles guarded the finished product like he'd been sworn by God to do it. He scooped the ice cream into wax-lined boxes and packed them in the ice chest, then sat right down on top of it so we couldn't get to it. A short while later, Aunt Addie called, and Jamie and I were sent upstairs to bathe and dress up in our finest go-to-meeting clothes.

When the party time finally came, the folks who'd been invited to the celebration began drifting in around eleven. Aunt Addie had decided to hold a brunch as she called it—a sort of social luncheon party.

The Parson Briggs and his wife were the first to arrive, and they were followed in quick turn by a parcel of ladies, some middle-aged, some older. Miss Martinson came in after Parson Briggs and set right into playing the piano the moment she arrived. She was an older lady, too, and all hunched over. Her fingers were long and bony, and she had one cocked eye, but she sure could play the parlor piano. For a time, Jamie sat on the bench and helped turn the pages for her music. Then Aunt Addie spirited him away to greet the ladies.

Jamie was the picture of etiquette and politeness. He wore his knee-pant suit with black wool stockings and a print neck scarf that hooked in back and looked the part of a Boston schoolboy I'd come across in a picture catalog in Hudson's Mercantile.

Of course, Aunt Addie made me greet the ladies, too, but I'd met most of them before when I arrived and wasn't too keen on doing it again. But I had no choice. I stood close to Jamie and smiled and shook hands and said hello as I felt I should and took my cues from Jamie who was used to doing it.

Aunt Addie was scurrying all around, making certain everything was running smoothly. Clarke-Jiles, all suited up and smiling broad, stood at the corner table dipping cherry punch with a crystal dipper into the smallest cups I'd ever seen. They scarce held enough for a swallow for a man.

Soon the ladies all formed into little bundles and set into chattering loudly. Clarke-Jiles finished dipping and joined the largest group. The ladies liked to talk with him because he was educated and polite and could tell a story with the best of them.

I was getting mighty hot and growing fidgety, so I sauntered up and helped myself to some punch when, from nowhere, Aunt Addie collared me.

"The punch is for our company," she said. "It's laced with wine. You and Jamie can drink the ginger beer. And, Clayton," she cautioned, pulling me over and whispering in my ear, "stop gawking and pulling at your clothes so." Seems I couldn't do anything right.

Miss Martinson played for two hours straight, stopping only long enough to down cups of punch Aunt Addie brought to her. I noticed, too, how Jamie had brought her punch and the Parson, too, had brought her several more. But she kept on playing and the tempo never faltered. Not a bit, though the music grew a might louder as time went on.

Around one o'clock, Aunt Addie disappeared into the kitchen and a few moments later came out carrying the birthday cake all ablaze with candles. I counted twenty-seven in all–twelve for Jamie and the rest for me. When she paraded through, Miss Martinson struck up a wild-sounding birthday song and pounded it through twice with the choirmaster of the church leading the ladies in the song. A greater chorus of pale, crackling voices was seldom ever heard in the history of the state. Some sang high, some sang low, with others in between. It didn't seem to bother the choirmaster none. He stood in the center of the parlor, smiling broad and beating out the tempo with his arms.

With the singing done, Aunt Addie cut the cake and Jamie and I were the first in line and got the biggest pieces.

"You boys make a wish for what you want most," she said and knifed the cake, "and blow the candles out."

I gully-whumped them good, scarce before Jamie could take a breath, with him blowing out the rest in a whooshing gust. There were ooh's of appreciation from Clarke-Jiles and the ladies, the ladies' cotton-gloved hands clapping a muffled applause at our efforts. After the racket died out, everyone gathered around the table where the food was stacked and helped themselves. Aunt Addie had a special word for it which I'd never heard used before and couldn't hope to say. She said it was Swedish for 'help yourself,' and Jamie and I helped ourselves a lot.

Miss Martinson stopped her playing long enough to eat and down another cup of punch before she went at the keys again. Clarke-Jiles, with Aunt Addie's blessing, had sat on the sofa seat and was deep into a tale about a European prince with the ladies all a-titter. Parson Briggs had cornered Jamie, and I was kind of set aside. I didn't mind none because all those bodies made the parlor a flood of heat, and all I could do was sit on the wall bench by the parlor stairs and think of swimming naked on the river. My button-on collar was choking tight, my legs itching fire, and I was sweating something fierce.

Tucked away and mostly out of sight, I couldn't help but hear some of the old ladies gathered around the stairs. I overheard their conversation, though I wasn't trying to.

One was saying, "Do you see the difference between those two boys?"

Another one answered, "It is positively amazing what a little breeding does."

"I agree," said another lady, one I'd caught notice of when I first met Aunt Addie at the station house. "That Jamie Hudson is such a handsome boy. And so well mannered. There's a world of difference between the two."

"Addie's nephew is handsome, too," one silver-haired woman chimed in.

"Yes," answered 'Mrs. Stationhouse', "but you can tell that he's a river boy·. There's nothing in his manner to tell me different, fancy clothes notwithstanding. Have you heard him talk?"

"Addie's such a brave woman," the silver-headed lady voiced, "taking in two young boys, and at her age."

"It's positively amazing," the first lady said.

The woman from the station house added, "She certainly has her hands full with that older boy. Why, did you know that when her husband died …?"

The voices began drifting out and I was growing mighty tired.

Suddenly, I was out along the river in front of Pop's old cabin, laying out on the raft I'd built, my shirt bundled under my head for a pillow, my eyes gazing off into a clear blue sky. My feet dangled in the cooling water, the raft swaying gently with the passing current. And Pop was there asking if I wanted to go fishing with him. And we were out together, Pop and me, alone in his fishing skiff, floating free and easy with the river. Pop was telling me a story about his boyhood and about his adventures with his own father and his brothers.

I was suddenly awakened by the shaking of my shoulder.

"Clayton, dear," Aunt Addie chirped, "stop your dreaming now and go help Clarke-Jiles and Jamie in the kitchen."

I realized then how I'd been dreaming. It all had seemed so real. Especially Pop.

It was going on half past the hour. Some of the ladies began floating out with the Parson Briggs remaining behind to chat with Aunt Addie about some church affair upcoming. The daydream I'd had put it into my mind to give Jamie a real birthday party. I gathered up Jamie, glanced at the parlor clock, and told him about my plans. He went along with them right off. Guess the ladies' boring carrying on had gotten to him, too. With Aunt Addie busy with the Parson, we slipped unnoticed out the kitchen door and scurried off to find Clarke-Jiles.

Clarke-Jiles was busy just inside the carriage house. He'd been free all of twenty minutes and already he was grooming down the horses.

It was a task he did as often as he could and thoroughly enjoyed it. He and I had grown to liking one another, and we were sort of kindred spirits, so I doubted he'd get too riled if I asked him for some of his special tobacco mixture.

Jamie sort of held back, scared of doing something which Aunt Addie, and the Parson, too, considered a foul and unhealthful habit. So, with Jamie half-hiding behind the sliding doors, I approached Clarke-Jiles who was just finishing currying down the large, dappled mare. He was all lathered up, sweating something fierce. His knot-muscled, dark brown chest dripped beads of water like he'd been swimming. I thought I'd polish him up some first before I asked him about the tobacco, so I complimented him on the look of the horses. He grinned broadly, as I'd expected, and started talking up a storm. I was sore put to get a word in lengthwise, but I did.

"Jamie and I'd like some of your tobacco," I finally got to say.

Clarke-Jiles looked at me kind of quizzically first off, then glanced up and snatched a sight of Jamie peering over from scarce inside the doorway. He grinned when he saw Jamie and I guess then he knew what I had in mind.

"Clayt," he said, hitching his thick-veined arm across my

shoulders and drawing me in close, his bass voice growing a serious note, "you know right well Miss Addie doesn't cotton to the pleasures of tobacco. She nips her wine a little, but that's what fine folk do."

"We ain't asking for much, Jiles. Just a handful of your special Virginia."

He looked at me again, then glanced over toward Jamie and back again to me. "Well," he drawled, drawing out the final letters of the word and pursing his lips up tight, "considering it's your birthdays and I haven't given you two a present. I guess it'll be all right this once."

He laid down his curry brush and stalked over to the wooden box which sat beside one of the empty stalls, opened it and took out a tin. Then he stalked back and opened it with the greatest ceremony, measured out a scant handful, and tipped it inside my trousers pocket.

"I expect you boys to be real careful now, you hear?" There was a stern-set caution in his eyes. "That special Virginny is some powerful stuff. It won't do having you comin' back here sick. I'd never hear the end of it from Miss Addie."

"We won't," I promised him with my solemn vow. "She'll never catch a breath of it."

I thanked him for his present and Jamie, who'd come up, thanked him, too.

"You boys be careful," he warned again as we scampered from the carriage house and headed toward the river.

Having not been in Waytown long, I wasn't too secure about my knowledge of the river thereabouts, and Jamie wasn't any help because of his bookish habits. But I'd adventured some and knew a place where the river met a creek stream and formed a shallow cove about a half mile down from the lumber mill. We headed there.

It was a pleasure being along the river once again. Near to town, the river gets kind of tame and civil. I wasn't too surprised that the trees weren't near so tall, most of the large ones having been logged out. There were mostly young ones--cottonwood, elm, and willow and cedars-- maybe twenty feet tall along the bank—and a scattering here and there of basswood, good for carving whistles. Along the water's edge grew a lot of willow saplings and cottonwoods which hadn't begun to gain full growth. But the river here was calm and slow-moving, reminding me of how it flowed wide and easy past Pop's old cabin. Here it felt a lot like home to me.

I loved the river. I knew Jamie liked it too, but he didn't say so.

He stayed quiet and followed me right along as we wound down along some narrow deer paths and clambered over an enormous log fall of an old bored-out willow that'd been old when the first Waytown settlers came.

We finally reached the cove which was tucked away and mostly out of sight from passing riverboats. The sun was high and bright overhead, and we sat down for a minute on the hot, dry sand to rest.

"Let's go for a swim," I said to Jamie, beginning to loosen my own neck scarf. "Take your clothes off but keep them off the ground or Aunt Addie will have one of her conniptions when we get back."

Jamie was shy at first about undressing, scared someone might come along or passersby see him from the river. But I quickly set his mind to ease. So we undressed, hung our clothes in a low willow crotch, and stretched out naked on the sand. I was beginning to feel free at last. Jamie was laid out comfortable as a porch dog, the sunlight playing off his pale skin and shooting glimmers of golden light off his collar-length straw hair. Jamie was a handsome boy, handsomer than me, and despite being three years younger, almost as tall, and slender as a pike.

"Let's go swimming," I said again following a spell of peaceful lounging. "Later we'll try some of Clarke-Jiles's Virginia."

Jamie shifted sideways from his lying flat position, cast a quick glance toward me then looked away and began digging his toes into the sand. "I can't swim, Clayt. I never learned how."

"I'll teach you then," I said. "It's as easy as swinging your arms and paddling with your feet. You won't sink because the water will hold you up."

Jamie was mighty skeptical that anything like swimming could be that easy. I reassured him, giving him a demonstration. The cove water wasn't deep, and I stood flat-footed on the muddy bottom at the deepest part with the water scarce coming to my shoulders. Jamie, seeing he wasn't too likely to drown in five feet of water and with me standing by, waded in and we set in to splashing and frolicking about for a time before I helped him learn to swim.

I held him around the waist while he kicked and paddled for a time, stretched out face flat across the water. Then I let him free. He did really well, catching onto it like a young duck in a pond. When we got tired of swimming we laid up in a bright and sun-drenched spot and I lit up the tobacco in a new cob pipe I'd carved out specially for the occasion.

Poor Aunt Addie. Had she known what we were up to she'd have swooned from a fevered fit. Together we sat back and smoked and sunned.

The smoke from Clarke-Jiles's Virginny was real strong—stronger than what I'd been used to. It wasn't too long before Jamie got to looking mighty pale and sick. I remembered the first time I'd smoked with the gang and those recollections set me to feeling sorry for him. But I'd smoked first when I was twelve and I reckoned, Sunday preaching aside, all in all, it wasn't too bad except when a body did it often.

It wasn't too soon after my musings when Jamie bolted upright of a sudden and sprinted off full tilt back into the trees, his bare rear shining pale. There were some mighty awful retching sounds and gagging, but he was soon back, looking kind of somber and chagrined, but a long sight better than when he'd left. I lit up my pipe again but thought better of offering some more to Jamie. I was careful, too, to let the smoke drift past him so as he wouldn't catch a whiff of it and lay him up sick again. We stretched out, soaking up the sun, free from the tipsy old hens in Aunt Addie's parlor, and soon set in to talking long.

"My folks were killed on the *Robert Lee* when she struck a snag and blew her boilers a piece above St. Louis," Jamie told me when I asked him about his parents. "I was staying with Grandma Price, but she took sick and died soon after she got the news, and I was left with nobody." He continued. "It was Parson Briggs who heard the news about an orphaned boy and traveled up to see me. I guess Miss Addie ('Miss Addie' was what Jamie always called her) had been wanting a boy to raise so I came to live with her, and she adopted me."

The Parson, I thought, reflecting back to Swainville, was good at saving more than souls. First, he'd pulled Jamie out of trouble, then me.

I told Jamie about my own adventures, the parts he didn't know, especially adventuring with Ronnie and about our special friendship. I told him about Ronnie's drowning and my being arrested in Swainville and the judge's ruling and got him all caught up to date. By the time we completed telling one another everything about ourselves, it was drawing on to dusk, so we traipsed back to the willow crotch and gathered up our clothes. It wasn't until then that Jamie discovered he was badly sunburned–baked red like a Missouri ham.

I should have known better, Jamie being so pale from the beginning and all, but I hadn't thought about it before. His body was burnt bright red all over, with tiny blisters forming across his shoulders and around his chest. He was in awful pain. I cooled him off as best I could with water from the cove and scoured all around for the blister weed Pop always used for burns but couldn't find any. I knew right then we'd be in frightful trouble when we got home. Especially me.

I felt I'd be right about Aunt Addie, and I was. She threw an awful fit. Carried on something fierce.

"Let's sneak into the house the back way," Jamie suggested. "That way Miss Addie won't catch us."

"That won't do any good," I said. "You have to come down for supper and she's sure to notice then." He knew, of course, I was right. Jamie's face was tinged bright red and he was hurting so he could scarcely keep his shirt on.

We had to face up to it, and we did.

Taking one close look at Jamie as he stood waist-naked before her in the parlor, Aunt Addie sent Clarke-Jiles full gallop for Doc Clarendon. The old doctor came rolling up in his one-horse rig soon after.

Aunt Addie had helped Jamie upstairs and into bed. After the doctor was in and tending to him, she came downstairs and glared at me meaner than I'd ever seen her look.

"Poor child," she snapped, "he's burning up with fever." She gathered some linens from the cabinet in the back parlor and hurried back to Jamie's room with not so much as a 'by-your-leave.' "Poor child," she repeated as she scurried up the steps, "he's ranting and raving so and likely as not to die."

I didn't know rightly what to do; go upstairs and look in on Jamie or stay below and hide out from Aunt Addie. But I ventured upstairs and kept out of sight, peering into the room from around the corner of the doorway. Doc Clarendon was at the bedside, placing some tiny pills underneath Jamie's tongue and smoothing his body all over with a light-green salve. Jamie looked an awful sight, rolling and tossing so and wincing in pain every time the doctor touched him. The old hom-e-o-pathic doctor's little "miracle pills" did work wonders. In was twenty minutes, by the clock, when Jamie's pain first slowed, then stopped like magic. Clarke-Jiles, who was also tending Jamie, caught sight of me and sneaked out into the hall.

"Aconite for the fever," he whispered, "Urtica for the burn. Jamie will be sound enough in no time. Stay clear of Miss Addie, though. She's powerful upset."

The doctor's tending brought Jamie back around okay, but he was raging hot with a fired fever that lasted for most of the evening. The fever broke around midnight. Aunt Addie was powerfully relieved. She'd stayed by Jamie's bedside through it all, putting cooling towels on his forehead and sitting by him in a rocker saying muttered prayers with the Good Book in her lap.

Doc Clarendon said the sunburn was "quite severe" but added how Jamie would heal up right fine. Jamie remained in bed, resting comfortably, but I was feeling awful low and not much better when Aunt Addie came down to talk with me.

"Clayton Sievers! Honestly! I've never seen the like of you. To take a boy Jamie's age out along the river to drown or burn up like he has. I don't honestly for the life of me know what to say!" she added in her harshest and most despairing tone. "It's times like these that I pray Mr. Hudson was alive. He knew how to handle boys."

I was so chagrined I couldn't speak. The two of us sat across the kitchen table and stared at one another for the longest time in silence. Her kind eyes were awash with water.

"If it wasn't counter to my good judgment," Aunt Addie spoke at last, "I'd take a switch to your behind." There followed another long, unbroken, tortured time of quiet. "Spare the rod and spoil the child. That's what the Good Book says." She echoed what Uncle Frank had said a short week earlier. She looked at me over the top of her silver spectacles, kind of sorrowful like, then her eyes teared up and flooded over. "And you were smoking, weren't you? Your clothes reek of it, and I could smell it on Jamie's breath." After another long silence she added, "It's a sin against the Lord Almighty and He will have to punish you for it, not I."

I felt awful blue. When Aunt Addie finished her talk with me, I went outside, strayed up and down the yard, and walked around the blocks of houses. A light glowed in Jamie's and my room all night. Aunt Addie was keeping vigil. I spent the night, sleepless, in the carriage house on the horse blankets and straw. I guessed I wasn't missed because no one came to find me. Everyone was concerned for Jamie.

All night long I tossed and rolled and couldn't sleep on account of knowing Jamie was lying up in bed, his flesh on fire. I even asked the Almighty to visit a punishment on me for my wrongdoing. But He didn't. I guess the way I felt for Jamie was punishment enough.

Jamie laid in bed three days, then was up and walking about the house for another two. Doc Clarendon came by often to look in on him as he made his rounds about Waytown.

On the second day I overheard him tell Clarke-Jiles, "It's dangerous for a boy as pale as Jamie to burn like that. It's almost like rolling in an open fire."

Aunt Addie had nursed and tended to Jamie, cooking his special-favorite foods and carrying them up to him the first three days. At length, the doctor pronounced him well. In a few more days Jamie was looking right again and fit and was back to being himself.

Despite his sickness, which had been my fault, Jamie and I remained friends. In fact, we'd been brought closer. He didn't blame me for getting him sick with my cob pipe, nor for his awful sunburn either. In fact, we spent a lot of time together.

School in Waytown had started up again, so we adventured most on weekends. Aunt Addie, after a bout of long and torturous consideration, allowed I needn't attend school any longer seeing how I'd gotten my schooling through the ninth grade and all. I'd always done my best to please Pop when he was living, but I never had a hankering for higher education.

As I said, Jamie and I adventured a lot along the river; when we could get from out Aunt Addie's watchful sight that is. After Jamie's incident, she was mighty watchful, of me especially.

Jamie had become a real swimmer, taking to the river as much as me. And he was always doing freaky things like covering his body and face with mud so he couldn't be recognized and lying in wait along the riverbank among the bushes, waiting for some passersby. When some boat carrying passengers churned up along the channel where the deep water was, Jamie would leap out from behind the brush, bolt naked and screaming wild, wave his arms and leap up and about and was like as not to scare the whillikers out of some ladies who were standing by the rails. He took a real delight in scaring women. I'd be lying by all the while watching him and laugh myself into a tizzy with his antics. He even took an occasional smoke from my pipe–now and again–though I'd got my own supply of tobacco from some men in town and didn't have to trouble Clarke-Jiles anymore. After Jamie's sickness, he'd closed his supply to me.

One afternoon when school let out, Jamie and I met together along the cove. Clarke-Jiles had driven Aunt Addie into town. When they were gone, I'd sneaked into Jiles's room at the top of the carriage house and 'borrowed' a package of picture cards–direct from France–which I'd heard him say he'd won in a poker game in town. I didn't let on to Jamie I knew about the cards, nor tell him where I'd got them because I didn't want him to get into trouble. I figured I'd be safe enough and get them back before Clarke-Jiles found them missing. When I sneaked those cards out of his 'special box'–where he kept his Virginny mixture, some keepsakes of his father's, and other special and important mementos that he valued I wasn't certain what would be worse if I was caught: Aunt Addie's wrath and her preachments about stealing or Clarke-Jiles's anger. I knew for certain, had he discovered those cards missing, he'd know it was me who took them, not Jamie. And I knew, too, he'd be angry as a stud bull caged up from his favorite heifer. But, despite the danger, I took my chances.

Jamie was waiting for me at the cove, already undressed and sunning himself on the bank. I joined him and we swam and splashed about for a time, then laid back a while. I lit up my pipe and we smoked a bowl together. Jamie had grown taller and was now a half inch taller than me. He'd filled out, too, and even had taken on a healthy, light-brown glow.

"Jamie," I said as we lay out, "have you ever seen picture cards?"

"Sure. My folks used to send me picture cards when they traveled."

"Have you ever seen real picture cards–from France?" I asked.

"No, but I reckon I've heard about them."

I smiled and reached over into my shirt pocket which was lying by. "Well, I've come across some of those picture cards."

Jamie was all of a sudden full of questions and could scarce wait to see them. But I made a great production of unwrapped them from the brown paper-and-string-tied package, keeping the backs toward him so he couldn't catch a glimpse.

"Let me see them, Clayt," Jamie whined, "let me see them!"

I played the mystery out as long as possible, milking Jamie's curiosity all I could. Then I showed them, one by one, and we ogled them over, close, together. They were mighty fine pictures and pen-and-ink drawings of exotic women. Orientals and Africans and European women with sleek long hair and wild eyes. Most wore only the scantiest of underthings, and a few were even naked. Well, those picture cards made our peckers stiff in no time, and we looked them over for the longest while.

After viewing the cards, Jamie and I took to swimming again (mostly to cool off our ardor), then ambled along the riverbank. We were on our way back some while later to gather up our clothes when we caught a sound of voices through the trees. They were girls' voices, and they were calling from our cove! Jamie and I fired dumb founded looks toward one another. That cove was our place, our private hideaway. It was about the only place I felt fully free, and Jamie could free himself for a time away from his books. He'd become quite a nature boy.

Real careful we sneaked up quiet, Indian fashion, just like Ronnie and I used to do when we were together and wanted to scare the gang. Jamie snaked belly-wise along the ground with me behind until we could see the cove clearly through the bushes.

Sure enough, there were five girls frolicking and splashing in the cove, and they were wearing only their cotton underclothes. It was just like the picture cards we'd looked over–only real. Of course, the girls were a lot younger and less well rounded. They hadn't caught sight of us, so we watched them from the cover of the bushes for the longest while. It was really something. When I was growing up with Pop and adventuring along the river with Ronnie, I'd never seen girls swimming. Their cotton underthings were wet and all that cloth clung altogether tight to them and nearly transparent. Jamie, who was watching every bit as seriously as me, would laugh quietly and point out the girls one by one and call their names to me in hush-quiet whispers. He knew all of them because they were in his school.

Then I saw her! It was Marie Ellis, the girl I'd saved from the steamboat wreck during the flood. My heart skipped and thumped, and, for a minute, I was all excited. Then my memory flashed quickly back to that eerie night and the roaring waters of the river at flood. I remembered Ronnie and his drowning in his trying to save her mother. I thought I'd almost forgotten that night, put it back in some dark, cob-webbed corner of my mind to rest. But I hadn't. It had all come flooding back.

Marie was frolicking with the rest of the girls. She was not as tall as me, with soft cream skin and hair as long as a comet's tail and light straw-colored like Jamie's. Just to set the record straight and shake up my recollections–make certain I wasn't seeing someone else who looked like her--I whispered to Jamie and asked him who she was.

"That's Marie Ellis," he answered. "She's the most popular girl in school."

"Does she live nearby?" I was trying not to appear more than just passing interested, but Jamie caught the hint.

"She lives in a gray-painted house near as large as Miss Addie's just on the other side of Bluff Hill Road. You must have passed her house a hundred times." He added, "Her father owns the dray works and the mill."

So, it was Marie Ellis after all. It wasn't hard to see why she'd be the most popular girl in school. She was the prettiest girl I'd ever seen.

The girls had rigged a rope line from one of the nearby trees and took turns swinging from it and bellyflopping and boulder-diving into the water, laughing and giggling and shouting to one another all the while.

"Clayt!" Jamie gushed suddenly, nearly forgetting to keep flat and lay his voice down low. "Our clothes!"

Sure enough. In the midst of all our excitement we'd clean forgotten about our clothes. They were lying nearly in full view just to one side some feet from the rope swing.

"What if the girls find them?" Jamie asked.

It did provide quite a predicament. We were both naked as two bolts of plain cloth in Aunt Addie's mercantile. If the girls were to spot them, they'd be certain to know we were hiding nearby.

"What if they find our clothes and keep them?" Jamie wondered aloud.

I knew we were both nervous and thinking the same thing. How could we explain to Aunt Addie our prancing into town stark naked? There was no way to sneak into town unseen.

We puzzled over it for a time, but it didn't take us long to hatch a really good plan. It was Jamie's plan mainly—one he came up with after he'd pondered it out a while. We'd creep back down to the river, smear ourselves all over with mud, and run back right into the middle of that gaggle of girls and snatch our clothes. So, we did. We kind of chicken-creeped down the bank slide and smeared all over with the river mud until we were covered thick. Not even Aunt Addie would've recognized us. Then we pranced back toward the cove, care-less as could be. Jamie, of course, got the idea to act out his wildman part and bolted right out from behind a clump of sumac with me following behind. There was yelling and war-hooping from Jamie and shrieks and startled screams from the girls who ran every which way like hens scattered by a fox.

"Get away! Oh, get away you filthy boys!" one girl shrieked. It was Marie Ellis.

They all scattered lickity-split into the trees so all you could see was their white behinds through the clinging fabric of their underdrawers. They carried on, shrieking, and screaming like Irish banshees while Jamie pounded out a wild dance, darting close up to the trees, then charging back while I gathered up our clothes. He played his part first rate. When I knew we were safe, I turned around toward the trees and yelled out. "This is our place. From now on you girls stay clear of it." Then, to make our point more emphatic, we gathered up the girls' clothes and scampered off for the deep woods. There were shrieks even louder than before. The girls screamed, hollered, stomped, and fretted as we ran off. Of course, we had no intention of keeping their things, so we tied them together into ropes with nice tight knots and slung them in the trees.

We waited hidden for a while until the girls, assuming it was safe, grouped and started a cautious search. Then Jamie and I strode back to the cove, washed off the river mud, got dressed, and left toward home, laughing and joking all the way.

Prejudice, which sees what it pleases, cannot see what is plain.

—Aubrey de Vere

CHAPTER 13

Market Time. Marie. "Nothing but a River Boy."

I COULD REMEMBER THAT TIME–not too long past–when I'd had nothing to do with girls. Always it was Sam Johnston, Charlie Michaels, ol' Mike Dearson, with his curled-up lip and lisping voice, and Ronnie and me together, swimming, fishing, holding pow-wows, and just lying out along the river and talking. Girls were just cream-faced, pale and pretty things to glance at from a distance and to make sport of in the schoolroom whenever Old Man Dodson's back was turned.

Girls weren't as much fun as boys. A boy couldn't talk to girls about his thoughts and secret longings, or sit with a girl on a sand shoal or on the riverbank and fish. Girls always squirmed when a boy threaded a worm onto a fishhook, and the thought of hunting anything generally made them sick.

But that was a while back and I was going on sixteen now. Somehow girls looked different. Marie Ellis especially so.

I wanted to see Marie, talk to her, ask her about what happened after the flood, the time the crazy man knocked me down and stole the skiff, leaving her mother and her shrieking and screaming through the blackness of that night. But I wasn't exactly certain how to go about it.

Jamie was too young to know, and poor Ronnie wasn't alive to ask for his advice. I'd have to find my own way.

I pondered on it for quite a spell. At first, I thought of sending a note to school with Jamie, him handing it to her sometime during the day. That didn't prove to be a good idea because I didn't want Jamie to learn that I was interested. Hanging out around the schoolhouse wouldn't serve either because that would've started talk. Waytown not being over-large, I figured maybe Marie had heard by way of the gossip line how I'd come to town and was living with Addie Hudson. Would Marie remember me? Had Ronnie introduced me by name to the women on the sinking steamboat? I couldn't recollect if he had. To be honest, all in all, it was quite puzzling.

As it turned out, all my planning and pondering turned out for naught. Seems I was destined to meet Marie by accident.

It was an early Friday afternoon. Clarke-Jiles had driven Aunt Addie and me into town, dropping us off in front of Hudson's Mercantile. Aunt Addie had an appointment with Mr. Mertinger to go over the record books. She usually did that on Saturday, the last day of the business week, but she'd also made an appointment at the millinery shop to have a new hat fitted. Aunt Addie had a reason behind everything she did.

She didn't hanker much to waste her time and effort. She'd do two things today so she didn't have to do one or the other thing tomorrow. "Procrastination is a sin," she said. Procrastination was putting matters aside for later. It was something I was good at.

Friday was fish day and, though none of us were Catholic, the Friday supper meal was always fish. Aunt Addie had given me a silver dollar, and with it I was to hike down to the steamboat landing and the open market and select a fresh fish for supper, one large enough to feed the four of us. "A dollar will be plenty," she said. But just in case, she handed me a fifty-cent piece too. Pop having been a fisherman for thirty years catching and selling fish up and down the river, Aunt Addie reckoned I'd be a good enough judge of what to buy. The task normally belonged to Clarke-Jiles, and he looked forward to doing it, because he could spend the afternoon leisurely shopping and talking with the folks he knew. But the rim of one of the carriage wheels had cracked–split open like the seam on a pair of worked-out trousers–and he was bound toward the blacksmith's to have it fixed. "Before I hit a hole and dump the whole rig into the street," he said, joking.

Aunt Addie never quite seemed to trust me when I was away from under her watchful eye. I reckoned it was partly because of Jamie's and my misadventure along the river, and partly out of fear I'd do something to embarrass her. Though she never said anything, I guess she knew the moment I was out of sight and the day was hot and sunny like it was, I'd doff my socks and shoes, roll up my trousers legs below the knees, open up my shirt or if away from town and out of sight, go about with none at all. And, of course, she was right.

The market along the wharf where the riverboats slid into land and let off passengers and cargo goods was jam-packed and crowded with people. Seemed how those with nothing else better to do in town had emptied to the landing. There were people shopping–women mostly–dragging tired and complaining little ones too young to be in school, behind them between the vegetable and fruit stands which lined the wharf. Here and there along the way, a pair of men would stand huddled up together, talking and passing a tobacco chaw between them, or a group of women parceled up together passing on the latest gossip. Between the red color of plump tomatoes and the green of loose-leaf lettuce which lined the aisleways in shallow boxes, and the rainbow colors of the women's' clothes, and the browns and blacks and grays the menfolk wore, the marketplace was a patchwork quilt of movement. I couldn't recall ever seeing so many people in one place.

When I was younger, I'd been to many a market sale with Pop, helping him haul and sort and sell his catch. Those sales had always been in small towns no bigger than a blink or a whistle. Waytown was a burgeoning community of some five thousand souls–a full-size city. The biggest I'd ever been to.

The fish market would be right down near the river past the radish and rutabaga stands and the turnip and asparagus boxes, so I headed there.

What Clarke-Jiles saw in the market sales I didn't know. All there was, was a lot of high and low-pitched voices calling, people pushing and shouldering by, bumping into one another. There wasn't a friendly face in the entire crowd. Leastwise none that I could see.

Every kind of fish the river spawned that could be trolled, netted, or poled out and was fit to eat was there. There were bullheads nigh on to a pound and a half apiece, and channel cat and blue cat, paddlefish and carp. Some were large enough for a small-size family to eat on for a week. I browsed for quite a time, not knowing just what to settle on.

Which one of us caught sight of the other first I don't rightly reckon. The fish market seemed an unlikely place for Marie and me to meet, but there she was, standing just on the other side. Her straw-colored hair streamed down, draping across her shoulders in the front against a flowing blue print dress with ruffles on the sleeves. She was staring hard at me.

I guess Marie thought she recognized me, then acted like she wasn't sure. We stood like we were frozen; like two dogs that meet in an alleyway, each one uncertain what to make of the other. My heart pounded like a piston on the flywheel of a steamboat, jumping up and down in starts before settling in on a steady motion. Marie made the first move forward.

Her sky-blue eyes sparkled as she sauntered over. "Aren't you the boy from …?"

"From the steamboat?" I said, finishing up her question.

"You are!" she nearly shouted, startling a couple of passersby who halted long enough to stare at us. "You're the boy who helped save Momma and me from the steamboat wreck!"

"Clayt Sievers at your service, Ma'am," I said, kind of bowing from the waist. No doubt the doing of it looked as funny as it felt. I didn't know how else to greet her.

"I'm Marie–Marie Ellis," she said, putting out her hand sort of limp for me to take. She looked good enough to hug. I was feeling more awkward than I'd ever felt before.

"I know. Ronnie introduced us on the boat, and I've seen you around town but wasn't sure how to meet you." (I certainly wasn't about to tell her where I'd seen her, or in what condition, or that I'd helped tie her clothes in knots). "I wasn't certain you'd recognize me."

"You took me by a start," she said. "I wasn't certain either it was you until just now. Where's your friend?" she asked, glancing around and no doubt expecting Ronnie. "The other boy?"

"He drowned. Leastwise I guess he did, falling overboard. I

haven't seen him since and I looked for him for quite a spell."

"Oh, that's so sad." The way Marie said it, with a sudden tearful look about her eyes, I knew she truly meant it. "Are you living here in Waytown?"

"With Addie Hudson. She's my aunt."

"I heard Miss Addie had taken in another boy–an orphan boy from somewhere down river–but I didn't know he was you."

I'd forgotten of a sudden why I was standing in the market. All I could do was stand there awkwardly with my hands shoved deep inside my trousers pockets and scuff the dirt with a naked toe. If it hadn't been for Marie carrying on the conversation, I couldn't have said a thing.

"Oh!" she gasped suddenly, "You've got to meet my daddy. He's around the market somewhere. I just know he'll want to thank you for saving my life and Momma's."

Her hand, which she'd held out earlier for me to take, and which I hadn't, darted out again. The next thing I knew, Marie was leading me around the produce stands, threading me like a needle through the clumps of shoppers. We stopped from time to time long enough for her to stretch up on her toes and glance around. She was searching for her father.

Being mid-afternoon, the marketplace swarmed like bees on flowers in July and Marie couldn't find her father right off. We sat down on a bench--actually a plank slung across two low kegs–to rest our feet. It was beside a melon stand that had closed, having sold all its offerings early.

I was mighty curious about what happened the night of the flood when the angry man stole the skiff away. So, I asked her.

"Oh, it was horrible!" Marie recalled. "I still have nightmares over it. The man must've been frightened to death of drowning or burning up. We lost an oar after he jumped in and cut us free and, for a time, all we could do was hold onto the sides and pray. He raved on like a wildman and bellowed out swear words something awful! I started crying, and Momma, too, and he yelled out, "You cut that blubbering out now afore I toss the both of you in the river." He was a horrible Godless man who cared only for himself. I comforted Momma as best I could. She was taking the trip awfully hard. And that horrible man only made it worse.

"The night was so horrible–and dark–we couldn't see past the boat. We bounded down the river out of control for the longest while, and all the time that man was cursing and straining at the one oar, keeping us from slamming into tree trunks floating down. By the time morning came, the river had quieted enough for him to row to shore. He ordered us to get out, and we had to walk the rest of the way to the nearest town. Momma had to borrow money for stage fare to get us home." Marie paused a moment. "I don't know what happened to that man, or to your boat."

"It wasn't my skiff really. It belonged to my Uncle Frank," I said, not telling her I'd stolen it from him in the first place.

"I thought about you, Clayt, all the while we were bounding down the river," Marie told me. "I didn't know what would happen to you, the steamboat on fire and you without a boat."

It felt good knowing Marie had thought about me on that awful night. Even now I was thankful for her thoughts and prayers.

Having rested up some and talked a spell, Marie set us off again. She said her father was a big man, dressed in a black suitcoat and gray silk vest so he shouldn't be hard to spot. We searched around the market for several minutes more before she found him.

Marie had gotten out of school at the end of the morning session. Mrs. Ellis, who Jamie had told me was nearly as prominent socially as Aunt Addie was, was having a dinner party that night. Marie had come down to the market with her father to help him with the shopping. We found Mr. Ellis a short while later, a wicker basket of salad fixings clenched in his hand.

Mr. Ellis wasn't the largest man I'd ever seen. Max, the barman back in Swainville, was taller and broader at the shoulders, but Mr. Ellis wasn't small by any stretch. His face was broad and flat, the skin of his face coarse and near the color of rust. Large, dark-set eyes blazed out from under a heavy growth of thick-matted brows, giving him a fearsome look. Two deep furrows fell around either side of his down-turned mouth. He had the sour look of a man whose stomach hurts him. Frankly, when I caught sight of him, a cold feeling shuddered up my back and I wasn't much certain I wanted to meet Marie's father.

Marie danced right up to him, her face all aglow. She was still leading me by the hand. When Mr. Ellis caught sight of the two of us prancing toward him, his daughter pulling me along beside her, his brow-ends crinkled down toward his nose. It was obvious he was a man of means, dressed fit to marry or bury like he was. Clenched along one side of his mouth was a brown-wrapped cigar which had to have set him back fifteen cents–maybe twenty.

"Daddy," Marie sang out, tugging me up to him, "I want you to meet a boy. This is Clayton Sievers," she smiled, introducing me to her father, "one of the boys Momma and I told you about who helped save us from the steamboat."

Mr. Ellis didn't speak a word. He just looked thoughtful at his daughter, then at me. Judging by the scowl that swept across his rusted face, it wasn't hard to tell right off he didn't like me.

I wasn't exactly what Aunt Addie would have called 'presentable.' No sooner had I vanished from Aunt Addie's notice, but I'd stripped off nearly every piece of clothing a civilized boy would wear. My feet were bare and dusty, and one toe was bandaged where I'd knocked it against a stone the day before. My trousers' legs rolled up around the knees, and the only things I wore to cover up my chest were the suspender straps that buttoned to the trousers waist.

"Oh, Daddy!" Marie sounded out, having grown impatient from her father's silent and scowling look, "this is the boy who saved my life!"

Mr. Ellis finally broke his quiet. "I thank you for helping my wife and daughter from the spot that they were in, though it was nothing more than any red-blooded man would've done under the circumstances." Marie looked shocked by what he said.

"Daddy," Marie asked, with a mixture of soothing and hopeful, "Can't we invite Clayton to supper tonight? I know Momma would like to meet him and she won't mind setting an extra place."

Mr. Ellis, who'd scarcely been covering his feelings about me all the while, guided Marie a step or two away and came out with his true thoughts on the matter.

"Girl, do you know who your mother has invited to supper this evening?" There was a stern and stolid look set about his face. "The mayor and his wife and the Claybergs and the Rollisons. What are they supposed to think about some young river tramp sitting at the supper table?"

"Daddy!" Marie gasped out, shocked by what she heard. "Clayt's no river tramp! He's living with Addie Hudson. She's his aunt!"

Mr. Ellis glanced a quick shot toward me, then turned back to his daughter. "So–he's the new boy Addie Hudson's taken charge of. Her nephew? I'm a might surprised a woman of her standing in this community would allow kinfolk of hers to wander about looking like river riffraff. Look at him," he told Marie. "He's nearly naked. Probably hasn't washed in days." (That wasn't true. I'd bathed that morning before breakfast). "Do you want this boy sitting amongst fine company at the supper table? Never you mind what he did for you. All he is, is a good-for-nothing river boy. That's all he's been or ever going to be. Addie Hudson notwithstanding."

One thing for certain; there wasn't any sign of the Christian love the Parson Briggs preached about in the soul of Mr. Ellis.

Marie was so shocked by her father's explosive words she went dumb mouthed. Water had begun to gather at the corner of her eyes, and a trickle ventured down her cheek. Mr. Ellis wasn't speaking low-voiced either, but loud enough for everybody near around to hear. I glanced about, close enough to see several smiling and approving faces in the crowd. They were women's mostly, and I recognized one of them in particular,'Mrs. Stationhouse'one of the ladies who'd come to Jamie's and my birthday party. Aunt Addie's friend.

Marie was sobbing softly now. And Mr. Ellis was standing as stern and straight as when we'd first met. All around me I felt the market folks' mocking faces and, without telling Marie goodbye, I tried to slink away unnoticed. Mr. Ellis, however, had other thoughts. He wasn't finished deriding me. Leaving his humiliated daughter behind long enough to catch up with me, he reached his hand out to my shoulder and spun me around to face him.

"I'll thank you once again, boy, for helping out my wife and daughter," he said gruffly, "but just because you did doesn't give you any special privileges. And I don't want to see you hanging round my daughter. I won't have her wasting her time on river tramps." He paused quietly and looked down on me, letting his words sink through. "I've made myself clear enough?" It wasn't a question but an order.

"Yes, sir," I said.

I don't know which of us felt more humiliated–Marie or me. Her father's words had cut me deep and hurt me something awful. If the truth was known, I felt lower than a snake whose end-piece had been rolled over by a wagon wheel.

About all I could think about heading home was what Marie's father had said. I scarcely remembered to gather up my clothes I'd stashed behind a bush on the road to the marketplace. Aunt Addie added quietly to my pain, too, when I reached home without the fish she'd sent me off to buy. In the goings-on, I'd forgotten all about it.

"Honestly, Clayton Sievers! What am I to do with you?" she voiced her disapproval.

With the carriage wheel fixed, Aunt Addie sent Clarke-Jiles thundering down to the marketplace before it shut up business to buy what I'd forgotten. Supper was an hour late because of me.

That night in bed I had a flight of dreams; dreaming in fits and starts, scarcely getting any rest. I tossed and rolled throughout the night. Jamie lay in the next bed, sleeping the sleep of a dead man. Nothing could wake him up short of a dynamite blast outside, and it was a good thing, too.

Nightmares interchanged with pleasant dreams. Mr. Ellis would bound out sudden from the blackness of my thoughts, steaming like a mad bull and taking on gigantic size. Good for nothing. GOOD FOR NOTHING. GOOD-FOR-NOTHING RIVER SCAMP he'd snort and bellow loud at me, and I'd take off running down the path past the landing wharf fast as my legs could fly. But he'd always gain on me. Suddenly, running along the river's edge, the scene would change. It was like a curtain being lifted from a window, the picture outside becoming sharp and clear. Mr. Ellis would vanish fast away, becoming Pop, soft-voiced, rowing a skiff or poling a raft along the current flow, singing a song to bide the passing time.

The river became green and lush along its banks, the dark-brown water changing to faded gold as it passed over a shallow bar. And the banks were lined with wildflowers and mint-green ferns, and I was floating past it on Pop's own raft. Then the picture changed again, and I'd be back, jammed into the marketplace, hearing Mr. Ellis's ugly voice booming out through the crowd. Jeering, mocking faces swirled around me and off I'd run again–never to Aunt Addie's home, but always toward the river.

Most of the next day I moped about the house. It was Saturday. Jamie had found a group of school friends his age he liked being with and they'd gone off somewhere together. Aunt Addie stayed around the house and settled into morning cleaning. She hadn't spoken to me during all of supper time the evening before, giving me her silent treatment, which showed her disapproval. I sat in the kitchen staring out the open porch door toward the carriage house. Pausing from her cleaning, Aunt Addie came in and sat down next to me.

"It isn't like you, Clayton, dear, being inside on a lovely day like this," she said quietly, breaking the silent spell between us. "Aren't you feeling well?"

"I don't want to go anywhere," I told her.

Aunt Addie smoothed out her apron, a long white one which looped around the neck and tied in back, just like the store clerks used in Hudson's Mercantile when they dusted off the shelves. She folded her hands and rested them in her lap.

"It's what I said to you last night, isn't it? Or what I didn't say."

"No, Ma'am."

"Clayton, dear, I love you very much. I love this family very much: Jamie, Clarke-Jiles, and you. It's just that…it's just that sometimes I don't know what to do with you. I didn't know John-Clayton well. I was fifteen when he was born, but I cared about him very much.

"Sometimes," she said, casting down her flower-blue eyes a spell, "sometimes I wish I'd known him better. He sounded like a fine man from what you've told me of him. And you're my brother's son. I only want what's best for you. Until some months ago I didn't have a son, then Jamie came, and some months later, you. I allow I don't know much about raising boys, but I'd like to learn."

"You're doing fine, Aunt Addie," I told her, speaking low.

"Maybe for Jamie, but not for you," she said. "Jamie's quiet and bookish. That's his rearing. The two of you come from different backgrounds. You're polite enough, Clayton. I can thank your father for that. But a family must grow together, to love and respect and trust one another. You haven't shown me yet that you're responsible. I send you to do a simple task and you forget, or you go off–the Lord knows where–for hours, without letting anyone know and worrying me something fierce. I get angry with you, Clayton, dear, but I love you all the same."

Maybe Aunt Addie was waiting for an answer, some sign from me, because she stopped there, and a long pause of silence swept between us. I wasn't showing it, but I was thinking hard about what she'd said.

"Well," she started up, her soft voice becoming crisp and clear, "I've my work to do. Try as she might, the saying's true: a woman's work is never done."

Aunt Addie seemed a might restive, maybe even nervous, and I guess I should've spoken to her, but I didn't. Sliding the kitchen chair back beneath the table and adjusting the green lace cloth, smoothing it with her fingers at the corners, she paused wordless to look at me, then disappeared from the room as quickly as she'd entered.

It wasn't Aunt Addie's fault the way I felt. I guess I should've told her so. Sometimes things are left unsaid that shouldn't be, and a body waits too long to make things right.

Clarke-Jiles was the sort of man a boy my age could admire and whenever I felt a lowness in myself like I did then, I knew I could talk with him, and he'd listen close and give me straight advice. Pop had been the same, but he was dead.

I found him working in the carriage house, doing some piddling chores he'd put off from yesterday. He didn't often do that, being bee-busy more often than not, but I guess everyone has the right to slow down now and again. Seeing I was troubled, he put aside his fiddling and led me up to his rooms on the second floor.

The quarters atop the carriage house were roomy, large enough for two to live there easy. Tall windows on the south and east brought in plenty of the outside light. With the windows open in the summertime, and a light breeze blowing in, the rooms kept cool. Come winter with the sunlight streaming in, the rooms would be warm and comfortable. A small, pot-belly woodstove lay up against one wall, the floor surrounding it made of tiles. There was a large clothes wardrobe in the bedroom and a double brass-rail bed, just like the old one Jamie and I had shared. His rooms had storage space a plenty and Clarke-Jiles prided himself on keeping his quarters clean and tidy should company drop by.

Clarke-Jiles listened closely as I told him what had happened in the marketplace on Friday; my meeting with Marie and listening to her father. He himself had had some experience in similar matters, coming from the South and being black, so he understood what I was telling him.

"Sounds to me you had some real trouble yesterday," he said after hearing me out, "and I know it cut you to the quick. I know it hurts 'cause I've been hurt myself." He lay back in his horsehair easy chair, took a long, deep breath, and let it out slow and noisy, which showed he was thinking. "Sometimes a body's just got to hear it out and take it for what it's worth, and what was said ain't worth nothing.

"Clayt, I'm going to tell you about people. It's no doubt something your poppa would've told you had he lived. People can be mighty unkind to one another. Sometimes without even meaning to. As I recall, the Good Book says three things about how folks should be treating one another. There's the Golden Rule: Do unto others as you would have them do unto you. There's Jesus's own 'Eleventh Commandment' which He added to those Moses carried down to the Hebrews, to love thy neighbor as thyself, and a piece about searching out the log in your own eye before you go looking for the splinter in another's. Preachers talk about these things at nearly every Sunday meeting and, as good God-fearing folk, the congregation listens to the words and nod approval with their heads. They leave the services thinking well of themselves and well of the folks across the way, see their faults and say that they'll do better. But they don't. Not by a long sight. And you know why they don't? It's 'cause humankind is weak. It's 'cause they've listened with their heads and not their hearts. Why, families can't get along with one another often times, and they's related! We can't expect folks to be loving and respecting perfect strangers.

"Take Mr. Ellis for example. He wasn't born in Waytown. He come from somewhere 'round Ohio and arrived in town about the same time I come to work for Miss Addie. He was a stranger then and folks who'd been born in Waytown and lived here all their lives were suspicious of him. He had to prove himself worthy of respect. He started up a dray works; dealt with folks fair and honest in his business. By and by he became successful and after a time became a wealthy man. He started dressing fine; built himself a large house above the river. His business grew and he gave folks jobs. He went to service every Sunday morning, even taught Sunday school; held a lot of civic posts in town. Why, he's even been mayor once, just like Miss Addie's late husband. But people didn't take to him right off.

"Miss Addie's husband?" he continued. "Why, the same was true for him. He was a Yankee. Come all the way from Boston to settle and set up business. He stepped into town with three strikes against his favor: he was a Northerner, he didn't speak nor act like a man from 'round these parts, and he had money. Oh, not near as much as Miss Addie has now, but money enough to make Waytown folks suspicious. He started into mercantiling; married up with Miss Addie a short time later. He treated folks fair, gave them value for their money, 'n stood behind what he sold. Waytown folks found him a good man soon enough.

"Same is true with me. I had to prove myself triple to folks in Waytown 'cause I'm black. But I worked hard and done it. If I was to leave Waytown, I'd have to prove myself all over again." Clarke-Jiles looked thought filled for a moment, then smiled. "There's folks here who don't think well of me, but that's the way it is. It doesn't matter if you're black or white, poor, or rich. It's all the same. You've got to prove yourself no matter who you are. A body's got to be worthy of folks' respect and, when you are, most folk accept you."

There had been short pauses between his talk so he could stoke his pipe bowl. Clarke-Jiles always thought better with his pipe. The sweet aroma of the smoke clouded up around him.

He continued. "What Mr. Ellis did was see you from the outside and make a judgment. It's what's in a body's inside which matters most."

Everything Clarke-Jiles spoke on made sense and I listened to him closely.

"But doesn't helping save Marie and her momma from the riverboat count for something?"

"Sure, it counts, and Mr. Ellis knows it and thanked you for it. Deep down inside I'm sure he's mighty grateful. But he's a proud man and pride's gotten in the way of him showing it to you. But what he's got is false pride, and false pride is a powerful hard emotion to overcome. You know you done the right thing, and Marie knows it, and her momma, too. Mr. Ellis knows it, but pride won't allow him to show it to you proper."

I guess all along I knew what Clarke-Jiles had been saying,

though I needed someone to tell it to me. I thought back to my experience in Swainville and to Maggie Lewis. Maggie was a good woman, giving help to strangers and to folks in need. But in general, Swainville society looked askance on her for what she was outside—a barmaid–and didn't bother looking inside, to her heart. I had a lot of living and growing yet to do, and a lot to learn about people and the world. They were all things Pop would have helped me learn if he hadn't started drinking heavy.

I wasn't certain about seeing Marie again, leastwise not so soon after the way her daddy had treated me. It wasn't the stern warning he'd given me to stay clear of her that bothered me, but how she'd look on me now–after what he'd said.

I didn't have to search out Marie; she found me.

A few days following the talk Clarke-Jiles had had with me which made a world of difference about how I saw things now, I'd ventured down to the cove where Jamie and I had gone so often. I wasn't aware Marie had followed me there.

It both surprised and pleased me to see her because when she came, I knew I was still all right with her. It was a good thing, too, the afternoon was gray and overcast, with heavy banks of clouds moving in over the horizon in the southwest, signaling the thunderstorm that was to break loose that night. Had the sun been blazing warm, showing itself a bright-yellow disc, I'd have been browning myself naked on the sand–a fine condition for a girl to see me in!

Marie had seen me loitering down the river path toward the cove and kind of stalked me, uncertain as me to her of what to say.

"I came to apologize for what Daddy said about you," she said after she'd sat down on the bare sand next to me. "I know he didn't mean a lot of what he said, and I think he's sorry for it."

"Has your daddy said he's sorry?" I asked.

"No. Not in so many words. But I know he is. He even said you can come to supper with us if you'd like. Momma said she'd like to meet you and thank you in person for what you did."

"Tell your momma what you've said is thanks enough for both of you. Your daddy's right by saying I didn't do anything more than what any thinking man would've done under the circumstances."

"But you're a hero! And a hero ought to be given proper thanks," Marie insisted.

"I ain't a hero. All a hero is, is a body who tries to help when there's a need and it works out well. There's nothing special in it. Besides, I don't think the time's right just now to impose myself on your daddy. Maybe later. We'll both know when the time's right."

"Clayt," Marie said. Her voice was petal-gentle, and her large eyes seemed to melt into me. "Please don't think poorly of my father. He's a good man, really. It's–it's just that sometimes he can be so impossible!"

A dark-shadowed cloud was sweeping in nearly overhead and carrying rain.

"Your daddy only wants what's right for you. He's wrong though when he said I'm good for nothing. Ronnie and I proved that on the steamboat. I think your daddy knows that."

"I know he does," Marie said, thoughtfully.

"He's right about one thing though. I am just a river boy, born and bred up along the river."

"Daddy, when he was angry, said Miss Addie took you in only because you were kin, that she isn't going to leave you anything when ...

"When she dies?" I said, finishing up her sentence. "That won't be for a long time yet. A lot of things can change by then. And I didn't come to Waytown on account of her money. I'm only glad she saw fit to take me in. I'd be living in an orphan home if she hadn't."

Marie and I talked for quite a spell, staying out along the cove under the shelter of the trees until the thunderheads rolled over, threatening sudden rain. She was no cream-faced, pale and pretty girl who pranced around asking folks to admire her. She was a real human being. And she liked the river, saying how it was a beautiful thing. I was more than a might surprised to learn she even liked to fish.

When she was younger and her daddy had had more time, he'd taken her fishing and she'd enjoyed it since. That knowledge cut a lot of my feelings about girls down to size; about them being the weaker sex and not enjoying much the same things as boys.

A lot of things changed following my talk with Clarke-Jiles, and my second meeting with Marie. Even Aunt Addie noticed I was somehow different. I did things for her around the house without her asking, things she'd had to do for me before. And I didn't let her down as much, though I had to allow I slipped back into my old ways now and again. But I tried to set things right.

Marie had allowed how it'd be nice if we would see one another from time to time. I agreed, though on the sly so as not to upset her daddy.

Mr. Ellis still didn't cotton to me any. I didn't know if he ever would. But, for some time, though, matters were mostly right for me in Waytown.

Best trust the happy moments. What they give makes man less fearful of the certain grave and gives his work compassion and new eyes. The days that make us happy make us wise.

–John Masefield

CHAPTER 14

Holiday Preparations. Tragedy Strikes! Orphaned Again.

THE CHRISTMAS SEASON WAS FAST approaching and Aunt Addie set in early to her holiday preparations. Earlier, when the season was ripe for the fruits which grow wild and free along the river, she'd sent Jamie and me along the river and into the hills on the west side of Waytown to gather up basketfuls of elderberries, choke cherries, and wild plums. She'd put them up in large containers and now that the holiday times were upon us, she was packaging jellies and jams in fine fashion as gifts for friends and as sale items at the church bazaar.

After school one mid-week afternoon, Jamie and Clarke-Jiles set out to chop down a tree to be set up in the parlor and to haul in a yule log. Aunt Addie said the yule log was a custom her late husband and she had shared. He'd come from Boston, and in those parts back East, the yule log had been a tradition in his family and many others. She'd even decorated it with clusters of holly berries and pinecones and bits of greenery.

Whigmaleeries and gewgaws Clarke-Jiles called them. That's because he nearly wrenched his back setting it into place on the iron grating inside the front parlor fireplace.

Soon the whole house took on a festive look, and I had to allow how Aunt Addie's decorations gave the place a special festive warmth and glow. The whole house, from the ground floor to the attic rooms, smelled of pine scent from the sprays of evergreen wreaths on the walls and windowsills. Holly strings were slung around doorways, and mistletoe cropped up in the strangest places. Aunt Addie kissed and hugged everyone in sight. She seemed especially happy.

On the twelfth night before Christmas, a scarce four months since my fifteenth birthday gathering, Aunt Addie, Clarke-Jiles, Jamie and I all crowded into the parlor to decorate the tree. Clarke-Jiles had popped the corn and Jamie busied himself stringing chains of it together to hang across the boughs. I sat opposite on the floor doing the same with a bowlful of cranberries while Clarke-Jiles worked setting the glass ornaments on the tree. When everything was done, I had to admit the tree was indeed a spectacle, all dressed out in colored ribbon, fruit and popcorn chains, and glass bobbles which glittered gold and red, blue and green and silver.

Since Jamie was the younger, he was given the honor of topping the tree with a large, gold foil angel with silver hair and holding a tiny hymn book in its hands. Candles studded the branch tips, and we lit them all. Clarke-Jiles turned the parlor lamps down low, and Aunt Addie sat down at the piano and played while we sang Christmas songs.

Aunt Addie's favorite was "Silent Night" but sung in German. Of course, Clarke-Jiles, having lived with her for a number of years, knew it well, but Jamie and I had to learn it new. The words sounded odd at first but weren't hard, so we learned them easy enough. Stille Nacht, heilige Nacht, alles schläft, einsam wacht.

Groups of ladies trooped in and out nearly every day around this time and when the parlor wasn't filled with their high-pitched laughter or quiet murmurings, Aunt Addie was out in the carriage, buzzing through town delivering gifts, or making personal calls and attending to her social circle and sewing circle, her knitting group and church doings.

Jamie at this time was still in school, but about to get vacation.

He and I already planned a camping trip up around Mason's Overlook, the high-peaked lookout three miles north of Waytown. Jamie was especially looking forward to it. He'd camped out but once and never in the winter. I'd made fun of him, poking jokes not to forget to wear his Union suit and keep it buttoned tight. He'd stay warm, I told him, as long as he didn't trip over his own two feet and roll down the hillside into the river. Jamie was growing rapid as a pea shoot; was kind of awkward and gangly, and forever falling over his feet which were growing faster than the rest of him.

Aunt Addie had decided to remain at home one afternoon, only a week before Christmas, and hole up in the kitchen baking pies and melting paraffin to pour into candle molds. She made the neatest candles I'd ever seen: all colors, some tall and slender like a willow shoot (she called them tapers) others squat and square. Many of her candles she set out around the house; others she gave away to friends and neighbors, and some she put up for sale in Hudson's Mercantile or gave to the church bazaar.

It was only a short while after noon-time lunch when it happened, just on the Tuesday before Christmas.

Aunt Addie had hustled Clarke-Jiles and me outside and into the carriage house where we set to telling stories to one another while working on the rig, making it all shiny and bright for Christmas. Jamie was still in school, the final day before his freedom started. Pies cooled on the screen porch off the rear side of the kitchen and, when the wind breezed right, the smell of spiced apple and mincemeat wafted in through the only open window of the carriage house.

We were just in the middle of a laugh from a story Clarke-Jiles had told when a dull sound, like thunder rolling in the distance, caught our hearing.

"What do you suppose that was?" Clarke-Jiles asked, cocking his broad face kind of quizzical. "It ain't likely to be thundering in December."

No sooner had he spoken but the thunder pealed again, this time snapping like a lightning crack. It sounded like an explosion, and close by, too, so we wandered out to have a look-see.

It wasn't a storm that greeted us. The whole back side of Aunt Addie's house was on fire! Already flames were shooting out the porch-side windows and licking up the outer wall near up to the second floor! For an instant both of us were dumb struck, standing like statues at the carriage house doors, staring out in disbelief.

"FIRE! FIRE!" Clarke-Jiles started yelling. "FIRE!" and rushed toward the horse trough like a man who'd been set afire himself. I reacted, too, only slower. Galloping inside the carriage house, I grabbed two feed buckets and a pair of woolen blankets and bolted out to meet Clarke- Jiles who was already sprinting toward the house.

Orange and yellow flames danced out along the porch and shot crackling sparks into the cool, crisp air.

"Miss Addie! Miss Addie!" Clarke-Jiles sang out, pitching his voice up loud and high. "Miss Addie. Are you a'right?" There was no reply.

We started feeding water buckets to the flames at the kitchen door, but it wasn't any use. The flames were fierce, and we couldn't get in close enough to douse them well.

Thick, choking, black smoke filled with a waxy soot billowed up along the backside of the house. The white frame boards soon turned dull gray and black with the rolling smoke and fire-charring flames.

"Miss Addie! Miss Addie!" Clarke-Jiles kept on calling out. "Miss Addie. Can you hear me? Are you there?" Again, there was only silence.

"Jiles" (which is what I called him mostly because it was shorter) "Jiles, we've got to get inside."

"Can't. Fire's too hot," he yelled back. "Got to pour more water on it."

I bellowed out, coughing in the thick soot haze and choking smoke. "Water's no use! We've got to get inside!"

The whole backside of the house facing the carriage shed, was now in flames. Night-dark smoke clouds billowed high into the sky and blanketed outwards over Waytown. Clarke-Jiles, realizing I was right, beat it back to the watering trough and soaked the heavy blankets I'd brought out. We wrapped ourselves snug inside of them and scurried off through the yard to the front parlor door.

The only way to get inside the house was through the front street-side door. But it was heavy, solid oak and Aunt Addie always kept it locked. We tried it to make certain, and it was bolted tight. Clarke-Jiles forced his weight against it in our clamor to get inside. It wouldn't budge. Again, he shouldered it. Again, it refused to move. By now, and desperate, Clarke-Jiles acted like a raging bull. His nostrils flared; I could picture the thick-knot muscles beneath the heavy blanket strain against his effort. Once more he charged the door. Its jam groaned against the force, then cracked, splintered, and sprung open, almost flying off its hinges as he forced his total weight against it.

Dense smoke billowed in thick, black clouds throughout the lower floor, seeping up the red carpeting of the wide staircase steps like ground fog in a cemetery. Through the swirling gray haze, we could see licks of flames–tiny fire fingers–searing up the walls, dancing against the patterned papered wall. The back parlor and beyond, the kitchen walls and ceiling glowed an eerie orange-red-yellow. When the door had cracked open, we caught a flash of heat so fierce it nearly knocked us back. Even through the wet blankets, we gasped for breath, huddled low against the floor where the air was clear. The candles on the Christmas tree slumped over, and along the windowsills, Aunt Addie's decorations melted into waxy puddles, the reds and whites and greens running in together.

We kneed and elbowed low across the floor, snake-like, but at a pitifully slow crawl, cutting a short pathway toward where we thought Aunt Addie might be. The heat was fierce, almost like a red-hot flat iron had been set against the blankets, making our backs grow tingly. We drew our breath in short, shallow gasps. The wet blankets steamed, and we were sweating something fierce.

All we could see was the bottom parts of the parlor furnishings, crinkled sofa skirts and chair and table legs as we slithered belly-low along the floor. Suddenly, the Christmas tree, set alongside the fireplace against the back parlor's wall, shattered into flames, shooting sparks like a dragging wagon tongue through the smoke-choked air. We neared the kitchen.

Greasy smoke and sparking flames clogged the room and there, lying gaped out and as firebird pink as any newborn, was Aunt Addie, unmoving and dreadful still. Clarke-Jiles, who was ahead of me, grasped her feet and pulled, dragging her tiny body like a sled on soft-bellied snow toward the door. There was no escape through the kitchen which belched a mass of flames, so we retreated the way we came.

We reached the street-side door none too soon. With a sound like a steamboat's giant wheel starting up, the parlor ceiling snapped, cracked, and buckled in, sending parts of the second floor crashing down. Just as sudden, the back parts of the house that we could see vanished in a sea of blazing yellow orange, the brightness of a sunrise.

On the front lawn, outside and safe, Clarke-Jiles covered Aunt Addie lovingly with his blanket, patting her fragile-looking hand and moaning softly to her. Clarke-Jiles looked suddenly smaller than he was, bending over her, soothing her like a body might an injured favorite dog.

The neighbors, realizing what had happened, had gathered around in groups, gasping, and muttering quietly among themselves. A Mrs. Sterling, who'd been a near life-long friend of Aunt Addie's, came rushing up through the crowd of lookers-on as soon as we'd crawled outside. Her heavy winter skirts flared out around her in the growing breeze. Kneeling beside Aunt Addie, Mrs. Sterling helped comfort her. But Aunt Addie lay unconscious.

Looking up, I saw how the kitchen flames had spiraled up the second story and now crackled through the roof. Jamie's and my bedroom was a mass of belching flames, surging and spitting around the window frames. The whole grand house was going quick. Smoke clouds, which appeared like awesome thunderheads, surged, and rolled skyward to be seen from all over Waytown. Townsfolk had poured out from shops on Main Street and from houses all around and hastened up the street toward us.

Someone had called the fire battalion and the horse-drawn firewagons clattered up the brick street moments later, the firemen decked out in their gold and red helmets and thick, black coats. The clanging of the fire bells sounded loud against the chorus of awe-struck voices crackling against the winter wind. It was useless to fight the fire.

Aunt Addie's house was a hell-flaming shell when the firemen arrived.

Some of the standers by had taken it upon themselves to form a bucket line from the horse trough and were dousing at the blaze, but there was nothing to be saved. All the firefighters could do was keep the flaming finger sparks from spreading to the carriage house.

As I watched, both horror-chilled and amazed, two gable-peaks caved inward through the roof. Flames flared outward around the roof like they'd been doors opened on a furnace.

The person we most wanted to see came driving up in his one-horse rig soon after. Doc Clarendon climbed down, clutching his doctor's bag and huffing vapor breath against the chilling air. I could tell Aunt Addie was bad from the first instant he bent down to examine her.

Miraculously, Aunt Addie wasn't badly burned. Though her face and hands were a bright cherry pink, her clothes were still intact. She lay half-conscious now, and breathing in wheezing, shallow gasps.

"We can't risk moving her very far," the doctor said. "Best we take her to the carriage house."

Several of the menfolk standing by helped roll Aunt Addie onto the blanket I had used and, under Doc Clarendon's direction, carried her easy into Clarke-Jiles's quarters. Clarke-Jiles helped the doctor attend to her while I waited downstairs for Jamie to come home. He arrived soon after.

"What happened, Clayt? How'd the fire start? Is everyone all right?" Jamie was all alight with questions.

"Aunt Addie was caught in the fire," I told him, my voice cracking as I said it. "Doc Clarendon's with her now. Jiles, too."

I told him what had happened to the best of my feeble knowledge. I could only guess, but I'd say the paraffin Aunt Addie had been melting on the stove caught fire and then exploded, spattering the kitchen walls and curtains with flaming wax. Aunt Addie had most likely been knocked unconscious by the blast. Being stretched out low along the floor had given her air to breathe and saved her from being badly burned.

The great old house was a total wreck; a charred cinder of smoking rubble, smoldering against the bleak blue gray of the December sky.

In a few hours, only the blackened skeletons of the fireplace chimneys stood out from the smoking heap like two brick phantoms in the declining light of dusk.

Dr. Clarendon stayed with Aunt Addie throughout the night. Mrs. Sterling assisted him as nurse. Jamie, Clarke-Jiles, and I camped out below near the horse stalls, nestled up tight on the loose hay straw, huddled in woolen blankets. All the warmth was in the woodstove in Clarke-Jiles's quarters so resting wasn't easy and none of us could sleep anyway. Our thoughts, unspoken, were always with Aunt Addie.

Come morning, none of us had eaten breakfast; wouldn't if we'd had a place to cook it. Around ten o'clock, Doc Clarendon stepped down from above and told us we should see her.

Aunt Addie lay on the brass-bound bed, covered to her neck by a cotton sheet. Her eyes were closed but her lids danced a nervous flutter-twitch. The doctor led us over to the far side of the room and in low-toned whispers gave us his grave prognosis.

"Miss Addie's dying," he announced, his gray eyes looking sad and heavy from lack of sleep. "It's not the burns, which are only minor, but the smoke and heat she breathed. It seared and clogged her lungs," he droned. "I've given her a soporific to help her rest and Cantharis has calmed the burn pain and eased her restlessness." His next news struck us especially hard. "She won't make it through the day."

The three of us gathered around her bed. Clarke-Jiles stood somber near the head with Jamie and me at the foot. Aunt Addie lay sleeping quietly, her breathing growing shallow.

I hadn't known Aunt Addie long, having only come to her in July. We'd had our misunderstandings and disagreements, sure, but her warmth and kindness, and the love she'd tried to share seemed to flow outward from somewhere deep inside her. Aunt Addie was a laid-back, flowers-pressed-between-the-pages person. Around me she was kind of pressed away and hidden, but then sometimes she'd open like the pages of a book and the petals of her kindness and gentle caring could be seen again.

I knew Jamie felt the same. We were all taking her dying hard, especially Clarke-Jiles who loved her so.

After lying quiet for quite a time with scarce a sign of life, Aunt Addie began to move slowly beneath the coverings. It was as if she sensed us being there. Her eyes flickered open slowly and she looked around at each of us. Doc Clarendon, sensing something only a doctor could, guided Mrs. Sterling from the room, leaving us alone with her.

Clarke-Jiles moved two her head, fluffed her pillow some, and cradled her hand in his.

She couldn't speak, and what words she tried to say were mumbled so silently we could scarcely make them out. Repeating over and over again came only parts of words, "my wi..." and there was a deep fear and sadness in her eyes which flashed toward me as she mouthed them. I don't think it was for herself.

We lingered near her for a time, until she tired and fell asleep, then passed back downstairs, the doctor and Mrs. Sterling remaining with her.

Less than half an hour later, the doctor reappeared, mouthing the simple words, "She's gone."

Aunt Addie's funeral was held on a blustery day with light snow breezing down, laying a thin, stark-white veil over Waytown. The Parson Briggs officiated, and many in the town attended. Most all the shops in Waytown closed in respect to Addie Hudson. Everyone who was anybody in town sat prayer-silent inside the church with more lingering around the steps and yard outside. Many of those who weren't prominent in the community but had felt her kindness sat or stood inside or huddled about outside. Marie Ellis and her mother sat a few pew rows back from Jamie, Clarke-Jiles, and me. Mr. Ellis wasn't with them.

The choir sang sad hymns and Nellie Martinson played the organ with more meaning in the tones than ever I'd heard her give. Parson Briggs preached the eulogy, saying, and rightly so, that scarce a finer woman, more loving, giving, and forgiving than Addie Hudson had ever lived as far as his knowledge went.

"Addie Hudson has her place in Heaven," his voice seemed to smile, then he spoke the final prayer.

Oft-times when a body dies–and he may have been a shyster or a huckster or a downright miserable and unkind brute–he's praised long and loud at his funeral. But all that the Parson voiced was heart-felt and true. Aunt Addie had been a remarkable woman all along.

The doings at the cemetery were brief, the snow flying down heavier and swirling in the growing wind. There lay scarce a doubt, but a blizzard was on its way.

Prayers were said, flowers sprinkled over the polished oak casket, and the box and body lowered somberly by the bearers into the freezing ground. And everybody wandered home.

The burial was on the day before Christmas Eve.

Clarke-Jiles had taken it upon himself to have a gravestone carved: a simple, red granite stone which bore the inscription: ADELINE SIEVERS HUDSON, 1822 - 1888, BELOVED BY HER FRIENDS AND FAMILY. R.I.P.

There are two things in which men, in other things wise enough, do usually miscarry: in putting off the making of their wills and their repentance till it be too late.

−Tillotson

CHAPTER 15

The Reading of the Will. River Tales. Moving On.

FOLLOWING AUNT ADDIE'S DEATH, THE three of us settled into the large and cheery apartment suite above Hudson's Mercantile. Mr. Mertinger, Aunt Addie's manager, had given it to us, himself moving into the upstairs of the carriage house until he could find a more suitable place to stay. We hadn't wanted him to move but he insisted, saying how he was a bachelor so he didn't need much room and the carriage house was plenty large and comfortable enough for him.

We hadn't had a Christmas; the tragedy of Aunt Addie's loss weighed heavy on the three of us. We settled into the routine of household chores and managed for ourselves as best as three men could. Each day Clarke-Jiles, otherwise seeming at a loss of what to do, drove his rig over to the house site to feed and tend the horses. Finally, tiring of the trip and not wishing to disturb Mr. Mertinger, he stabled them at the local livery.

Two weeks to the day after Aunt Addie's funeral, Clarke-Jiles, Jamie and I were sitting in the office of the local attorney-at-law, Jeremy Benjamin Settles. The office was decked out tastefully in black leather armchairs and thick-stuffed horsehair couches. We were gathered there for the reading of Addie Hudson's will.

Mr. Settles began by peering down over the top of his half-spectacles and reading the traditional, formal opening of a will: "Adeline Sievers Hudson being of sound mind ..." and after those preliminaries, he settled down to go over the heart of the document.

"Adeline Hudson left a considerable estate," he began, then read directly from the will.

In the event of her death, she wrote, her beloved houseman, friend, and devoted companion, Clarke-Jiles Franklin Davis, would be gifted the cash sum of $10,000 to do with as he, in his free will, chose. He was also given guardian ship of the inheritance of Aunt Addie's estate for one James Price Hudson, minor son, adopted, until he achieved legal age. Willed to Jamie was the bulk of her estate with Clarke-Jiles given a share as well of all properties real and personal, the house (which, of course, lay in ruins), land she held title to along the riverfront, and Hudson's Mercantile. She'd also remembered Mr. Mertinger with a handsome sum, her circle at the church and the church itself with monies—ten percent of the cash money in her possession—to be divided evenly. Parson Briggs also received a tidy sum: far more than he was paid as pastor or likely to earn by outside labors. I received no mention.

After reading the will in total, Mr. Settles addressed me, "Mrs. Hudson had mentioned to me some while back that you were to be included in her will for half of her adopted son's estate. However," he added, blinking over his reading frames, "she passed away before she could change this document. I'm sorry, Clayton, but there is nothing I can do as, while you are relation, you are not legally her son. You may, however, seek a remedy in a court of equity."

I saw no good use in fighting Aunt Addie's will. Just knowing that she'd thought of me was plenty enough. Pop had been a poor man and I'd grown up free along the river. I didn't see any present need for money, and I didn't want a share of Jamie's. And I told them so.

Following the formalities, with some exceptions, we went back to living life as regular as before. Jamie and I made our camping trip to Mason's Overlook, Clarke-Jiles thinking it'd be good for us to get away for a spell.

We stayed out three days, settled down in a makeshift lean-to, the two of us had slapped together. The campsite was nestled cozy between a stand of young evergreens which kept the blast of the chill winds away. It'd snowed only lightly while we camped out, and that made the going easier, and being away from town broke up the flood of well-wishers and sympathizers–all friends of Aunt Addie's– who'd come to visit Clarke- Jiles, Jamie, and me following the funeral. "If there's anything we can do's" had poured out from all of them and, of course, there was nothing anyone could do. Life is for the living, and we chose to live our lives as regular as possible.

Saying that young'uns should have something at Christmas time, Clarke-Jiles had given each of us a present; gifts he'd bought and laid away in the carriage house and of course, hadn't been destroyed. Jamie's was a set of Bret Harte stories and he loved them because he was heavy into reading and especially liked Western stories. "Outcasts of Poker Flat" and "The Luck of Roaring Camp" were among his favorite tales which he read to me while we settled in around the fire one night.

Jiles's gift to me was a Remington .22 rim fire rifle with dark mountings, an oiled stock, and genuine checkered pistol grip. It was a honey of a rifle and something I'd always wanted. Pop had had a similar one, though I think it was a Springfield single-shot and he had taught me how to shoot and handle it when I'd turned ten. With several boxes of cartridges and a quiet afternoon, I did the same for Jamie.

Mason's Overlook only looked the part of being uninhabited and wild. It wasn't like the finger point where Ronnie and I had stayed. A lot of folks camped these woods. They were mostly boys like us who stayed out here during their summer days off from school, coming out to swim and fish and keep out of the hair of their folks in town.

But the Overlook got its share of men who wandered in to rest a spell before moving on. While Aunt Addie was living, several times these men would stop by her house to get a meal, chopping stove wood or doing some chore to earn their handout. The work done and the meal served and eaten, they'd head on up to the Overlook to set up camp before moving on upriver. "Wanderers in the desert" Aunt Addie called them. Others called them hobos or vagrants or bums. It took me some time to see the difference.

Jamie and I had found some cans, bean tins mostly, around some old campsites we'd wandered across and when we had a handful, we found a bank to set them against and use for rifle practice.

I told Jamie the importance of handling a rifle safely: never touching the trigger until ready to shoot, never pointing it in another body's direction, and never pointing it unless you were meaning to shoot and what was behind was clear. Jamie caught on fast, being a quick study at nearly everything and, while he was scarce an expert, I felt he'd do just fine. Before the afternoon was over and the target cans looked like riddled sieves, Jamie had learned enough for me to feel easy going hunting with him. That night we had a stew—I bagged a squirrel and Jamie had gotten himself a juicy rabbit.

Guess Jamie caught sight of a far-away look in my eyes as we sat cross-legged around the fire early that third evening. We'd both been mighty quiet, Jamie reading a Bret Harte tale silently to himself and me sitting by and thinking.

Putting down his reading, Jamie asked me, "Clayt, are you all right?"

"I'm all right," I said. "Just thinking."

"About what?"

"About being here—along the river again. And about Aunt Addie's dying."

"You want to leave Waytown and Clarke-Jiles and me, don't you?" he asked.

I was powerfully surprised—downright astounded—and showed it, too. It was as if Jamie had crawled inside my head and could hear what I was thinking. Since our first adventures along the river together we'd grown close. We shared our secrets. In some ways we were as close as Ronnie and I had been. I found it as easy to talk to Jamie as I had with Ronnie. And, while he was but twelve-years-old, he was more grown-up than me in many ways.

"Town life just isn't for me," I told him. "Leastways not now. I get the feeling of being all cooped up. Along the river, I'm free to be myself. In Waytown I have to smile because it's expected; I have to be perfect when I don't feel like it. Jamie, I'm just not free to be me."

Jamie was silent for quite a spell. "When do you plan to leave?"

"Soon as I can. A few days maybe."

"Think Clarke-Jiles will let you leave?"

"He'll let me. Isn't no reason for him to keep me here. He's got his hands full now with raising you, keeping track of your inheritance and his own. He'll be working close with Mr. Mertinger in the business at the store. He doesn't need me getting under foot and being in the way."

"You aren't in the way, Clayt," Jamie said.

"No, but I feel like I am sometimes," I smiled.

We talked out my plans for a long space, then talked about Jamie for a time. Jamie was already thinking about becoming a lawyer someday; maybe rising to a judge's bench. At the least, he thought he'd be a teacher. Leastwise he'd be heading off to some college someday. In whatever he chose to do, I knew he'd be good at it, and I told him so.

The soft glow and crackling of the fire and the crimson licks of color it cast over the evergreens and the thin veil of virgin snow, set us into a lull of quiet once again. Jamie went back to his reading, and I sat still, thinking about leaving Waytown.

For the longest while, it'd been silent around the camp. The eerie quiet was broken, though, by the snap of dry twigs and pine needles in the distance behind us.

Jamie and I both looked at one another and sat upright, listening to the sounds. They were moving nearer. It was a popping sound, slow and even, like the noise footsteps make on snow when it's crisp and cold outside. There weren't any animals bigger than a deer, a coon, or a bobcat maybe around these parts, and animals when they're creeping up on something don't make a steady noise.

Just as suddenly as the sounds had come, they stopped. The shattering silence was broken only when a pine bough I'd set on the fire exploded with a crack like a rifle shot.

"Haloo there!" a man's voice sounded from somewhere in the darkness beyond the fire's reach. A moment later it called out again. "Anybody 'bout?"

Jamie and I looked at one another and didn't answer. Supposing it was someone with a gun and meaning harm? I pulled my rifle close then realized there weren't any bullets left. We'd used them all that afternoon.

The crunching noise drew closer; heavy footsteps making the snow crust pop.

"Haloo in there. Anybody spare a cold man a cup 'o coffee?"

Just at the edge of the clump of evergreens surrounding camp, a tall, dark figure of a man stood out in the campfire light. Neither of us could make him out well. I clutched the rifle, thinking, loaded or not, the sight of it would scare him off it he was meaning mischief.

"We've got coffee," I called out to the shadow figure. "Come on up where we can see you."

The shadow man approached until he stood near on to the fire.

The flames from the extra sticks we'd added set a flood of glowing light against the man.

He was old, looking about in his fifties, late, and appearing like he'd seen better times. He wore a heavy short coat that, like himself, had seen better days. The trousers he wore were heavy wool but thinned and torn out in places and baggy about the waist like a body wears who's lost a lot of weight, and held up by what appeared to be faded red suspenders. As the man stepped closer toward the fire's warmth, he caught sight of the rifle slung across my lap and backed away, putting his hands up, bent outwards from the elbows.

"Now hold it there, young'un," he called in a sort of gravel voice, "you wouldn't be a-pepperin' a man who's only cold and hungry would ya?"

I reckoned to myself I wouldn't unless he was to make a rapid move. All I could do was point the barrel in his direction and maybe back him off.

He looked harmless enough, standing in front of us, shivering a bit with a sudden wind blast that carried with it a few flakes of snow. I invited him inside the lean-to, Jamie pouring him out a cup of steaming coffee, the silvery vapor swirling upwards around the rim like morning mist rising along the river.

The man plopped down like a heavy sack of flour, his back against the growling wind, his front side toward the fire.

"Name's Hank Short," he grunted. His voice was hoarse and wheezing as he spoke. "Come up from round Hortonville a time back. Been lookin' for steady work to keep belly 'n soul together. Ain't found none yet," he wheezed.

He rolled the tin coffee cup around in his gloveless hands, warming them before he tasted it. He winced and puckered up his wind-raw lips.

"Who learned you young'uns to make coffee? This here brew's 'nough to make a man's hair fall out!" He took a longer sip, drawing in cold January air along with it. Both Pop and Uncle Frank had liked their coffee strong, and that's the way I brewed it. I'd always taken mine with a little cream–when I had it.

Jamie and I introduced each other to him.

"An' fine-lookin' young lads you are, too," he said, his voice becoming less pitiful sounding as the warming brew thawed out his throat. Then he glanced over at my rifle. "You've no need for the squirrelin' piece. As you kin see, I come unarmed," and he threw back his coat to prove it. He hadn't a gun, nor any knife that was visible. I set the rifle back on the blanket roll, still in reach if I should need to flash it.

Hank Short proved to be quite the talker when he'd warmed up to it, carrying on near non-stop.

He said he'd been a gambler on the steamboat circuit for a time when riverboats were in their heyday, and following that had worked at being a lumberman, a flatboat poler, and, during the Confederacy, a message runner. Now, he said, he was a wanderer mainly, and a rum-and-whiskey-drinking man without a steady income. He'd been acquainted with the river–both sides of it–from the gulf at New Orleans to Keokuk and then some as well along the Ohio. "I come up some on the good times 'n rolled back more on the bad," he told. Living along the river all his life, he knew it likely better than any man alive, he said.

Jamie and I told him briefly about ourselves, beginning to warm up to him, seeing he looked harmless. He poured himself another cup of coffee then started in about himself again.

"Ever hear tell 'o a man named Devol?" Hank Short began.

Jamie and I looked over at one another, both drawing up a blank on that name, and shaking our heads no that we hadn't. Even if we'd recognized the name, there was no doubt but Hank Short would've told us about him anyway. He hadn't even had a sip of whiskey and already he could talk a stream more words than Uncle Frank ever did when he was good and primed.

"First met Devol in '52 when I was a young tad 'bout eighteen. I'd just signed aboard the *Katie* as a prentice fireman learning how to feed the boiler fires 'n keep a head 'o steam up. Not as easy as you young'uns might think. There's more to being a fireman than jus' stokin' wood or shovelin' coal. Gotta watch the pressure. Pressure goes too slack, you gotta stoke more in. Pressure goes too high, you gotta let off steam or split a boiler out or, worse, blow yourself to the other side o' Heaven.".". He was about to go on about the finer points of steamboat work when he caught himself and continued on about the mysterious man, Devol.

"Devol was quite a gambler. Best gamblin' man the Mississippi ever seen. Why, by fifteen he could play with the best 'o 'em and beat 'em cold. Devol'd play straight or crooked dependin' on his mood and who he was gamblin' with. If he thought some river slicker was playin' him for a fool 'n out to cheat him, he'd cheat right back so slick even another gambler couldn't tell how he done it. Poker, keno, monte, faro—you name the game an' ol' Devol was a master hand. He knew 'em all and no man bested him. Not one." Hank Short sure could spin a tale. As he talked, he scratched his face which bore a week's stubble growth and drew out the words he wished to stress. Jamie and I listened closely. "Why, he could pull off capers with them cards slicker'n my pap's razor strap. Learned some good tricks from Devol on the run 'tween N'orlans 'n St. Looie. Never could do 'em near as good as he could though. He had the touch. Yes sirs, Devol was the slickest rascal on the river."

Our long-talking visitor paused only enough to catch his breath and ask the favor of another cup of coffee, the pot being nearly empty now.

Reaching inside the deep folds of his coat, he brought out a pint bottle of Shaker's whiskey. "Give a man the shakes if'n he drinks too much o' it," he snorted, chuckled to himself, and drained what was left into his cup.

"I 'member one trick o' Devol's that was like to set everyone on their heels. It was just before the War 'tween the States. Out of Baton Rouge was an old steamer fitted up like a wharf boat 'n gamblers o' all descriptions set up there. Devol was one o' 'em. A crony o' his and Devol got into their heads a way to cheat the other gamblers. When no one was aboard one night they rigged a wire from round the rear wall to a loose board under Devol's favorite chair—the only one he ever sat in. His 'lucky chair' he called it." At that point in his yarn, Hank Short screwed up his grizzled mouth and scratched his chin. "Funny how a body grows attached to a certain place. Me? I weren't never like that. Liked to wander a might, see folks, things, 'n places."

"Wild Bill Hickok was like that," Jamie piped out. "He always had a set place he sat when he was playing cards. He had a 'lucky chair' too. Only one day he didn't sit in it and got gunned down by Jack McCall–right there in a Deadwood saloon." That was the first Jamie had spoken in the longest time. He knew all about the West from his reading–all about its heroes and its villains.

Hank Short looked hard at Jamie. "Smart boy for jus' a striplin'," he allowed. He stretched out lengthwise near the fire. "As I was sayin', Devol'd rigged his chair 'n was sittin' in on a game 'o stud."

His crony was peeping through a hole in the wall behind the other player. They'd rigged a nail to pop up under his shoe by pulling on the wire."

"One tug on the nail was a pair, two tugs a set 'o threes. More for straights and flushes. Yes sirs, 'twas quite a system them two rigged and no'un caught on for the longest while. Over time, Devol said he made nigh on to thirty thousand dollars with that trick."

"Course, the better Devol got at gamin', the more his reputation spread, and it weren't too long 'fore his name 'n face was so well reckoned he couldn't scarce get no'un to sit in with him. He'd move on then, farther upriver, or over to the Ohio or 'long the Missouri toward Omaha. Usin' another name, he could always ferret out a game where his face weren't known."

Our guest was well warmed now. His face, which had been pale from the chill, glowed pink now from the fire and you might say his pump was primed with the coffee and whiskey he'd drank.

"'Nother thing 'bout Devol which I'd heard tell of 'n saw jus' once was his head. He had a skull thicker'n a cattle horn. Could stave in doors with it; take blows direct from clubs 'n fire pokers that'd split a normal man's head clean open. Saw it happen once," Hank Short recalled. "Was on the turnback leg from St. Looie. The *Katie'd* took on passengers from the trip downriver. One 'o 'em was a duded up gentleman, a sugar seller coming back from a business trip. He set in on a game with Devol 'n several others. Devol was playing straight that day, but still winning more than losing. This here gentleman in his frockcoat 'n high-topped silk hat asked Devol if'n he was the man with the iron head. Devol 'llowed he was. "Then I'll wager you five-hundred dollars you can't take a strike from my cane," the gentleman said. He was carryin' an ebony walkin' stick with a gold knob head and flashed it in front of Devol. The gambler said, "Make it a thousand and I'll give you one good crack."

"You're on," said the gentleman. The gentleman reached inside his wallet and brought out ten hundred dollar bills and laid 'em out 'long the table like a fan. Devol stood up 'n walked over to the center 'o the room. Quite a crowd gathered round 'bout that time 'n was peerin' on, wagerin' bets themselves. "Whenever you're ready, sir" the gambler said and braced his feet apart. Well, the gentleman reared his cane back, its gold knob jus' a-glitterin', and swung it like a scythe a-cutting grass round a farmyard. Whaamp!

That ol' cane came crackin' right 'cross the gambler's forehead, swayed him 'n staggered him back a step or two, but didn't knock him down. Why, there weren't so much more'n a dent o' red in the skin. Ahh's and ooh's o' amazement scattered up from that there crowd. The gentleman stood by, disbelieving. A strike like that should've brought down a steer in a slaughter pen.

"Thank you," was all Devol said and walked back to the table like nothin' more had happened than he'd stubbed his toe, gathered up his money 'n left."

In my imagination I could just hear the cane cracking across the gambler's head. Hank Short had added pictures to his story, slapping himself across the forehead as the cane struck home and reeled back from the fire. I thought back to Swainville and the fight I'd witnessed between Sam and Eric and pondered on what might happen if Sam and the Great Devol butted heads together, each one bragging they had the hardest heads along the river.

Seeing how Hank Short had spent more of his life along the river than on the land, I decided on asking him about the *Channel Belle*, checking on Uncle Frank's old tale and seeing if it was true.

"The *Channel Belle*?" Hank Short said after I'd asked him about her. "Why, sure I 'member the *Channel Belle*. It weren't that long ago, jus' after the war began, when she went down carryin' cargo 'n cases 'o silver bars and gold coins bound for N'Orleans."

So the tale Uncle Frank had told was true all right–about the gold at least–I hadn't doubted the truth about the boat.

"Can you tell me where she lays?" I asked.

Hank Short got a glimmering flicker in his eyes and searched me over for a time.

"Got it into your young head to go lookin' for the *Channel Belle* maybe, boy?" he smiled. "Well, if'n you can find her grave you're a darn sight better man than most. Folks been lookin' for her since

'62 'n ain't never found her yet. River's flooded heavy more'n a dozen times since then. She's buried right heavy under mud 'n sand. Ain't nobody goin' to find the *Channel Belle*. But," he said, tilting over to one side and leaning against his elbow, his free hand reaching inside his coat. "I can show you a piece 'o her." And from out of the flowing folds, he pulled a coin. It was shiny like a brass lamp that's just been polished. An Eagle–a ten-dollar gold piece.

"This here Eagle," Hank Short said, handing it over to Jamie and me to look at, "come from the *Channel Belle*. Found it while stompin' a bar one day 'bout ten years back. There it was sittin' bold as you please, high 'n dry 'long the sand. It's my lucky piece. Never spend it 'n with it I'm never broke."

I looked it over closely, then handed it to Jamie who glanced it over and passed it back to me. It was gold and beautiful; shiny like it just came off the coin press, but the date on it said 1860.

"How do you know it came from the *Channel Belle*?" I asked our visitor.

"You a-doubtin' the word 'o Hank Short, boy?" I'd never been good at tact. Aunt Addie had told me that. "I know 'cause I found it where she sank, and I know where she sank 'cause I looked for her once," he said, sounding a bit hurt, like my questioning him was calling him a liar or, at least, I was accusing him of telling some tall tale. "The river shifts," he began, "'n over time some parts get deeper, other parts dry up. My guess is when she snagged herself, she split bottom 'n dumped her cargo, the gold boxes bein' in the lower hold. Over the years, 'n with the river floodin', those boxes come open 'n this here piece washed up. Most 'o that gold's either at the bottom or washed all the way down to the delta by now."

"But what if it isn't?" I asked. "What if that gold's still there? What if someone can find it yet?"

"Whoa, young'un! You're askin' a parcel lot o' questions."

Hank Short leaned back and was thoughtful for a time. "Reckon maybe she could be found if'n a body knowed right where to look."

"But you know where she lies. You just told us so," I clamored.

"I said I know 'bout where she lies, not the spot exact. All I know is she's underwater. And if'n she's under water, how's a body gonna find her and dig her out? You answer me that, boy." It was a question that was hard to answer.

"But what if she's dry?" I asked, keeping up the pressure on him.

"Who's goin' a-diggin' through twenty foot 'o sand 'n mud?"

Hank Short answered. "A body'd have to know the spot exact."

"Can you tell me about where she lies? Where was it you found the Eagle?"

"Well, I reckon I can tell you that. Found the piece restin' on a shoal bar near the end 'o an ol' channel cutoff. Now where was that spot exact?" He set into scratching his temple with the knuckle of his right hand, pondering on it long. "Reckon it was 'bout five miles southward from a place called The Landin'. Can't recall right clear. It was a time ago, boy. Was at the mouth 'o a channel cutoff. That I'm sure of."

I pumped Hank Short until he ran dry of answers. I couldn't get him any closer on a reckoning of where the *Channel Belle* might lie than south five miles from somewhere called "The Landing" at the mouth of a cutoff channel.

The coffee pot had run dry, and the hour was growing late. Our visitor had talked on, rambling like a non-stop stage with a tight schedule to meet. The three of us were all tuckered out. I added a stick or two of wood, just enough to keep the fire burning low, and the warmth coming out when it died down to embers.

"You'll stay the night?" Jamie asked Hank Short. He seemed to like him.

"A tired man thanks you for the invite, boy," he said with a hearty thanks. I passed him one of the blanket rolls and we laid back to our separate dreams.

The morning came, cold and brisk, but there was no snow in the air. The sky was a cloudless, pale blue. Our fire had burned down to cold ashes in the night and stirring around and rousting ourselves out of the blanket rolls was a might uncomfortable. There were only the two of us–Jamie and me. Hank Short was gone. He'd probably stolen away at sunrise as sudden as he'd come on us the night before. The blanket roll I'd given him was gone, too.

"I wish he'd stayed," Jamie said. "I was going to ask Mr. Mertinger and Clarke-Jiles if maybe they'd have a job for him. He seemed like a nice enough man, and he could have used the work."

I recollected Aunt Addie's words about wanderers in the desert. "I don't think Hank Short's cut out for work," I told Jamie, "least not the steady sort." Our conversation turned to other things and thoughts about our mysterious visitor were set aside.

We packed up our camping gear and without making breakfast, headed back down from Mason's Overlook toward town.

For the next couple of days, Jamie kept quiet about the plans I'd told him about leaving Waytown and going back to live where I'd been born--Pop's old cabin--and where I seemed to be most comfortable--the river. I'd been putting off my plan to tell Clarke-Jiles, not being certain how he'd react to my going home. I still wasn't sixteen and I didn't know how the law would look toward my leaving. But I'd made up my mind to leave and got up the nerve to tell Clarke-Jiles so.

Telling Clarke-Jiles my plan didn't seem to bother him. To be truthful, he didn't seem at all surprised.

"I had a feeling you were hankering to leave Waytown," he said after I told him what Jamie and I had talked about. Clarke-Jiles had just helped Mr. Mertinger close up the mercantile, ushering the last of the customers out and bolting the framed glass doors behind them.

Mr. Mertinger had been teaching Clarke-Jiles all about the business he and Aunt Addie had run, seeing as how Clarke-Jiles was an educated man--a high school graduate with a signed diploma hanging framed above his work desk to prove it. It was an accomplishment he was powerfully proud of. He was always saying how important a good education was and in that, he sounded like Pop. His own family, having been raised up serving the plantation owners and working the cotton and tobacco fields, never had the chance to learn. Clarke-Jiles was different, though.

Having learned to work hard, side by side in the fields with his folks when he was only five or six, getting his schooling at a free school for black folk following the War, then coming to work for Aunt Addie had given him a real sense of responsibility. Now he had Jamie to care for and raise, and a mighty handsome sum of money to look after. He was in charge of Jamie's inheritance, not to mention his own, which Aunt Addie had left him. Mr. Mertinger reckoned he'd make a downright fine accountant, having caught on lightning fast to bookkeeping chores.

With the store closed and locked, Jamie, who helped sweep up after school off somewhere with a group of friends, Clarke-Jiles sat down to talk with me a spell.

"I knew you'd be moving on someday," he said, sitting behind his work desk in the ledger room and me pulling up a stool beside him.

"I didn't reckon on it being quite so soon. Of course, with Miss Addie gone, the world's been topsie-turvied a might more than any of us thought. Matters are different now. Where I used to curry down the horses and run errands for Miss Addie, now I'm tending store and keeping ledgers. Jamie's sprouting like pokeweed in a bean patch and I've never raised a youngster before. Just looking out for him and his money interests will soon enough be a full-time task. Lawyer Settles has agreed to help, but it's a powerful responsibility."

"I don't want you thinking I'm leaving," I told him, "because of you and Jamie. It's just that ..." Clarke-Jiles smiled that broad, warm grin of his and shot his hand up, cutting off my words.

"It's just that you're a boy; a young boy who's restless and wants to be at home." I glanced around while he paused to fire up his pipe. "Maybe," he said, after a few thoughtful puffs, "if you'd been in Waytown longer, and Miss Addie'd live, well, maybe you'd feel this was home. And, Clayt, it is your home whenever you want it to be. Jamie and I will be here for quite a spell to come, and you're always welcome to come stay with us whenever you have a hankering."

We small-talked together for a time then I told him my plans. I'd be moving back to Pop's old river cabin–providing Uncle Frank wasn't still there–maybe take up Pop's old trade of fishing, myself becoming a riverman.

"I reckon there's nothing amiss with that," Clarke-Jiles allowed. "You're fast on sixteen and old enough. The law might look on it differently, but I'm not going to tell them. Why, there's boys your age working sixteen hours alongside their fathers; some not much older are settling down and getting married. I don't think that's good, but it's the way the world works."

I promised Clarke-Jiles I'd write him often and keep in touch with happenings between him and Jamie.

"You'll do right fine for yourself, I reckon," he said, "and if you don't, there's always Waytown to come back to."

Even though I'd only known Jamie for a short while, I'd grown to look on him like a brother. And Clarke-Jiles, too, was a special sort of man; warm and friendly and even-tempered, always smiling even when he was being serious. It was going to be hard to leave them. And leaving Marie behind wasn't going to be easy either. We'd come to liking one another a lot.

The next afternoon, I met Marie by lingering near the schoolhouse.

I'd spent the most part of the day at the mercantile helping Mr. Mertinger unload packing crates of store goods that had come in by express wagon and sweeping up in back and setting the storeroom straight. By three o'clock, I'd set off toward the school, arriving just before the bell sounded.

The morning had opened with a blustery breeze blowing in from the north, threatening snow, but only a few sparse flakes had fluttered down. By afternoon the wind had slowed, the sky settling into an ivory white with a parcel of gray-edged clouds hanging down like muddy cotton puffs.

Marie stepped out from the schoolhouse door amid a gaggle of laughing girls. Her coat collar was hunched up against the chill and her hand hidden in pink knit mittens. Her best friend, Marcie Allen, was first to see me leaning against the picket gate. The other girls saw me, too, and set in to tittering and smiling amongst themselves.

"Mind if I walk a girl home?" I asked Marie as she came up.

"That depends, Clayton Sievers, on which girl you mean," she said. And she smiled. I saw another girl nudge an elbow into Marcie Allen. They bent their heads low together, whispering. Marcie shot a wink toward Marie, then the other girls started up the road toward town.

"Oh! That Marcie Allen!" Marie snapped, pretending to be angry. "Sometimes I could just kick her! She says you're sweet on me."

"I am," I said.

"That doesn't give her the right to say it all the time."

We ambled on up the road, far behind the others. All the school kids except the group of girls Marie liked had vanished fast as a flock of sparrows seeing a hawk as soon as school was out. I knew Jamie was among them somewhere, but I hadn't seen him. Or maybe he'd stayed behind.

"Marie," I said, "I got to talk to you."

"You are talking to me, Clayton Sievers. Or hadn't you noticed?" She shot her 'little girl' smile at me which disappeared when she saw I had something serious to say. "What is it, Clayt?" she asked.

"I'm leaving Waytown. Tomorrow. I'm going home."

"Home? But Waytown is your home. Clarke-Jiles, Jamie and you."

"I'm going back where I was born. To my Pop's cabin along the river."

"But why? There can't be anything there but some old cabin. There are no people there."

"There's people. Mrs. Hawkinds lives just a short piece down the road, and the Meyerses–Ronnie's folks–less than a quarter mile further."

"What have Jamie and Clarke-Jiles said about you leaving?"

"I told them both and they understand."

Marie looked somber. "Is it because of Miss Addie's will?" Daddy's been gloating, seeing he was right about her not leaving you any money."

"She would have left me some if she hadn't died so sudden. The lawyer said so. And I didn't want her money. It's just that I want to go back. There's things I need to do I can't do in Waytown."

"What sort of things?"

"Just things." I shrugged my shoulders. I couldn't tell her because I wasn't sure myself.

"Will you be coming back?" she asked.

"Maybe. Jiles says I'm always welcome here. And I promised I'd write."

"You'd better promise me you'll write, Clayton Sievers. Every other day, or at least once a week."

"I can't promise that often. The way the post is, you might not get a letter until spring. I'll write though if you promise to write back."

"You know I will. I'll tell you everything that's going on with me and Waytown, with school, and Jamie and Clarke-Jiles, too."

We didn't talk for a time. Just walked up the road together, nearing town. Marie held my hand.

A lot of the town kids had gathered at the grocery, hunched up around the woodstove and getting warm. Mr. Huffmeier, the proprietor, ran a fountain there which was popular with kids and adults alike. I bought Marie a cherry phosphate and me one, too. We sat beside one another on stools at the counter. We talked about my plans some more, in general terms, then I walked her home.

We'd come up beside the front porch of her large, gray-boarded house. The front parlor window was half-hidden by the bare branches of winter-dead bushes which ran all along the rail.

"Clayton Sievers," Marie said, looking up at me, "I've never done this to a boy before, and I don't want you thinking you have any special privileges because of it." Suddenly, she put her mittened hands up on my shoulders and kissed me a glancing peck on the cheek, then shot up the porch steps like a startled rabbit. The spot where her lips touched was warm and kind of tingly. "If–if you don't write–I don't know what I'll do with you." she stammered, then disappeared inside, the door clicking closed on its latch behind her.

I strolled along the street back toward Hudson's Mercantile, not knowing what I'd done or said to make her act so strange.

Clarke-Jiles said he'd talk to the schoolmaster about allowing Jamie to come to school late and the next morning, around nine o'clock, the two of them walked me to the stationhouse. Clarke-Jiles purchased me a ticket which would take me about five miles from Pop's cabin. While we waited for the stage to load, he handed me a fistful of dollars.

"For things you'll be needing," he said, smiling his broad smile and settling his arm up along my shoulders. "There's more if you're needing it," he said. "All you need to do is write and ask."

Jamie, who was toting my carpetbag with him, a gift from Mr. Mertinger, handed it to the driver who slung it up on top the coach. I could see I was going to share the coach with five other travelers, so I shook both their hands and clambered aboard so I could get a window seat. A few minutes later there was a whip crack, the driver shouted out to the four-horse team, and I was off. Jamie and Clarke-Jiles stood on the boardwalk in front of the stationhouse, waving as the stage rolled out.

As the stage pulled up the short hill, south toward the river road, I glanced behind to catch a look at Waytown. It was the last I'd be seeing of it for some while.

The crisp late January air and the moisture from the river had settled a white frost over everything. The roofs of the houses and stores looked whitewashed and glinted in the morning sunlight. Fired chimney stoves sent up whorls of white smoke into the ivory-gray sky.

All along the river road, leafless trees hung heavy with the glimmering, crystal frost, their branches, dark-brown or black, looking like fire charred skeletons. An occasional fir tree, its bright green needles hidden beneath a blanket covering of white, flashed past the coach window to become only a vivid memory.

It wasn't too long before I set into kind of a half-sleep. The other passengers on the coach were quiet, a couple glancing now and again out the windows to watch the scenery flow past. One lady sitting across from me knitted on a sweater for her grandson. The old man next to her snorted fitfully in his sleep.

The stage made stops at every small town and village between Waytown and Hortonville, Hortonville being where I'd get off, buy provisions, and walk the remainder of the way to Pop's old cabin. The stage was making a mail run, stopping to drop off a bag of letters and parcels and pick more up, letting off a passenger or two and taking on another. During the slack times between layovers, I lulled. The jolts and bumps of the rutted stage road and the steady clomping of the horses' hooves against the hard pack set me into dreaming about the river and Pop's cabin and being home again.

Six hours after driving out of the Waytown station, the coach pulled into Hortonville. Me and the woman who'd been knitting were the only two remaining who'd boarded early that morning. I knew the layout of Hortonville well. Pop and I had come here often in the past to sell his catch at the open market and buy supplies. Of course, Ronnie, the gang, and I had come to town as often as we'd had money to spend.

With the money Clarke-Jiles had handed me, I headed toward the dry goods store and bought what I'd be needing: flour, dry beans, smoke pork, and bacon. I gathered up some boxes of wooden matches to light the cookstove with and bought a new pair of gloves I'd be needing for the cold winter days. The buying done and the goods loaded in a gunny sack slung across my shoulders, I ambled down to the landing along the river and followed a snowed-over dirt path trail the five miles to the cabin.

Somehow, I hadn't worried about Uncle Frank. That last meeting between me, Aunt Addie and him, I'd got the feeling he wouldn't be lingering long. Still, I wasn't certain of it. But, when I reached the cabin, Uncle Frank was gone.

The cabin appeared to have been deserted for some while. There wasn't any firewood cut and stacked against the cabin wall. The outhouse doors were flung open wide and heaped with a drift of snow that'd gusted inside. The cabin was dark and cold and bare. Uncle Frank had taken everything that was useful to him when he left. But the cooking gear was there–the pots and the cast iron skillet and the plates and cups–but I couldn't find the spoons, forks, or knives anywhere. The cookstove was heaped full of cold ashes. Shoveling those out and cutting kindling for the fire were the first things I did to set the household right. There was oil enough for the lamps, and by the time darkness fell, the cabin was lit and warm and cheery as I'd remembered it when Pop and I were together.

What we want is to see the child in pursuit of knowledge, and not knowledge in pursuit of the child.
–George Bernard Shaw

CHAPTER 16

Passing Time at Home. The Search for the *Channel Belle*.

DEPENDING ON HOW A BODY feels about life along the river, time can pass quick or slow.

Having been born and raised along the river's banks, knowing every bend and twist of its easy-flowing channel for near two dozen miles in both directions of Pop's old cabin, I felt a deep love for the river.

Pop had said in many ways the rivers is like a woman; always sturdy, yet sometimes fragile, fickle and unpredictable in turns, often restive, at moments violent raging, but most often calm and placid and loving.

The river is the flow of life itself. Pop always reckoned it had a personality all its own and called it 'she.' But I'd been along it, too, and ventured some along its shoals and bars and banks, experienced its easy-going life and its violence, too. I'd met some of the people that passed up and down along it, seen its moods, felt its currents, and experienced joy and sorrow on it. In many ways, the river was a mirror reflecting life. It wasn't, however, a personality but a thing; a thing of Nature and a thing that'd been born of God. In my thoughts about it, Pop and I disagreed. To him the river was 'she',a woman-like being. To me, it was just 'the river.' I loved it, however, as much as he had.

Almost five months had passed since I'd last seen Jamie and Clarke-Jiles, been at the church for Aunt Addie's funeral and at the cemetery for her laying-away. I'd sent a couple of letters to Marie via the post in town and had received many back. Things were going well for her, she said, and because Jamie was such a poor writer–loving the books he read, but hating letter writing–Marie kept me posted on his doings, too.

I'd grown since I'd seen them last, standing now at nine inches past five feet, and had filled out some. The river life agreed with me.

I'd wintered in Pop's cabin. This winter had been a particularly easy one; I hadn't needed to lay up in the cabin for long stretches of days on end, but had gotten out to walk along the bank, fish, and watch the ice flows drift past the landing.

There were times when it snowed heavily, though. On those times I'd hole up inside, near the crackling and spitting warmth of the pinewood fire and read. Pop had loved to read, doing a lot of it when he was sober. He wasn't the reader Jamie was by any stretch, but he could read, and he'd enjoyed it.

Pop had laid away a good collection of books. He'd read parts of them aloud to me when I was small. Now that I wasn't in school and under Old Man Dodson's glowering eye, not being forced to read and cipher, I found I enjoyed it more.

Among the dozen or so books shelved above Pop's favorite chair was a red-leather copy of *The Collected Works of Shakespeare*. Mother's name was penned in a fine-flowing hand just inside the cover. I'd never read any Shakespeare, and I admit the reading was mighty rough, the language not being mine and sounding strange and different from what I was used to. Mother had folded down the corner points of some of the pages, no doubt marking off her favorite plays, and I read those first. One of them was titled *A Midsummer Night's Dream*, and I liked it a lot, mainly because of the venturings of the fairies in a wild and tangled forest and all the trouble they caused which turned out right fine in the end. But my best-liked play was *Romeo and Juliet*, a love tale with a mighty sad ending about a comely girl a sight younger than Marie and a handsome boy my age from the feuding House of Montague.

I'd had to read it several times through before I could understand it all and before I could see how the ending wasn't fixed and it always set me into dreaming. The dream was always with Marie as Juliet and me as Romeo together at the end–but without the dying.

In some ways we were similar; me coming from the wrong family and Mr. Ellis, like Juliet's father, not wanting any doings with the 'House of River Boy'. During the months I'd wintered along the river, I hadn't been a hermit. I'd walked the short road down to Mrs. Hawkinds' place and visited with her a spell. She treated me to home-baked rolls and the put-up jams and jellies she was famous for.

Emma Hawkinds had aged some since I'd seen her last. She was going on toward seventy and looking every bit her age. Bad bouts with rheumatism had laid her low for quite a spell and it was obvious she wasn't feeling well. Her last daughter, Jenny Ann, had gotten married to the liveryman in Hortonville. Mrs. Hawkinds said Jenny Ann had wanted her to close her home and come to town to live with them, but she wouldn't hear of that. "Parents haven't a right to go bothering their youngsters less'n it's necessary," she told me. Emma Hawkinds was a strong-willed woman, a river woman, caring for herself, insisting on staying put and living by herself until she wasn't able anymore. Jenny Ann visited her often though, bringing needed goods from town and staying with her when she was laid up in bed.

Uncle Frank had called on her before he left, she said. He wasn't a happy man, she recalled, saying how he ranted on and bad-mouthed me after Ronnie and I had slipped away, and again when he'd come back from Waytown. "An ungrateful welp," he'd called me, "deserving of the wrath of God." Seeing how's Mrs. Hawkinds had gotten only one side of the story, I told her mine.

Noting how she couldn't any longer help herself as much as she was used to, I worked double duty chopping wood for her and me as well. In a week's time I'd laid up enough kindling and stove wood alongside her house to last her quite a spell. And I did some repairing chores, too, fixing some busted windows, putting a handrailing on her porch and patching up some shingles where the roof leaked. She offered to pay me for the work, but I didn't take the offer. She'd done a lot for Pop and me, and I was grateful for it.

The hardest thing I did though was getting up nerve enough to visit Ronnie's folks and tell them how he died.

There was a new grave in the Meyers family plot–a wood-fenced cemetery I had to pass by to come up to their cabin. It'd seen the burying of Mrs. Meyers's folks, Mr. Meyers's youngest brother who'd died in an accident a short while after returning home from the war, and a parcel of new-born children. The earth was mounded neat on top of the new grave and a simple white granite marker announced who lay beneath:

MOLLY MEYERS
and the date of her birth and death. It was Ronnie's mother.

The entire family was at home when I arrived: Mr. Meyers; Annabel, the oldest daughter, who, at sixteen, was turning into quite a specimen of womanhood; Crystal who looked like her mother; the twins, Tracy, and Trent; and 'course, the youngest, Micky. The only one missing from the gathering was Johnny and, of course, Ronnie, who I'd come to tell them about.

There was quite a ruckus when I arrived unannounced and poked my head in through the door. Mr. Meyers, who I thought would be like to throttle me because Ronnie and I'd run off, greeted me with a handclasp a brown bear couldn't scarcely match. He seemed mighty pleased to see me. I could gather from his look he knew there was something wrong when Ronnie wasn't with me.

He didn't ask any questions, just set the two girls into brewing up a kettle of spiced cider and setting out some rum cakes Crystal had just baked.

"So," Mr. Meyers said, sitting in his easy chair nearby the spitting fire, "the river boy's come home." He nestled up real cozy into the hide-covered seat and lit up his briar pipe with a flash stick from the fire.

Ronnie's father had a reputation along the river of being a hard dealing man. A loving husband and a good provider for his large family, he'd been a might heavy-handed with his sons. That was the reason Johnny had set out on his own and Ronnie had run off with me. On this afternoon, however, he seemed unusually calm and quiet.

"Seein' how's Ronnie didn't see fit to comin' back with you," he said, starting up the conversation again, "least maybe you can tell me what he's doin'."

I felt more than a might uncomfortable and squirmed a little in my chair. The twins and Michael had come over and sat around their father on the floor. I didn't know where to start or how to make the telling easier, so I came right out with it.

"Ronnie's dead," I said. A hush fell over the room and the cabin was completely silent for a moment. Crystal had come up with a plate of cakes, and Annabel, who'd been pouring cider, stopped.

"Ronnie died in the river flood last year saving the lives of a woman and her daughter caught on a steamboat wreck," I told them.

Mr. Meyers sank back, thoughtful, in his chair. "The *Aster Queen*," he said with unusual softness for a riverman, "I heard tell of it."

From behind me Annabel began to cry. The twins shot silent glances at one another, and Michael, who didn't know Ronnie well, sat silent, looking toward his father.

"Ronnie's dead," Mr. Meyers repeated, mostly to himself. Then after some time he said, "We had our differences, and heaven knows I was a might heavy handed with him, but I always liked that boy."

He asked when and where and how it happened and I told him, building Ronnie's memory up real fine, without overdoing any. I told them about our stay out on the land point and our finding the sunken packet boat and all about the flood and Ronnie's rescue of Mrs. Ellis. Everyone listened in rapt attention.

"I reckon how that sounds like the boy," Mr. Meyers voiced, thoughtfully tapping the burnt-up ashes from his pipe bowl. "Took a lot after his ma, always doin' things for others. That's what the Good Book says to do, and I guess he done it. Seems a might hard though. First Johnny goes off to the Lord knows where, don't know how to write him 'bout his ma. The wife died two months back, and now you come to tell me Ronnie's dead." After a long pause he said, "I reckon there's no second-guessing the will of God. You'll be comin' to the funeral service, I reckon?"

Funeral service? The words carried a mighty peculiar sound. How could you have a funeral service without a body? Then Mr. Meyers went on to make it clear.

"A man ought to have something to show for his livin', and I guess Ronnie deserves a place next to his ma. I'll cut a wooden marker 'til I get into town to get a proper one."

I thought I'd best be leaving, considering the circumstances, but Mr. Meyers wouldn't let me. So, I stayed at the Meyers's place for several hours, telling about my stay in Waytown and the friends and family I'd found there. Mr. Meyers was interested most in Clarke-Jiles, a man who'd been born into slavery and who'd truly found emancipation under President Lincoln's order. Many hadn't, especially those living further south in the heart of what had been plantation country, free, but forced to work for a meager living and a far sight from being equal. Mr. Meyers allowed how it was a good thing, he not having any prejudices to a body's color or religion, so long as they didn't impose themselves or their beliefs on his propriety. In that way of thinking, he was just like Pop.

"What counts," he said after I told him about Clarke-Jiles's inheritance and his seeing to Jamie's affairs, "is what a body is for real–on the inside–and how he deals with folks. That's what matters. Are they good folk, hard workers, and worthy of respect?" I allowed how Clarke-Jiles was all of those and more. Clarke-Jiles was a friend. And family.

Before I left for home, Mr. Meyers went out to the shed and found a piece of lumber to use as Ronnie's headstone until he could buy a real one like he'd said. He'd plane it smooth, then carve in the letters that'd be Ronnie's name and dates. The stonemason in Hortonville would chisel the real ones in stone.

That Sunday after Meeting, Reverend Archibald Dooley, who'd taken over the parish when Parson Briggs left Hortonville for Waytown, presided over Ronnie's graveside service. The day was bright and cloudless, only the slightest hint of a breeze blowing in from across the river.

Reverend Dooley was a short, stout-set man, dressed entirely in black from head to foot except for the white-collar piece he wore that marked him as a man of God. Standing next to Mr. Meyers, who was a thick-muscled mountain of a man, the preacher appeared almost like a boy. Of course, too, he was younger by some dozen years and without the gray sprinkles in his hair that Mr. Meyers had.

The family had turned out, looking sad, and dressed in their go-to-meeting best. The suit Aunt Addie had bought me and which I thought I'd never use again, came in mighty handy. It'd been Clarke-Jiles who'd told me to pack it with me and I was glad he did. "A body should dress fine when the occasion comes," he'd said. "Clothes are what folks look at first and pass their judgment on. If you're dressed well, they take you for a man of substance. A mean-dressed man is looked down on."

The service was short but meaningful. Though the Reverend Dooley had never known Ronnie, he recalled he was a fine boy and a credit to his family. While Ronnie wasn't the finest student, he'd showed a zest for life, he said, giving love and friendship to others. That's what mattered in the eyes of God, he told. He read from the Twenty-third Psalm and recited the Lord's Prayer, those gathered around joining in. He was certain, he commented, that for all he'd done, Ronnie was now living enclosed in the loving arms of his Almighty Father, in a sun-lit city paved with streets of gold. The service was mighty fine.

Ronnie would've liked it. I had a feeling how maybe he was there, in spirit form, to witness it. Following the doings at the cemetery, the family wandered off with the Reverend Dooley. I lingered for a time nearby. Mr. Meyers had done a proper job on Ronnie's makeshift marker.

RONALD WAYNE MEYERS
1873 - 1888
LOST WHILE REDEEMING LIFE

The words were engraved deep into the wooden marker-board and blackened with paint so they stood out. Wayne. It seemed odd, but I'd never known Ronnie's middle name.

I'd told Mr. Meyers about Emma Hawkinds' troubles and he allowed how he'd look in on her from time to time and have the twins do chores for her. They were only turned eleven, but they'd learned responsibility working side by side, taking responsibility with the household chores and helping him as might be needed.

Things had changed some around home. When the weather was favorable, I scouted out the gang to renew the friendships and tell them about Ronnie's passing. Only Sam Johnston and Charlie Michaels were left.

"You know, ol' Mike Dearson got hisself married up," Charlie told me the afternoon the three of us were together near Bertram's Levee. "Married Bessy Toole some months back." Mike Dearson married. Ol' Mike with the puckered lip and lisping voice. And Bessy Toole, a good-looker, too! It was a wonder.

"Can't say right where he's livin'—somewheres inland a piece,"

Sam recalled.

The more we talked, the more I saw how things had changed. Charlie Michaels seemed almost as care-free as ever, cracking jokes and telling tales. Sam Johnston appeared more sober. While he wasn't in trouble at home, he said how he was thinking about moving out, being on his own. Like the river, the gang was changing. I pondered some on thoughts of Ronnie, how, had he lived, he might be changing, too.

Nearly fifteen dollars was left out of the money Clarke-Jiles had given me. With some of it I bought additional provisions from the store in Hortonville, closed Pop's cabin, and left the landing in a skiff I'd purchased from a man in town. It cost five dollars, was worn out and had seen its better days, but it would get me to where I was going.

It was the first of June when I closed and latched the cabin door and sauntered to the landing to pack the skiff. The sky was bright and endless blue with not a cloud in sight. For eight months, throughout the late fall and the wintertime, I hadn't felt the hotness of the sun on my naked skin. The brownness of the summer before had left me. The first thing I did before leaving the landing one last time was drop the suspender straps and doff my shirt. I kept the shirt nearby, knowing I'd need to slip it on again before too long to keep from getting burned.

It wasn't going to be easy, searching out the *Channel Belle*. Her wreck was the real reason I'd left Waytown. From the stories Uncle Frank had told, and what Hank Short had said about her, I had some idea where she lay. With some work, and luck, I might find a piece of her. At least enough to make the search worthwhile.

The river was a delight to be floating on again, seeing how it was a year since I'd been on it last. The warming, early-summer sun drifted down on me, slowly restoring the light-brown color my skin had lost. The river hadn't changed. It really never did. New bars and sandbanks cropped up here and there, and the channel shifted time to time like the undulating coils of a snake, but the river itself remained the same.

The only difference between this trip and others I'd made was I was working the river alone. Before, I'd always been on the river either with Pop and, later, Ronnie. I should've been lonesome, but I wasn't. Drifting along, nuzzling against the bankside as close as possible to keep from the current's tug, I began to notice even more of the river than I had before. Fox, raccoon, and whitetail tracks lined the banks where the water had receded some and left behind a mud slope. I discovered, if a body was careful enough, he could even catch sight of birds' nests holding young ones. The nests had been built in the low brush branches which lined the riverbank. About old enough to fly, the young birds, all fat and feathery, peeped and cheeped, peering from their leafy hideaways, waiting for their parents to bring them food. Whenever I came too close, a parent bird would set into a flutter of excitement–chirping loud, even diving low across the water in front of me to draw my attention away.

Signs of beavers' work lay all along the bank. Small willow saplings and cottonwoods were gnawed clean through. Their chiseled stumps stood dying along the shore. The river was alive with sights and sounds, the smell of evergreen and cedar. It was early summer. With the river coming alive, I had no thoughts of loneliness. I grew to appreciate the freedom and the solitude.

Always I laid the skiff in toward the land side, keeping out of the current that would drag me back. I'd row for a couple of hours then tie up and rest a spell before pulling out again. With dusk setting in, I'd lay up along a sand shoal, build a fire out of driftwood, cook up a plate of beans and smoke-pork, and sleep until dawn the next morning.

On the middle of the third day out, I sighted the land point where Ronnie and I had stayed but passed it by without looking at it close. Too many painful memories came flooding back, so I headed on. Ronnie and I had made the point in one day's travel, the two of us rowing together, catching one another a breather from time to time. Rowing by myself and stopping to rest or camp made the headway slower. I wasn't used to all the work.

Waytown lay some sixty miles south by river from St. Louis, and Hortonville about forty south from Waytown. Somewhere between lay the rotting hulk of the *Channel Belle*. I hoped to find her, but the finding wasn't going to be a lark. Others had searched her out without luck. Leastwise, I was going to try.

One evening, while camped out along the shoreline where the river had cut an inlet, after finishing up my supper meal, I sat down beside the fire to read. I'd packed a couple of books along that Pop had had, figuring I'd read them in the quiet hours. One was a thin book titled *Essays and Counsels, Civil and Moral*, by a man who'd lived in England two-hundred years before, Sir Francis Bacon. I wasn't certain what the 'Sir' stood for, and if it was a name, it was sure a funny one. Most of the writings in the book were short and all started with the word 'of' in headings. There was "Of Truth," "Of Love," "Of Marriage and Single Life," and several more. I settled for reading one called "Of Studies," which was only one page long. The page top had been curled over, whether by Pop or by my mother, I didn't know. I read it over several times, thinking about each idea, the book's thin page illuminated by the growing moonlight.

The reading wasn't difficult, though there were some words I didn't know and had no way of finding out their meaning. But most of what I read made sense. Two things I read stood out as being important: "studies perfect nature and are perfected by experience: for natural abilities are like natural plants that need pruning by study; and studies themselves do give forth directions too much at large, except they be bounded in by experience." Thinking back on my time in Old Man Dodson's schoolroom, it seemed all his knowledge came from books. And he'd used heavy-handed ways to teach it. This Sir Francis Bacon spoke about that, too, and it hit Mr. Dodson straight on the nail head. "To spend too much time in studies is sloth; to use them too much for ornament is affectation; to make judgment wholly by their rules is the humor of a scholar." I thought I understood it, but I couldn't find the humor in the schoolmaster.

One other sentence I found struck like what Pop had told me, and it too had come from Bacon. "Reading maketh a full man, conference a ready man, and writing an exact man." Suddenly, lying in the moonlight, I found Pop's own words floating back to me. "I want you to get that schoolin' a yours," he'd said. "Schoolin's mighty important and I don't want you to grow up bein' just a stupid riverman like me."

In education, I'd gone beyond what Pop had had, completing the ninth grade. Pop had made it through sixth grade and started on the seventh when family matters went bad, and he was forced to leave. When he married Mom, who'd finished up her studies, she spent time teaching him a lot of the learning he'd missed. Pop had allowed, had things gone different with him, he would have been a businessman in some town along the river, maybe even St. Louis, rather than fishing his life away on it.

Those thoughts floating through my head, I decided, right there and then, squatting on a sandbar in the river, I was going to return to school. It didn't matter if I found the *Channel Belle* or not or harvested up her treasure. Rich or poor, I was going to become the kind of man Pop had wanted me to be. An educated man. Like Clarke-Jiles, I was going to hang a diploma on my wall.

Where the *Channel Belle* lay wrecked, I wasn't exactly certain. If she lay underwater, like Hank Short had said she might, I knew I'd never find her.

From what little I could remember Uncle Frank having told me, and the directions I'd been able to pull out of Hank Short from his visit with Jamie and me that night on Mason's Overlook, I knew she lay up a cutoff from the old river channel.

To anyone willing to listen, it wasn't hard to learn about the river's changing moods. Oft-times, experience was the better teacher. Uncle Frank had spent forty years moving along the river selling wares. Pop had lived nearly thirty on it passing up and down its banks on rafts and in fishing skiffs. Hank Short had gathered his experience by riding lumber rafts when he'd been a logger and for a spell as a crewman on the great steamboats. I'd listened to all three of them and learned the river's ways.

In my mind I patched together what must have happened the night the *Channel Belle* went down.

It had to have been a foggy night. The captain, grown weary from the day-watch run, had settled into his cabin for the night, leaving the pilot in the wheelhouse to steer the river. Considering the value of the cargo it was carrying, and the destination it was bound for, both the pilot and the captain should've been on watch that night.

The river shifts constantly, like a living thing. It changes depth by shifting mud and sand 'round with its current. New bars and shoals develop overnight, and old ones vanish. Heading upstream, the main channel might be on one side and on the downstream trip scarce a few days later, the channel may have shifted to the other, or be somewhere in the middle. Log jams and snags spring up which a body has to be constantly watchful for.

With a heavy fog that night, fog-patches settling in here and there and the moonlight shining down, throwing deceptive shadows, the pilot on the *Channel Belle* steered a wrong turn. It's easy enough to do. Thinking he was still in the main channel, which on that trip churned the downstream side near into shore, in fact, he'd run the cutoff.

The ship was loaded heavy and running faster than she should have in the fog. The water in the cutoff was growing shallow. A brutish snag, perhaps a whole, uprooted tree, had jammed into the bottom mud where the channel had been a few days earlier. The river bottom was rising up, the steamboat's paddle churning half-speed. The snag was waiting for the *Channel Belle*. A sudden shudder must have rumbled through the boat as the claws of the heavy snag ripped its bottom open, sending the river showering into her hold. Held fast, but not knowing she was sinking, the pilot ordered the engines stopped.

About this time, the captain, knocked loose from his bed, was charging up the wheelhouse stairs in his sleeping suit, cursing up a storm. In my mind, the scene was like a vivid dream, full of sound and color. By then, the chief engineer had found out the hold was flooding fast and yelled up the voice tube to the wheelhouse. Too late, the captain realized his boat was in a cutoff and the way ahead lay blocked. Barking orders, he commanded the engines fired up and the paddlewheel jerked into full reverse. The cutoff wasn't a narrow spot, but about a quarter-mile wide. Knowing his boat was headed toward the bottom, he chose to steer her into shore and beach her.

There, her valuable cargo could be removed, packed into another boat, and perhaps his own boat could be repaired. Those were the sound thoughts of an experienced river captain. The river, however, had other ideas.

Her bottom seams ripped open, her heavy cargo pulling her down rapidly, the *Channel Belle* was a doomed boat. When the water slapped against her fired-up boilers, it was over. The piercing sound of the explosion barreled through the boat, and she cracked open like an egg. The *Channel Belle* carried no passengers that trip and only a skeleton crew, the authorities not wanting to draw attention to her golden cargo.

She hadn't been a large boat. Perhaps half again as big as the sunken packet boat Ronnie and I had found grounded in the cove some miles back from where I was now.

The engineer and the fireman had been killed right off when her boilers blew. Of the three men left onboard, the deckman, who sounded out the river's depth with a weighted line, had been thrown overboard and was swimming for his life toward shore. The pilot and the captain perhaps had been knocked unconscious by the blast, the sharp-edged shards of the shattered wheelhouse glass cascading down upon them. The *Channel Belle* settled to the bottom fast, taking the captain and the pilot with her.

Leastwise, that's how I imagined it. The deckman, who'd managed to save himself, lived to tell the story as he saw it to the authorities. Hank Short had said the deckman was probably asleep. If he'd done his job correctly, his line soundings would have warned him the bottom was shallowing up and he would've called the wheelhouse. A body's got to be ever watchful on the river.

It was war time, and the nations–the Confederacy and the Union-- were hopelessly divided. The authorities in St. Louis were the only ones who knew the true value of the cargo that'd been lost. With other concerns to worry about, they decided not to search her out.

As Uncle Frank and Hank Short both said, following the war, people heard the tale and began to search. By then, the river had flooded several times. Heavy rains upstream and the spring thaws following winter had moved her hulk around and buried her with sand.

Hank Short had told me where he'd found the gold piece, and, following his directions, I headed there.

Eight days of plodding headway upriver, taking time out to rest from the ache of rowing, and to pitch camp at night somewhere along the bank or on some small tree-studded island in the river brought me within sight of the channel cutoff. Hank Short, who knew the river better than me, had allowed how this cutoff was the only one for a hundred miles along this stretch of river. The other lay south beyond Hortonville, below Pop's cabin. I was headed north.

Once the river forms a cutoff, it seldom becomes a true part of the river again. It was still a cutoff, the river having moved its course permanently further east. What had been low banks of new sand some twenty-five years before was now built up high, and good stands of cottonwood and willow thickets sprouted on them. The river flowed peacefully now and, as I rowed the skiff along, I felt a tingly sensation rise up inside of me. I knew–somewhere along this quarter-mile funnel stretch–I was passing near, or maybe even over the wreck of the *Channel Belle.*

I spent two full weeks oaring the skiff along the banks of the cutoff, allowing nothing to escape my notice. The skiff inched along at a snail's crawl but a foot or two from the bank, beginning at the cutoff mouth and moving to its closed end and up along the opposite side. It was a task and torment I repeated a dozen times. With each sweep past the now-familiar banks, there was nothing new to see. Not a single piece of the *Channel Belle,* nor anything that looked like it'd come off a boat wreck showed itself. All in all, it was mighty discouraging.

Having had no luck making skiff sweeps for several days, I took to walking slowly along the bank, wading in the knee-deep, sometimes chest-deep water, feeling out the bottom with my toes. It proved the most successful way of searching. By the end of the third afternoon of this wading search, I'd brought up all sorts of river treasure.

There was the sand-crusted shell of a long-dead turtle; the broken-off neck of an old whiskey bottle I came near to stepping on; the rusted remains of a Barlow knife some hunter or river wanderer had lost. I even found a nail keg, still in solid shape, maybe fallen from a flatboat a long time back. It still held nails, but they were so rusty they weren't worth saving.

The river had sludged in a lot from the time this section had been the channel. I'd given up on the wading search, having located nothing of value. Along with my provisions I'd brought the ax from Pop's cabin, using it for cutting the firewood I burned at night. With it I cut a pike-thin pole. I rested the oars inside the skiff and used the pole to push the skiff along the middle of the cutoff. Hoping maybe it'd strike against something solid–the planking of a sunken riverboat–I used it to probe the bottom. Even with the sand and river mud that had shifted in, plugging the cutoff in the first place, the water was shallow in most places.

My search was getting nowhere. After several hours of poling the skiff and probing around the bottom, I'd hole up and rest a spell. I was always plum discouraged and tuckered out.

It was nearing the end of June. I'd been out along the river for nearly a month. And for a month, I'd come up empty handed.

Looking for the *Channel Belle* wasn't all work. I took time for some pleasure, too. I didn't have any real fishing gear–a cane pole or anything–but made do with a pole cut from the branch of a tree, and some line I always carried in my pocket, along with a sharp-barbed hook folded in a bit of heavy paper. On a hot afternoon, after a long day's searching, I'd stalk around the riverside of the cutoff and lay out the line and fish. The river was alive with fish, and I never had a problem poling out a channel cat or bullhead or carp for the evening's supper meal.

On one such afternoon, the river brought some visitors. A man and his boy, about thirteen I'd guess, came poling a small raft from the down-current side and landed on the bank where I was fishing.

The man I judged was in his middle thirties and appeared to be a riverman. He had a mustache and wore scuffed-up leather boots. The boy was rail slender and, like me, barefoot, shirtless, and browned like a leather saddle.

"Haloo there," the man called out as the raft came scraping up to shore. "Mind if the boy and me come ashore for a spell?"

Of course, I reckoned I didn't mind. The river's free, and they were the first folks I'd seen close up for the longest time.

"How's the fishing?" the boy asked, dragging himself naked footed up the bank.

"Can't complain. Caught two yellow cat. That's enough for supper."

"You live 'round here?" the man asked, coming over and sitting next to the boy who'd squatted next to me.

"No", I said. "Came upriver from down south a piece, heading north."

"Seems we're doin' the same, 'cept we're heading down," the boy said.

"I'm Cal Benson," the man said. He held out his boot-sole hard hand for me to shake. I took it and introduced myself. "My son here's Jason. I was kind of hoping you lived 'round here and could tell a man where he might find work."

"You're not a riverman then?" I asked. He sure enough looked like one.

"A riverman? No," he kind of snort-laughed out, "I wouldn't know the first thing about the river. I'm a wheelwright by trade. Times being hard where I come from, and working for another man, I lost my job a month back. The boy and I've been riding the river since."

I was sorry to hear it. A man with a boy to support and being out of work can be mighty hard to take. "Most of the towns along here are small," I said, "don't know if you'd find much work. There's Hortonville, about thirty or forty miles down that's got a blacksmith's shop. You might try there."

"Mighty grateful for the tip," Cal Benson said. "I think I'll do just that."

They stayed some and rested up. We talked a spell and I even let Jason use my pole and do some fishing. It was obvious from the way he cast the line out he hadn't done much fishing. I showed him how and he seemed mighty pleased. He was a quiet sort who didn't talk much. I even invited them to stay for supper.

"Thanks for the invitation," Mr. Benson said, "but we'd best be moving on. I figure we can get another eight to ten miles before nightfall. Sooner I find work, sooner I can send for Jason's mother back in Bridgeway. She wanted to come along, but a raft trip's too much for a woman."

I could see they were pretty well provisioned, or I would've offered up some food, though I didn't have a lot to give away. They might not know the river, but the weather was good, and I reckoned they'd make out fine.

It'd been some pleasure having folks to talk to. Living along the river gets mighty lonely at times. The two of them laid by only about an hour, then set off again.

"I want you to have my fishing pole," I said to Jason. "It'll give you something to do while you're on the raft."

His brown eyes lit up bright. "Gee, thanks!" he beamed. It was like I'd given him a dollar.

I watched as the boy pushed the raft into the river, jumped onboard and kept a lookout until it rounded a knob-bend below the cutoff and vanished out of sight.

At about the middle of the cutoff, a low sand shoal had pushed up from the riverbed. It was nearly bare except for a single elm about thirty feet tall that'd sprouted from it, surrounded by weeds and wildflowers and grasses.

I could only make a guess on how far the *Channel Belle* had come, steaming backward from the blind end of the funnel before she exploded and settled to the bottom. I thought on it for a long spell. A feeling, no more really than a fleet-footed passing thought, settled over me as I moved along the island. If the *Channel Belle* was anywhere, it was here.

The day drawing on toward dusk, I shored the skiff and set up camp at the bottom of the elm on the island. I soaked a small pot of dry, white beans in the drinking water I carried with me and filleted the cats I'd caught. Then I set off to find some wood to build a fire.

The island was only about two-hundred feet long and maybe a third as wide. Wood along this stretch of sand was scarce and I found but a few small sticks of scrap that had drifted down and lodged into the sand. They were dry and brittle, bleached stark white, and cracked open in deep splits by the sun. They were enough to get the fire started but not enough to keep it burning long.

I guess I could have rowed across to the other side and hewed out some fallen wood with my ax, but I was feeling lazy about that time. I found a spot where the sand was especially dry and, using my cupped hands as a shovel, scooped a hollow in the sand and began digging out pieces of buried driftwood. I must've been feeling powerfully lazy because, all along the bank, just beyond the island and across a narrow stretch of water, was all the dry wood a body could've wanted lying loose just for the asking. My shoulders began to ache as I hollowed out a dish into the sand, but I was turning up a fair-size pile of wood to burn. When I had an armload, I wandered back below the elm and set the fire going, laid back, and cooked up a mess of fish and beans.

Night was falling fast, and the river flowed so still and quiet, it was almost eerie. Meeting Cal and Jason Benson after so long a time of being alone set me into thinking. If only Pop was here, or Ronnie was still alive, or even Jamie and Clarke-Jiles were along to talk to. That would have helped pass the quiet of the nighttime.

In a couple of hours, the fire had burned down low. A chill was growing in the river air and hovering over the island. I needed to gather up more wood, set in a good stock for the night.

It was easiest looking where I'd dug before. By scraping in the sand, I gathered up more pieces–good-size ones that would keep the fire blazing bright. As I reached down inside the hole, one thin and kind of narrow piece, wouldn't give. I tugged on it harder and pulled it loose. It was about to go into the kindling stack until I noticed it wasn't any ordinary piece of driftwood.

When I looked it over closely, I could've sworn my heart leaped straight outside my chest! The muscles in my gut grew tight and, for an instant, I could scarcely breathe. I held in my hands a thin, narrow strip of flat-planed wood with a groove cut into it. A shard of glass jutted out of dry, white caulking along the groove. It looked like a piece of window frame. A piece of window frame from the wheelhouse of a steamboat!

Like a body gone crazed from too much sun, I scooped and dug and shoveled until my arms were like to break. More pieces of shattered frame came loose. A piece of broken glass sliced into a finger as I dug, but the cut wasn't deep and didn't matter. Nothing short of dying would've mattered then. I continued scooping sand. About three feet beneath where I'd hollowed out the driftwood was more wood frame, and larger chunks of board. I was squatting right above what must have been a sunken riverboat and it had to be the *Channel Belle*!

Forgetting all about the sharp ache in my arms and back, I scooped down until I'd dug out a waist-deep hole in the sand. It wasn't long after that I hit solid wood. It had to be the top side of the wheelhouse, or the deck of the *Channel Belle* herself.

I was sweating like a plough hand, even in the river chill, my head was spinning loose, and my body ached like crazy. I heaved myself out of the hole and laid back on the sand to rest. It wasn't five miles above the land point where Ronnie and I had camped those weeks before the river flood. Here she was, the *Channel Belle* herself--it had to be--lying buried for over a quarter-century under scarce three feet of sand! And Clayton Sievers had found her when Hank Short and Uncle Frank and the dozens of others who'd searched for her had failed. If only Ronnie had been here alongside me, it'd been a boyhood dream come true.

The quick thought about Ronnie brought some sorrow flooding back. I almost cried, dredging his memory up.

If I'd had a lantern along, I think I would've dug throughout the night, even if my shoulders busted from the doing. I had to rest a spell, so I laid up for the night, lying stretched out underneath the elm tree, gazing up into the jeweled, black blanket of a cloudless night sky.

I couldn't sleep. I tossed and rolled and turned like a body thinking if he falls asleep, he might never wake up come morning.

First my head was filled with thoughts of treasure, then with thoughts of doubt. If what I'd found was the *Channel Belle* would there be anything aboard her? I had no way of knowing it was the *Channel Belle*. It could've been another boat snagged up and come to rest. More doubts flooded in. A boy my age couldn't hope to find a thing folks had been searching for for years–just stumble across it in the dark. But I hadn't just stumbled across it; I'd worked hard in finding her. I'd blistered my hands working the sounding pole along the cutoff bottom. I'd worn my skin wrinkled wading along the bank line and scraped my feet raw along the graveled bottom. If this was the *Channel Belle*, I'd found her fair.

When the first light of morning broke, the sun rising over the low, tree-crowned ridge in the eastern sky, I set back to work. I hadn't bothered stopping to cook breakfast. By mid-morning I was feeling sharp hunger pangs and was growing weak from all the work I'd done. I laid into what food I could cook up quick enough and started in again.

The digging wasn't easy by any stretch, and by the time I was tuckered out again, I'd only dug out the smallest piece of the sunken boat. I needed tools–a shovel and a mattock–something to give me a fair advantage digging. Scooping out the sand by hand, I wasn't going to make it. The only sensible thing to do was row the skiff into a nearby river town and buy up what I needed. But first I spent considerable time covering up the hole I'd made, burying it up right fine, and smoothing out the sand. There hadn't been any heavy traffic along the river near the cutoff in the weeks I'd been along it, but I wasn't going to chance on some passerby stumbling across where I'd dug. I even doused my cooking fire, carrying off the larger pieces and tossing them into the river, and spread new sand over the ashes where the fire had burned.

The hour was growing late when I packed up and left the island, bound upriver for the nearest settlement.

That friendship will not continue to the end which is begun for an end.
—Quarles

CHAPTER 17

A River Town Gone Wild. I Meet Up with Martin Markham.

WAUD'S LANDING WAS THE NAME of the tiny river town I hauled myself into. Hank Short had called it just 'The Landing' in his account to me the winter before. Though I'd never set foot in the village, no doubt Pop had many times when he was living and fishing along the river. It was small, smaller by at least a hundred souls than Hortonville, the town near where I grew up. But it looked like Hortonville and the dozens of other towns Pop had told me about so long ago. The flat-roofed Main Street buildings looked the same, the narrow, dirt path, wheel-rutted street looked the same, and the handful of whitewashed, picket-enclosed houses looked the same, too.

Waud's Landing wasn't four miles upstream from the sand island and the cutoff and, if I hadn't been so stiff-muscled and sore from my digging, I could've made it into town and bought the tools I needed. But dusk had settled in over the village before I'd anchored the skiff to shore. I'd have to wait until morning came to get the supplies I needed.

Even before I'd reached the town and oared into the mooring place, from about a quarter mile off and echoing across the river, I heard the shouting yells of voices and what sounded like the blasts of pistol and rifle fire. By the sound of the ruckus in the streets, it appeared how maybe the war'd broken out all over again.

I slipped up the main road cat-cautious, kind of slinking around the outer buildings until I could see what the whoop-de-doo was all about and judge if it was safe to stay around.

Every storefront and house in town that I could see from my crouched position behind a hogshead cask was lit up bright. People of all ages, from those that appeared in their sixties and fifties on down to boys and girls my age, and younger children, pranced about in the street. Fireworks sparked and whizzed off everywhere. The night air snapped with the sound of cannon crackers–tight little packages of powder about half the length between a body's wrist and fingertip.

When they exploded, a sound like a thunder peel rolled through the town and across the river then rippled in echo back. Older girls and half-pint children tossed ladyfingers into the street. They cracked off like pops from my .22.

Some older boys had caught hold of a mongrel dog, tied a string of firecrackers to its tail, and set them off. With the first sharp crack the dog must've leaped two feet off the boardwalk, then took off barking and howling something fierce and running about in tight, wild circles. Most folks who viewed the spectacle laughed at each frantic leap and howl. I didn't think it was funny much. The poor hound looked as if it was about to keel over dead of fright. Just because an animal's dumb doesn't make it right for them to be ill-treated, any more than it does a person.

I still hadn't discovered what all the celebration was about, but it seemed safe enough to venture out from behind the hogshead. Paper banners had been stretched taut across the street between the roofs of two store buildings. Red, white, and blue with no lettering on them, the colors were beginning to fade in the low light of evening time.

As I stood on a corner of the boardwalk, leaning up against a building, a man seeming in his middle thirties came staggering up the street. A small boy tagged along behind him. It was obvious the man was drunk.

"Wazza matter, young'un," he slurred, "a-standing here 'n no crackerworks ta throw?"

"I just came into town," I said. "What's going on here?" I asked him. "What's the celebration about?"

"Sselebration?" He looked puzzled and didn't answer right off, but reached down and grabbed away a string of firecrackers the little boy was carrying. "Here. Yoos sshoot 'em off. Day wazzout crackerworks ain't Independence."

So that was it. I'd spent so much time out along the river I'd lost all track of time. When I'd found the *Channel Belle* I hadn't cared. It was the Fourth of July the town was all roared up about.

The little boy looked mighty sad by his father's drunken generosity. When the man wheeled and staggered off again, I handed them back to the child. From between clenched lips, quivering like he was about to cry, he forced up a smile at me.

Waud's Landing boomed, thundered, and sparked like a place in riot. Wagons which had brought folks in from outlying farms clogged the streets. The horses, startled and shying at the clamor, had been bound up tight to the hitching racks to keep them from galloping off. There wasn't a solitary place of quiet in the town. Rockets whizzed upward to the sky trailing colored sparks behind. Roman candles danced multi-colored balls of rainbow fire skywards like blazing fountains, sparklers fizzed and crackled from every corner.

From somewhere through the alarm, I caught the faint noise of dancing music blowing toward me through the breeze wafting from the river. I sauntered toward it, pushing through the crowd.

A clearing sat at the village's far edge. Crammed tight with lively folk, it was fired up brighter than the town. Illuminated paper lanterns swayed easy in the night air, suspended from paper banner strips that appeared to dance to the tempo of fiddle music. Around the sides of the dirt dancing circle, lumber planks had been set on barrel tops like tables and smaller kegs saw service as sitting stools. On them, menfolk lined up drinking while the women mostly gathered grouped in tight circle-clumps, giggling, laughing, and having a merry time. Some of the older folks pranced to the fiddle music, the women's fancy, soft skirts flying out around them. Independence Day, I figured, was about the only time these folk felt like cutting free; the remainder of the year's days being passed in ploughing, planting, and harvesting and, for the townsfolk, going about their daily living. A body's got to cut loose sometime, bust the bottled-up energy free, or someday burst open like an over-filled balloon.

I wandered about the crowd, elbowing past the drinking, laughing groups of merrymakers. Guess I looked a lonesome sight, standing by with no one else to talk to because before long, a young man came stepping up to me and said hello.

Though older than me by several years, he was young; about twenty-one or two at most by the look of him, smooth-faced with thick brown hair. He was built about like me–lean bellied and straight–but his skin that showed was light, not milk-cream pale, but looking like he hadn't seen much sun. Blue, stove-pipe trousers belted around his narrow waist, not like the buttoned, cloth suspender straps I wore. He had on a tan, coarse-cloth shirt. The deep-set eyes that glistened out from under brows the same color as his hair, were the bluest I'd ever seen on man or woman. Clear, with no sign of drink, they showed he hadn't been around the party long. They didn't have the glazed-over, bloodshot look the other menfolk around there had. I could've sworn I'd noted him someplace earlier but couldn't recollect where or when.

"Name's Martin Markham," he said, smiling and holding out his hand for me to shake. "What's yours?" he asked. I pumped his palm a time or two. "Clayt Sievers," I told him. His handclasp was firm and solid.

"Glad to meet you, Clayt," he beamed, beginning to get familiar. "Been round Waud's Landing long?"

"Since nightfall. I came upriver by skiff."

"Come to celebrate the Fourth I bet," he said, nodding his head.

"To be truthful, I didn't even know about it. I've been out along the river for quite a spell. Seems like time slipped by me."

"It does that easy enough." He snapped a white-toothed smile at me.

Martin Markham was a smooth-talking young man, and downright friendly for a stranger I'd just met. I took it into account he was just lonesome as I was and had been searching out a similar friendly face to talk with for a spell.

"How about me buying a couple of beers and us get out from all this to-do? Find a quieter place to talk."

"I'm not old enough to drink," I said.

"Age doesn't matter much. It's how you handle it. You look like you could take a beer," he said. There was a man pouring from a keg nearby. Martin Markham elbowed a path over to him, planted down a two-bit piece, and returned with two mugs of thick-headed beer.

"How old are you?" he asked as we slid side-saddle through the crowd, bound toward a quieter place along the dirt street away from the crowd. "Sixteen, maybe seventeen be my guess."

"Fifteen," I said, hoping he wouldn't catch the beer away and sort of pleased I looked older to him. "I'll be sixteen come next month."

Being nearly sixteen didn't seem to faze him and we settled out along the dark bank, the fiddle music soaring up behind us.

I'd never drunk beer before. Aunt Addie would have had a conniption if I'd tried it when I lived with her. For her, it was bad enough smoking my pipe now and again. Once when I was younger, I'd sneaked a swallow from Pop's whiskey jug. It singed my throat like fire and hit my stomach like a spoonful of molten lead. The beer was cold and tasted somewhere between bitter and sweet. I was a might surprised how it went down easy.

"Where do you come from since you're not from hereabouts?" he asked me.

"From around a small town along the river south a piece. You've probably never heard of Hortonville."

"No," he said, sounding thoughtful, pursing his lips out, showing he was considering it. "Don't guess I ever heard of Hortonville. I come from St. Joe way. I'm kind of new to these parts."

I knew where St. Joe was, and he was a long piece from his stomping grounds. St. Joe lay on the other side of the state, up along the Missouri.

"What brings you from St. Joe to these parts?" I asked, taking another swallow of the beer he'd bought me. It tasted good and slid easy down my throat.

"Looking to make a little money; set myself up in business," came his answer.

"What kind of business you looking for?"

He laughed. "Any kind that turns a steady profit. The kind of profit a man can build a good life on."

"A dry goods store?" I asked.

Martin Markham kind of scoffed at that suggestion. "No. A body can't make the kind of profit I'm wanting in the dry goods business, unless, of course, he's well established. I was thinking more on railroad jobbing or warehousing maybe. If I can't find what I'm searching for round here, I'll be moving elsewhere 'til I do."

We finished our beers about the same time and, without asking if I wanted more, he grabbed my mug away and bounded off, sauntering back a short while later with two more. We talked some more about odds 'n ends, small talk mainly–where we come from and things we'd seen that seemed interesting enough to tell one another about.

I wasn't used to drinking, and by the end of the second beer, I was beginning to feel kind of woozy and sleepy but good as well. Martin Markham talked up a steady pace and didn't seem to notice any different. Laying back, my legs stretched out in front of me, I let my eyes close. I hadn't heard him leave, nor did I hear him come back until he returned and slapped a fresh, foaming mug into my hand.

That beer flowed down as easy as the first two had, though I hadn't really wanted it. If he'd asked me, I would've told him no. He was sure a friendly sort, seeming to enjoy my company. I reckoned he was a good person and was fast growing to like him. The flow of steady talk kept up for a while longer, then he started in to asking me all sorts of questions. What was I doing out along the river alone? Didn't I have a family? Where was I headed to? About then my head was becoming like a cloud pushed along the sky by an easy breeze. I found myself answering his questions nearly as fast as he could ask.

I reckon somehow the *Channel Belle* cropped up in the conversation. He asked me all about it, having never heard the story before, and I told him everything.

"You think you've found it, then?" He was growing interested. "I think so," I said. "Can't be certain until I dig her out."

"You'll be needing some help then, Clayt. One fifteen-year-old boy ain't gonna uncover it alone. Not too easy anyway." I had to admit to the truth of that. Even with the proper tools, the digging would take a long spell. And, if there was cargo-treasure to be un-covered, hauling it out and toting it to where I could see it would be more than I could do alone.

"Tell you what I'll do," he said, suddenly popping to life like a puppet whose strings had just been pulled. "I'll make you an offer. My services in helping you uncover her for an equal share of whatever there is we find. Fifty-fifty. A fair split."

I knew I needed help, and the offer sounded honest. I accepted and we shook hands on it. Suddenly, I was feeling awfully tired and dizzy. All I really wanted to do was sleep.

The bright sun's golden disc rose sharply over the eastern ridge come morning. What woke me was a ray of blinding light gleaming in through a glass windowpane. My eyes were filmy when I first pulled them open. Then I noticed my head. It felt like tiny people prancing to fiddle music inside it. I had that washed-out, wrung up feeling I recall Pop describing to me once. He called it a hangover. Having never had the feeling then, I hadn't appreciated what he'd said.

The smell of frying eggs and sausage filtered through the air. Once I came awake and glanced around, I found myself lying in a bed with a blanket slung over me. I was inside a tiny cabin. Martin Markham was standing over a woodstove, one hand on a skillet handle, the other holding a flapjack turner. I was about to slide out of bed when I noticed I was altogether naked.

Martin Markham turned and saw me sitting there. No doubt I look sort of puzzled.

"Morning," he called, shooting a white-toothed grin toward me from across the room. "How you feel?"

"Like a stagecoach ran over me." I ached all over, worse than from yesterday's digging.

"Seems you had a few too many beers last night," he smiled.

"How many?" My head was thumping something awful.

"'Bout five if I remember right." I could count maybe three. "Oh," he said, seeming to have just remembered something. "You had a little accident last night. Guess you couldn't handle drinking after all. After you passed out I washed out your clothes. They're hanging up outside." He looked a might embarrassed and shrugged his shoulders. "Sorry 'bout that. Same thing happened to me when I was around your age, and I should've known better." He set the skillet off the stove plate and stepped outside. "Your pants and drawers are mostly dry," he said, tossing them over to me when he returned. "Shirt's still damp."

"Where am I?" I asked, pulling my trousers on and sliding over to the table. My head rattled with every step. "How'd I get here?"

"The cabin belongs to a friend of mine. Name's Wiley Jakes. I carried you here last night like a wounded dog."

"Where's–" I couldn't remember the friend's name and gestured my hand some in the air to prime my recall.

"Wiley Jakes. He's out buying up the supplies you said you need. To dig up the *Channel Belle*? You remember that don't you?" I guessed I did, though I wasn't too sharp on recall just then. I couldn't remember inviting anybody else along except Martin Markham.

He walked a cup of coffee over to me. It was black as grease and near as thick. It tasted sour, but I knew I needed it. He sat down next to me and slid a tin plate of eggs and sausage in front of me. "You're not too hungover to eat, I hope," he chuckled. "We're all going to need our strength if we're going to find that boat." Just then the cabin door creaked open and in strode Wiley Jakes. Leastwise I guessed it was. Martin Markham introduced me to him, and it was.

Wiley Jakes was older than my new-found friend by some twenty years or more. His face showed signs he hadn't shaved in several days, and his skin wasn't near as pale as Markham's. He had broad-strut shoulders, but where Markham tapered to the waist, Wiley Jakes sort of blossomed out.

"Got the 'quipment you said to get." Jakes's voice was rough and sandy. "Cost me seven dollars."

"I'm sure my young friend here'll see his way clear to paying you back." Markham turned to me and smiled the same white-toothed grin he'd shown earlier. "Couldn't help noticing as I undressed you last night, you had money in your pocket." He pointed to a shelf near the woodstove. "It's over there, Wiley. Help yourself." Jakes fired a glance toward me with a look like he disapproved me being there. I didn't know I appreciated it much, Markham rifling through my pockets. But then I guessed he didn't have a choice if he was washing out my things.

Jakes didn't say anything. He just grunted and stalked over to the shelf, sliding some bills and coins into his pocket.

We finished eating and Markham dumped the cups and plates in the sink without bothering to wash them. I stepped outside. My shirt was line-dried enough to wear. I buttoned it up, tucking in the tails at the trousers waist, and ambled back inside.

The cup of coffee began to set things right, and before long I was feeling better. Markham and his friend Jakes were busy packing supplies together which they thought we'd be needing along the river.

Wiley Jakes spoke but little; of the two of them, Markham was the talker. It wasn't hard by any stretch to see how Markham was the leader in their friendship and held command. Jakes's face always wore the same expression: like a man who'd just bitten into a lemon, or like the face you sometimes see an old woman show who's not especially pretty and has spent her life searching for a man to marry she'd never found. The look was a pinched-lipped sourness about the mouth.

The packing done, Jake closed the cabin with a hasp and rusty padlock, and together we headed off toward my skiff.

The streets of Waud's Landing were all but dead and silent. The roistering of the night before had kept many of the townsfolk to their beds, and no doubt nursing party wounds. About the only traffic along the main street was a pair of scruffy mongrel dogs which padded about the boardwalks sniffing and sifting with their snouts through the truck 'n plunder of the celebration, finding scraps of food that been dropped. The general store was set for business as usual. Wiley Jakes had bought four long-handled shovels and a mattock pick there that morning. Why he'd bought four shovels when there were only three of us, I couldn't reason right off, unless maybe he was expecting one to break. The storekeeper hailed Wiley as we walked past, no doubt in appreciation for the business. Wiley only kept his tight-mouthed look, saying nothing. From his cheery look, the storekeeper was among the few menfolk in Waud's Landing who'd kept his senses about him and gone home early from the celebration.

We arrived at the spot on the landing where I'd moored the skiff and I was surprised to see another man squatting on the clay bank nearby. Markham hailed him with a friendly greeting and gave a quick wave of his hand.

"Good to see you could make it, Sam," Markham called out. Then he said, as we moved closer, "You look like some dog dragged you through a thistle patch."

"Feels like it, too," the new man grunted. "This trip had better be worth me getting up so early."

Markham saw my face drop some, and he turned around to me. "This here's Sam Richards," he grinned, introducing me. The other man looked mighty glum. "He's a friend of mine like Wiley here."

I was a might upset by all of this. I'd only invited Martin Markham to come along to help me dig. Next thing I knew, he'd taken charge of everything and sprung Wiley Jakes on me. And now another man, Sam Richards. Though I tried to hide my thoughts, Markham was remarkably perceptive.

"It's going to take more than our two backs digging if that boat's buried like you say." He wrinkled up his brow, the smooth skin of his forehead crinkling. It appeared he was waiting for me to speak. I didn't. "Don't worry about Sam and Wiley here taking more than their share of whatever we find. It's still a fifty-fifty split 'tween you and me. Whatever we find, you get half. The three of us," he motioned, making a sweeping gesture, "will split the rest."

What he said did reassure me some. I still wasn't thinking clearly, but his offer seemed fair enough.

The fourth member of our treasure-finding party looked about Wiley's age. Why the two men took orders from Martin Markham who, in the morning sunlight, looked young enough to be the youngest kid brother to either of them, I couldn't rightly reckon. He had a way about him that made me think of Ronnie. Leadership was written all over him. He spoke well, was heaped with energy, and held the same commanding nature Ronnie had had.

Sam Richards was still parked on the bank as Markham, Jakes, and I packed the skiff. He had a sizeable rock jug with him, and every now and again he'd pop the cork and take a swallow.

"A taste o' the hair o' the dog that bit 'im makes a man feel better," he rasped. I reckoned it was just an excuse so he could get drunker than he was.

Between the four of us and a skiff-load of supplies—food stuff and tools mostly—we were loaded full enough so we could scarcely move. But the cutoff lay but four miles distant, and we had the river current with us on the downstream trip. Picking our way slowly and hugging close into bankside, there wouldn't be any trouble with the passage, even loaded over-heavy like we were.

The difficulties, hardships, and trials of life, the obstacles one encounters on the road to fortune, are positive blessings. They knit the muscles more firmly and teach self-reliance. Peril is the element in which power is developed.

—Pythagoras

CHAPTER 18

The *Channel Belle* Comes to Light. A Dead Man's Hand. A Treasure Lost.

THE SKIFF MOVED DOWN EASY along the river, following the channel current. Overloaded like we were, our provisions and supplies high- heaped in the middle, Sam Richards and Wiley Jakes sitting stern-side and Markham and me in the bow, none of us could scarcely move. We rode low to the water, the river lapping only about four inches from the gunwale top. But we made good time.

Sam Richards seemed to be biting off more of the hair of the dog than he needed. He appeared to be getting worse off more than better. His seat companion, Wiley Jakes, sat silent the whole downstream trip, staring with a sort of gloomy look off into the water, watching the scenery pass by him, but taking no interest in it.

Markham and I talked together some. He had the whole expedition organized down to the finest details and he spent his time talking over those details with me.

"When we reach that cutoff channel of yours, Clayt," he said, sounding serious and down-to-business like, "first off we'll be setting up a camp. Wiley there can handle that. You and me'll head

215

off and reconnoiter some before we set in digging. I want you to be certain of the spot you found those window pieces, so we don't wind up like a pack of coon dogs who've dropped the scent."

Only three of us would dig right off: Markham, Wiley Jakes, and me. "If we find what I think we're going to find," Markham went on, "this skiff of yours isn't going to be big enough to carry it. Sam there used to do some small-time lumbering–nothing fancy–but he knows how to handle an ax. I'll get him started building the raft we'll use. Besides," he said, glancing over toward Richards who was nodding off by now, his head bouncing back against his shoulders, his hands dangling loose between his legs, "Sam looks like he can use the work." I snickered some at that. Richards, dozing off in his alcohol dream, looked like a man who needed work all right; about as much as I needed to be back in the loving care of Uncle Frank.

We must've appeared a pretty seedy group, the four of us. All except Markham who was crisp and clean and bright blue-eyed-- just like he looked when we first met. A short while later we skinned into the cutoff. Richards finally woke up and peered around as we neared the island.

"I've been all 'long this here stretch 'o river," he grunted, snapping upright on his board, "and I ain't never seen no sunken boat." I pondered some on the thought of him ever seeing a sunken boat.

"I can assure you," Markham rejoined, casting a solid blue-eyed stare at Richards, "if Clayt here says there's a boat buried on this slice of sand, there is one."

Richards coughed and cleared his throat. "Just sayin' that if there is, what makes you so sure there's treasure on 'er?" I answered up before Markham had the chance.

"This is just the place the *Channel Belle* went down," I said, growing annoyed by now. I didn't much like Richards, and I didn't like him calling me a liar. "She's buried here all right, and no one's ever claimed her treasure.'' I paused and gazed steadily at Richards. "We're going to be the first." My words sounded mighty confident, but deep down inside I wasn't sure at all.

Richards was about to slur out something more when Markham reached in and cut him off.

"If we stand round here any longer, jawing instead of working, we're gonna to be that much longer waiting to get what we came here for."

Markham's words ended the matter quickly. He proved to be a master organizer. It was amazing how we all fell to as he started assigning us our duties. I was a might perplexed at Jakes and Richards, two older men taking orders from someone so much younger. And without a sign of disagreement. Sure, Richards grumbled some just beneath his breath when he found he had to throw his shoulders into work and build us up a raft. But he did, taking up the ax and a long, coiled length of rope and rowing the skiff across the river to the bankside.

Everyone and everything seemed to be moving as smoothly as a newly oiled pocket watch. Sam Richards was off working in a stand of timber, the steady whack, whack, whacking rhythm of his ax blade slicing into tree bark and bouncing in echo back across the water. Markham and I set into our reconnoiter, and Jakes worked to set the campsite. I don't know which of us was the most miserable– Richards sweating off his drunk of the night before, or the three of us sweltering on the bare, shadeless sand.

In the early afternoon heat, it wasn't long before the three of us were stripped to the waist and shedding sweat like water spaniels. I was used to being in the open. Markham wasn't. His slab-muscled chest was hairless as my own, but his skin was pale as a sheet of writing paper. Inside half an hour, he was already beginning to take on a shade of pink about the neck and shoulders. My mind drifted back to Jamie's and my birthday celebration. It'd been nearly a year since I'd brought him back, broiled and blistered. As we worked, I told Markham about it.

"It's the wise man that takes advice," he allowed, reaching for his shirt and tying the sleeves in a knot around his neck to protect his shoulders. "Wouldn't do having the brains of this outfit laid up with heat fixation or a bad burn now, would it?" He fired up that striking grin of his again, which seemed to be his trademark, his teeth so white they reminded me of the first trackless snowfall of winter.

Wiley Jakes joined up with us a short time later and we set in close to our digging. I'd found the spot where I'd finger-clawed the sand only the day before. Markham reckoned it was as good a place to start as any. None of us talked much except for an occasional remark from Markham or a muttered grunt of toil from Jakes. With the help of the shovels and two extra backs, the digging went faster than when I'd begun it. But it wasn't any easier.

We'd been shoveling not quite an hour when, suddenly, from the waist-deep hole, a heavy thud echoed up from Jakes's diggings. He threw his full shoulders and back into it, using the shovel tip like a spear. The cracking and splintering noises of splitting wood sounded up from the hollow of the hole. Jakes was growing excited.

"I hit something! I hit something!" he kept on shouting.

"Well, keep on digging, man!" Markham sang out.

Markham and I sidled over to where Jakes was working. Sand started flying from the hole; the bright new shovel blades flashing fires of sunlight on their backward swing. Sure enough, there was wood all right, and plenty of it coming fresh into the light after a quarter century and more years. That is, of course, if what lay below our feet was the wreck of the *Channel Belle* herself.

What was coming up were pieces and bits of shattered decking and window frame like I'd found before, then bits of window glass and more frame and decking. Jakes stopped shoveling long enough to rest and stare down into the hole. "Well, I'll be damned if the kid ain't right about a boat." Markham and I took a minute to rest up, too.

"Clayt," Markham said, blue-eyeing me, "I think we've found your boat. And I'd bet a straight flush for a full house it's the *Channel Belle*." If he was at all excited, he didn't show it. His face wore the flat look of a gambler. But the rest of us looked different. I was shaking some and Jakes was worse off than me. Turning back to work, we lit into digging like lustful sinners fleeing from the fury of God.

It wasn't long after that we struck into solid planking, painted white, splintered some in places, but solid mostly. We'd spread ourselves out so we weren't bumping backs and elbows, and the diggings took on the look of a moist, gray cavern. It reached up over Markham's head who must've been no less than six foot tall. We couldn't keep up this rollicking pace of digging long, so we rested up. Markham stripped off his shirt again and wrung the sweat from it enough to fill a water glass.

"There'd better be somethin' down here worth all this damned digging," Jakes wheezed out, slumping up against the side, and mopping down his brow. Markham didn't offer a reply, and I kept my quiet, too. Richards, on his side, must've been resting, too, because the beating of his ax had stopped and the island and river stood quiet, except for the crow cries overhead.

"We can't be sitting here," Markham said, calling up his energy again. "There's work to do and gold to find," he sparkled. We were off to work again.

I couldn't, for the soul of me, figure where Markham got his strength. He'd drunk as much as me the night before; was up by sunrise cooking breakfast. He was built well, but not burly like Jakes or Richards, and I'd noticed how his hands were smooth–almost like a woman's. In his digging he set a furious pace I couldn't hope to match. It almost appeared he was in a race against Jakes and me.

What we'd been digging on was the Texas deck–the roof of the steamboat's wheelhouse. We'd opened the front side, near where the wheel lay. River silt and sand had filled it mostly full, except for the wheel itself which stood out stark bare from its pinion housing. It was free and only its bottom spokes were buried.

"There's no use in wasting time on this," Markham said. "What we want's buried in the hold."

Jakes snorted. "I'm mighty glad to hear that. I figured you'd be having us three uncover this whole damned boat while Richards lollygags with that raft."

"Not likely," Markham smiled. "Sam will be joining us soon enough, but even with the four of us, digging out the whole of her would take the rest of the summer and then some. No. We're going to do this scientific." We halted work again while Markham laid out his whole plan to us.

"I reckon that the heavy goods–the quicksilver, silver bars, and the gold--would be laid out amidship to settle out the weight. The whiskey's probably behind it and the copper up toward the bow. If we dig at the stern side of this wheelhouse, that should put us right about center. I'm thinking that the hold is mostly empty. The boards would've kept out most everything except the water. So, once we've dug down to it, there won't be much left to do but carry what's down there out."

Markham's 'scientific' plan made sense. Even Jakes saw the sense in it. But, judging by the shadows that the falling sun was throwing down, there wasn't but little light left, and any digging to be done would soon be done by lantern light. The three of us were all tuckered out and shoulder-sore from scooping sand, so we left the hole and plodded back to camp. A short while later, Sam Richards hauled the skiff back in, looking powerful grumpy. No sooner had he gotten back than he popped the cork and started in at his jug again. Jakes stretched out, laying his head up against a rolled blanket, and Markham, too, for a piece, until he decided to help me cook supper.

The chill of the river at evening time started to waft in on us, and the blaze of the cooking fire was a mighty welcome warmth. With supper served up and eaten, Jakes and Richards amused themselves with a game of stud and passed the jug between them. Markham didn't drink. He just sat still and silent, peering off into the growing darkness.

He seemed to be pondering something hard. I traced a barefoot trail to the river's edge and cleaned up the supper ware, using sand to scour out the scrapings and dunked the plates and cups into a bucket I'd set out beside the fire to boil. Thereafter, Markham fired up the lanterns.

"It's round seven o'clock," Markham noted. "I reckon we've got some hours of good work ahead of us before we sack out for the night." He gunshot that cold blue-eyed stare of his at Jakes and Richards who'd pretended not to hear him, and they responded like two farm dogs to a farmer with a club.

Three of us settled into digging out the silt and sand and Richards toted it by bucket-load clear of the digging site. In less than an hour we'd uncovered the whole back side of the wheelhouse. It glowed plain in our lantern light. It seemed an eerie sight, like the uncovering of a grave.

The shovel work had uncovered a gaping hole in the hind wall of the wheelhouse. The white-painted boards had been cracked open like a cannon shot had blasted through. There was sand piled up inside and, as it fell away from the digging, I glanced down to see what appeared to be... No, it couldn't be, I thought–the finger of a man's hand!

Whatever it was, it glowed a ghostly white in the beam of the glimmering lantern and I stooped down to dig it out by hand. The instant I touched hold of it, I knew what it was all right. A finger bone, and more–a bright, bare skeleton of a man's whole hand! There was more, a lower arm, but I stopped digging. A chilling cold crept up my back and lodged like a quaking shiver at the base of my neck. 'The chill off the river air,' I thought. 'A dead man's hand can't cause anyone hurt.' Markham stopped long enough to snatch a look at my ghastly find.

"Probably the captain," he nodded. "Poor devil."

"Or the pilot," I chimed up.

"Are you two gonna play with some dead man's bones all night, or lend a hand with this?" Sam Richards snorted, the tone of his voice sounding mighty sour. He'd been hauling out the heavy buckets and didn't appear in any mood to dally about.

We worked until after ten by my reckoning, then laid it up dog tired for the night.

Before laying out my blanket roll, I hollowed out some pockets in the sand for my hips and shoulders. There was no sense in sleeping uncomfortably. Jakes and Richards sat propped up beside the fire, dealing cards and polishing off the jug, talking softly between themselves. Markham seemed to prefer my company to that of his two friends and stretched himself out near me.

By the looks of him I could tell Markham was as tired as me, though he didn't act it. Sleep doesn't always follow body weariness, especially when the mind's cranked up, so we sat up to talk a while.

"How you holding up, Clayt?" Markham asked.

"'About as good as expected, I guess. My shoulders sure are sore," I told him.

Markham responded with a laugh–not a full laugh, but a kind of grunt from inside his throat and a snort of air puffed through his slender nose. "Seems to be a common hazard in this salvage business. Maybe I can help," he said. Without my asking, he set his hands against my shoulders and commenced to knead the muscles near my neck. At first it hurt, but shortly set in to feeling good as his slender fingers smoothed across my back. His hands held a surprising strength.

"Do you think there might be a sign in finding that hand?" I asked Markham as we sat out on my blanket together.

"You don't impress me as the superstitious kind," he whispered, then kind of laughed from out the darkness. "There's no harm in a pile of bones. None that I can see."

Somehow, I wasn't so certain. Up north of Pop's old cabin–just beyond the land point where Ronnie and I had camped, not far distance from where we sat, were some Indian burial caves. I'd never seen them, but Pop had explored them; Uncle Frank, too, when he was younger. Anymore, there wasn't anything there except bones, maybe some pottery pieces and an arrow point or two. Over the years, white folks had cleaned the caves out of anything of value or to use as souvenirs. There was a load of stories about the walking spirits of the Indian chiefs who'd been buried there; about what would happen if the sacred ground was bothered, or the bones disturbed. I didn't know about the truth in those old river tales, but river folk are a superstitious lot by nature. Pondering on it some in the silence of that starlit night, I guessed a white man's bones couldn't do me harm. Leastwise I didn't see how.

Markham's hands working over me set me relaxed. Soon we were both laid out, cradled in the blanket rolls and drifting into dreams.

Come first light and following a warming breakfast of beans and bacon and Markham's grease-thick coffee, we started in to digging once again. By noontime we'd shoveled, scooped, and bucket-hauled out more sand than I ever cared to see. The work was slow and tiring. Richards had muttered and grumbled his way back across the river to continue his raft-building effort, and Jakes looked like he could use a drink. Only problem was, the jug had been drained the night before and Sam Richards had forgotten to bring another along. The knowledge of it seemed to please Markham mighty well, though he didn't voice his thoughts aloud.

By later afternoon, the sun had turned the kiss of pink along Markham's chest and back to a light-colored, fall-leaf brown, and the appearance of it seemed to please him. Maybe it was a memory from his boyhood, or the thought of working out-of-doors along the peacefulness of that river stretch. When I'd first met up with him, his hands had the look of a card dealer's softness, not someone who worked hard labor. Now they were blistered about the inside of the palms and growing calloused. I realized I knew little about Martin Markham. He'd come from along the Missouri near St. Joe. He'd told me that. How he'd met up with the likes of Jakes and Richards is what I pondered on. While they drank and dealt cards around the firelight, Markham stared off into the surrounding darkness. When they were rowdy and boisterous, he was silent and firm. When they grumbled about doing work, he'd just gaze over to them and flash a smile. And why he'd happened onto Waud's Landing, a dozing river town not likely to offer much to a man his age or the quick-set sharpness of his mind–and decided to stay a spell– I couldn't reckon. But he held his life and thoughts close in and didn't seem bent on speaking about them none. I liked him, despite his self-held secrets. There was a glimmer about his deep-set, stark-blue eyes which would oft-times look square into my own, that showed he liked me, too.

By the third full day of digging, I was quick to reckon how, without having met up with Markham and his bringing along Jakes and Richards, I couldn't've done the work myself. Not even with the tools, and not in weeks or months.

It was after nightfall on that third full day that Richards finished up the raft he'd been working on, and our shovel tips struck the cargo hold. Markham had been right in his reasoning. Most of the hold was clear except where some sand and river mud had washed in where the bottom had snagged out and she'd flooded. I'd been right in my speculation, too. The river had flooded out her boiler which exploded and cracked the top deck like an egg. That accounted for the hole in the backside of the wheelhouse. The explosion hadn't been enough to sink her though. The sawyer snag had done that.

We hollowed out a cavern in the hard-packed sand and supported it with planking from the boat deck. When we broke through the cargo hatch, Wiley Jakes got so excited he dashed off toward camp to grab the lanterns, racing like a rabbit from a bobcat. Each of us held a lantern.

The bottom of the hold was hip-deep in river seepage. The air below was rank and foul-smelling, just like the pirated packet boat Ronnie and I had stumbled on. Markham and I rolled up our trousers legs which was silly and didn't do any good. The brown, rank-foul water oozed up around my belly button and was cold enough to shoot shivers through me. There was no doubt in anyone's mind as we entered the tomb-dark hold. This was the *Channel Belle*!.

Kegs and casks and boxes a-plenty were scattered about the hold. Row on row of them, sitting easy for the taking. Jakes and Richards were like two kids turned loose at a church school picnic. Ax swinging, Richards cracked open the first keg he came to.

"There's quicksilver here!" he shouted, the pitch of his coughing voice ringing in a hollow echo through the hold. "Just a-look at 'em all! There must be a hundred here!" I made a quick count in the dim light of my lantern. There was nigh on to forty I could see, maybe more hidden in the murky water.

Jakes worked the bow side, the rank water sloshing about his hips as he pulled himself along. There was a prying sound from his shovel blade and a moment later a graveled shout.

"Copper! Cases and cases of copper! Most of it's still shiny!" A few moments later, another shout. He'd found a chest, three foot by two, filled with silver bars.

"Hey, Jakes," Richards called from the other side. "Here's some good sippin' whiskey for you," he yelled, splitting open the thin top of a large oak cask.

"That's worth the work itself," Jakes shouted back, hurriedly wading through the slime to where Richards stood.

"Here. Have a taste," Richards said, holding out a tin cup he'd tied to a rope loop from around his belt. Jakes took a swig one instant, choked and spit it out the next.

"Chr—! Ya tryin' to poison me, you damned fool!"

"What'd you think it'd be," Richards laughed and snorted, "fine Southern sippin' whiskey? After sitting in the river for thirty years?"

"You dad-blamed fool! I oughta crown you with this here shovel handle!" Jakes threatened. Jakes spent the next minutes spitting 'poison' whiskey and muttering words a body doesn't hear but seldom. Markham shook his head at his partners' antics and went about his business of examining everything he could lay a hold on. I did the same and steered clear of the two older men as long as possible.

I don't know what time it was. In the darkness of the hold, I couldn't tell. But I knew we'd spent some good hours traipsing through its dark and foul rot.

"There ain't no gold down here," Richards grunted aloud. He'd looked through nearly every box. "You find any gold?" he shouted out to Jakes.

"I ain't found none. You found any, Markham?"

"I've come up dry as you." There was a ring of disgust in his voice.

"I bet there never was no gold. I bet they jus' said there was so some damn fools like us would go lookin' for it," Jakes growled. "I bet them St. Looie bankers packed it out on another boat and used this one as a decoy in case she was pirated. That's what I think."

"You might be right, Wiley," Markham said from his vantage on top a whiskey keg. "But I don't think so. The gold's not here, sure enough, but I'd stake a hundred dollar bet it was here. Once."

"What?" Wiley grunted. "How do you know? You mean some piker's been here ahead of us and taken it?"

"Hardly. If they had, would they have left all this here?" Markham made a sweep with his arms from bow to stern. "It's obvious. When this boat struck that snag, it ripped her bottom out. The gold cases were probably sitting just at the bottom of that set of cargo steps." He waved his hand languidly toward the open stairway descending from the cargo hatch. "And, what's at the bottom of those steps? A gaping hole, that's what. I felt it when I stepped down.

"There's river bottom at those steps, not wood." Markham paused to be dramatic. "A hole 'bout twenty feet across."

"So, what you're saying," I spoke to Markham, "is that the cases of gold…"

"Fell right through the snagged-out bottom and right into the river," he finished what I'd begun to say. "It's the river's now, and none of us, or anyone else, is ever going to find it." Markham's words rang hollow through the musty hold. All of us stood silent for a time. "But" he said, starting up a-sudden, "just because there's no gold doesn't mean we haven't found a treasure."

"Say what you mean, Markham," Richards grumbled.

"I mean, I've been estimating the value, Sam, of just what's here, while you and Wiley there were playing games."

"And–?" Richards asked with anticipation ringing.

"I'm not certain of the exact market value, mind you, but I'd guess–between the four of us–about five thousand dollars. Apiece!"

"Eeeyah!" Jakes shouted out. "That's a powerful sum of money for a three-day backbreaker." Richards agreed with his partner, only louder still until my ears hurt with their ringing,

"All that matters now is getting the stuff we've found out of here and up onto Sam's raft and what's left over in Clayt's skiff," Markham said softly. "With some real work from all of us, we can have it out by tomorrow nightfall."

That night, come sleeping time, none of us could rest for thinking about the haul we'd make come first light. I didn't sleep at all--leastwise I didn't think so–and if I did it was by fits and starts. Markham's words kept flooding through my brain. Five thousand dollars. Apiece. That was more money than an average man could hope to make in three or four years by hard and honest labor. Then it snapped clear suddenly. Something I hadn't reckoned on before. My deal with Markham was fifty-fifty; his half split between himself, Jakes, and Richards's cut was a bit over three thousand.

I thought and thought about it. Perhaps the oddest thing is how memories flash back to crowd the mind, charging in and out and rambling back again, much like a troop of ducks or a gaggle of geese in a thunderstorm. The most money Pop had ever held was a hundred dollars. And that's when he and Ronnie Meyers' father went in together on a logging trip and hauled out a stand of walnut which they sold way upriver in St. Louis. There was poor Aunt Addie lying on her death bed, her eyes flashing painful looks at me because she hadn't changed her will to favor me as well as Jamie. Now here I was with a fortune in my pocket. Wouldn't the gossipy folks in Waytown be shock-eyed floored when I came rolling back, a river boy turned rich?

Since I scarcely slept all through the night I caught a sort of snaky feeling, that kind of slithery feeling you sometimes get when you're being watched in secret. Jakes and Richards had fallen into dreams of wealth, and Markham was lying close by, still and silent.

The amber glow of the campfire cast an eerie yellow-orange over his blanket roll, and glittering flickers across his face.

I couldn't tell for sure, due to the way he lay, but I felt his eyes were wide open and probing me like a schoolboy does a beetle. Perhaps it was no more than the play of my imagination. Or maybe I was asleep and it was all a dream.

At the first glimmering light of morning, the chill from the river still hanging heavy in the air, Jakes and Richards oared the skiff across the narrow stretch of water to float the raft back, and Markham and I set into rigging a pulley rope to lift the stores up from the hold of the *Channel Belle*.

If Richards was good at anything, save grumbling, it was raft building. He'd gone full out. Downright proved himself a craftsman. What he'd built looked like a lumber raft, the kind that loggers use to float raw timbers with. Cottonwood logs, longer than all of us stretched lengthwise together and near as thick as a thin man's waist lay lashed together with scarce a space between. Like a dozing grandfather not wishing to be disturbed, the heavy platform moved grudgingly and labored. My skiff bobbed high up and easy, tied behind. Jakes and Richards poled her across the narrows and landed her near the wreck.

If three days of hard digging through hard-packed sand had been rough-going enough, pulling pony kegs of quicksilver and hoisting copper ingots, and the chest of silver bars wasn't any easier. Not one of us had ever put in one day's work like that.

As the whiskey'd gone sour, we left its casks behind, but cleaned the hold of the *Channel Belle* of everything else of value.

We hoisted out the copper first because it was lighter. There were twenty-six coffins, as Markham called the long and narrow boxes.

Sixty pony kegs of quicksilver came next, each weighing fifty pounds apiece, and finally the chest of silver bars which took all four of us to lift. The four of us took turns; two working the hold, the remaining two on the hoisting rope and pulley. We worked straight through without a break until the job was done. I'd never worked so hard. And I was certain Markham hadn't. We were all tuckered out and with sand clinging to our sweat.

When the raft was finally loaded and the cargo lashed, Jakes and Richards slumped down on what little free space was left. My arms felt like line sinkers the rivermen use; my legs as if they'd been hollowed out, the blood and bone replaced with lead. The first thing I did when the job was done was plod heavily up to the river's edge, shed my clothes until I was stark bare, and plunged into the water. It was my first river swim since the four of us had come together to claim the *Channel Belle*. It felt mighty good—the river licking at my skin, carrying the grime and sweat away. I free-floated in the shallows and let the river's gentle flow lull me. I was too tired to swim.

Martin Markham arrived a short time later. He set in to doffing his clothes, too, and a moment later joined me.

"I haven't swum since I was your age," he called soft-voiced and wading out toward me. "It feels as good as I remember it."

Markham appeared an odd sight. Where he'd worked shirtless in the sun was a brown shade, but the rest of him was white. From his narrow hips on downward he gleamed the sickly, pale color of a catfish's belly. If I hadn't been slug tired I might've broke out laughing.

We didn't say much to one another except to pass the time of day in small talk. Having waded and paddled around some, we lay out along a shallow shoal and let the river lap over our legs and stomachs. Markham was mighty quiet but kept looking over at me from time to time. It seemed we were too pooped to talk. After about half an hour, we gathered up our clothes and ambled back toward camp. About the time we got there, Jakes and Richards arrived. Markham was just pulling on his trousers.

"See you've been skinny-dippin' like some pale-assed kid," Jakes grunted, catching sight of him, "'stead of workin' like us."

"Just because you don't know the pleasure doesn't mean I don't." There was a steel edge to Markham's voice, the first time I'd ever heard it. Then, just as sudden, his tone changed. Markham had a surprise for Jakes and Richards. "Boys, we leave tonight. Our job's done here and it's time to cash in on our good fortune. But first," he said, his eyes brightly flashing, "a little drink to celebrate."

Jakes and Richards had been near to drying out, going two full days without a drink. They were mighty shocked and pleased when Markham reached into his blanket roll and came up with a pint bottle of whiskey. A broad, almost boyish smile flashed across his beardless face.

"Well, I'll be damned," Richards snapped. "You been holding out on us, Markham?"

"I've been saving this for a special occasion, and I can't say I know a more special one. A drink to our good fortune, gentlemen," he sang out, and went over to the fire where the plates and cups were set and poured some into each. "Tonight, we celebrate, because tomorrow we'll be rich!"

Richards and Jakes each took a cup and drained it off right quick. Then Markham sauntered up and handed a cup to me. "Clayt," he said, "if it hadn't been for meeting you, well…it goes unsaid. To your health, my young friend, "and he touched the cups together and we drank.

I was never much for the taste of whiskey, had never been too keen on it seeing what it'd done to Pop and made a wildman at times of Uncle Frank. But that day was an exception, and I drank it slowly in sips. All the while Markham watched me, ignoring Jakes and Richards who'd taken up the remainder of the bottle and seeing who could drain it first.

I was thinking that maybe it was the heavy, almost endless labor I'd done, or the swim that'd pumped me dry of strength, but a short while after drinking, my head began to reel. A funny, light-headed feeling swept over me before I staggered, wheeled around, and dropped.

When I came to, the blackness of night had crept up the river. The raft was heading slowly upriver, hugging the bank, with Jakes and Richards poling along each side. A warm glow of lantern light broke the gloom ahead of it. Markham was squatting beside me, his back leaned up against a copper coffin. I tried to move and shake free of the thundering in my head, but couldn't. My hands and feet were tied! I was trussed up tight–like a hog before its slaughter!

"Clayt." It was Markham's voice. My eyes were foggy, like a gray film had settled over them. I couldn't see him clearly. "Don't try fighting," he spoke, seeing me struggling against the bindings. "Those knots of Sam's would hold a draft horse."

"I–I don't understand. Why am I–what am I tied up for?" My head had stopped its spinning, and my eyes had begun to sharpen some. Between my ears and along across the forehead, my head still thundered like horses on a gallop.

Markham was settled in the shadows just in front of me. Jakes and Richards still moved their poles slowly from front to back.

"I'm truly sorry I had to do this to you, Clayt. It was my idea to leave you behind–just row you across the river and tie you to a tree. You'd get free in about a day, and Wiley, Sam, and I'd be gone. But we took a vote–democratic like–and mine was the losing ballot."

"What vote? What ballot? I–I don't understand any of this!"

"Guess it's time to tell you about myself," he sighed, "seeing how it won't matter now. When I was younger than you are now, my pa was the greatest artist along the Missouri from Sioux City to St. Louis. He wasn't an artist like you might be thinking. He didn't work with brushes on canvas, but with people. My pa could trick a land deal slicker than waffle syrup, or a rich woman of her jewels. And when he wasn't scamming folks, he was a gambling man. Went by the name of Devol. 'Course it wasn't his real name. He caught a bullet in his head when I was seventeen. Before he died, I'd learned to win at cards and carry on a con. He taught me a lot of what he knew. All I had to do was learn to play the game smooth and easy."

"You planned this whole thing out? Before we even came here?"

"Right down to the fine line of it." Markham smiled in praise of his smartness.

"But how'd you reckon I had anything worth stealing?"

"That's part of the artistry, Clayt. A conman gets a feel for people like I got a feel for you even before we met. You looked like a boy with something heavy on his mind and I made it my business to find out what that something was."

"And you got me drunk on purpose and pumped me about the *Channel Belle*."

"I gave you a few beers because I knew you couldn't handle drinking. A few right questions and you started talking. The powders did the rest."

"Powders?" I said. "You're not making any sense."

"It's what I poured into your drink back there a piece." He waved his hand off into the darkness toward the island behind us. "And the same thing I slipped you the night we met when you weren't looking. You passed out and I carried you to Wiley's shack. And you didn't have an accident. That was part of the ploy. I had to make it appear you did and that I'd taken care of you. To build your trust. All I did was strip you, wet down your clothes, and hang them out to dry. You were never seriously drunk, at least not from drinking beer."

"Then Jakes and Richards are friends of yours.

"We work together. I met Wiley when I was nineteen. He supplies the back work and I supply the brains. We've been a pretty good team so far. Sam there, well, he's helped me out before. Keep him in whiskey and he's happy." Markham moved a little closer to where I lay. "You don't recognize me, do you?"

"Should I? Other than back at the celebration?"

"We've met before. In passing." I strained, through my fuzzy thoughts to remember where I might have met Markham earlier. But through my headache nothing came clear.

Markham jogged my memory. "We saw each other about a year ago. In a saloon where I was playing cards."

Suddenly I remembered. In Swainville. Sure enough! The young man in the saloon where Maggie Lewis worked! Markham was the man who'd stolen the gaming money during the fight between Sam and Eric!

I could read from the look on Markham's face he knew I remembered. "You stole two hundred dollars from the card game that night."

He smiled. "It wasn't my best show. For some reason, that night I was losing. Even a card shark loses sometimes. I needed money bad, and when I saw the chance, I took it."

"They set out after you. If those men had caught you, they'd've strung you up."

Markham laughed. "All those men were good for was chasing shadows. I watched the whole commotion from a building roof across the street. When folks set out hunting something they look down, and around, and under, but never up. I waited until I knew it was safe, then made tracks out of town." There wasn't any question about it. Markham was a master.

"So, what are you planning to do with me?" I asked. It was the curse of the dead man's bones all right. I was certain of it.

"That's the sad part of it, Clayt, and I hate to do it. I tried telling Wiley and Sam it was good enough to tie you up and leave you. We'd be long gone when you got loose, and it'd be your word against the three of us if you told your tale to the authorities. This is the first time they wouldn't listen." His voice seemed to crack when he spoke. "I don't like my hand in murder."

From the time I woke up on the raft I had the feeling of it–deep inside. They were going to kill me.

"You don't have to kill me," I said to Markham. "I'm not going to say anything. And, like you said, it's my word against the three of yours."

"Can't take that chance. The stakes are too high. You see, Clayt, I'm good at what I do–really good–but I've never liked it much. I don't have the heart for it. After this expedition we're parting company; Wiley and Sam their way and me mine. With the stake split three ways instead of four, I can set myself up honestly. Maybe somewhere in the eastern states."

"But you still don't have to kill me. I'll give my part to you. Take it. It's yours."

Markham's face took on a real slack-jawed look and his voice quavered. "If I don't kill you, they've promised to kill both of us. I haven't any choice. I'm sorry, Clayt, I really am." He reached out and laid his hand up on my shoulder. There was a pause of deep silence between us. "Under other circumstances," Markham spoke soft-voiced, "we could have been good friends."

About that time, Jakes's gravel voice sounded up from along the quiet of the river. "Are you gonna jaw with that kid all night, or are you gonna get it done?"

If it hadn't been for Uncle Frank's old tale about the wreck of the *Channel Belle*, and Hank Short's telling me where to find her, I wouldn't've been about to become food for the river fish.

"Go on, Markham. Get it over with," Richards taunted from the darkness. "If you don't have the stomach for it, I'll slice his belly open 'n yours 'long with it."

My mind flashed bright with ways to escape, except there weren't any. I was bound so tight I couldn't move. If Markham dumped me into the blackened river, I'd be drowned for certain. There wasn't anything I could do.

Markham grabbed me by the naked ankles and started hauling me toward the raft end. Richards saw the movement while he walked his pole back.

"Cut 'im first. That kid's just slippery enough to get free 'o Wiley's knots."

I knew it was over when Markham pulled his Barlow knife flipped open, catching the glint of lantern light along the blade.

"Give me your hands," he whispered, leaning over my face and glancing close over his shoulder to see where the two men were. They were at the raft front, just beginning to walk their poles back.

I reached my hands out toward him not knowing what he was about to do. Richards and Jakes moved slowly toward the back of the raft. Richards's shadow loomed up in the yellow glimmer of the lantern light. Suddenly, Markham grasped my shirt and ripped it open, buttons popping to the raft-boards. The knife blade flashed in an upward motion, Markham bending over me. The blade split my hand open, blood flowing out along the steel edge. The next instant he cleaved my wrist ropes free and rolled me overboard. A lazy splash sounded as I hit the water and as the raft's light dimmed ahead, I heard Markham's voice ring clearly. "I slit him from belly button up and kicked him overboard. He was near dead when he hit the water. Nothing but fish food now. Satisfied, Richards?"

I couldn't see it clearly, but I was certain I saw Markham hold up the bloody knife blade for Richards and Jakes to see. And then the raft and the men were gone, and I was floating on the inkiness of the river. With my wrist ropes slashed, it wasn't difficult to work the knots at my ankles free, the water helping to loosen up the tightness of the ropes a bit.

The raft was gone and the treasure of the *Channel Belle* with it. But leastwise, thanks to Martin Markham, I was still alive. And Sam Richards and Wiley Jakes–those two river pirates–were none the wiser for it. Markham had pulled off his slickest con of all.

When he rolled me off the raft, it was poling up about five yards from shore. A raft that heavy-loaded couldn't easily fight the steady river tow with only two men poling. Now Markham was free to help. Once I'd freed my ankles, I stroked easily into shore. There was a deadfall cottonwood right along the bank, and I curled up next to it, drawing my legs in tight, staying warm as possible in the chill of a river night.

The Lord Almighty received prayers from me that night–more than He ever had before. I thanked Him for helping save me, and prayed long for the soul of Martin Markham, too. It was the least I could do. By his kindness I was still alive.

What men call accident is the doing of God's providence.

–G. Bailey

CHAPTER 19

An Unexpected Discovery.

I'D BEEN ROLLED OFF THE raft only about a mile's distance from the diggings on the island. By mid-morning I was making a path along the western edge of the river, returning to the wreck site. What I hoped to find there, I didn't know. The *Channel Belle* was picked clean. The four of us–Markham, Jakes, Richards, and I–had made certain of that. Not so much as an ounce of quicksilver had been spilled. All that remained in that rotting and musty hold was polluted whiskey of no use to anyone.

The loss of all that remained of the *Channel Belle*'s treasure, and the money it would bring weighed heavy on me. But I had my life, which, all in all, was of greater value.

Pop had said once there's folks meant to have wealth and prestige and power and all the fine trappings that go along with having money. And there's those that aren't and who, like Pop and Ronnie's father and thousands like them, have to bend their backs and scrape hard to eke out just a simple living. I guessed that I was one of them.

Unless a body's fortunate enough to inherit it, like Aunt Addie from her husband or Jamie and Clarke-Jiles from her, making money was mostly a matter of hard effort, with a little luck thrown in.

It took me only about an hour's hike to back track and reach the point where the sand island loomed up just ahead, my pace being slow, but not undeliberate. I crossed over at the narrows between the landside and the island where the river ran shallow, rising up to only about my waist. And there was the gravesite of the Channel Belle, that once-proud treasure-hauler, its prizes gone upriver with Markham and his river pirate friends. I peered down into her cavernous, ink-black hold from atop the digging site and felt tears welling up about my eyes. They weren't for my loss of wealth, but for her violation. I wondered if it'd been right to rob her, to disturb her moldering bones and those of the men who'd died aboard her. Come spring and the next good flood, she'd be buried up and rest again beneath the sands of the shifting river.

The campsite had been picked clean, too. All that remained were the cold, gray-white ashes in the fire pit and one bent-up tin plate someone'd forgot to pack. The plate reminded me I hadn't eaten in one entire day since the morning previous. There was a powerful churning and hollowness inside of me, as I didn't have fishing gear, nor anything to make it with, much less to cook a fish when I caught it. I recalled seeing a berry bush just a short way above the island. The day was fast growing on past noon and there was no sense of lollygagging around the island any longer and measuring my disappointment. My skiff had gone on along with the raft upriver, and the only way to get back to town was walk. I fished through my trousers pockets and found I had some dollars left from what Wiley Jakes had taken when he'd bought supplies. He'd been honest enough to take only what he spent. Leastwise, I could buy a decent meal when I reached Waud's Landing. Afterwards I'd contact Clarke-Jiles for a ticket back to Waytown.

I scuffed along the island, past the digging site, and waded out into the water. But instead of taking to the landside direct, I shuffled through the shallow water toward a sandbar lying about fifty yards ahead. From it I'd cut over across to land and walk the four miles into town.

The bar was partly under water, but shallow enough to see through the brownish water to the sandy bottom glinting from below. The water lapped easy around my ankles, making eddies in the river, and the soft sand gushed up between my toes as I sloshed along. Safe in the shallow water, schools of fingerlings–minnows mainly and tadpoles--flashed in silver swirls around my feet, picking at my skin thinking it was food. I stood still and watched them for a spell swarm in and out between my legs. When they were gathered all about, I raised one foot slow so as not to disturb them much, then stomped it down. I didn't kill them and hadn't meant to but did it just to see them scatter. The gray sand swirled up clouds of grainy pellets, making the water black. Then, as my foot stepped forward, it struck hard into something jutting up from the bottom.

"A snag! Damn it!" I yowled, holding up my foot and prancing a wild dance step around the water. The snag had split the toenail back; the skin around it was scuffed and bloody. It throbbed and stung something awful, like an angry wasp had lanced its stinger into it.

To take revenge for my stubbed toe, and to make me feel better, I reached down and grabbed that snag and pulled. It wouldn't give. I pulled again, harder, and still it hung in tight. That snag didn't have the feel of a chunk of tree stump, or a buried log. It was smooth. I stood still long enough to let the swirling sand clouds settle and when the water was clear to see into, I stooped down and tugged even harder at the object. The sand gave its hold grudgingly, with a sucking sound, and I got both hands around one corner of that hunk of wood. In all that to-do, I'd forgotten about the soreness in my toe.

Whatever it was, that snag was heavy and would scarce budge except when I yanked hard. Then I saw it. It wasn't a tree snag I was shagging loose, but a box—an old wooden saw-board box with rusted nails jutting out one side. One corner end I managed to heave out just above the water. A board came loose where the top was nailed shut and I tugged on it until it sprung up.

A bright yellow glimmering bounced up and glinted against my eyes. It was almost blinding. Gold! I reached inside and jerked up another saw board, and then another until most of the top was free. The whole box was stuffed full of gold! Coins! Hundreds of gold coins—thousands of them from what I could see. Shiny new as the day they were minted. It was almost like I'd drunk another of Markham's powders. My heart thumped and hammered, and my head got woozy; my knees went weak and trembly. The coins were scattered loose inside the box and heaped to the top. I shoveled my hand inside and pulled a palmful out. The ones I held bore dates from 1858, 1859, and through to 1862, the year the *Channel Belle* went down. Every one I could see was a Double Eagle! In a small handful alone, I held two-hundred dollars!

It was the real treasure of the *Channel Belle*! Or part of it at least. Markham, Jakes, and Richards had sweated so hard to scheme me out of my rightful findings, and all they'd come out with was quicksilver, copper ingots, and a single chest of silver bars. Heaped up between my two cupped hands lay solid gold.

Hundreds of dollars of it. Thousands inside the box. It'd been sitting on this bar–so close. We could've most reached out and touched it from the digging site.

I had no way of knowing how much there might be lying around nearby, or if it was in easy reach. Uncle Frank, in his tale about the *Channel Belle*, recalled there'd been cases of it. Tens of thousands, hundreds of thousands of dollars' worth. Maybe as much as half a million. But one case lay at my feet. My mind spun on like a forty-niner with the fever. Hank Short, traipsing along a bar, had found a single gold piece–an Eagle. There must be more!

The fever'd struck me sure enough. And hard. I gandered a quick look around, up and down the river. Where I stood on the sandbar gave me a clear view for quite a distance. The river lapped along as usual; there was no one on it in sight except me. It wasn't long before I set off stomping up and down the bar, probing the sand with the point of a willow pole.

I searched the bar and the surrounding shallow river bottom as best I could. It wasn't an easy task without the skiff. Where the river ran deep, there was nothing I could do but watch the ripples and swirling eddies sweep by. The water was too deep to dive in, too muddy to see into underwater, and the current too swift to remain in one position long enough to do any good in hunting out the bottom. Besides, how long could I hold my breath?

The river yielded other treasures than the first I'd found when I'd first come to the sand island cutoff. My pole poked into an old, crusted barrel hoop off a hogshead cask, brought up a roll of fencing wire some farmer had ordered that had never arrived, and plenty of sodden logs. But there was no gold anywhere. I was still floating in disbelief on what gold I'd literally stumbled my toes across. The fever pitch was high.

I stalked along the banks and waded through the shallows, poking and prodding with the pole, scooping out sand-bowls with my hands in likely places, below the cutoff end and above the cutoff mouth, inside the cutoff funnel, and outside along the river's edge. But the river yielded up no more golden treasure. Then the thought struck me and my senses came drifting back. Whatever other boxes of gold remained, the river had carried away, or buried under mud and sand I couldn't dig through. I had no way of knowing where they lay. Whatever gold remained from the *Channel Belle* belonged to the river. Perhaps forever.

No one was around. The river snaked along green banks, lulled still and silent but for crow calls from the high treetops. The gold couldn't be left in open sight. In case someone happened by, I couldn't let them stumble over it the same as I had.

I stalked back to the bar and the gold. The box jutted end up from the water where I'd forced it loose. I let the box down easy, scooping my hands down around its sides and hollowing out the sand until it sank down under water. Then I buried it with sand. A body could walk right over it and never see its hiding place. A dying cottonwood that showed the blackened spiral scar of a lightning strike stood exactly on the other side and I used it as a marker. Satisfied I could find the spot again and making double-certain the box was hidden, I dashed off upriver toward town.

I sprinted all the way. If I could've sprouted wings, I'd've flown. In my excitement I'd forgotten all about the hunger pangs gnawing at my belly, and the split and bloody nail on my toe. And there wasn't time to stop and catch a bite of food. There was only time to find myself a skiff and row back to the gold site as quick as possible.

An old man, stooped, white-haired and grizzled, sat at the wharf side, a homemade fishing pole dangled slack between his hands. A battered skiff was moored nearby. I skipped up to him, nearly out of breath.

"Mister, whose skiff is that?" I asked him, pointing toward the paint-chipped boat.

"Whatta ya want to know that for, Sonny?"

"I need to rent a boat. I've got money. I can pay."

"Well, seems to me you're in an all-fired hurry." I was, but it was sure-fire certain he wasn't.

"Mister, please, tell me who that skiff belongs to. I need it bad."

"You tell me what you're a-needing that there boat for, and maybe I'll tell ya who owns her."

"I need it. I need it to catch up with some friends of mine who are on a raft heading upriver," I lied.

"Two scurvy-lookin' fellers and a younger man with 'em?"

"Those are the ones. You saw them?"

"I was fishin' here last night–'bout ten o'clock–and saw these here three fellers come polin' up on some big raft jus' a-heaped with things. The young fella, he come and sat a spell with me while the other two went on into town. Nice young fella. Didn't say me his name, though."

"That's him. That's my cousin," I said. "The other two's my uncles. I got separated from them a while back. Please, mister, who's skiff is that?"

The old man eyed me over some. He'd been holding a wad of chaw inside his cheek which he spat out thoughtfully. "I guess that there skiff is mine."

"Can I rent it from you? I'm really in a hurry to catch up with them."

"Guess ya can," he droned, setting aside his pole, "seein' I won't be needin' it right off. Cost ya a dollar. Ya got yourself a dollar, sonny?" I dug down inside my trousers' pocket and fished the old man out a gold dollar. "Where ya bound for? I gotta know so's I can get my boat back."

"My uncles and cousins are heading to Cloverville," I said. "That's where they're dropping off their goods."

"You'll never catch up to 'em in that there skiff. Current's 'gainst ya rowing upriver."

"I don't need to catch them, mister," I said. "All I need is get something they forgot up to the next town with a freight wagon station and get it packed up to them. I'll leave your boat there."

The old man scratched his head. "That'd be Snookerson–'bout seven miles up. Got kin 'o mine livin' there can fetch the boat back. Okay, Sonny. Ya can take the skiff. But I want it back, ya hear?"

"Yes, sir," I said. "You'll get it back." I thanked him and thundered off toward the battered skiff. "There's no oars in the boat," I called up to the old man who sat silent, eying me.

"All's ya said is ya wanted to rent a boat. Didn't say nothin' 'bout no oars. They'll cost ya extra." He thought the whole thing mighty funny. I paid him out another dollar. As I cast off, I started rowing hard downriver. The old man looked a might perplexed. "Say, Sonny! You're a-headin' in the wrong direction!"

"I know," I shouted back to him. "I got to gather up the things I'm going to freight. It won't take long."

The way I oared, like Satan himself was hot-hoofing me, I arrived at the scorched cottonwood in less time than it'd taken me, Markham, and his crew of thieves. I rowed directly even on a sight line from the tree and wedged the skiff into the bar. Everything was the same and undisturbed. The gold box still lay where I'd buried it.

The box was so heavy I couldn't lift it in one piece. I scooped the gold coins out and heaped them in the skiff, then hoisted the empty box out and placed the coins back inside. A tattered canvas tarp lay in the bottom of the skiff, and I used it to hide the box.

I moored the old man's skiff at the dock in Snookerson like I promised, but not before I slipped into a small inlet to the river that ran alongside the bank a short way outside of town. There I hid the skiff really well, covering it with leaves and brush so as no one was like to find it, and scampered off to find the sheriff.

The sheriff was a silver-headed, tall, thin man with a slight stoop to his shoulders, and he was more than a might skeptical about my tale of the *Channel Belle* gold I'd found. But I convinced him enough to follow me and have a look-see for himself. I'd've liked to have had a picture of that old sheriff when his face went slack-jawed at the sight of all that gold! From speaking with him earlier, I caught the feeling he was an honest and upstanding lawman; that I could trust him with my secret. But I'd learned fast from the likes of Markham, Jakes, and Richards not everyone's to be trusted.

Wheelbarrowing the box into the jailhouse in Snookerson was no easy task. We had a mighty struggle with it. The street was bare of folks, so no one saw us. The effort took a real toll on the sheriff, considering his advancing years and rheumatic joints. But we got it there and the sheriff locked the chest up sound and safe in his jail cell.

"I reckon that's the most money Snookerson's ever had all at once inside its limits," he groaned out, dropping heavily into his desk chair in his office.

"I reckon it's more than most towns have seen," I said.

"Have you counted it yet?" he asked. From the excitement at having discovered it, I hadn't bothered on a proper count, coin for coin.

"No, sir. I reckon I'll keep that for a surprise when I get to

Waytown."

I didn't have any money left, except fifty cents, from renting out the skiff, so Sheriff Robeson loaned me enough to send a telegram on to Waytown which I addressed to Clarke-Jiles personally. I had to wake the telegrapher to do it. I supplied him with a tip because he sure looked sour!

Some hours later, Clarke-Jiles's reply came back. He'd make arrangements, the telegram said, for the safe transfer of the gold by guarded coach into Waytown come morning and caught hold of Lawyer Settles who'd handle the legal work. By the sound of his message, he was right happy to hear from me.

I pondered some on the thought whether the gold would be mine or not to keep. With all the work I'd done and coming within a cat's whisker of being murdered for the effort, I hoped I'd get something for the trouble.

Along with Clarke-Jiles's telegram followed a wire for money which I could get at the bank come morning. It was enough to pay the sheriff back and purchase a ticket for the stage ride up to Waytown. Before I left Snookerson, the sheriff and his wife served me a welcome supper meal, a room to sleep in overnight in their quarters above the jail, and a hearty breakfast come morning. They were both mighty fine and caring folk.

Beware, as long as you live, of judging men by their outward appearance.

    –La Fontaine

CHAPTER 20

A Jubilant Return Home. "Respectability."

NEWS TRAVELS FAST ALONG THE river and, when the stage from Snookerson pulled up at the Waytown station house, I was startled to see what seemed near half the town turned out for me. Seems I'd become a local celebrity of sorts.

Clarke-Jiles was there, standing proud in a clean, dark suit, and Jamie, too, and Marie Ellis, of all folk. Jamie, Clarke-Jiles, and I had scarce shaken hands when Marie came bounding up and clenched me about the waist like I was her long-lost kin.

"I knew you'd come back someday, Clayt," she cooed, "and now you've come back rich! Oh, Clayt, I'm so proud of you." Of a sudden, and before I knew just what was happening, Marie, her arms still clenched around my waist, tip-toed up and kissed me. Right against my lips! Her lips felt mighty warm and my heart set into hammering a might inside my chest. But it was a strong embarrassment, right there on the public street, right there in front of all those townsfolk. "Won't Daddy be surprised?" I reckoned he would have been more than surprised if he'd been there to witness it! I think we were all a might surprised. Me especially.

It was a darn sight better greeting I received now than when I'd first clambered off the coach in front of that same stationhouse with Parson Briggs scarcely a year before. I'd been greeted by Aunt Addie then, and by the hushed whispers, hen-cackling, and disapproving stares of her lady friends. Now, near total strangers traipsed up to shake my hand and slap me on the hind parts and across the shoulders and compliment me on my find. The boardwalk running along the stationhouse roared a buzz of laughing voices and swams of friendly smiles. What all the to-do was about I couldn't rightly puzzle out. The way those Waytown folks carried on, you'd have thought it was them who'd found a treasure. I was certain I wasn't any different than I was a year before. Leastwise, I didn't feel truly different. With my shirt torn loose and my trousers ripped and muddy, it was certain I looked the same.

When the greetings and all the fanfare had had a chance to settle, Marie went back home to tell her folks about what had happened. She'd learned the news from Jamie. The town had learned the news from the telegrapher, who'd told the paper editor, who'd printed an extra edition and sent newsboys around the town. Clarke-Jiles held the paper in his hands. The bold-type banner headline read: LONG-LOST TREASURE FOUND. LOCAL BOY MAKES GOOD. I didn't have time to read the story right off, but when I did, it turned out it was mostly lies made up to sell.

In the afternoon after settling in with Clarke-Jiles and Jamie again in the rooms above Hudson's Mercantile, Clarke-Jiles and I walked over to talk with Lawyer Settles. I informed him about what had really happened to me along the river–how I'd met up with Martin Markham and Jakes and Richards, and how the three men had overpowered me and planned to slice me up and drown me in the river. With the descriptions and names I gave him he, acting out his part as an officer of the court, informed the county sheriff and the search for those river pirates began.

Surprisingly, it wasn't too long after that two of the men were found: Sam Richards and Wiley Jakes, caught hot-handed with a share of the goods they'd stolen from me. The sheriff took them without a struggle in some town just south of St. Louis where they'd tried to turn their ill-gotten gains into cash money. They were snagged easily because they'd got drunked up and raised riot in some tavern. That sounded like Jakes and Richards all right.

Martin Markham, however, was nowhere to be found. Good to

his word, he'd parted company with the likes of Jakes and Richards somewhere along the river route. In a way, I was glad he hadn't got himself arrested and hauled back to stand trial. He was a conman, sure, and a mighty smooth talker, but if it hadn't been for him slicing through my wrist ropes like he did that night, and faking that he'd murdered me, I'd have died for certain. And with no one who cared the wiser for it.

Markham stayed in the front of my thoughts for a long while. I hope that now, having fathered up money enough, he'd established himself in more honest enterprises.

The trial of Jakes and Richards was the biggest event to hit Waytown in anybody's memory, together with "The Golden Boy" as some folks called me. Lawyer Settles served as prosecuting attorney, and the circuit judge who came to hear the case turned out to be none other than The Honorable Nathaniel Bellman—the judge I'd been brought before back in Swainville.

Richards didn't speak a word throughout the trial; just sat still, sober-faced and solemn, no doubt wishing he had a drink. Wiley Jakes, though, talked a blue streak and, under Lawyer Settles's close examination, admitted to everything. I'd oft-times pondered on why the men had suddenly turned against Markham, had forced him into attempting to do me in, threatening his own life, too.

"That young tramp was turnin' honest," Jakes growled from the witness box. "Said he hadn't the belly for no more work together. We'd been making money with him along 'n then he starts in whimperin' how he's not cut out for it no more. He was gonna let that kid go free so's he could head off for the nearest law."

The trial lasted only one short day. The jury was out for little less than an hour before bringing in their verdict. Guilty. Mr. Ellis, Marie's father, was the foreman, and he spoke out the jury's finding.

Despite his stiff-braced stance from the jury box, after he'd pronounced the verdict, he rifled a wink toward me, and I could've almost sworn he smiled.

For their part in attempting to plot my murder, the sentence Judge Bellman called down on Sam Richards and Wiley Jakes sent both packing to the penitentiary for quite some stretch. The judge said that, under law, he couldn't take the goods away they'd helped remove from the wreck of the *Channel Belle*. It was theirs by rights of salvage. But he did divide it up to give a rightful share to me. The rest would be held in trust for them when they got out of prison. By then they'd be mighty old men.

Following the trial, the crowd of lookers-on in the courtroom and those adventure-seekers gathered around the front doors to the courthouse, went wandering off to talk up the happenings in their homes and bars. Judge Bellman himself, recalling my face and name from the Swainville hearing, came up to me and shook my hand.

"I see you've done well by yourself," he said, then glanced about the group of friends gathered around beside me. "I'm happy to have been of help to you in this affair, Mr. Sievers."

The free-booting adventure along the river was finally over.

Things settled down right well for me following the trial. Using some of the money Aunt Addie had left him, Clarke-Jiles had built a house for Jamie and himself on the cleared property where Aunt Addie's old house had set. It was built of brick and while not so grand as the other house had been, it was airy and spacious and comfortable. I'd told Clarke-Jiles I planned on staying on in Waytown for as far into the distant time as I could see. Come mid-August, the workmen laid in the finishing refinements on the house, and the three of us moved in.

Jamie and I settled into our own spacious rooms across the hall from one another. We no longer had to share a bathtub; I no longer had to listen to him wheeze and snore.

With Clarke-Jiles and Mr. Mertinger working closely together, business at Hudson's Mercantile had grown upwards at a steady pace.

A new rail line had been laid out along the edge of town following the river road and Waytown was fast becoming an important stop-off point for rail passengers and cargo goods, replacing the steamboat traffic which was all but dying out. Waytown had hopes of growing larger and along with it, the mercantile business. Clarke-Jiles had decided to expand. A new addition to the building was being added, and a second Hudson's Mercantile was being built in Cloverville with plans for another elsewhere.

Clarke-Jiles was already envisioning a string of such stores, all bearing the Hudson name, all up and down the Missouri side of the river.

The money, and a share of the goods I'd found from off the *Channel Belle,* was put in the safekeeping of Lawyer Settles. He took steps necessary to see if any rightful owners could be found to lay claim to the recovered treasure. Some time passed, but no one came forward to claim it. It turned out the records had long been lost as to where the gold and other cargo goods had come from. The treasure from the *Channel Belle* turned out mine to keep.

The case of gold I'd crashed my foot into along the sandbar contained both Double Eagles, twenty-dollar coins, and ten-dollar Eagles. One hundred thousand dollars' worth. I asked Lawyer Settles and he agreed to handle it. He invested the money out at interest which brought in several thousand dollars yearly without me even having to work for it!

It was more income than I ever dreamed of owning, and it was every penny mine to keep.

"How's it feel, Clayt, being rich like that?" Clarke-Jiles asked me one evening at the supper table. I had to allow it felt mighty good and I told him so. I wasn't exactly certain how much a hundred thousand dollars would buy, but I wasn't hell-bent to spend it. My thoughts flashed back to Pop; my only wish that he was living and sharing in my good fortune.

Folks in Waytown were downright pleasant to me for the longest while. Some had jokingly begun calling me the Waytown Rockefeller after some rich man named John D. Rockefeller who lived back East somewhere and had gone from nothing to riches much like me. Folks stayed polite and friendly, but the newness of the joke soon wore off.

Two letters came in addressed to me, arriving by mail coach at the Waytown post office. One was from Ronnie Meyer's father. It said his oldest daughter, Annabel, had taken up a steady interest in ol' Sam Johnston, one of my old-time friends who'd been in Ronnie's gang. It was looking mighty serious and while they were both too young now to marry, Mr. Meyers was keeping a steady, watchful eye on both of them. Annabel would be turning eighteen soon and he'd give consent then. He offered me a hundred dollars for Pop's old river cabin and property. If he could buy it, Sam and Annabel would move in after they were married. The cabin was in good condition and the price offered seemed a fair one, so I accepted. Lawyer Settles handled the details of the sale deed for me.

I wasn't sad at selling Pop's cabin. The way it was, sitting cold and empty, it wasn't doing good by anybody. When Sam and Annabel moved in, they'd bring laughter to its old walls once again like there'd been when I was younger and Pop and me were together--before he started drinking. It would be like it was when Pop and Mom first married and had started up their lives together. Better. I'd help see to that. One thing sure, I'd give them a wonderful wedding gift.

Words from the past, from Pop when he was mostly sound, flooded back to memory. 'There's no wrong done in giving folks a start," he'd once said. "Givin' too much makes folks beholding or makes them weak."

When I'd closed the cabin up, before I set out searching for the *Channel Belle*, I hadn't planned on coming back. A body's future lies ahead and not in the past. Someday I would go back. Visit Pop's and Mother's graves; remember the pleasant times and the fun with Ronnie and his gang. Maybe recollect the harsh times, too. But not right now.

The other letter I was especially happy to receive. It was from Maggie Lewis.

Dear Clayton,

News finally arrived in Swainville and l congratulate you on your good fortune. l can't imagine anybody finding so much money! I couldn't be happier for you. You'll remember Max, the man I've been working for these past six years. Well, the good news here is that he has asked me to marry him. I've learned that my husband who went off is dead, and it is legal for me to marry. I've loved Max for some time, and he loves me in return. l know that everything will work out fine for both of us. If you're ever back to Swainville, please feel free to look us up.

May good fortune and God be with you always.

Your friend, Maggie Lewis

I felt especially happy for Maggie, now that she'd be marrying Max. The two of them settling down together, Maggie would become an 'honest' woman again in the eyes of the populace of Swainville. Swainville womenfolk would come to call on her, sit and have tea with her; talk about local gossip. Maggie would be likely to take part in a sewing circle. She'd be good at that. It was a puzzlement to me. Maggie Lewis was a good-tempered, God-fearing woman, always helping those less fortunate who stumbled across her kindness. In marrying up with Max, she'd have 'position' in the town, be recognized for the good woman she was. Yet she wouldn't change any from what she'd always been.

I wrote her back, wishing her all the happiness she deserved and asked her to tell me when the wedding date was set so, if I could, I would be there.

Toward the end of August, Jamie and I celebrated birthdays together. Jamie had sprouted into a tall, handsome thirteen-year-old and I entered on my sixteenth year. No one played the parlor piano this time, though Clarke-Jiles had bought one just like Aunt Addie had, he and Jamie both learning to play. The Parson Briggs and his wife weren't there, and none of Aunt Addie's women friends showed up either. None of them were invited. Clarke-Jiles had some cronies over and gathered up around back smoking pipes, swapping tales, and having a merry time. He tapped a pony keg and seemed at home drawing beers and playing host. Friends of Jamie's and my own ages were in force this time—some twelve in total. We drank punch and lemonade, sang songs, served up a giant birthday cake Clarke-Jiles had the local bakery make. It was heavily frosted and decorated elegantly.

I'd sent Marie a special invitation and she accepted it. Her daddy seemed happy to allow her to come. Only short days before, Clarke-Jiles, Jamie and I had dressed up fine and had supper with the Ellises at Mr. Ellis's personal invitation. I wished Aunt Addie could've seen me then, Pop, too, if they'd both been watching from above, because I came to supper dressed up proper: brown trousers and a linen shirt, even a string tie flopping at my neck.

Through the supper hour, Mr. Ellis, whenever I glanced his way, seemed a might ill-set and, following the meal, which Mrs. Ellis had done up fine, called me into the parlor. It didn't seem like him to hem, clear his throat, and paw some at the carpet with his shoe-toe, but he did.

"Damn it, boy," he finally spat, "it's mighty hard sometimes for a man to admit he's been wrong, but I sure called you wrong."

"Mr. Ellis," I said, attempting to interrupt. He raised his hand and stopped me mid word. "No, boy, don't apologize for me. It was I who was in the wrong all along. And, don't get me wrong, it's not that you have money now that matters. It's who you are." He paused, flashed a glance down to the carpet, then up to me again. "I always prided myself on being a sound judge of character. I judged you by how you looked and how you talked. Somehow, I forgot my roots before I settled down in Waytown. You're a fine young man, Clayton Sievers, and," he said, reaching out his thick-palmed hand, "I'd be mighty proud to call you friend."

Mr. Ellis had never been a bad man. Clarke-Jiles had told me that and, of course, I knew it. I shook his hand some pumps and we stalked back into the dining room together, his arm resting around my shoulders. It seemed in a flash I'd gone from being a rapscallion river boy to a young man respectable in the community. The truth told, nothing had really changed, leastwise inside of me, except my having money.

Jamie and I had taken our party friends down along the river. One boy, Rance Hardin, between my and Jamie's ages, played banjo and could kick up quite a storm of music. He worked alongside his pop who owned the lumber mill, enjoyed fishing and camping out, most everything I did. And we became good friends.

Marie Ellis was most special though. A body has a special feeling when he comes to like someone a lot, and a feller knows when that someone feels the same toward him. It was that way between Marie and me. Mr. Ellis, every bit still stern and proper, had mellowed out and allowed we could see one another. Of course, in the evenings when I came calling, her daddy made certain we had proper chaperoning.

At Sunday church time, all of us would sit together in one long pew row: Clarke-Jiles and Jamie, Mr. Ellis and his wife, and Marie and me together. We'd often hold a picnic on those late fall days when the river runs calm and clean, and the shocks of maple leaves are changing gold-brown and red, with scarlet-tinged sumac and Virginia Creeper hanging in dazzling clusters among the trees.

At long last, things were finally falling into place for me.

I hadn't forgotten Pop's words to me, nor the promise I'd made when I was out along the river. School in Waytown had started, and the opening day found me walking toward the schoolhouse with Jamie and Marie. We met up with Rance Hardin strolling from the opposite way, looking a might uncomfortable in his new-bought school clothes.

School in Waytown wasn't like that in Hortonville. Old Man Dodson's schoolhouse had been a single room, the boys and girls of every age gathered in together. The Waytown schoolhouse was two stories tall and built of brick, and there wasn't one teacher but several. In high school I had three new teachers to grow used to. None of them was like Old Man Dodson.

A young man named Mr. Sollstrum, the new principal who'd come to Waytown, was nothing like I remembered Old Man Dodson being. There was no shiny birch switch dangling threatening from the chalkboard in his classroom though he did have a paddle in his office. "It's for decoration only," he said. "A reminder of a past that needs to end. A similar one was used on me, but I never intend to use it. We're coming into new times here and I want to see such punishments ended. As long as I remain principal, they will." Mr. Sollstrum, along with the other teachers, didn't make fun of students and didn't use the dunce cap like Mr. Dodson had done to humiliate and embarrass the youngest kids, or someone who he thought hadn't done right by him.

I reckoned how everything was going to be just fine. Having been away from school for nearly two years, it was a powerful uphill jaunt settling back into working with the books. Rance, who was a whole year younger, but in the Tenth Grade the same as me, shared several of my classes and helped me out a lot. So did Marie and Jamie after school. After a time, I caught on quick. I wasn't being forced to read and cipher and bend over history books like I'd been under Old Man Dodson's fiery stare. After a time, I found I liked school and soon was doing well.

Living in Waytown, in a fine new house and with new friends I could count on, I felt that I belonged there. The free-spirit welled up inside me from time to time and when it did, I'd accept the call and head upriver in the handsome new skiff I'd bought. Oft-times Rance Hardin would come along, to keep one another company. In some ways he was like lost Ronnie, joking and given to telling tales. We'd swim and wade among the shallows, pole out a catfish and cook it up for dinner.

Come late fall I'd grown another inch. I even had a pencil strip of light-brown fuzz sprouting on my breastbone. If Ronnie could've seen it, he'd been mighty proud.

Sometimes I'd go out alone. The river lapped gently on those brief trips, flowing brown, with silver patches of sunlight flashing in the distance. The skiff would snake along banks alive with redbud and fragrant cedar, skim past barren shoals and the dying stumps of washed-out trees. Despite all the good fortunes that had come to me, a river boy is what I'd always be at the heart and center—where it counts.

ABOUT THE AUTHOR

Lyle Morgan holds two doctoral degrees, one in English literature (with emphases in Shakespeare, Late 19th & Early 20th Century British literature, English linguistics, and writing), and another in medicine. He has traveled extensively throughout Europe, and in 49 of America's 50 states, and studied in England, Austria, and Germany.

He taught at the University of Nebraska-Lincoln and until his recent retirement was a full professor at Pittsburg State University in Kansas where he directed the university's composition program, the English Department's education program, as well as having served as Chair of the Pre-medicine and Health Sciences program of the College of Arts & Sciences.

Morgan has authored books on medicine and healthcare which have been translated into several languages. He has appeared in editions of *Who's Who in the World, Who's Who in America*, and *Who's Who in Medicine and Healthcare.*

Additionally, Dr. Morgan is a long-time member of the Boy Scouts of America where he has served in numerous positions both on the troop and district levels as well as on camp staffs, council boards and in regional and national activities. An Eagle Scout, he has been awarded significant district, council, and regional awards including the District Award of Merit, the Silver Beaver and Silver Antelope awards. A Vigil Honor member of the Order of the Arrow, he is a Sachem in the Tribe of Mic-O-Say of the Heart of America Council, a Chieftain in the Tribe of Lone Bear of the Ozark Trails Council founded by the Tribe of Mic-O-Say. In 1995, he received the rare distinction of the Distinguished Eagle Scout Award by the National Eagle Scout Association.

www.ingramcontent.com/pod-product-compliance
Lightning Source LLC
Chambersburg PA
CBHW070743180626
46818CB00007B/2962

* 9 7 8 1 9 6 0 4 9 9 3 6 3 *